I0645951

VETERINARY
TECHNICIAN

Visit us at www.boldstrokesbooks.com

By the Author

Veterinary Partner

Veterinary Technician

VETERINARY TECHNICIAN

by

Nancy Wheelton

2021

VETERINARY TECHNICIAN

© 2021 By Nancy Wheelton. All Rights Reserved.

ISBN 13: 978-1-63555-839-5

This Trade Paperback Original Is Published By
Bold Strokes Books, Inc.
P.O. Box 249
Valley Falls, NY 12185

First Edition: January 2021

THIS IS A WORK OF FICTION. NAMES, CHARACTERS, PLACES, AND INCIDENTS ARE THE PRODUCT OF THE AUTHOR'S IMAGINATION OR ARE USED FICTITIOUSLY. ANY RESEMBLANCE TO ACTUAL PERSONS, LIVING OR DEAD, BUSINESS ESTABLISHMENTS, EVENTS, OR LOCALES IS ENTIRELY COINCIDENTAL.

THIS BOOK, OR PARTS THEREOF, MAY NOT BE REPRODUCED IN ANY FORM WITHOUT PERMISSION.

CREDITS

EDITORS: VICTORIA VILLASENOR AND CINDY CRESAP
PRODUCTION DESIGN: SUSAN RAMUNDO
COVER DESIGN BY TAMMY SEIDICK

Chapter One

Ronnie pedaled as if her life depended on it. Her butt lifted off the seat of her bicycle, and she pumped as if her past was chasing her, and no matter how hard she pedaled it was right over her shoulder and would run her over if she didn't keep moving.

Sweat trickled down her back and her thighs screamed. Happy and exhilarated, she grinned. There was nothing better than sailing along the road at full speed. In rural Saskatchewan, cars were rare, and the roads ran straight and flat, perfect for racing. Perfect for escaping.

Her arms jolted, her front tire slipped, and the bicycle slid out from under her and flew into the ditch. Ronnie landed face first in the muddy, wet snow in the middle of the road.

An engine roared as a rusty brown pickup truck fishtailed past her. It spun on the same patch of ice she'd hit and stopped ten feet away in the other lane, pointed in the direction it came from. A big man leaped from the truck and sprinted toward her.

Ronnie stood and brushed the snow and mud off her clothes, wincing at the aching already starting in her hip. She'd hit the frozen ground hard.

"Are you crazy, lady? I could've killed you. What're you doing out here?"

The man didn't scare Ronnie. He yelled with the anger born from fear when you come close to killing somebody by accident, something she was familiar with. "Sorry. Hit that patch of ice and lost control of my bike."

"I almost ran over you." The man tilted his head and studied her. "Are you hurt? Do you need a lift?"

Ronnie limped along the road, slid down into the ditch, and climbed out carrying her bicycle. She pulled her water bottle from its holder and drank deeply. "No, thanks." She remained at the side of the road with her bike leaning against her leg while she took several more sips of water. Her hip throbbed, but she was alive and full of energy and could ride for hours more.

"But I saw you crash, and your pants are torn."

Ronnie slid her finger into the tear on her leggings that had been gradually opening wider with each wash. Someday she'd get around to mending it. "I'm okay. It was torn before."

The man glanced at her leg, his expression showing he was unconvinced. "Okay…"

He shook his head as he stomped to his truck. He jumped in and edged his truck in a circle glancing once more at Ronnie before driving away.

Ronnie smiled and waved and could see him saying, "Crazy woman," as he pulled away.

She tucked her water bottle away and scanned the barren wheat fields to the horizon. After stretching she planned to continue her bike ride. If she put her bike away every time she fell, she would never leave her driveway. Growing up in Winnipeg, Manitoba, Canada, she understood the dangers of cold weather cycling and took precautions. It was May first and the temperature in Thresherton, Saskatchewan, danced between minus five and plus five degrees Celsius as if nature was waffling about whether to let winter go.

Today Ronnie rode her old mountain bike. It moved well in the small amount of snow still coating the roads. She used her stationary bike through the winter, but nothing made her happier than being outside and riding far and fast.

The man's reaction didn't surprise her. He was the third person to offer her a ride since she'd left Thresherton, but she hadn't fallen in front of the other two. People either thought she needed help or was crazy for being on a bicycle this time of year. She felt crazy, almost claustrophobic from being trapped inside all winter.

She counted only two farms in sight. The average size of farms in Western Canada was increasing, and consequently, the number of farm families was decreasing. Small towns disappeared when the population dropped too low to sustain them. Thresherton, where Ronnie lived, was an exception. Its population was six thousand and growing. Folks who lived on the surrounding farms drove into town to shop, go to school, or for other services. Their business helped keep Thresherton thriving. She liked the small town vibe, for the most part. For now, anyway.

Ronnie adjusted her helmet and mounted her bike. As she pushed off, the front tire skidded in the snow and she hit the ground yet again, landing on her other hip. No big deal, except for the matching bruises. She stood and brushed the dirt and snow off her clothes and groaned as another pickup truck stopped beside her. Tired of men thinking she needed rescuing, she whirled with every intention of snapping at the driver. At the last second, she swallowed her words when she recognized the woman driving the truck. It was Dr. Lauren Cornish, a veterinarian at Prairie Veterinary Services in Thresherton.

"Hey, are you all right?" Lauren asked.

Ronnie laughed. "Thanks, I'm fine." Lauren was a few inches taller and a few years older. She had short brown hair, deep green eyes, and a strong body with delicious curves a lover could curl against for life. The enticing thought warmed her all over and Ronnie lied. "I damaged my bike when I fell. The wheel's bent."

Lauren flicked on her hazard lights, climbed from the truck, and came around to Ronnie. "Do you need a lift or can you fix it here?"

"I wouldn't say no to a lift." Ronnie had said no to a lift three times in the last two hours, but this time an alluring lesbian offered. Lauren smiled and Ronnie melted a little. It felt less important now to finish her ride. She had her priorities.

Lauren shifted her equipment to create a space in the bed of her silver four-door pickup truck. "Want help to lift it?"

"No, thanks. I've got it." Ronnie lifted the bike and caught her finger in the chain. She gritted her teeth as she slipped the bike into the truck. She could have stopped and rescued her finger, but she wanted to appear tough. She got the bike in and tugged her finger out of the chain, trying not to wince.

After stowing the bike, Lauren and Ronnie climbed into the truck. Lauren shifted to face Ronnie and stuck out her hand. "Hi, I'm Lauren Cornish."

Ronnie swallowed her sigh of disappointment. She'd met Lauren twice, but Lauren didn't remember her. It was like being back in high school and your crush not knowing you were alive.

"You're Sharon Yakimoto, right? We haven't technically met."

Ronnie grinned. Lauren had recognized her after all. "I prefer Ronnie, thanks. Only my mother calls me Sharon."

"How do you like Thresherton?"

"Thresherton is a nice town and people are getting used to me." She smiled to take any sting out of her words. She was of Japanese ancestry and didn't mind being the only Asian in town now that people had stopped staring at her.

Lauren focused on the road as she drove. "You teach at the school in town."

Ronnie blinked at Lauren in surprise. She hadn't mentioned her profession to Lauren either time they met.

Lauren seemed to sense her surprise and she laughed. "You teach English. My girlfriend's daughter, Becky Anderson, is in grade four. She told me you're an awesome teacher, and she enjoys your class."

Ronnie dug into her memory. Becky Anderson was the tall one. "Becky's a good student." It was her policy to say a child was a good student even if their grades weren't great. Ronnie saw no downside to being positive. Becky was a solid B minus in English, and when what they studied interested Becky, she was alert and attentive. "She wrote a short story about her farm. It was full of warmth and very funny."

Lauren laughed. "That's her. Becky loves the farm and especially the cattle."

Ronnie fiddled with the strap of her helmet. So, Callie Anderson was a lesbian and Lauren's girlfriend? *Callie is tall, blond, strong, fit, gorgeous, blah, blah, blah.* At five four, Ronnie was tall for her family, and Callie towered over her. Ronnie mentally shrugged. Lauren was spoken for by an Amazon. No point in pursuing that angle, then.

After twenty minutes of light conversation, Lauren dropped Ronnie at home. She thanked Lauren for the lift and unloaded her bike. She opened her garage and leaned the old mountain bike against an inside wall. Her plan had involved another hour cycling, but she'd stop now that she was home. She was cold and bruised and wanted a hot shower.

Lauren was out as a lesbian in Thresherton and a topic of local interest. Ronnie bemoaned her luck. "I fall across the path of the one cute lesbian in town and she's taken by the only other attractive lesbian in town."

There *had* to be other lesbians in Thresherton. One RCMP officer pinged her gaydar, but the cop didn't interest her. She preferred softer women to whom smiling was the natural state of their face. Every time she saw the cop, she was frowning. Perhaps it was part of the job?

Ronnie opened the door and stepped into her back hallway. While she unlaced her shoes, she heard the ponderous steps of Dover as he came to greet her. Her father had given her the black Labrador retriever puppy. Dover was her pal, protector, and best friend. "Hey, Dover. Miss me?"

She squatted in front of him. "Hi, old man. You have a good day?" She petted him and looked into his soft brown eyes. His gray eyebrows matched his gray muzzle, and the sign of his aging made her heart ache. She gave him a kiss on the top of the head as she rose to her feet. "Ready for lunch, buddy?" In the kitchen, she filled a small bowl with senior canned food and kibble and set it beside his water bowl. She quickly scanned her supplies. She had enough dog food for two weeks.

"I talked to your vet today."

Lauren had examined Dover a month ago and told Ronnie that he could live a few more years, but to expect more hearing and vision loss. "And she remembered me." She shook her head at the way her stomach had flipped when Lauren had pulled over, and trudged upstairs.

Ronnie turned on the hot water in the shower and went into her bedroom. She removed the dry cycling clothes draped over her exercise bike. They could be worn again. She glanced around her bedroom and hung them on a hook on the wall. She loved hooks. She should install more. In her head she could still hear her mother nagging at her to pick her clothes up off the floor. She'd be nagging if she were in Thresherton right now. Her mother thought clothes were on your body, in the laundry, or on a coat hanger. Ronnie shook her head. Her mother should have installed a row of hooks in her bedroom and saved them both a lot of aggravation. She grinned with relief. He mother was a province away and couldn't criticize her hooks or house. Or her.

She stripped off her clothes and draped them along the arms of the stationary bike to dry and headed into the bathroom. After her shower, where she analyzed and then ignored the bruises from her mishap, she searched for clean clothes. Most people would search through their dresser drawers, but her laundry never made it into the dresser. If she was lucky, there was something clean in the last laundry basket she'd hauled upstairs.

Ronnie dug through a basket and found a clean T-shirt. The second place to search for clothes was the bottom drawers of the dresser. The place where she stashed the clothes she seldom wore but was too miserly to put in the trash. A mismatched outfit of sweatshirt with worn elbows and track pants with a torn knee spelled success. If she wanted clean clothes, she had to do laundry.

In a fit of energy, Ronnie scooped the dirty clothes off the floor and dropped them into the hamper. She contemplated the dripping clothes decorating the exercise bike and then shrugged. They had another workout in them.

Hamper clutched against her chest, Ronnie marched down two flights of stairs to the basement. Why had the previous owners installed the washer and dryer in the basement? She'd put them beside the bedroom. Why hump dirty clothes downstairs, just to cart them upstairs when they were clean? She loaded her washer, started it, and listened to it bang. A trickle of water emerged from under the old washer and wended its way to the drain in her basement floor. Mystery solved why the washer was in the basement.

She shrugged, jogged upstairs to the kitchen, and closed the basement door. She turned on her music and cranked the volume. If she couldn't hear the washer there was nothing wrong with it.

Ronnie opened her refrigerator and contemplated the contents. She closed her eyes, hoping when she opened them again, she'd find fresh food. Ronnie sighed. If she wanted fresh food, she had to shop, but to shop, she needed clean clothes.

Dover leaned against her leg. "Hey, buddy, your lunch is looking yummy right now. Maybe I'll just share yours. Or should I buy groceries?" Ronnie laughed as she scanned her outfit. "Imagine if the town saw Ms. Yakimoto dressed like a hobo at the grocery store. I'll blame it on teachers' salaries." She pulled a box of pasta from the cupboard. It would have to do.

The unsteady pounding of her washer overwhelmed Ronnie's music. The washer needed replacing, but her mortgage consumed more than half her pay. One day her washer would die, and if she was lucky, only quit working. But if the washer went the way of her last relationship, it would explode and blow the basement apart. She turned up the music.

Ronnie prepared her lunch, switched off the music, and dropped onto the couch in front of the television. She put the remote on the floor and changed channels with her big toe while she shoveled food into her mouth. She paused to glower at the contents of her bowl. The pasta had a thin smear of tomato sauce with a few flecks of basil, but there was no more cheese. Without melted cheese her meal was boring. Everything tasted better with melted cheese, but she'd grated the last of the cheddar into her bowl.

Now she was desperate. As soon as she had dry, presentable clothes she'd have to shop or eat Dover's food. Dover's canned food resembled pate. Maybe she could spread it on toast. "Dover, I'm losing it." Dover's expressive gray eyebrows rose as he contemplated her.

At last, the raucous rumblings of the washer stopped. Ronnie turned the television volume down. She either had clean clothes or a dead washer. She jogged downstairs, tossed her clothes in the dryer, and returned to the couch.

Ronnie scanned the freshly-painted walls of her living room with satisfaction. It had been a big job, but worth it. One day she'd get the baseboards put back on. It was an annoying job, but they were collecting dust in a neat pile stacked behind the television. She'd bought the paint on sale, but the costs had added up by the time she'd bought rollers, brushes, spackle to patch the walls, and a ladder to reach the ceiling. Painting the other rooms would have to wait.

Decorating cost money and she needed to earn more before she could spend it on anything other than basic living. She could teach summer school or find another job. A job would give her less time to train on her bicycle, but she had to pay her bills. She enjoyed teaching English to grades two through eight, but she wanted a break in the summer, and kids weren't the only ones who found summer school tedious.

Ronnie's shoulders slumped as thoughts of school punched their way into her weekend. English teachers had a ton of papers to read and grade. Thirty compositions written by the seventh graders languished on her kitchen table. She needed to digest and would start work after thirty minutes with her Xbox.

Two hours later, Ronnie paused her game and snapped off the television. She snagged her bowl off the coffee table and headed to the kitchen. She dropped her bowl on the counter on top of a huge pile of dirty dishes. Who snuck into her house and used her dishes? Ronnie sighed. If she wanted clean plates, she had to wash the dishes. Maybe later. "Dover, when did I become such a slob?" She glanced at Dover and read *since forever* in his eyes.

She dragged herself to the kitchen table she'd never used for meals. It was for work and she was falling behind in her marking. Members of the public thought schoolteachers earned a fortune for working eight to four, Monday to Friday. Teachers spent hours preparing for class and marking papers evenings and weekends. Ronnie plopped into a chair in front of the pile of papers and snatched her red pen. If she wanted to have grades for the students, she had to mark the papers.

Cycling, walking Dover, teaching, and marking papers was her life. It was all she did these days. It wasn't exciting, but it was peaceful and the life she'd chosen. Maybe she wouldn't live in Thresherton forever, but she was here now and there was work to do. She groaned and began to read the first composition.

CHAPTER TWO

Valerie Connor jotted numbers into the neat boxes and columns on the sheet fastened to her clipboard then scanned the sheet with satisfaction. One side listed all the products by category and how much she wanted to keep in stock. Today was inventory day at Prairie Veterinary Services, and she was recording the amount of each drug in stock at PVS and noting which ones to order. It was a veterinary technician's most boring job, but it was still necessary. Accurate inventories and ordering ensured they didn't run out of the drugs they used most often. The veterinarians often forgot to tell Val when they used up a drug. She frowned. Looking after veterinarians was like catering to small children who put an empty milk jug in the refrigerator and never understood why it was empty the next time they were thirsty.

"Got you." She pounced on a bottle of fifty-milligram amoxicillin. She knew she had one. Somebody had shoved it behind some taller bottles.

Val enjoyed the job of organizing the pharmacy. Rows of drugs on their labeled shelves were all turned with the English labels facing out. She sighed with satisfaction and then grimaced. The veterinarians would have it messy in a day.

The veterinarians treated a wide variety of animals which meant there were plenty of products to keep track of. Prairie Veterinary Services was a mixed animal veterinary practice in Thresherton and was located seventy-five minutes southeast of Saskatoon. The veterinarians drove to the farms when the large animals required treatment, but often farmers transported livestock to PVS for surgery.

Val glanced over her shoulder when the outside door banged open. "Hey, Lauren."

Dr. Lauren Cornish entered with one of her veterinary kits in each hand. The kits resembled large fishing tackle boxes with drugs, needles, syringes, gloves, and other equipment to examine and treat large animals. "Hey, Val." Lauren placed her kits on the floor and headed outside.

A minute later, Lauren returned with another kit and a bag of dirty coveralls. After she washed her hands, Lauren leaned against the counter and grinned at Val.

"What?" Val asked.

"Inventory, again? Didn't you just do it?"

"It's been two weeks."

"Can you get us some fifty-milligram amoxicillin, please? I needed some for a kitten yesterday. Had to send them home with hundred milligram and a pill cutter."

Val stared skyward. "I found it. *Someone* shoved it behind the tetracycline tablets."

Lauren shrugged. "Somebody must have been in a hurry to clean up."

"It's not *cleaning up* if the stuff is not put away properly. It just makes more work." Val shook her head.

"Why not just put all the antibiotics on one shelf? Then we can browse the choices and pick one."

Val frowned at Lauren. "Why? Everything is alphabetical. This has been my system for six years. Amoxicillin goes with A not T for tetracycline."

"You're the boss." Lauren glanced over the shelves and grinned.

Val squinted at her and noted the big goofy smile. Lauren and Callie Anderson were in love. They'd only told each other the weekend before, but both were full of goofy smiles. "I'm really happy for you."

"Pardon?"

"Three months ago, you were alone and miserable. And now you have Callie."

"I'm the luckiest woman on the planet. I love her. Callie is amazing. So smart and tough and beautiful. And she loves me. Everyone should be as happy."

"Sign me up."

"Okay." Lauren waggled her eyebrows. "Guess who I just saw?"

"A hot lesbian searching for a sexy femme veterinary technician to make her very own?" Val scoffed and returned to her task.

"Maybe."

"Are you messing with me?" Val dropped her clipboard on the counter and turned to face Lauren. "You better not be messing with me, Cornish." Callie and Lauren, in the way of happy lesbian couples, had made their single friend's happiness one of their main missions in life.

Lauren raised her hands in mock surrender. "I'm not messing with you. I met Gwen and Becky's English teacher thirty kilometers from town on a bicycle. Can you believe it? It's only May first. The woman must be a fanatic. Yesterday was freezing and we still have snow on the ground."

"It's dangerous to cycle on the snow. She could slip under somebody's tires. Not exactly responsible, is it?"

"Crazy, eh? And it's cold. I'm keeping my snow tires on for at least another month. Callie isn't even poking around her farm equipment and that's her first chore each spring."

"Hello, Lauren? Focus on the *important* topic, please. What does winter cycling have to do with being a lesbian?"

"Sharon Yakimoto, she prefers Ronnie by the way, told me there was something wrong with her bicycle so I offered to drive her home." Lauren shook her head. "I tried to help her lift her bike into my truck, but she insisted on doing it on her own."

"Wow, she must be gay. Because straight women aren't at all independent." Val didn't attempt to disguise the gentle sarcasm in her voice.

"Well, the sensible solution would've been to accept the offer of help." Lauren laughed and gasped for breath. "Wait." She laughed again and spoke when her control returned. "She caught her finger in the chain or something, and I could tell she was barely managing to keep it together. Instead of rescuing her finger, like a sensible person, she continued to lift her bike. She hung on and slid her bike into the bed of my Bowie unit, but she was white as snow." Lauren leaned against the counter, looking smug.

"You think she was trying to impress you?"

Lauren shrugged.

"Interesting. I wondered about her. She's sporty and athletic. When I saw her last at the school, she was in dress pants, a button-down shirt, a sweater vest, and running shoes."

"I know the look you mean. Cute."

Val shrugged. "Cute yes, but not very professional."

Lauren winked. "There wasn't a spot of pink on her cycling outfit, and it was clearly something she uses often."

Val smiled at Lauren, who announced the information as if it were part of a checklist. The color of a person's clothes didn't indicate their sexual orientation unless they were adults wearing rainbows at gay pride and perhaps not even then.

Val stared at a point on the wall while she tapped her bottom lip with her finger. "The couple of times she's been into PVS, I got a gay vibe from her. She inspected your chest with more than casual interest and longer than was polite." Val laughed. "Always a potential sign of a lesbian."

Lauren hung her head. "Has she been here? Have I met her? I guessed at her name because of Becky talking about her at home."

"Yes, Lauren. She was in a month ago." Exasperated, Val rolled her eyes. "How is it you remember every pet you see, but their owners are a mystery? Her dog is Dover."

"Oh, that's right. The ancient black lab with arthritis. He's a great dog. She loves him. I felt sorry for her because he hasn't many years until he's blind and unable to walk."

"Dover is a sweetheart. Now, how do I meet Ronnie?"

"What about Christine?"

Val waved her hands. "Fizzled away last month and probably should have been sooner. I'd been hanging on because I thought a poor relationship was easier than being single. Don't worry about me. I know better now."

"I'm so sorry. I've been so hung up on my issues and getting to know Callie that I never noticed." Lauren squeezed Val's hand. "Did she cheat? Like the one before?"

"No cheating. Not like Margery. But Christine wasn't interested in meeting Gwen or my parents. My mom was *not* impressed. What a disaster." Val fiddled with the papers on her clipboard. "The next time I'm attracted to a woman, I'll ask how she feels about my having an eight-year-old daughter right from the start."

And then she'd find out if the woman was dependable and planned to settle down in Thresherton. Her checklist differed from most people's. Sure, she yearned for a gorgeous, intelligent woman, but those characteristics ranked secondary or tertiary. Did Ronnie fit the above characteristics? She had gorgeous covered, but was she ready for a relationship with someone with a child? Was she happy in small town Thresherton and planning to stay? Was she reliable and stable? They were jumping the gun questions, but there wasn't any point in wasting time with someone who didn't meet her criteria.

"Gwen and Becky like her. She must be good with kids," Lauren said.

Val shrugged. "True, but there's a difference between being generally liked by children and being a good parent."

"So, find out. Do some research when you see her on Friday at the school open house." Lauren winked. "Or get Gwen to write an English composition on her lesbian mom. It's a novel way to out yourself to the cute teacher. Get it? Novel?" Lauren grinned.

"You're a nut." Val tapped Lauren on the shoulder with her clipboard and Lauren shrank away in mock terror. "Now get to work."

"Yes, lots to do." Lauren winked and headed out of the treatment room.

Val continued with the inventory. When she'd counted the same row of bottles three times, she gave up and set her clipboard down. Was Ronnie single and available? Was Val even interested? Not a chance. She was going to stay away from women for a while. She had other projects and wanted to spend more time with Gwen. Maybe next year she'd try a dating service and see if they could fix her up with Ms. Right. They couldn't do a worse job than she had.

CHAPTER THREE

"Good morning, everyone. Settle down please." Ronnie waited patiently for the chatting to stop and the students to take their seats. She could yell at them to hurry, but that wasn't her style. There was plenty of time to teach the lesson. "It's okay if you want to chat, but the more time you take now the more work you'll have to take home with you for the weekend. Your choice." That did it. The threat of homework had her students in their seats ten seconds later. Not that she gave the grade three class much homework.

She glanced at the two parents sitting at the back of the room and smiled as a third one slipped in and took a seat. "I'd like to remind everyone that today is our open house. Your parents will be moving from classroom to classroom watching you work and watching me." She gave a comical shudder and the class laughed.

Ronnie smiled at the three parents. One was on her phone, one smiled back, and the third frowned slightly. She gave a half-shrug. Not everyone got her sense of humor. "I need you to concentrate on your work and try to ignore your parents. They're here to see a typical day at Thresherton Public School." The students had turned to look at the parents and were now refocused on Ronnie. The frowning parent with the rich red hair was smiling at Gwendolyn Connor. Ronnie didn't need a science degree to match Gwen's red hair to the red hair of her mother.

"Who would like to start reading today?" Three hands shot up. Ronnie smiled. "Thank you, Gwen, please start." While Gwen read, Ronnie studied her mother. Mrs. Connor was an attractive redhead with a beautiful warm smile directed at Gwen. For a parent, it would be a pleasure listening to your child read. Gwen had a quick, nimble mind and read well.

Ronnie let Gwen read longer than she should, but Gwen obviously enjoyed it. She would prefer it if every child took a turn reading, but she had a policy of not forcing them. Some kids struggled with the words and others were horribly shy, as she had been at that age. She made it her business to sit with the quiet students and have them read to her at least once a week, so she'd know who needed extra help.

"Thank you, Gwen. Who's next?" The class took turns reading for twenty minutes and then she left them to read on their own.

Ronnie sat at her desk and pulled out the grade sevens' compositions. She had six left and had promised to hand them back after lunch. She'd have to hurry. Every so often, she scanned the students to see that they were working. Gwen was reading from a book that was much smaller than the assigned one. Ronnie walked over to have a look. "Horses?"

Gwen grinned up at her. "Yes, Ms. Yakimoto. A whole book of them." Gwen half turned to look at her mother. "My mom gave it to me." Gwen held the book up. "It has pictures and tells about each breed. What they look like, where they're from, and fun stuff like that."

Ronnie glanced at Mrs. Connor who winced slightly and then gave her a small, polite smile. "How did you like the reading assignment?"

"I'm done. It was okay. Easy, but okay."

"Would you be willing to help Toby? Sit and read with him."

Gwen frowned and glanced over her shoulder at the large boy seated at the back. She shrugged.

"How about Lisa?" Ronnie asked. When Gwen brightened, Ronnie sent her over to sit beside Lisa.

Ronnie studied Toby as she walked toward him. He wasn't reading but was clearly drawing something. She'd work with him herself. "Hi, Toby." Ronnie pulled a chair over. "Let's read together. You start." She pretended not to see the excellent drawing of a spaceship. Toby sighed, opened his book, and in a halting voice, started to read aloud.

He wasn't a bad kid; he'd just prefer to be somewhere else. It was Friday and in a few hours they'd both be free.

Ronnie glanced outside. It was a sunny day, and at this rate the last of the snow would melt away soon, then there'd be no crashing on the road like the week before, when Lauren Cornish had given her a ride. With the snow gone, she could get her racing bike out, hit the roads, and ride until she couldn't stand up. On her bicycle, life made sense. Her mind cleared of everything but the chore of maintaining her balance and setting a steady rate of pedaling. Alone, against the wind, she found peace.

She concentrated on Toby. The grade seven assignments would take up her whole lunch hour now. She sighed. It was her own fault for watching that movie. She'd intended to only watch thirty minutes, but then the couch had been comfortable and Dover was curled beside her quietly snoring. She hadn't wanted to leave him and had fallen asleep. She'd woken in the middle of the night and gone to bed.

"Thanks, Toby. Good job." Ronnie reached the front of her class just as the bell rang. The students rose and chatted noisily as they packed up.

She picked up an assignment. She had ten minutes between classes, enough time to mark one.

"Ms. Yakimoto, this is my mom."

Ronnie looked up into two pairs of identical intelligent blue eyes and smiled. She stood and shook Mrs. Connor's hand. "Hello."

"I'm Valerie, Val Connor. Pleased to meet you, Ms. Yakimoto."

"Ronnie."

"We've met before, but I didn't know if you'd remember."

She didn't and just managed to keep from blurting that out. "It's nice to see you again."

"Bye, Mom, I've got to go."

Val kissed Gwen on the cheek and smiled at her as she left the classroom, then she turned back to Ronnie. "Gwen did a lot of reading out loud."

"She likes to. I don't make anyone read out loud who doesn't want to." Ronnie moved a chair close to Val. "Would you like to sit down?"

"Thanks." Val sat. "How do they learn to read then?"

"I sit with them individually." Ronnie slid into her chair. "And more of the kids would volunteer to read if their parents weren't here. I was horribly shy at Gwen's age. I can still picture the face of my third grade teacher as he pulled me to the front of the class when my mother was visiting. I caught my mother's critical look and proceeded to trip over every second word. I almost peed my pants." She laughed. "I don't want some poor kid twenty years from now reliving a nightmare with me in it."

"That was mean of him." Val studied her for a second. "You care about the kids."

"I do. I want them to learn, but have a little fun doing it." Ronnie shrugged.

"Sorry about the book."

Ronnie blinked and tried to relax her clenched hands. They'd gone from an intense conversation about her mother to Val apologizing about a book, and she couldn't keep up. "What book?"

"The book about horses. I never intended her to bring it to school."

"Oh, that's okay."

"It is?"

"Sure. I know that if Gwen is reading her own book it means she's finished reading the schoolbook. She's good like that."

"You wouldn't prefer she read something else?"

"Such as?" Ronnie squinted at Val, completely unsure where the conversation was going.

"Another schoolbook." Val waved toward the two low shelves of books at the front of the class.

"I prefer to leave it up to her." Ronnie shrugged. "And you." She grinned and casually spun the tires of a tiny toy bicycle she kept on her desk.

"Me?" Val pointed to herself.

"Sure. Help her pick another book to read when she's read the schoolbook."

"Isn't that *your* job?"

Ronnie smiled, not in the least put off by the question. "I teach the books I select for the whole class. It's good when parents are involved in their kids' extracurricular reading." She raised her hand when Val opened her mouth. "But if you want me to help Gwen pick out extra books, I'm happy to do that. There are some fun ones I think she'll like."

"Fun? What about something more intellectually stimulating? When I was her age my mom started me on the classics like *Tom Sawyer* and *Black Beauty*."

"You and our mothers went to the same school of parenting. Mine was always yelling at me to 'put the comic books down and read a real book.'" Ronnie shook her head. "My mother yelled so loud my brothers joked that she rattled windows on the next block." Ronnie wagged her finger and raised her voice slightly. "Sharon Grace Yakimoto, your brain is going to wither away to dust if you keep reading comic books." Ronnie laughed.

"I wish I was more like *my* mom, and we never yell at Gwen. I just want what's best for her."

"Sorry, I didn't mean to imply—I have a book in mind. It's good quality literature, and still fun."

Val's shoulders relaxed and she smiled. "Thank you. Please help her. What's the book you're thinking of?"

"*Anne of Green Gables*."

Val's frown was back in an instant. "The one about the redhead."

"Yes, Anne had red hair, but she's also a feisty young girl, with a quick mind and great imagination. She'll appeal to Gwen. Have you read it?"

"No." Val squared her shoulders.

Ronnie studied Val. Her modest skirt and matching jacket made her look as if she were headed for a job interview, or maybe she was a lawyer or banker. She looked about thirty and held her purse primly in front of her. "Really? You've never read it?"

Val sighed. "I was teased in school about my red hair and people called me Anne Shelley. I wouldn't be caught dead reading the book after that."

"Shirley."

"Yes, really. I didn't read it."

"Not surely, I mean Shirley as in the name. It's Anne Shirley."

"My mistake." Val glanced at the students filing into the classroom. "I should probably go. You have another class and I want to slip into Gwen's math class. Thank you."

"Okay, good-bye." Ronnie gave a small wave as Val darted out of the classroom. Val was petite, several inches shorter than her, and so beautiful when she smiled, with her white teeth and smattering of freckles across pale skin. She had longer hair than Gwen, but it was tied up in a tight updo. Probably trapped for the day.

Ronnie ran her hand through her loose hair. She'd worn her hair in a tight ponytail as a child because her mother said it was tidier. It had pulled and given her a headache. If you wanted a tidy cap of hair, why not just cut it off? And as soon as she'd reached high school, she had cut it off. Her mother had been pissed for days and said Ronnie looked like her brothers. If the old witch could see it now.

Ronnie brushed the bangs off her forehead. She'd needed a cut for ages and after school she'd call for an appointment and see if they could squeeze her in. She needed a cut every four weeks and should book ahead, but she always figured she could go last minute.

Ronnie watched tall, blond Callie Anderson stride into the classroom and fold herself into one of the chairs at the back. She draped one jean-clad leg over the other and leaned back. Ronnie tugged at her collar as the temperature rose. Callie's long blond hair was down and caught casually with a clip at the back of her neck. What would it feel like to bury her face in it? Callie was taken, but no harm in looking. She looked away and smiled as her next group of kids filed in.

"Class, please get out your books and remember that today is our open house. Your parents will be moving from classroom to classroom watching you work and watching me." Ronnie shuddered and smiled as the grade four class laughed.

Chapter Four

At lunch time on Monday, Ronnie flipped open her laptop and scanned her school email account. It had been three days since she last looked. She needed to keep up or she was going to miss something important. Fortunately, there was only one from the vice principal listing several parents who had complained about how slow she was to return assignments. She leaned back in her chair and bit into her sandwich. She'd thought the open house went well on Friday, but apparently, parents had still complained about her. What else was new?

It had been interesting speaking with Valerie Connor. Beautiful, but buttoned up. The young professional ready to make the world her own. Ronnie slapped her forehead and pushed papers around until she found a scrap. She wrote *FIND BOOKS FOR GWEN.* She'd promised Val a list. Better not forget that or Val might be disappointed in her.

Ronnie shook her head to dispel the uncomfortable thought and opened the next email from the physical education teacher, Linda Strobel. She liked Lin, who was into cycling too, although she didn't compete like Ronnie. She read the email about a sports day for the kids. "Good idea." She finished her sandwich and headed to the gym to find Lin.

Ronnie stepped into the gym and leaned against the wall to watch Lin do laps. As she passed, she held up her finger. Ronnie nodded and waited.

Lin returned and grabbed a towel off the bleaches to mop her face. "Hey, you. Thought I might see you. Ready to get fit?" Lin laughed and playfully whipped Ronnie's stomach with the towel. "Just kidding. I want to go cycling with you again soon. But only a short distance."

"We can ride together. No problem. When you're done, I'll head out for a longer ride."

"Ha, so my whole ride is your warm-up?" Lin flicked Ronnie in the stomach with the towel again.

Ronnie shrugged. "We all have our specialties. I couldn't hit the basket with a basketball if I was standing beside it."

"You stand under a basketball net."

"That proves my point. So, I saw your email about a sports day. What's the plan?"

Lin sat in the bleachers and opened a bottle of water. After a long drink, she spoke. "I'm thinking of a fun day of sports. Not like track and field day. All the kids should have fun at a sports day, not just the athletic ones. What do you think?"

Ronnie settled beside her. "I agree completely. We preach fitness to these kids, but only the most athletic get on the teams and the others need exercise too. More kids would play if there were less pressure to win. When is it?"

"June forth. So, will you be in charge?"

"What? Me?"

"Yes, figure out the sports, organize the day, coordinate with parents. Stuff like that. You've got a month."

"Isn't that your job?"

"I'll help, but I also coach girls basketball and volleyball. And I have to run the track and field day. Please, Ronnie. Please." She drew out the plea and held her hands up in prayer.

"And I don't coach anything so I have the time?" Ronnie hung her head and groaned. "You want me to organize kids and parents? I can barely organize Dover and me. Have mercy."

"I'm desperate. No mercy." Lin punched Ronnie in the shoulder. "Ask for help and delegate some of the organizing. You know Valerie Connor, right? Her daughter Gwen's in your class."

"She was here last Friday for the open house."

"Val will *love* to help. She was awesome last year, and I've never met anyone more organized. Tell her I've already ordered the prizes."

Ronnie flinched inwardly at the thought of working with a woman as uptight as Val criticizing her every decision. At least Val wouldn't be able to yell at her. "Do I call her or something?"

"You'll figure it out."

Ronnie stood when the bell rang. "I have a class now. Send me her contact info and I'll do something."

"Don't you have her email already?"

"I don't encourage the parents to email me. I'm not spending half my evening answering them. If they're really concerned, they can make an appointment to meet me." Or email the vice principal.

"I'll also send you the master schedule Val put together last year. It's all in a computer spreadsheet. Have fun."

Ronnie scowled and pointed at Lin. "Next time we ride, we're doing hills."

"Is that my punishment?"

"It's just phase one."

"Bring it on. Hey, you ride horses, right?" Lin asked.

"Western. Since I was eight years old. Why?"

"Starview Farm has horses and they board them too. Anyway, last summer they had beginners riding lessons, but they're not offering it this year because they have no instructor. My girls are bummed. They want to learn to ride."

"I'm not a riding instructor."

"You're a teacher and you're a rider. Why don't you see if you can get hired to teach this summer?"

No summer school teaching and she could be outdoors. "It would help with the house payments. Maybe I'll go talk to them. Thanks for the idea."

"My kids would think I was a hero if I found them lessons. I'll send you Starview's info."

"I have it. Last fall I rented a horse a few times, just to hack around and keep my hand in. They're good people and take care of their horses. I'll think about it. See ya, Lin."

"Have fun with sports day. Call Val."

"Yes, boss." Ronnie headed back to her classroom. Val was beautiful, but so uptight, just like Ronnie's mother. And of course, Val had a spreadsheet. Ronnie groaned.

❖

After breakfast and a walk on Saturday morning, Ronnie loaded Dover in the car and headed to Starview Farm. She was proud of herself for only waiting three days to follow up on Lin's tip about a possible job teaching riding.

She parked beside the barn and headed inside. There was lots of activity at the farm, people mucking out stalls and others saddling or grooming horses. She waved to Mandy Trevor. "Hey, kid. Your mom or dad around?"

"Hey, Ronnie." Mandy jogged over and Dover trotted to meet her. She kneeled to pet him and kissed him on the nose. "How are you, Dover? Cute boy." Mandy fussed over him and then stood. "Mom's in the office. You taking a horse out?"

"Not today. Just here to visit. Thanks." She headed to the farm office and tapped on the open door. "Hi, Claire. Mandy said you were in here. Do you have a few minutes to talk?"

"Sure, close the door and have a seat." Dover walked over to Claire and pressed against her knees. She bent and petted him. "Hello, Dover. You look good." Claire ruffled his ears. "Such a good boy." Claire held up a dog treat so Ronnie could see it. "Okay?" Claire asked.

Ronnie nodded.

"Here's a cookie for you." Claire continued to pet him and then looked up at Ronnie. "What can I do for you?"

"I've been riding Western since I was eight," Ronnie said.

"And you're good."

"Thanks." Ronnie shrugged. Compliments still caught her off guard. There weren't many in her house while she was growing up. "I heard you might need somebody to teach beginners riding lessons."

"You ever teach riding?"

"No, but I am a teacher." Ronnie glanced up as a somebody opened the door and entered Claire's office without knocking.

"You should hire her. She's a great rider," the intruder said as she walked in behind her.

Had this person been listening in on their conversation? Ronnie focused on the woman's face. "Irene? Irene Schmidt?"

"It's me."

Ronnie stood and embraced her. "What a surprise."

Irene hugged Ronnie back. "For me, too." Irene faced Claire. "Ronnie and I grew up in Manitoba. We spent Saturdays and all summer at the same stable riding and generally getting in the way. Typical barn rats." Irene poked Ronnie. "Your dad had to drag you home at the end of the day."

"He did, but I loved it at the barn."

"And our experience got us summer jobs at the stable. Hey, let's get a coffee."

Ronnie sat. "Maybe later. I'm sort of in a job interview."

"But it's over, right? You got the job?" Irene asked.

"We're still talking," Ronnie said. She dipped her head, uncomfortable with Irene's rudeness and presumption, behaviors she'd gotten used to when they were kids. Clearly, Irene hadn't changed much.

"Irene, would you excuse us for a bit?" Claire rose and herded Irene out the door, closing the door behind her. "So, you know Irene?"

"I haven't seen her since high school."

"She's an excellent trainer and gives some private lessons. She taught the beginners last year, but…"

"Did you have a good group?"

"We started with fifteen and ended with six."

"*Nine* quit?"

Claire nodded. "Irene should stick to teaching older kids and adults. She was too impatient with the little ones."

Ronnie nodded. It made sense. When they were working at the barn, Irene hadn't been very warm toward the kids and had even bullied the younger ones. "I teach grades two to eight. Kids want to learn, but also have fun. There needs to be a balance."

"Glad you see that. I'll discuss your proposal with my husband and one of us will call you." Claire stood and shook Ronnie's hand. "Will that suit?"

"Absolutely, and thanks for your time." Ronnie headed out the door. The interview had gone well despite the awkwardness created by Irene. It was nice of Irene to try to help her out though. Ronnie searched the walkways between the stalls for Irene. Coffee with an old friend would be great.

Ronnie turned a corner and leaned against the wall to wait. Irene was speaking with a girl who looked about fifteen or sixteen.

"I want you to groom Balius again and do his feet as well," Irene said.

"I did groom him."

"Groom him until he shines. Oh, and I told Mandy not to give him any grain tonight."

"Our lesson was over an hour. He worked hard."

"Not hard enough."

"But—"

"Your parents hired me to train him and teach you. I say no grain."

"Okay, Irene. I'll just text my mom and tell her I'm going to be late."

"Good." Irene looked up. "Ronnie, hey. You get the job?"

Ronnie spotted the tears the girl was trying to brush away as she passed. Apparently, Irene wasn't great with older kids either, and what was the point in withholding the horse's grain? If it was meant to punish him, it wouldn't work. He wouldn't understand, he'd just be hungry. Ronnie shrugged. She wasn't a trainer. Maybe Irene knew best. "Not sure. There'll be some more discussion first. So, you train horses now?"

"Full-time, mostly in Saskatoon, but at a few outlier places like this. And you?"

"I'm a schoolteacher here in Thresherton. I teach English to grades two to eight."

"Schoolteacher? You traded Winnipeg for Thresherton? But it's so boring here. What do you do with your spare time?"

"Teaching is great, and so is Thresherton." She had no idea why she felt the need to defend the little town she hadn't even lived in very long, but she couldn't help it.

Irene leaned down to pet Dover, but he moved behind Ronnie. "Is this skinny old dog Dover? You still have him?"

"Dover's old but doing well. Say hi, Dover. You remember Irene?" Dover pressed harder to the back of Ronnie's legs and hid his face.

Irene pulled a cookie out of her pocket. "Here, Dover, you want this?"

Dover didn't budge. He generally loved any people food he could get. Ronnie frowned. Maybe she needed to take him to the vet again. "He just ate. Guess he's full. Or maybe he'll eat it off the floor," Ronnie said. "So, where shall we go for coffee?"

Irene dropped the cookie on the floor and crushed it into crumbs with the heel of her boot. "Not today, but I have time for a smoke. I have to make sure Miss Moneybags grooms her horse properly, then I have another nag to train."

Ronnie and Dover followed Irene outside and around the corner of the barn.

"Give me your phone," Irene said and held out her hand.

Ronnie unlocked her phone and handed it over. Why had Irene tried to pull her out of a meeting for coffee when she clearly didn't have time? It was weird.

Irene fiddled with the phone. "There, now you have my phone number. Text me and we'll do something. Now for a smoke." Irene pulled out a joint, lit it, and took a deep puff, then she handed it to Ronnie.

Ronnie stepped back. "No, thanks." Pot was a waste of time and she was done with it.

"Come on. We smoked all the time in high school."

"I'm not a kid anymore. And I should get going anyway. See you later, and thanks for putting in a good word for me with Claire. Text me next time you're here."

Ronnie and Dover jumped in her car and headed toward home. Dover looked out the window and barked at any cows they passed. She petted him and played with his ears. "You weren't very friendly with Irene." Dover turned and raised his eyebrows as he studied her. "Something there, eh, old friend?" Dover licked her hand. "I wish you could talk."

Dover returned to barking at cows and Ronnie concentrated on her driving. It was nice to see Irene and she could use some friends, but the whole encounter and been odd and unsettling. And why had nine of Irene's students really quit? "It's a mystery."

Dover didn't comment as he was busy barking at a field of Charolais cattle. The sign at the road said Poplarcreek. "Those are Becky Anderson's cows. Better stop barking." She rubbed his ears and Dover settled with his head in her lap. She petted him as she drove and smiled as the contact gave her a sense of peace and contentment.

CHAPTER FIVE

Val peered through the window of her house and watched Becky, Gwen, and Becky's dog, Max, as they played a complicated game of tag in the backyard. Gwen, the light of her life, and Callie's daughter, Becky, were friends, but opposites in appearance. Becky was a grade ahead and nine months older than Gwen but appeared much older because she was tall. Becky had dark brown hair and brown eyes, a complete contrast to Callie's blond hair and blue eyes, but Callie hadn't given birth to Becky. Callie's late wife, Liz, was Becky's birth mother.

Val grinned at the antics of the trio. "You go, Gwen." Gwen was quick and agile and dodged when Becky reached for her.

Max, the border collie, yipped happily as he chased Becky and Gwen. He was healthy and fast on three legs and loved by everyone.

Val opened the back door. "Come in please, you three. Dinnertime."

Becky and Gwen dropped their game and ran for the door, laughing and poking each other. Val enjoyed having Becky stay with them. Lauren was surprising Callie with a weekend at a cabin in Prince Albert National Park. A cabin in the middle of May wasn't every woman's idea of a romantic weekend, but it was for Callie and Lauren. A snug cabin with a hot tub and a wood-burning fireplace sounded heavenly to Val, too.

Gwen and Becky shed coats and boots and washed their hands.

"Girls, the pizzas are ready. You can each carry yours to the table. Watch the cheese—it'll be very hot and can burn you." Val stepped toward the stove to help the process. Each of them had prepared a pizza and decorated them with the toppings they preferred.

They'd spent a fun afternoon cutting toppings and rolling the pizza dough. Gwen and Becky had done their best, but the cutting was uneven. Some of the pepperoni was a quarter inch thick and other slices almost transparent. Val had wanted to cut them herself and cut them all the same thickness, but it would've spoiled Becky and Gwen's fun.

"And, Max, here's your food." Val placed a bowl of kibble and canned food on the floor for the collie. He never received table scraps, so expected none of the pizza, but he bounced around with Becky and Gwen from excitement and sheer joy.

Val cut her pizza and lifted a piece to bite it. Becky was struggling with hers. "Hey, Becky, your pizza is just a little thin in places. That's why you can't pick it up."

"Sorry, Val."

"Oh, that's okay. It takes practice." There was a thin side and a thick side to the pizza. Val had offered to roll out Becky's crust to make it even, but rolling was the fun part. Still, she'd had to practically sit on her hands to keep from interfering.

"Just roll the thin side," Gwen said as she demonstrated. Becky followed suit and grinned with her mouth full of rolled up pizza.

Dinner wasn't a quiet meal. Val gave up trying to follow the conversation as Gwen and Becky leaped from topic to topic. Becky and Gwen discussed a television show, Becky's latest painting, and the indoor soccer club at school. Val grinned. Gwen did ninety percent of the talking. Becky smiled shyly and only offered a few comments as she wolfed down her pizza.

Val had talked a lot at Gwen's age. Her mother had encouraged her chatter and had always taken the time to listen and respond. Val let Gwen talk all she wanted. It was dinnertime, not the library.

Val shuddered. In a few years, their conversation would include boys, or not, who knew. Becky and Gwen would talk about dating and kissing, and whether it was boyfriends or girlfriends didn't matter. But time moved so quickly, and she wasn't ready for them to be that grown up.

After dinner, Val carried her dishes to the sink. "Girls, can you two clean up the kitchen, please? I'm going to my room."

"Yes, Mom."

"Yes, Val."

Val stretched out on her bed. Emotional exhaustion overwhelmed her, and even the noise in the kitchen couldn't keep her awake. Her house was a two-bedroom bungalow with a living room, large storage closet, and a generous eat-in kitchen. It wasn't big by any means, but it suited her and Gwen just fine. Becky and Gwen would do the dishes and get them fairly clean. With any luck, the dishes would be still in the drainboard and not put away, then she could wash them properly after Becky and Gwen were in bed.

Val listened to the silence. They'd gone quiet. It always worried her when they fell silent, but she didn't need to be concerned, really. They were good girls and always cleaned up after their cooking projects. She would stay put and not spoil their fun. They would be fine in the kitchen.

Val curled around a pillow. It was going to be a quiet weekend. She missed having a girlfriend to meet or to at least call and talk to. Did Ronnie like to talk on the phone or text? Was she a chatterer or an action woman? Val rolled on her side and thought about her, as she had done since meeting her at the school. Ronnie was an athlete. She would be all action.

Her phone rang, interrupting her mental picture of what Ronnie would be like to spend time with. Val glanced at the number but didn't recognize it. "Hello?"

"Is this Mrs. Connor?"

"It's Val." She almost said Mrs. Connor was her mother, but she'd given up trying to correct strangers. To everyone else she was Val or Ms. Connor.

"Hi, Val, this is Ronnie Yakimoto. Do you have a few minutes to talk?"

Heat built in Val's face and she was relieved nobody could see it. Had Ronnie somehow known she'd been thinking of her? "I have time. How are you tonight?"

"Surviving. I went for a bike ride today and overdid it. I'm lying with my feet propped up, trying to find something to watch."

"Good luck with that. Most of the stuff on television is garbage." Val winced at how judgmental that sounded. "We just had dinner and I left Becky and Gwen with the dishes."

"Becky Anderson?"

"The very one. She and Gwen are good friends."

"Speaking of the kids...I wanted to talk to you about school."

A sinking feeling took over and Val sighed. "Everything okay?"

"Yes...well, no...I mean, maybe." Ronnie cleared her throat. "It's about sports day this year. Lin wants me to organize it. I told her I would be hopeless, and she said you might help."

"Oh, she did?"

"She said you did an awesome job last year. I'm looking at the spreadsheet you built and I'm impressed."

"When does she want to do it?"

"June forth."

Val sat up. "Are you kidding me? That's three weeks away."

"Can't be. It's at least a month."

"It's three weeks, and I assumed it wasn't happening this year because I never heard from her."

"What if we just follow the same schedule you made for last year?"

"But, Ronnie, we have to organize parents and teachers and order the prizes. Why would she give us only three weeks?"

"Lin said she'd ordered the prizes."

"That's something." There was a minute of silence. "Are you still there?"

"Yes."

Val barely heard Ronnie. "Ronnie?"

"It's my fault. Confession time. Lin asked me a week ago. I kept meaning to call you and get things in motion, but time just flew."

"Three weeks isn't enough time."

"It has to be. I can't disappoint the kids. They'll be expecting it. I'm such an idiot."

The crushed tone in Ronnie's voice was more than Val could bear. Ronnie had procrastinated, but she was asking for help and Val couldn't say no. "Yes, I'll help you, but we have a lot of work to do."

"Thanks, tell me what to do."

"On page one of the spreadsheet is a list of about ten names. Do you see it?"

"I do. Some are teachers."

"Yes, and the others are parents. Contact them all and set up a meeting for Tuesday night at seven p.m. at the school. Get whoever will or can come."

"But it's already Saturday."

Val covered her mouth to keep from laughing out loud. Ronnie sounded just like Gwen when she felt she'd been given an impossible task. "It is, but we've only got three weeks. We'll use your classroom and get coffee and snacks."

"I guess I'd better get calling people. Thanks. You saved my life."

"Glad to hear it. See you on Tuesday." Val hung up and burrowed beneath her comforter. Just talking to Ronnie had made her day and now she had a project. A nearly hopeless one, but a project all the same, and one that would put her in Ronnie's orbit, where she could see what kind of person she was. Why had Ronnie done nothing for a week? Val shook her head. If she wasn't so happy, she'd contemplate strangling Ronnie for her procrastination.

There was a knock at the door and Gwen said, "Mom, are you all right?"

Val shot upright. "Come in, honey. I'm okay. Just being lazy."

Gwen opened the bedroom door and grinned at Val. "You're resting. That's not lazy. Becky says Lauren often has a nap after work."

"Does she? Lucky her."

"Are you coming back to the kitchen?"

Val was right, the silence had meant they were up to something. Becky and Gwen had a surprise. Gwen could hide nothing. She blushed, a clear sign she was excited. Val stood and drew Gwen into a tight hug.

"Mom?"

When Val let go, she registered Gwen's worried expression. It was unusual for Val to disappear after dinner. "I'm okay and I'll be there in five minutes." She kissed Gwen on the top of the head and plodded to the bathroom to splash cold water on her face and pull herself from the gloomy place she'd been wallowing in. But the gloom was gone. A short conversation with Ronnie even about an impossible project had cheered her up.

When Val arrived in the kitchen, Gwen and Becky presented her with dessert. They had baked a simple white cake and dished out three portions smothered in a chunky berry sauce, a tasty concoction of Callie's.

"This looks delicious." Val settled into a chair at the table and dropped a generous scoop of French vanilla ice cream on her cake and berries. She would need her energy. It was going to be a busy few weeks, but she would see lots of Ronnie. She would see her at the school and it would be strictly professional, but nice all the same. "Girls, would you like another sports day this year?"

"Yes, please. Last year was awesome," Becky said.

"It was so much fun and I got to be a team captain. I never get to be a captain," Gwen said.

"What did you like best?"

Val ate her dessert and listened to the girls dissect sports day, listing what they liked and making faces at what they thought were baby games. She tried to concentrate, but her mind returned to her conversation with Ronnie. She'd sounded desperately in need of rescuing and there was truth to it. That kind of procrastination meant she probably wasn't relationship material, but she could be fun to spend time with anyway.

CHAPTER SIX

Ronnie closed her binder and let her head drop to the desk. "Oh my God. What have I done?"

Val laughed. "You volunteered to run sports day. This is just the first meeting, wait until we get closer to the day."

"But I had no idea it was so much work." Ronnie was struggling not to whine.

"What did you think? You'd give the kids a few balls and set them loose for the day?"

"Can we?"

Val laughed. "No, and you're stuck now."

"I know, but oh my God."

"Put the tasks in order. Start one, finish it, move on to the next. It's doable, just barely."

"I caught that 'just barely.' Everyone here tonight is questioning the timeline."

"But they were all here."

"That's because I told them you were helping me. And I quote, 'Oh, if Val's there then it will all work out.' People have a very high opinion of you."

Val blushed. "I try to do what I say I'm going to. Now stop whining. Copy down all the lists we wrote on the white boards."

"All of them?"

"Yes, and then type them up and circulate them by email."

"What if I just took a picture of them?"

"Fine, take the picture and then type them up."

"Bossy."

"You ain't seeing nothing yet. Don't take this wrong, but if you'd rather do this without me, I'm okay with that."

Ronnie held up her hands in submission. "No, no, I'll do whatever you say. But is this a 'my way or the highway scenario'?"

"Yes, so, when will we meet next? We haven't even talked about food," Val said.

"Food!" Ronnie threw her hands up and laughed.

"And drink. Did you think the kids were going to play all day without being fed?"

"I saw that page in your spreadsheet, but I was hoping it wasn't for sports day. Can't their parents send them with lunch or something?"

"No, and the next meeting is Thursday night. Call the parents and teachers under the food heading on page two of my spreadsheet."

"Okay."

"Gwen's at Poplarcreek tonight. Do you want to get a coffee or a drink or something?"

"No, thanks. I've been told I have to copy all this down, type it out, and call a bunch of people."

"Okay, night, Ronnie."

Ronnie pushed her papers into a pile. She liked joking with Val and loved the blushing, but then the fun was gone. Val had looked a little downcast when she left, her smile a little forced. She thought of their conversation and nearly smacked herself in the head.

Ronnie dashed outside and ran into the parking lot, but Val was already pulling away and couldn't see her waving. She had Val's phone number but not handy in her phone. It was just as well. She'd crushed on straight girls before and it never ended well.

Ronnie trudged back to the classroom and took pictures of the lists. She'd take them home and type them out.

On Thursday night, Ronnie pulled a couple of bags of cookies from her desk. Next, she fetched a selection of sodas from the staff lunchroom and started a pot of coffee. When she returned with the coffee, Val was already there. She'd pushed two desks together and set out some containers of food.

"What've you got?" Ronnie asked.

Val jumped. "Hi, Ronnie, just some squares and sliced fruit."

"Home baking?" Ronnie had supplied store bought cookies for the Tuesday meeting too. Evidently, that wasn't quite up to par.

"There's no other kind. Do you think we could have plates tonight? The napkins worked on Tuesday, but the fruit is wet."

An hour later, Ronnie had a sense of déjà vu. She was sitting with her head on her binder and groaning loudly.

"Stop that," Val said. "You hardly have to do anything about the food. The cafeteria staff will take care of it, and the custodians will see that the garbage and recycling are set up."

"I was just trying to be dramatic. I suppose I should copy down those new lists?"

"Yes." Val smiled and nodded. "Good night."

"Would you like to get coffee?"

Val glanced at her watched. "My parents are expecting me in thirty minutes to pick up Gwen. I need to get her home to bed. She has school tomorrow, well, of course you know that and you do too…" Val blushed and dropped her face in her hands. "Feel free to stop me any time."

"I like listening to you. What if you stayed here for a little longer and we chatted? There's sodas left, or I could make fresh coffee."

"I'd like that and soda's fine."

Ronnie pushed two of the children's desks together, nose to nose, and fetched two sodas. She and Val sat and sipped.

"So, Gwen's with your parents. Would I have met them in town?"

"I don't know. My mom works part-time in the library and my dad works for the railway."

"I haven't taken out a book or taken a train since I arrived."

"No books?"

"Oh, I'm a reader. I have a stack at home that I'm working my way through. I buy them faster than I can read them. How about siblings?"

"I'm an only child."

"What does your husband do?" Ronnie asked.

Val coughed and held a napkin over her mouth. "You thought I had a husband? I asked you to coffee. I wouldn't do that if I had a husband."

Ronnie nearly spilled her soda as she set it back down. "Not coffee between friends?"

Val shifted nervously. "Ronnie, I'm gay. I thought you knew that. Most everyone in town knows."

Ronnie sat back. She assumed there must be a man in Val's life. Val acted almost matronly, and her life seemed to revolve around her job and her child. Ronnie had made a foolish assumption based on preconceived ideas. What an ass.

"Callie and Lauren are too," Val said.

"I knew that. I just—I'm embarrassed."

"That's okay. I'm glad we sorted that out." Val sipped her soda and looked at Ronnie over the can, her eyes alight with amusement.

"I'm gay too."

Val laughed. "I figured that."

"So, is this the point in the conversation where two lesbians start talking about their exes?"

"Let's not."

"Agreed." Still, Ronnie couldn't help but wonder what kind of women Val went for.

Val glanced at her watch. "I wish I didn't have to run off, but I can't be late."

"Not for your parents?"

"Especially not for my parents. Next meeting is Tuesday night. First group again."

"Yes, boss."

Val hesitated at the door. "And I can stay later on Tuesday if you want to go for coffee."

"I'd like that." Ronnie smiled as Val hurried out. So, Valerie Connor was a lesbian. That was interesting. Ronnie pressed her temples as a familiar throbbing started. Making friends with a straight woman had seemed safer, but just because Val said she was gay didn't mean she was single. "We'll just be friends. No problem."

On Tuesday night after the meeting, Ronnie followed Val to the Thresherton Diner and parked beside her. They entered and found a table for two at the back. "That went better tonight," Ronnie said as she perused a menu.

"Everyone's good about getting their work done. Almost everyone." Val tilted her head as she looked at the menu.

"I got the lists typed."

"Yes, but you emailed it this morning. Most people didn't get a chance to read it before the meeting."

Ronnie put her hand over her heart. "I'll do better. Today's list will go out this weekend."

"Tomorrow."

"Can we negotiate and say Friday?"

"Thursday it is."

Ronnie laughed. "No wonder Gwen always has her homework done."

"It's how we roll in the Connor house. I'm starving. Late day at work and I didn't get home for dinner."

They ordered entrees and then sat back to sip their sodas. Ronnie started to ask a question just as two women came to their table. They were introduced to Ronnie, chatted a few minutes with Val, then moved off. "You know everybody?"

"Pretty much." Val waved to another group sitting by the window.

Twice more, people came over to visit. One was a farmer and questioned Val about the antibiotic he was using to treat his cattle. She asked him to call the clinic in the morning. Ronnie had wanted a quiet chat. She didn't expect the flood of people.

"It will stop when our food arrives. I promise."

"How do you know?" Ronnie asked.

"Happens every time. People here feel like it's rude to come up while you're eating."

Val was right. After their plates arrived, there were a few more waves and hellos to Val, but nobody stopped by. It was very civilized to leave them while they ate so their food wouldn't get cold.

"Thought that was you." Irene grabbed a chair and pushed it to their table, then she straddled it and stole a French fry off Ronnie's plate.

Ronnie frowned at the interruption. "Val, this is Irene Schmidt. Irene, this is Valerie Connor."

Val shook hands with Irene and returned to her meal.

"This is amazing. I haven't seen you in ten years, now I see you twice in two weeks," Ronnie said and tried to smile at her joke. She didn't want to see Irene. She wanted to visit with Val.

Irene took another fry. "So, you all set up for lessons?" She punched Ronnie. "Hope you can handle a bunch of whiny kiddies."

Val's head shot up and she frowned at Irene. "Excuse me for a second, Ronnie." Val headed over to the group by the window.

"She a lezzie? Hot date?" Irene asked.

"None of your business."

"Pardon me." Irene stood. "You need some weed?"

Ronnie shook her head furiously.

"Your loss, Grandma. See you at the stable." Irene snagged two more fries and left.

Ronnie returned Irene's chair to the table beside them and sighed. This wasn't the night she'd hoped it would be.

Val returned. "Sorry about that. I wanted to say hi to my cousins." Val continued with her meal.

"I should be the one to say sorry. My friend is the one that interrupted our dinner."

"It's what Irene would do."

"I know her from high school, my wild and crazy days. How do you know her?"

Val stabbed at a fry with her fork. "Gwen took riding lessons with her last summer."

"You don't seem happy about it."

"I never spoke to her directly. Irene only wanted to teach the best students. The ones to whom riding came naturally. She wanted the others to go away, but needed their fees."

"Claire told me about Irene teaching. I get the impression Starview has already decided Irene was a mistake. I guess they lost money on lessons last year."

"When Gwen quit, I recovered most of our money."

Ronnie leaned back. "You look like a fierce Celtic warrior." Val's hair glowed red in the light and her scowl was fierce. "I'd have refunded all your money just so you didn't separate my head from my shoulders."

"Maybe I am descended from Celtic warriors. My grandmother's family were Scottish Highlanders."

Ronnie wanted to stay away from the subject of family and returned to the subject at hand. "Claire Trevor asked me to teach beginners riding this summer."

"She did? I'm so excited and Gwen will be thrilled. She likes you. When is sign up?"

Ronnie grimaced. "Sign up?"

"When do we register for the class and pay?"

"I don't know. Claire sent me an email, but I haven't looked at it."

"Ronnie…"

Ronnie winced. She was always at least two steps behind when it came to Val. "I promise to look tonight and email you."

"Callie too. Becky will want to come."

"Yes, boss."

"Stop that." Val squeezed her forearm. "Have you been riding long?"

Ronnie swallowed as the light caress on her arm sent electricity shooting to all points in her body. "I rode Western when I was Gwen's age. We lived on the edge of Winnipeg and there are horses just outside the city. There was also a stable breeding Thoroughbreds, and I worked there every summer in high school. I spent most of my time with the foals and mares in the broodmare barn."

"Did you want to be a jockey?"

"For about five seconds. Sometimes I exercised the horses on the track, but I prefer riding Western. I wanted to buy a horse and learn barrel racing, but I couldn't afford all the expenses. You can buy a decent horse for not too much money, but boarding is the big cost."

"I can't afford one, that's for certain."

"Irene and I worked together. She was so amazing with the horses. We worked in the broodmare barn together for a year, then she moved to helping the trainers. Now she's a full-time horse trainer, with clients and everything." Ronnie shook her head. "It's impressive."

Val removed her hand and resumed eating. "She should probably stick to training horses."

Ronnie wanted to kick herself. Val had no use for Irene, and even the mention of her name sent a wall up between them. She dug through her brain for another topic of conversation. "Do you remember my dog, Dover?"

Val smiled and nodded. "Nice old gentleman."

"I had him in a couple of weeks ago. Dr. Cornish wrote a prescription for him. He's doing well on the new painkillers."

"How long's he been on them?"

"Two weeks."

"You got them right away? Sorry, that sounded bad."

Ronnie laughed. "I deserved that. No, I don't procrastinate when it comes to Dover. What he needs, he gets."

"That's very sweet."

"He's my best friend."

"That's also very sweet."

They finished their meal and lingered over coffee, talking about whatever simple things came up, until it was clear the restaurant was trying to close. Ronnie walked Val to her car and headed home. She let Dover into her backyard and then sat on the patio steps. She really needed to get some furniture out here.

It had been a pleasant evening, and even though sports day was a lot of work, spending time with Val each week was awesome. The most fun she'd had in months, or maybe years. And Val was so beautiful. No doubt she was taken, but she was nice to look at and fun to talk to. She'd be a good friend, and Ronnie could use more of them. Especially one as smart and funny as Val. And if Val had a girlfriend there would be no pressure. Maybe she'd even get two new friends.

CHAPTER SEVEN

There were several more meetings leading up to sports day, but she and Val never had a chance to meet alone again. Ronnie sighed. Others in the sports day preparations group had picked up on the pattern and joined them at the diner after meetings. Ronnie made several new friends, but for some reason she wouldn't analyze, she missed seeing Val alone. Sports day had been a huge success, and it had been amazing to see the kids having so much fun. Even the ones who usually avoided the active stuff got involved, and Ronnie had made sure to give them extra support. Watching Val run around with the kids hadn't been a hardship either.

Ronnie hooked Dover's leash on, picked up the bag, and headed out the door. She was expected at Val's house in an hour. Plenty of time for a walk at Dover's speed. She rolled her shoulders. It was the Sunday after sports day and she'd planned to sleep half of the day and then catch up on her marking, but Val had invited her for coffee, and she couldn't refuse. Didn't want to refuse.

Ronnie arrived on time, knocked, and Val answered. She had to keep herself from looking at Val's beautiful legs framed in white shorts. "Hi, Val, I brought Dover with me. I hope that's okay."

"Sure, come on in."

"I think his feet are clean. Let me check." She bent and started to lift his paws.

"He's okay. Bring him in." Val headed inside. "Gwen, Ms. Yakimoto is here and she has her dog with her." Val winked at Ronnie over her shoulder.

Gwen burst out of one of the bedrooms with Becky behind her. A border collie followed them and bounded over to greet Dover. "Hi, Ms. Yakimoto," Gwen said. "This is Max, Becky's dog."

Ronnie watched Dover politely accept the sniffing and licking from Max. "This is Dover." She tried to pet Max, but he never stopped moving.

Gwen squatted down and petted Dover. "We're going outside. Do you think Dover would like to come?"

"He would, but he's an old dog, so if he lies down in the shade to rest, you'll let him, right?" Ronnie asked.

Gwen and Becky nodded in unison, then turned and darted out Val's back door followed by Max.

"Come on, Dover," Gwen called from the backyard.

Dover looked up at Ronnie. "Go ahead, buddy, go play." Dover trotted out and Val closed the door behind him. Ronnie peered out the kitchen window at the action.

"He'll be fine. Gwen will take care of him and Max is energetic but friendly."

"I'm sure he'll be fine. It's just fun watching him almost run around. He loves to play with kids but rarely gets to. Look at him go after Max. He'll be sore tomorrow, but he can rest all day."

"I'm making coffee, or would you prefer tea?" Val asked.

Ronnie dragged her eyes from the window and focused on Val. "Tea please. Are we waiting for anyone? Your girlfriend?" Ronnie nearly rolled her eyes. *Smooth. Real smooth.*

Val fumbled the box of tea and almost dropped it on the floor. "Girlfriend? No, I'm single."

"Oh, I, oh…" Ronnie slid into a chair, not sure if she was happy or scared. Excitement surged in her chest, but she wasn't sure if it was the good kind.

A few quiet minutes later, Val set a mug in front of her. Ronnie sipped the much too hot drink and glanced around the room, searching for something to say. "This is a nice room. Looks like a page from a decorating catalogue." Thankfully, Val took up the topic change and put her out of her misery.

Val nodded. "I copied it from a catalogue. Right down to the neutral colors and inspiring sayings on the plaques."

"It suits you."

Val laughed. "What? Beige and folksy?"

Ronnie struggled for an answer. Val had backed her into a corner and was having fun with her. She'd been here before. Val loved to tease. "Organized. Everything in its place." That was a word that fit Val perfectly.

"Thanks. I like it, but speaking of organized, I wanted to talk about sports day."

"Thanks again for all your help. You saved my life."

"You can stop saying that. We did it together and you were pretty great."

"Thanks."

Val rested her chin in her palm. "The kids really like you. You were a lot of fun."

"So were you."

Val shook her head. "I was the taskmaster. Pushing them from place to place. You made it fun. I especially liked the way you solved the conflict between javelin and shotput. I didn't realize I hadn't given them enough room on the field when I scheduled them. What an idiot."

"You're allowed to make a mistake." Ronnie laughed. "But I'm eternally grateful that you caught it in time. Imagine if the events had started? One group of kids lobbing shotputs onto the others' heads and the other group retaliating with spears. Sort of a public school medieval war. We'd have made the evening news."

Val laughed. "Not sure how it worked with them going at the same time. I wasn't sure if the next thrower would have a shotput or a javelin."

"Neither did they. In the end the javelin kids were competing with the shotput kids. There were no injuries, and everyone went home with all their body parts intact."

Val laid her hand over Ronnie's. "Everyone had fun. That's what it was all about."

Ronnie stared at their hands for a second before she gently pulled hers away. "That's what life should be about."

Ronnie drank three cups of tea and chatted with Val about the other events and how much fun the kids had, and then she gave Val the thank you present she'd purchased.

Val held the plastic bag. "What's this?"

"Sorry, I didn't have anything to wrap it in. It's not much." Ronnie shrugged. "Just a little thank you for helping me."

Val pulled the object out of the bag. "It's a hat."

"Not just any hat. A ballcap, and it has a large opening at the back for your hair. I know you like your hair back and you said you couldn't find a hat to fit."

Val put the hat on and pushed her bun through the opening at the back. "It's perfect."

"And now you have the brim to protect your face and eyes. Sorry, it's fluorescent green. It was the only one I could find with the hole at the back. I looked in about six stores."

"I love it." Val laughed. "I'll still need a bucket of sunscreen, but I like the hat. It'll be better than being in the sun. Callie was worried I'd get sunstroke. She can fit her ponytail through the back of a regular ballcap, but I have more hair."

"You have beautiful hair. Very thick and luxurious." It was the truth, but it took on new meaning now that she knew Val was single. She needed to watch her step.

Val blushed. "Thanks, and thanks for the cap."

Later, when Gwen brought an exhausted Dover inside, Ronnie thanked Val for the tea and rose to leave, but Dover collapsed, panting at her feet after drinking a bowl of water.

"He's not walking home," Val said. "Will you stay for dinner or would you like a lift home?"

She thought about the way Val's hand had felt on hers. "Home, please. Are you rescuing me again?"

"If I can."

They drove to Ronnie's house. Val put a restraining hand on Ronnie's arm as she tried to get out of the car. "Did you want to ask me anything?"

Ronnie shook her head as she scrambled for an answer. Did she have a question? Was she supposed to ask anything? She looked at Val blankly.

Val waited a second and then smiled slightly. "Ronnie, I'm a lesbian, single, and a mom. I'm very busy, but I like people and I'm always happy to make new friends."

"Friends are good. I like friends. Thanks for the lift." Ronnie leaped from the car as if it were on fire.

She stood by her door and waved as Val drove down the street. Dover had already gone inside and was no doubt passed out in his bed. It had been a pleasant interlude and she was sorry she'd turned down Val's invitation to stay for dinner. But being friends with a hot, single lesbian wasn't easy. Things always got complicated, and she wanted life to be simple. She walked inside, plopped on the couch, and watched Dover sleep. Ronnie sighed. She had so many things to do and all she wanted was to be sitting with Val, watching her laugh and smile and blush when she was embarrassed. She'd made the right decision to come home, even if it didn't feel like it.

Ronnie yawned so hard she thought her jaw would dislocate. She downed half a cup of cold coffee, yawned again, and rested her head on the papers on her desk. Her classroom was empty, so she'd close her eyes, just for a minute…

"Ronnie?"

Ronnie lifted her head and blinked. Val was smiling and not trying to hide it. Ronnie brushed the wetness off the side of her face and glanced down at the wet spot on the papers. She'd put on an impressive display of sleeping and drooling. She stood and was about to jokingly ask if she'd been snoring, but the comment suddenly seemed inappropriate.

"Good morning. Have a seat. How are you?"

Val smirked. "Not as tired as you."

Ronnie winced. "Busted. Late night of grading papers. Always a rush this time of year." She'd been up all night grading papers and tests. School was done for the season in two weeks and she had to get the grading done. It had been a mistake to watch a movie first.

"What if you did them sooner?"

"Pardon?"

Val blushed. "I mean what if you marked them right away instead of letting them pile up?"

"How do you know I don't?" Ronnie grinned and sipped her coffee.

"Gwen told me. I guess all the work on sports day got in the way of marking."

Ronnie coughed and dabbed at the drops of coffee that landed on her sleeve. "Yeah, well..." She sighed. Of course, Gwen had told Val about waiting for grades. Some kids had complained about her. She sighed and gave her standard answer using her robot voice. "That's a good idea. Thank you for the suggestion. I'll try to do better." Today the parents were visiting and harassing the teachers again.

"Yikes. Guess I'm not the first one to mention that."

She instantly felt bad when Val seemed to shut down. "Sorry, you're the fourth one today, and I agree it's a bad habit. I grew up in a strict household. It was manageable until my father died, then my mother became this machine who scheduled everything and if you missed a deadline it was a disaster."

"I was taught not to miss deadlines. Was your mom just trying to teach you to be responsible?"

"Maybe, but it was too much. When I left home, I stopped organizing anything. Stopped being on time. I swear I wouldn't have made it to class if my friends hadn't gotten me out of bed. I never kept track of any dates, I just assumed people would remind me."

"Did it work for you? Does it?"

"Mostly, although I was, and am, probably pretty annoying. Like when I called you three weeks before sports day begging for help."

"Did I sound annoyed?"

"No, you didn't, but you should've been. Why weren't you?" This impromptu discussion about her family must mean she was really tired. She never talked to anyone about that stuff.

"What would've been the point? And I didn't mean to hassle you about marking assignments. Gwen just gets excited and likes to tell me her grades, but she can learn to wait." Val shrugged. "Probably best she learns now that you don't always get what you want." Val sighed softly.

"My turn to say yikes."

"Am I wrong? I planned to go to university and never made it. But I'm happy with my college diploma and the job I have. It *is* possible to be happy with what you have and to not want more."

Ronnie flashed to her planned career as a university professor. Teaching English, writing books, and traveling the world to discuss books. "Nope. I agree. I like teaching, and it wasn't my plan." Ronnie shuffled her papers. "So, I guess we should talk about Gwen. Would you like to ask me anything about her?"

"Not really. She had a good grade in English and likes your class, loves you." Val blushed. "Thanks for the books you recommended for her. I wouldn't have been able to suggest as good a selection as you did."

"My pleasure. How did you like them?"

"Me?" Val pointed to herself.

Ronnie grinned. "Gwen told me you read them after her."

Val blushed so deeply the red slid down her neck and throat and disappeared into the cleavage of her dress. How could she have thought Val was thirty? The blush and averted eyes made her look about twenty. Ronnie dragged her eyes up. It was not a good idea to get caught ogling the parents, but fortunately, Val was looking out the window

"I didn't read them all. I don't have the time, but I read the *Anne of Green Gables* series. Very enjoyable. I'd have loved them at Gwen's age."

"I'm glad." Ronnie folded her hands on her desk and watched Val look out the window.

After a few seconds, Val turned back. "Anything I should know about Gwen?"

"Great student. Helpful to the other kids. A pleasure to teach, and before you tease me about standard answers, it's all true."

"Thanks. Do you have some suggestions for the summer? For Gwen to read?"

"I can put together a list, but isn't the summer for fun?"

Val straightened. "She has fun and some of her fun is reading. I plan to let her pick any book she likes to start, but the next book should be from your list. Challenge her a little." Val picked up her purse as if to leave.

"No offense meant. Okay, I've got some ideas." Ronnie mentally listed books in her head. She'd put a list together for Gwen of good books, but nothing too heavy. Summer was for fun, not being forced to read the classics. "I forgot to mention that she always does her homework."

Val looked confused. "Of course."

"You say that like there's no other option."

Val set her purse down and tilted her head. "There isn't."

Ronnie laughed. "Plenty of options. At Gwen's age, I only occasionally had my homework done. Pulled a lot of all-nighters to get assignments done."

"And you haven't changed."

"Ouch." Ronnie laughed.

"Sorry, that sounded like a dig. I didn't—I mean it was…"

Ronnie laughed harder and wrapped her desk with her knuckles. "You got me again. And I bet you haven't changed either." She cupped her chin in the palm of her hand and studied Val. "I bet you always have your work done early."

Val shifted in her seat. "I don't, but I try. I'm my mother's daughter and she was all about punctuality and meeting deadlines." She lifted her chin. "Nothing wrong with that."

Ronnie raised her hands. "Absolutely nothing wrong." She glanced at her watch. "We still have a few minutes."

Val put her purse down. "How's Dover doing? He's a sweet dog."

"Enjoying the summer now he's willing to move around more. Dover's old but still wants to explore."

"Good. Keep him moving, but not so much it hurts him."

"How long have you been at PVS?"

"As a veterinary technician, six years, but I worked there in middle school, high school, and while I was at college. I guess it's been fourteen years."

"Fourteen. Wow." Ronnie hadn't even had a job for four years.

"I love what I do."

"Gwen writes stories about the animals that come in to PVS. She told me you tell her about them."

"I hope she doesn't use any names?"

"People and pet names are changed to protect the innocent. She has this cute little disclaimer on the bottom of her stories. I particularly like the one about the three-legged dog."

Val glanced toward the open door of the classroom and back at Ronnie. "Lauren, Dr. Cornish, saved him and he has a good home now."

"You worked on him too."

"Nursing care, bandages, all the regular stuff."

"Well, I'm impressed and so is Gwen. She's proud of you." Ronnie smiled as the blush returned and disappeared into Val's cleavage. "I guessed it's Becky Anderson's dog, Max. Becky described him in a story and his adventures at her farm. The two stories fit perfectly together, and then on Sunday I met Max."

"I'll have to ask to read Becky's story too." Val looked toward the door. "I see a couple of parents waiting. I should probably go." She stood and held out her hand.

Ronnie leaped to her feet and took the proffered hand, holding it longer than was necessary. The flowing green sundress Val wore was a better fit for her than the stodgy suit she'd worn at the first parent-teacher meeting. Val looked more like Gwen's big sister.

Val glanced at the door again and Ronnie reluctantly released her hand. "See you in a few weeks for Gwen's riding lessons."

Val smiled and left.

The thought of waiting almost three weeks to see Val again stuck in Ronnie's throat. She could engineer some way to see Val, but was it a good idea? Probably not.

Ronnie plastered on a smile and greeted the next parent, then she sat to listen to their thoughts on how she could do her job better. She glanced at the door where she'd last seen Valerie Connor. A beautiful, funny woman. Ronnie sighed. In two weeks, she'd be done for the summer. Two whole months of freedom. She held that thought tightly and focused on the scowling parent sitting across from her.

CHAPTER EIGHT

Callie pulled up at the school, and Becky and Gwen jumped out of Callie's SUV to head in and get ready for their basketball game.

"Have fun, you two," Callie said.

Val stepped out of the SUV and hugged Gwen. "Be sure and do whatever the coach tells you."

Gwen shrugged. "If I get to play."

Becky playfully punched Gwen in the shoulder. "We slaughtered the Tigers last time. We'll be so far ahead by halftime the coach will have to let you play."

"Oh, fantastic." Gwen enunciated each syllable and rolled her eyes.

Becky grabbed her bag from the back of the car and hugged Callie. "Bye, Mom. Come on, Gwen." Becky jogged away with Gwen racing after her.

Callie snagged a small cooler from the back of the SUV. "Sorry, Gwen doesn't get to play a lot."

Val shrugged. "She's happy though and she gets to participate in practice. Let's hope Becky is right, and she gets to play today."

Val and Callie walked toward the arena. Val glanced at her watch. They'd arrived early so the girls could change and warm up, so it was still thirty minutes to game time. "My goal is to find Gwen a sport that suits her better."

"She's a good volleyball player."

"Still helps to be taller and be able to spike the ball."

"I don't think any of the kids are tall enough for that yet." Callie skidded to a stop and squeezed Val's upper arm. "How about horseback riding? Don't have to be tall for that. The girls have beginners riding lessons this summer. Maybe with the right teacher Gwen will be able to make that her thing."

"True. I'm glad Becky signed up too."

"I'm glad Ronnie's teaching. You told me that woman last year was a bitch."

Val frowned. "She was a bitch. She's not involved this year, even though she's still around. Ronnie promised."

"Good. Have you seen Ronnie lately?"

"Not since the last parent-teacher day."

"Come on, Val. That was a week ago."

"I'm busy, she's busy." Val shrugged. "What do you want me to do? She's nice, but she's Gwen's teacher."

"You mean after all that time you two spent sweating over sports day that *nothing* happened?"

Val shrugged.

Callie shook her head. "Valerie. What are we going to do with you? Eligible women don't show up in Thresherton every day."

"But what if she leaves?"

"Everyone can leave. Even you. There's no crystal ball for life. If you like her, go for it."

"Not sure I have your confidence," Val muttered as she followed Callie inside to some seats in the bleachers. Val tucked her legs under her, and Callie draped hers over the seat in front of them. "Maybe I'll see her at Gwen's riding lessons."

"I forget. How many lessons are there?" Callie asked.

"Every Thursday morning for eight weeks. Ronnie said the kids will learn to care for the horses too. Grooming, saddling, and whatever else."

"Hey, do you need help getting Gwen to riding class? You work Thursday mornings, don't you?" Callie asked.

Val sighed. "I do. I could ask my dad."

"Nah, drop her off at Poplarcreek before work. I'll take her to the lesson and then she can slave on the farm in the afternoon. Farms are a hotbed of child labor."

Val laughed. "She'll love it. Thanks, Callie."

Val sat up as the girls jogged out of the changing room, dribbling basketballs. She winced. Gwen was easily the shortest on the Thresherton Public School team, but she was laughing and dodging around some of the taller girls. She was quick and nimble, but when she raised her arms to shoot, the ball hit the bottom of the basket and bounced away. Becky caught it easily and effortlessly popped it in the basket.

"Where's the coach? Who's that?" Callie asked.

Val looked to where Callie was pointing, and her breath caught. "That's Ronnie."

Callie leaned over. "You're right. She's not the coach."

"Is she coming our way?" Val straightened her shirt and tucked a stray strand of hair away. It was reflexive, and when Callie smirked at her she wished she'd had more self-control.

Ronnie darted around the people seated and arrived in the row in front of Callie and Val. "Mrs. Anderson?" Ronnie asked.

"Callie's fine. Everything okay? *You* okay?"

Val looked down to keep from laughing. Ronnie's face was pale and she looked like she wanted to run away.

"I need help. The basketball coach was in a car accident. Not injured, but her car is totaled, and she's stuck in Saskatoon."

"What can we do?" Val asked.

"Hey, Val. Callie, I need a coach. I need help. I haven't played basketball in a hundred years and I was never any good. I said I would fill in because without a teacher present the girls would have to forfeit, but I can't *coach*."

"Where's the assistant coach?"

"Sick at home with the flu. Please, Callie, I'm desperate and Becky said you used to play in college. The team is having such a good season and I don't want to screw them up."

"That's very nice of you. Not everyone would step in," Val said. Ronnie had stepped in at sports day when she was needed. She was unbelievably generous with her time.

Ronnie swiveled to glance at the girls. "They would've been so upset to miss this game. Couldn't have that."

"Well, I know the team pretty well, and I've never missed a game." Callie stood. "Happy to help." She turned toward Val. "Keep an eye out for Lauren, please. She's hoping not to be late."

Val had started to get up with Callie, but she wasn't being asked to help. The rules of basketball were a mystery aside from the fact that the girls bounced the ball from end to end and tossed it into the basket. "Sure. I'll wait here." She smiled at Ronnie, who was grinning in relief and bouncing on her toes.

"Thanks, Callie. You're a lifesaver," Ronnie said.

"No problem." Callie headed down the bleachers to the waiting team.

"How are you, Val?" Ronnie asked.

"Good. Under less stress than you."

"I know, eh? Well, I'd better go. See you."

"Have a good game."

"Thanks." Ronnie lingered for a few seconds, then turned and followed Callie down through the bleachers to the team.

Val groaned. She'd had a chance to invite Ronnie to join them after the game, but the words had stuck in her throat. She scooped a bottle of water from Callie's cooler and sipped as she watched Callie expertly put the girls through proper basketball drills. It was nice of Ronnie to pitch in even when she couldn't coach. Callie was directing Ronnie and had set her up to catch rebounding balls. Clearly, Ronnie was prepared to work at whatever would help the team. A generous person and easy on the eyes.

"Got another one of those?"

Val jumped as Lauren scooted into the seat beside her. "Hey, Lauren." Val pulled the cooler out and opened the lid. "Callie packed water and soda."

"Water please." Lauren accepted the bottle, unscrewed the cap, and took a long drink.

"She also packed you a sandwich. She didn't know your schedule. We're planning to go out to eat after the game." On game days the girls had a light snack after school for energy, but the big meal was after the game.

"I'm good. I got lunch at two thirty between farm calls. Why's Callie down on the floor?"

"Coach was in a fender bender and is stuck in Saskatoon. Assistant coach is home with the flu. That's Ronnie Yakimoto down there too. She's covering as the teacher, so the girls don't have to forfeit, but she was up here a few minutes ago begging Callie to coach." Val laughed. "She really looked desperate. I thought she was going to pass out."

Lauren laughed. "Good for Callie and Ronnie. There'd be tears if the girls missed this game. It's the playoffs and the winner plays for league championship. Callie's a good coach. She can do it."

Val watched as Lauren caught Callie's eye and waved at her. Callie and Lauren took a second to really look at each other, and Val felt the warm waves of love pass between them. She wanted that. Where did she go to find that kind of love? Callie hadn't left her farm, and love had come to her, but not everyone was as lucky as Callie.

Val grinned as Ronnie jogged after a basketball. She'd been trying to dribble it and it had escaped. Ronnie was incredibly athletic and fit in well with the team, even if the basketballs wouldn't cooperate.

Val and Lauren shared some light surface conversation and discussed patients until the game started. Val watched Gwen play, but when she was benched, she studied Ronnie. Often Ronnie sat beside Gwen but jumped up each time Callie wanted her to do something.

"Gwen's playing a lot tonight," Lauren said.

"Callie's being very kind. Becky said that Gwen would be allowed to play once our team was well ahead and couldn't lose."

"Ouch."

Val shrugged. "It's the reality and Gwen knows they need to win this game." Val slapped her hands on her thighs in frustration. "She's so fast and agile, but as soon as she tries to shoot, nothing."

"Callie could work with her some more."

"Maybe, but Gwen will have to ask her."

When the game was over, Thresherton had won by twenty points. After the students and coaches shook hands, they all raced to the changing room. Callie jogged up the steps of the bleachers two at a time. She dropped into the seat beside Lauren and pulled her into a deep kiss.

Val smiled and then looked away when someone started cheering and clapping behind them. Why was two women kissing such a big deal? People needed to grow up. She glanced at Lauren's red face, but Callie turned and waved in the direction of the cheering. Val snuck a look over Lauren's shoulder. "It's just Mark and Tracey Renfield."

Lauren turned and waved at Callie's good friends.

"So, pizza tonight or something healthier?" Callie asked.

"What do the girls want?" Val asked.

Callie raised her eyebrows and smirked.

Val nodded. "Pizza it is. Lauren's joining us."

Callie looped her arm through Lauren's. "Good. I invited Ronnie as well. She deserves it."

"Ronnie? Ronnie's coming?" Val asked.

"Yuppers." Callie winked at Val and kissed Lauren on the cheek.

Fifteen minutes later, Becky and Gwen joined them. Ronnie wasn't with them and Val felt a stab of disappointment.

"Ms. Yakimoto said she would meet us at the restaurant. She wanted to run home and change and let Dover out," Gwen said.

"Which restaurant? We hadn't decided yet," Val said.

Callie hugged Becky.

Gwen shrugged. "I told her the pizza place, but if that's wrong, she said you can text her. You have her personal cell number."

"Oh, that's news," Callie said and nudged Val.

It wasn't news. Ronnie and Val had been in touch many times while they planned sports day. Val ignored Callie's teasing and opened her arms. "Come here, you." She squeezed Gwen tightly as she went in for a hug. "You were awesome tonight. So fast, and I saw you take the ball away from a couple of the Tigers."

Gwen laughed. "I did, from their center forward. I don't even think she realized I was down there."

Lauren hugged Becky and then Gwen. "You just scooted in under the radar. I saw that. Great moves, Connor," she said.

"Tonight is a pizza night," Val said. She scooped Callie's cooler off the floor and the group trooped outside to Callie's SUV.

"I better take my truck in case I get an emergency call and have to leave. See you there," Lauren said and waved as she jogged away.

Val, Callie, Becky, and Gwen jumped in Callie's SUV and headed to the pizza place. Val was glad Ronnie was coming later. It meant she would get a few minutes to prepare. Callie was right. She needed to go for it. She'd started a dozen texts to invite Ronnie for dinner or coffee, and then she'd decided to phone her instead, but never got the nerve. Once, she'd passed her on the road when Ronnie was out with her bicycle. Ronnie had been sitting on a tree stump drinking water and taking a break. It would have been so easy to stop and chat, but she just plowed right by. Something about her made Val so nervous she couldn't think straight.

The pizza place was crowded with kids and parents, but they snagged a table for six at the back. "I'll get the pizza, Callie, you sit."

"I'm sure it's my turn."

"No, it isn't, and besides, you worked, Coach." Val headed to the counter and stood in line to order. The line moved slowly, and she sighed as it took fifteen minutes to move two places.

"Best pizza in town," Ronnie whispered into Val's ear.

Val jumped as the hot breath hit the back of her neck. "*Only* pizza in town."

"I've had it at the diner and the Italian restaurant. Even the bakery tried for a while. The crust was good, but their sauce was tasteless. Nope, this is the best."

A girl behind the counter waved at them. "Hi, Ronnie, you getting the usual?"

"Not today, thanks, Stephanie. I'm with a group."

"Hey, you two," Lauren said. "I'm looking forward to this. I haven't had pizza in months. Are we buying?"

"Not this time. Callie and the kids are at the back," Val said. "What took you so long?"

"Phone call about a lame cow." Lauren squeezed Ronnie's shoulder. "Hey, Ronnie, great game." Lauren left them to join Callie and the girls.

Val turned and found herself inches from Ronnie. She swallowed and forced words past the lump in her throat. "They know you here."

Ronnie shrugged. "I'm a good customer."

Val winced. Ronnie wasn't embarrassed and shouldn't be. "Did I sound judgy? I wasn't trying to be."

"You're fine and it's the truth. It's not like there's a hot supper or caring woman waiting for me at home. Just whatever leftovers I can scrape out of the refrigerator."

"I'm sorry."

"Don't be. I'm not. It's a trade-off against knowing that my house is the way I left it in the morning. Nothing will be moved, used, or disposed of without my knowledge. And Dover doesn't care how messy I am."

"Sounds comfortable."

Ronnie leaned close. "Maybe. But if I let it, sometimes loneliness creeps in and stays all night."

"Do you let it?" Val locked eyes with Ronnie. Ronnie's expression was serious, and Val could see a hint of deep pain that Ronnie covered up well.

"Sometimes I can't stop it," Ronnie said.

"How can I help you?" Stephanie asked.

Val jumped as they reached the counter. She glanced at the smiling girl poised over an order book and then looked back at Ronnie. The moment was gone and Ronnie was smiling at Stephanie.

"I hope you like pineapple on pizza, because I never have pizza without it," Ronnie said as she studied the list of posted ingredients.

"Poplarcreek is not a fan." Val smiled and joined in the fun of ordering, but she would find a way to reconnect with Ronnie. She longed to understand her more, and it would be lonely in Thresherton without family or friends. Ronnie needed friends, and she would happily help with that. "Two large deluxe pizzas, please and add pineapple to one."

Chapter Nine

B ye, honey. And tell my little brother lunch is here after church."

"Yes, Aunt Marilyn." Val kissed Marilyn on both cheeks and grinned. It was funny hearing her dad referred to as a little brother. "I'll tell him. Gwen and I'll be here to help with lunch. You're supposed to be resting."

"Pish. Only a little sprain."

"Maybe it's time to give up jumping off ladders and climb down to the bottom like the rest of the world?"

"Takes too long, and I have windows to clean."

Val pointed at Marilyn. "And save the ironing for me. That's too much standing."

"Only tablecloths. I don't iron sheets anymore. Wash them and put them right back on the bed."

"Don't you like the smooth neat surface and the crisp seams? I iron Gwen's and mine. We like it that way."

"It's a lot of fussing."

"Maybe. But it's the way we always did it at home. My mom taught me to iron pillow slips when I was eight." Val smiled and shook her head. "See you Sunday." She waved, jumped in her car, and headed down Marilyn's laneway. When she was forty feet from the road, a bicycle shot by. It was ridden by a slight figure in a black outfit with a red and black helmet. Ronnie was out cycling again.

Val turned and slowly followed the bike. She didn't want to speed past and risk spitting gravel in Ronnie's face. She'd take the next left and leave Ronnie the road. An instant later, the bike stopped. She couldn't pass now without it seeming weird and she didn't want to. The more time she spent with her, the more she wanted to spend with her.

Val slowed beside the bike. "Here you are again." She did a mental head slap at her inane remark.

"Hi, Val. I ate a ton of pizza after the game yesterday." Ronnie straddled her bike.

"You wanted to work it off?" Val cringed.

"It gave me a lot of energy. You out for a drive?"

"Helping out my aunt. She lives close to here. You've got a nice day for this."

"Have we been reduced to talking about the weather?" Ronnie laughed.

Here goes nothing. "It was nice visiting after the basketball game. I had fun. We should do it again." As Val spoke, Ronnie shifted to look past the car.

"What's that?" Ronnie pointed.

Val swiveled her head. "Smoke. Lots of people burn off the wheat straw after they harvest the wheat."

"I thought they baled the straw for livestock bedding."

"There's more straw than anyone needs." Val tapped her bottom lip. "But it's a big fire and too early in the year for straw. Straw comes after the wheat harvest. You know what? I'm going to head that way and check it out."

"Wait, I'll come with you. If that's okay."

Val popped her trunk. "Jump in." She studied the smoke while Ronnie loaded her bike. It was a huge fire and the smoke floated into the air in an ominous puff.

Ronnie jumped in and grabbed the seat belt.

Val took the next corner and drove as fast as she could on the gravel road. She grimaced. "The smoke's coming from the Henry place."

"You know them?"

"A bunch of homophobes. Friends of mine, a lesbian couple, live next door to them. My friends have an organic farm and sell eggs, goat milk, and goat cheese at the market in Saskatoon along with a variety of organic vegetables. It's Saturday, so they'll be at the market." Val shook her head. "A year ago, Maury Henry sprayed pesticide upwind from their farm on a windy day. The chemical settled on their vegetable patch. There was no reason for Maury to spray his land and his reward was a large fine. My friends had to plow under their entire acre of vegetables and start again."

Val turned in the laneway. "Never mind, though," Val said. "We still have to help, even if they are jerks." They stopped in front of the house as flames roared from one end of the big barn. "Check the house." Val quickly called the fire department.

Minutes later, Ronnie ran up to Val. "There's no answer at the house."

"No time to track them down now. The fire is at the east end of the barn and the wind is blowing from the west. We have time to let the horses out." They sprinted to the barn. Most of the stalls opened with little effort, and the horses stumbled out, shaking their manes and stomping in panic. The horses seemed to be running out of the barn, but the air was thick with smoke and she couldn't get a clear look.

Several of the stall doors wouldn't budge. "I don't understand." Val spoke through her coughs. "The door won't open."

Ronnie tugged on a door. "The latch and hinges have rusted closed." Ronnie ran to a workbench of rusty tools and returned. She hefted a chisel and sledgehammer. "Stand back." She placed the chisel and hit it once, twice, and three times before the latch broke. "Help me." Ronnie grabbed the unlatched door and Val grabbed below her. They hauled it open against the squealing protestations of rusty hinges. They repeated the process on three more stalls.

Val tried to speak but her eyes ran with tears and her throat burned with smoke. She pointed to herself and to a horse shaking in the walkway by its stall door. She gripped the horse's halter and heaved. She expected the animal to fight her. Instead, it attempted to follow but staggered a few steps before finding its footing, then it stumbled toward the barn door.

They continued yanking open stall doors and shooing the horses outside. The horses' movements were erratic as they surged outside into the large paddock and as far as they could get from the fire. Val released another horse as Ronnie led two horses from the barn, one followed by a small foal. Flames engulfed the east door, but the north and west doors leading to the pasture were still useable.

Val led another horse outside, then searched for Ronnie. The flames had consumed the roof and now blocked the north door. She raced through the paddock and climbed the fence. She needed to find Ronnie and keep her safe. No other option was acceptable.

Val pulled the collar of her shirt over her mouth and nose and charged into the barn through the west door. She dashed along the passageway and spotted Ronnie running from stall to stall. When Ronnie saw her, Val grasped Ronnie's hand, and they sprinted outside.

Outside in the fresher air, well away from the flames, Ronnie hugged Val and rocked from side to side. "I was terrified when I couldn't find you. I was searching for you in the barn."

"Me too. I ran inside to find you." Val stared into Ronnie's red eyes and watched tears streak through the ash on her cheeks.

Ronnie stepped back and coughed. "My eyes are killing me, and I'm dried out."

Val hid her face as she rummaged through her car and passed Ronnie a bottle of water. The tight hug had been surprisingly wonderful, but was just in the spur of the moment. Ronnie had clearly just been relieved to find her safe, but it was nice and made her thoughts spin and her skin tingle.

"You first," Ronnie said.

Val tipped the bottle and moaned as the cool liquid coated her dry and burning throat then she handed it back to Ronnie. Ronnie took a long drink.

Val peered down the laneway and saw pickup trucks rolling in with flashing green lights followed by a fire truck. "The volunteer firefighters are here."

A woman holding a clipboard leaped from the first truck and scanned the farmyard until her eyes landed on them. She jogged over. "What happened?"

"We were just passing and saw the smoke," Val said. "There's no answer at the house. We think all the horses are out of the barn."

"Thanks." The firefighter with the clipboard ran back to a cluster of firefighters, one of whom raced to the front door of the house.

Val watched firefighters pointing and gesturing to the barn on fire and a second smaller barn which wasn't on fire yet, although a covered wooden passageway connected the two buildings. The passageway was for moving animals and supplies in the winter, so the owners wouldn't need to go outside in the snow. When the gesturing ceased, a volunteer raced to a tractor. He started it and drove at the passageway. Val covered her mouth with her hands and gasped as he headed into the smoke.

The tractor backed up and drove again at the passageway, splintering wood and creating a gap so the fire couldn't take that route.

"Stay here." Ronnie sprinted to the clipboard woman, spoke with her, and returned as several of the firefighters headed toward the small barn. "I told them we hadn't checked the small barn for people or animals, so they're going to." She took several more swallows of water and glanced toward the main road. "We're blocked in for a while by all the firefighters. Let's have a look at the horses."

"Do they look thin to you, Ronnie? I'm always in the clinic and I don't see many horses for comparison."

"They're a little thin. Not emaciated, but certainly not overfed."

"I can't believe we had to bust four stalls open. Maury Henry isn't looking after them properly. The ammonia in those stalls we busted open was horrific. It stung my eyes." Val cupped Ronnie's cheek. "Your eyes are red from the ammonia and smoke, but not too bad." She moved her thumb to caress Ronnie's cheek and then slowly lowered her hand. Her breathing was a little fast but had to be because of all the smoke they'd inhaled. Didn't it?

"Let's go," Ronnie said.

They climbed the fence and headed toward the animals. Val helped Ronnie shoo the horses into the next paddock, even farther from the fire. Once the horses were in the pasture and safe from the fire and commotion, Val and Ronnie rested against the fence, watching as the flames consumed the rest of the barn.

The firefighters appeared to be concentrating on the small fires started by sparks and on protecting the house and other buildings on the farm. Val said, "If a grass fire starts it could burn across the fields to my friends' farm. I'll send them a text and let them know what's happening."

"Is there anything else we can do?"

"If the fire gets away and heads to their farm, I'll let their goats and chickens loose."

"And I'll help you."

"Thanks, Ronnie."

Ronnie scanned the horses. "Some of the horses are burned."

Val touched Ronnie's face. "You're burned too." The heat was intense, and Ronnie looked as if she had a bad sunburn. Smoke had blackened the skin over her cheekbones and the tip of her nose.

"You are too."

Val shared a long look with Ronnie and then shook herself into action. "The horses need a vet. I'm calling Lauren." Val jogged to her car and pulled her phone from the console. "Hi, Lauren. The horse barn at the Henry place burned down and the horses need help."

"Is Maury home?"

"No, but some of the horses are burned."

"On my way."

Val texted her friends with the organic farm and tucked her phone into her pocket. "Lauren will be here soon. There's not much I can do. If I were a vet, I'd be more useful." Val shrugged, helpless and frustrated.

"Really? Lauren couldn't have rescued them faster than we did. Sure, she's got the drugs and bandaging, but you were pretty awesome."

"I'm just glad you were here. Not sure I'd have had the courage to run in there alone. I was so scared when I couldn't find you outside."

Ronnie held her hand. "Me too."

"Let's sit in the car and rest." Val led Ronnie to her car. The seats were covered with ash from their clothes, but Val didn't care. They were safe and they almost hadn't been. She and Ronnie were dirty, smelly, and had almost gotten killed, but in that instant, Val didn't want to be anywhere else.

CHAPTER TEN

"There she is." Ronnie pointed to Lauren's truck as it parked on the main highway. Lauren pulled on coveralls and boots, picked up a black case, and headed toward them.

Thick, dark smoke billowed from the blackened pile of lumber that had been the horse barn. A few orange patches of fire collapsed into puffs of smoke as the firefighters sprayed them with water. They'd managed to keep it from burning anything else, which was a small miracle.

Lauren walked over. "Are you two all right?"

Val shrugged. "We're fine."

"The tips of your noses are black. Were you in the barn?"

Ronnie said, "We got the horses out."

"That was incredibly dangerous."

Val briefly outlined what they had done.

"I'm not sure if you were brave or crazy." Lauren shook her head as she scanned the paddock. "But show me the horses you saved."

Val and Ronnie walked with Lauren and they made a quick count of the horses and checked for injuries. Lauren stepped away to call PVS and returned. "We've tried every number we have on record for Maury Henry and nobody can find him."

"Judging by the condition of the horses and the mess in their stalls, nobody's been looking after them for a while," Ronnie said.

Lauren nodded. "I'll call the SPCA. They have the power to remove the horses or authorize treatment. I'll let them decide."

"I'll check in with the firefighters," Ronnie said. She jogged away and returned as Lauren got off the phone.

"No animals in the small barn, fortunately. Just some junk storage."

Val nodded toward the laneway. "Firefighters are leaving now."

"You two go. I'll stay and wait for the SPCA," Lauren said. "They're on the way."

"I'll stay too," Ronnie said.

"I would stay, but I need to pick Gwen up from her friend's house," Val said.

"Val, I'm going to ask to take some of the horses to Callie's," Lauren said. "Can you help me later to treat their wounds? They could use your gentle touch."

Ronnie feathered her fingers over her cheek where Val had caressed her earlier. Her touch had been gentle and light. Just a whisper of a caress had soothed her.

Val blushed. "Sure, Lauren. Text me when you need me."

Ronnie coughed and wished for another bottle of water. "Do you mind taking my bike? I'll pick it up later."

"No problem. Lauren, can you give Ronnie a lift home?"

"Sure." Lauren shook her head. "Look at what's left of the barn. You two took a horrifying risk, but you're very brave running into a burning barn to save horses." Lauren shuddered when she focused on the blackened remains of the barn.

Ronnie squeezed Val's hand. She didn't remember taking her hand again, but it was comforting to hold it. "We did what we had to."

"We did. And I'd do it again." Val smiled at Ronnie and let go of her hand. "See you two." Val climbed into her car and drove off.

Ronnie frowned after the departing car. "I'm happy we saved the horses, but it was a huge risk. I should have made Val stay outside. What would've happened if Val had died or been seriously injured?" She'd lost track of her and had been running frantically from stall to stall while she kept one eye on the building fire. Would she have left the barn without Val? Not a chance. "She has responsibilities. Gwen needs her. Nobody needs me."

"Whoa, hey, Ronnie. We'd all have been devastated if Val was hurt, but you're important too. We don't want anything to happen to you." Lauren laughed. "Besides, you'd need an army to stop Valerie Connor from trying to help animals or people in need."

"She's got a big heart."

"She does indeed."

Ronnie and Lauren stared at the blackened barn. "So, Callie tells me you're teaching riding this summer and you know all about horses?"

"Been riding since I was eight, and I worked at a broodmare farm when I was in high school."

"Excellent *and* you've been around foals. Will you help Callie and me with some horses? Please? I've done some foalings, treated colics, and sutured wounds, but I'm not an expert at handling horses. I'm a city kid and it's not the sort of training you get at vet school. I wouldn't take horses home without extra help. Callie was stressed and overwhelmed this winter with all the cattle work she had to learn. I won't put her in that dark place again with the horses."

"I want to help." Ronnie grinned. "Just try to keep me away."

Lauren laughed. "Good. We'll all be open to some lessons on handling horses."

When the SPCA arrived, Ronnie and Lauren met with them to discuss plans for the horses, then they headed toward Thresherton. "I need to phone Callie. It'll be speaker phone," Lauren said.

"Am I in the way?" Ronnie asked.

"Not at all. I just need to ask her about the horses." Lauren pushed buttons on the phone. "Hi, love."

"Hi, honey. You on your way home soon?"

"Home. I like the sound of that, very much. I'm on my way now."

"Maybe you should move in?"

"We've only been together four months. I can't let you see all my bad habits at once." Lauren shot Ronnie a quick smile.

"I miss you and I want—" Callie said.

"Ronnie's here with me."

The warmth in Lauren's and Callie's voices was almost startling in its tenderness. Ronnie wished she were anywhere but listening to an intimate conversation between people who were obviously so much in love. It was a reminder of what she didn't, and likely wouldn't, have.

"Ronnie?"

"Hi, Callie. Lauren's giving me a lift home."

"Bicycle problems?" Callie laughed. "You ever thought of carrying a tool kit?"

"Very funny. No breakdown this time."

"Is your horse barn useable?" Lauren asked.

"Horse barn? It's in good shape. Does somebody need my barn? They're welcome to use it."

"The SPCA is coordinating homes for about twenty horses. They've been caught in a barn fire and nobody can find the owner. The SPCA is asking for volunteers to house the horses. I volunteered to offer veterinary services, but the horses need places to go. Can we put seven in your horse barn?"

"Only seven? What about the others?"

"The SPCA is arranging volunteers for the rest. We can only take the number we can house. I selected a mare and foal and a heavily pregnant mare. I can check on them often if they live at Poplarcreek with us. They're a nice little group of quarter horse mares and geldings."

"Okay, but I know nothing about horses or foaling." Callie chuckled. "I see lessons in my future."

"I'll take care of the medical side and Ronnie's going to help."

Ronnie said, "I've worked with broodmares and have been riding since I was a kid. The horses need proper nutrition and we should figure out what we're dealing with temperament wise. I'm not an expert, but I know enough to get us by."

"Thanks, Ronnie."

"Lauren will drop me at home. I'll change into work clothes and come out and help get ready. If that's okay." She winced, not wanting to be presumptuous.

"The more help the better."

Lauren dropped Ronnie at home and told her she was getting supplies from the clinic and then heading back to the horse farm.

That afternoon, Ronnie joined Callie and Mark, Callie's neighbor, at Poplarcreek. They did another clean in the horse barn. The barn held six roomy box stalls in good condition. The stall walls and doors were smooth wood for the first four feet and then topped with steel beams.

The stalls had removable interior walls, so they joined two together for the mare and foal. They also joined two stalls for the pregnant mare, so she would have more space when her foal came.

Attached to the horse barn was a dry lean-to where horses outside could shelter from the wind and rain. It had a big door that led to a paddock. Mark helped Callie and Ronnie build a pen in one corner for two horses and set up a watering trough, then Mark had to head home.

"We've got lots of bedding," Callie said. "The wheat harvest was excellent last year, and I have hundreds of bales of wheat straw. I also have a decent supply of hay suitable for horses. I'd planned to sell it to Starview Farm, but it'll more fun to use myself."

They bedded the stalls and were just finishing when Lauren arrived home. Callie dumped a bale of straw in a stall and kicked it to spread it around.

"This looks great." Lauren surveyed the barn.

"You're home. I love saying and thinking that." In three steps, Callie was in Lauren's arms. She hugged Lauren and kissed her on the cheek. "We're ready."

Ronnie turned her back and fussed with the straw that was already spread over the floor of the stall. She was happy for Lauren and Callie, but she felt like she was intruding on something not meant for her.

"Hey, Ronnie."

Ronnie turned. They were standing side by side with an arm draped around each other's waist. Callie's smile reached her eyes and she leaned closer when Lauren spoke.

"Three horses will arrive tomorrow morning. The next four will arrive in early afternoon." Lauren's voice was rough and her words slow.

"Lauren, you're exhausted and you need a shower." Callie's nose wrinkled.

Ronnie had scrubbed hard to remove the smell of smoke from her body before she drove out to Poplarcreek, but she probably stank too. It was a foul, smoky stink wafting off Lauren's clothes and hair. Not the pleasant smell of a campfire.

"You're right." Lauren rubbed her eyes and sat on a bale of straw as if she would sit there forever.

Callie tugged on Lauren's hand. "Come inside."

Lauren pulled Callie down beside her. "I have to follow the first trailer and check it every thirty minutes to make sure the horses are okay. They're all a little weak."

Ronnie shook her head. "I think the mare and foal you picked are strong enough."

"I hope so."

"Enough. Shower, food, and bed until you have to go out again. Come on." Callie stood and pulled Lauren to her feet.

"I'll come back tomorrow," Ronnie said.

"Do you want to stay for dinner?" Callie asked.

Ronnie tugged at the filthy T-shirt glued to her with sweat. "All I want is a shower. I'm going to head home."

"Thanks, Ronnie." Callie took Lauren's hand and towed her toward the house. Ronnie watched them go. The invitation to dinner had been nice, but she hadn't wanted to intrude.

Ronnie glanced around the horse barn one more time and nodded at their preparations, then she brushed stray wisps of straw off her jeans and climbed into her car. As she drove, she did a mental inventory of her refrigerator and sighed. She could go for another pizza, but not as filthy as she was. Delivery was an option. She stopped at the side of the road and fished out her phone. She smiled at the text from Val, and tears burned her eyes as she read the invitation to dinner.

Thanks. I accept. It's been a long day.

And your fridge is empty and you don't want to be alone. I'm the same. Come when you're ready and bring Dover. Don't worry about bringing anything.

Ronnie put the phone down to blow her nose. She was unbelievably touched by the offer. She didn't want to be alone and Val had figured that out. Ronnie sniffled and headed home for another shower. Val had the biggest heart of anyone she'd ever met. She helped wounded animals and wounded people. It would be nice to feel like someone wanted to take care of her, even for just a little while.

CHAPTER ELEVEN

The next morning, Val and Gwen arrived at Poplarcreek for breakfast. Ronnie was already there, and Val gave her a shy smile. Dinner the night before had been casual and quiet, and they'd watched television and chatted a little before Ronnie had gone home, exhausted. Val had nearly offered to let her sleep on the couch, but pushed the thought away. Surely Ronnie would want her own bed, and she didn't live that far. Still, it would have been nice to see her first thing in the morning.

Callie explained the plan for the day and looked at Becky. "I'd like you to stay at Val's house for a couple of days. Just while the horses get settled."

"Mom, I'm almost ten. I'm not a baby. I'm helping." She crossed her arms and stood firm.

"Can we stay, Mom? If Becky's not coming home with us?" Gwen asked.

Val focused on Gwen. "The horses aren't very pretty and might be hard to look at, but I suppose it's okay with me. Okay with you, Callie?"

"Yes, as long as Gwen and Becky understand that Ronnie's in charge of everything to do with the horses."

Ronnie shook her head and raised her hands. "Poplarcreek is your farm."

"I know nothing about handling horses. Lauren told me you'd be in charge and would train us."

"But surely Val—"

"Don't look at me." Val shook her head. "We rarely have horses come into the clinic and when we do, I don't handle them. I help with the surgeries and equipment. Count me in when it's time to treat the burns, but knowing how to safely handle a horse is completely different."

Callie focused on Becky and Gwen. "That means we do what Ronnie says. We have to be careful. We also don't know if they're nice. Okay? Becky? Gwen? Ronnie is the boss?"

"Yes, Callie," Gwen said.

Becky grinned at Ronnie. "Yes, Mom. What do we do, Ms. Yakimoto?"

"Hang back while we unload them and don't get too close to their hind end in case they kick. The rest we'll figure out as we go."

After breakfast, Becky loped upstairs with Gwen. Val squeezed Callie's hand. "You'll need Becky's help with the horses. It could be a good project for her."

Callie smiled. "She can work like a real farm kid and do chores before breakfast on school days. But she's my baby, and I worry she'll get hurt."

"I worry about us all," Ronnie said. "We don't know what training or temperament the horses have. When they're stronger, their training, or lack of it, will appear. Because of the way they've been treated, they could be moody."

Becky bounded down the stairs with Gwen at her heels. "The trailer's here," Becky said.

Val pulled on her boots and headed outside with the others. Although the situation was awful, she was happy to get more time with Ronnie.

The horse trailer backed toward the horse barn as Lauren parked her truck at the house. Ronnie focused on the driver of the truck towing the trailer. "Hey, that's Irene driving."

"Great," Val muttered.

Gwen skidded to a stop beside Val and took her hand. "That's Irene. From lessons last year. She's not nice."

Val squatted in front of Gwen and gave her a hug. "No, she's not nice, but I'll make her behave. If you want you can wait in Becky's bedroom until Irene is gone."

Gwen shook her head. "I want to see the horses."

"Okay, honey." Val straightened and faced the trailer. Irene had better behave or else. "But for now, you hang back. I need to get a closer look."

"Okay, Mom."

"Irene, eh?" Callie said.

Val laughed. "Oh my God."

"What?" Callie asked.

Val grinned and shook her head. Callie and Becky were standing beside each other in identical poses. Arms crossed over their chests and scowling in Irene's direction. Gwen would never have to worry about a lack of support from Poplarcreek. Both Callie and Becky were ready to do battle for her.

Ronnie walked over to the cab of the truck and spoke with Irene, then she directed her while she backed the trailer up. When the truck stopped, Ronnie opened the back doors and Irene got out to join her.

Val had been walking toward the trailer but slowed when Irene hugged Ronnie. Val squared her shoulders and resumed walking. Ronnie had more friends than just the Thresherton crowd. It made sense. There was no need to feel threatened and she had no right to. But she couldn't picture Irene and Ronnie as friends. Ronnie was generous, friendly, and caring. Irene had been a self-involved, arrogant bitch at riding lessons the year before, and the impression she'd made since wasn't much better.

Lauren jogged over and climbed into the trailer, then she jumped out and smiled. "The first mare isn't so much standing as leaning against the wall of the trailer, but she's upright."

"That's good news," Callie said from behind Val.

"Sorry, everyone. Meet Irene Schmidt," Lauren said. "She volunteered to move the horses and she did an exceptional job of driving."

"I'm the best all right." Irene shook everyone's hand and slapped Ronnie on the shoulder. "Ron and I go way back. We worked on a horse farm near Winnipeg when we were in high school. Funny that we both live in Saskatchewan now." Irene shook her head. "Anyway, if you've got me and Ron on your team these horses will recover, no problem."

"They're going to need a vet, too," Val said.

Irene shrugged. "Sure, there'll be something for Lauren to do."

Val bristled at Irene's remark, but Lauren didn't notice it or chose not to comment. Val took a deep breath and swallowed her response.

"Irene's going back for the second load when we're done here," Lauren said.

Val peeked inside the trailer. The mare's legs trembled with the effort of remaining upright. The foal lay in deep shavings at the mare's feet.

Irene hooked a lead on the mare. "Ron, I'll lead her toward the barn. Let's see if the foal will follow."

"I'll run ahead and open doors," Callie said as she jogged away.

When the mare was fifteen feet from her foal, she dug her heels in and tugged on the lead, refusing to abandon her baby. Irene pulled harder, then she walked the mare in a circle and tried again. Irene slapped the mare on the rump with the flat of her hand, but she didn't budge. "She's not going anywhere," Irene said.

"Is that necessary? The hitting?" Val asked through gritted teeth.

Irene rolled her eyes and didn't answer.

Val hid her annoyance by focusing on Ronnie, who was watching the foal. Twice, the foal struggled to its feet and tried to follow its mother. Each time it collapsed after a few steps. Ronnie waved Val over. "Let's help the baby. He's too tired to walk."

Val followed Ronnie into the trailer. The next time the foal tried to stand, they caught it. Val grimaced at the patches of red, raw, burned skin on the foal's back. The foal shook on weak legs when she and Ronnie lifted it off the trailer.

"Let's carry him," Ronnie said. Val and Ronnie linked arms under the foal's belly and carried it. They passed the mare on the way to the barn and the mare followed them. After they lay the foal in the deep straw, Val and Ronnie exited the stall so Irene could lead in the mother.

"I'll get the other mare," Ronnie said.

Lauren entered and ran her hands along the foal's legs and over its body. "No new wounds. I knew he'd lie down for the trip, but I was worried the mare would stumble and step on him."

"Why didn't you separate them?" Val asked.

"Now I'm teaching horses 101." Irene scoffed. "You can't separate a mare and foal. At the Henry place, we tried, but this old mare kicked up a fuss, screaming and pawing the ground until she got her foal back."

"Well, she has no reason to trust humans," Val said. "No matter how wounded and exhausted a mother is she'd use her last ounce of energy if her baby needed her protection."

Irene shrugged. "She's just a drama queen. Some horses *and* people are."

Val was about to respond when Ronnie entered with the pregnant mare and put her in the double stall they'd prepared for her.

"Well, folks, if you're all set, I'll head back for the rest," Irene said.

"Want some company?" Ronnie asked.

"Love it. The drive will give us a chance to catch up. I'll tell you all about the world of professional horse training. Riveting stuff."

"I bet you have a shelf full of awards."

"I do. Come on." Irene hooked her arm through Ronnie's, and they left the barn.

Callie studied Val. "They're old friends?"

Val nodded as she chewed her bottom lip. She didn't need to say anything.

"Lauren, is Irene a lesbian?" Callie asked.

Lauren squinted at Callie and shrugged. "Don't know. I just met her today and all our talk was about the horses. The SPCA called her."

"Well, I don't think she is," Callie said. "She doesn't ping my gaydar." Gwen and Becky appeared after Irene left and crowded around the horses. Callie shooed them from the barn. "Girls, the horses need rest. There'll be work for us when Ronnie's back."

Val turned to study the horses, but her mind was elsewhere. It didn't matter if Irene was gay or not. There wasn't anything between she and Ronnie, and there wouldn't be. Ronnie was a free spirit—a procrastinator, someone who loved freedom and having her own space. She could leave their small town at any moment, and she wouldn't put her heart, or Gwen's, through that. Friendship was the only thing on the table. But why did that make her sad?

❖

Ronnie and Irene arrived with the second group of horses in the afternoon, followed by Lauren in her truck. Val, Callie, Becky, and Gwen went outside to see them.

"This morning we put the mares in stalls *A* and *B*," Lauren said. "I thought we'd put the two geldings together in the pen in the lean-to barn. They stayed close together at the farm and I'm hoping they're friends. They'll be horses *D* and *E*."

Ronnie nodded. "And the other two go in stalls *C* and *F*."

"The last two are another mare and a yearling filly," Irene said. "I don't think the filly has ever been on a lead before today. She doesn't bite or kick, but she bucked when Ronnie loaded her. She's a handful. I'm glad you're here." Irene squeezed Ronnie's forearm.

Val schooled her features into a neutral expression. Ronnie and Irene looked decidedly chummy, but it was none of her business. Still, she stared at Irene's hand as it slid down Ronnie's arm and wished she could slap it away. She wasn't jealous of Irene. She was protecting Ronnie form an evil bitch who clearly couldn't keep her hands to herself.

Ronnie and Irene unloaded three horses without a problem and walked them to the barn. "Now for the teenager," Ronnie said.

Val watched the young animal circle the compartment in the trailer and jumped at the loud clang each time it kicked the side. "Ronnie, you can't mean to go in there. It's too dangerous," Val said. "Get Lauren to sedate her. Something to calm her down."

Ronnie laughed. "We don't need drugs. She's just scared. Now, everyone but Irene stand well away from the trailer and be quiet and still. No sudden movements or noises that might startle her."

Callie herded Becky and Gwen away from the trailer. "Her stall is ready," Callie said.

"What can I do?" Val asked.

"Irene and I've got this." Ronnie gingerly unlatched the door to the last compartment and whispered soothing words to the young animal. They opened the door just wide enough for Ronnie to slip inside. Irene held the door closed, but not latched in case Ronnie needed to escape quickly. Val moved so she could watch Ronnie work.

Ronnie stepped toward the filly and the horse backed away. With eyes wide, the horse tossed her head to escape the human.

"Hey there, girl. Hey, horsey *F*. I won't hurt you." Ronnie approached the animal. "Hey there, girl. I'm your friend." Ronnie clipped two leads on the halter as the horse huffed but stopped tossing her head. "I'm ready."

Irene opened the door all the way and fastened it to the side of the trailer so it wouldn't accidentally swing shut. "You're in the way," she snapped at Val. "There's no room for spectators."

Val jumped aside and moved to where she could watch but wouldn't be scolded again. The filly stepped forward, but Ronnie blocked her way. Irene gripped the second lead. The horse lunged for the edge of the trailer, but they were ready for her and held her head. When they jumped off the trailer the filly minced and kicked out with her hind legs. They led the filly to her box stall and released her. The horse charged in a circle for two minutes and then settled.

Irene patted Ronnie's shoulder. "I thought she was going to drag us down the road." Irene shook her head. "Still, you're a sucker. She's too young and wild to bother training."

"What other choice is there?" Val asked.

"Ron, just how naive are your friends?" Irene smirked. "I mean dog food, lady."

Val fumed and opened her mouth to respond, but Ronnie spoke first.

"Not happening." Ronnie shrugged off Irene's hand. "Everyone deserves a second chance. She's a beautiful animal, and yes, she's going to be a project."

"Lots of people thought she was too dangerous, but I couldn't leave her there," Lauren said.

Callie slipped her arm around Lauren's shoulders and squinted at Irene. "She'll get a second chance at Poplarcreek."

"Nobody opens her door though," Ronnie said. "Nobody goes in there, but me."

Becky stared through the bars at the filly, her eyes filled with tears. "Are those burns on her side? Nobody will hurt you here, girl."

Val held her breath as the filly stopped charging around and approached Becky to sniff her hand, then snorted and backed away.

"See? She wants to be friends," Becky said, wiping at her eyes.

"Okay, there's too many people in here. The horses need to settle," Ronnie said.

"We'll check on the cattle." Lauren and Callie left, towing a reluctant Becky, and Gwen followed without a word of protest.

"I'll head out too." Irene pointed at Ronnie. "You've got my number. Text me when the horses are ready for training. You know I'm the best."

"Will do, and thanks."

Val smiled as Irene left. She kept her hands in her pockets to avoid waving. *Bye-bye you arrogant creep. Nobody needs you here.*

"Do they know what started the fire?" Val asked.

"The fire inspector thinks mice chewed the electrical wiring and that started the fire. Completely an accident."

"Well, that's something anyway," Val said.

They stood watching the horses munch hay for a while before Val asked the question bothering her. "What happened to Maury Henry?"

"When I went back with Irene, an officer with the SPCA told me he ran out of money and had trouble buying feed. There's no way he can afford to replace the barn or pay a vet to treat the horses, so he surrendered them to the SPCA."

"But that doesn't explain why they were standing in manure. Some hadn't been out of their stalls in weeks or months."

"He laid off his hired man and couldn't keep up with the cleaning. I guess he has a bad back," Ronnie said.

"Was that his only choice?"

"I don't know, but I'd hate to be in that position. You didn't seem to have a very good opinion of him, though, so maybe it's not a huge surprise." She motioned toward a tool bag. "I'd like to groom and clip them to make them more comfortable. Eventually, we'll get a farrier to trim their hooves."

Val helped Ronnie put the two geldings and the other mares in the crossties. She held their heads while Ronnie clipped. She was quick and efficient and kept up a steady stream of chat as they worked, and although she didn't say anything of real import, it was still nice to listen to her.

"I need to talk so they get used to my voice," Ronnie said.

"You seem to know what you're doing with those clippers."

"It's been a while, but it's coming back. Thank goodness Irene said she'd help me train the horses."

"That is lucky." Val injected as much perkiness into her voice as possible when what she really wanted to do was curse. She didn't need any competition, but who was she kidding? They weren't an item, nor would they ever be. So why couldn't she push away the flutter of jealousy?

CHAPTER TWELVE

Ronnie flailed around, reaching blindly for her phone as it rang. Why didn't people text? She could sleep through a text. "Hello?" She cleared the frog out of her throat and tried again. "Hello?"

"I woke you up." Val sounded apologetic.

"No, I was awake." Why did she lie about being wakened? Would it shame her forever to have been caught sleeping? And why was it "caught" sleeping? "I was reading." She'd been reading an hour ago and managed two pages before she dropped the book on the floor and curled around her pillow.

"I was wondering if you'd like to do something today. I mean unless you have other plans. I left you alone all week because of the horses and the last week of school and all…"

"It was a crazy busy week."

"And now you're relaxing and catching up on your sleep. Sorry. Another time maybe."

"Wait, wait." Ronnie sat up and rubbed furiously at her eyes. "I'd like to do something as long as it doesn't involve reading, computers, or horses. I need a break."

"How about flowers? The garden center is having a sale to clear out their annuals."

"I can never remember what's an annual and what's a perennial."

"You plant annuals every year…annually. I can help you plant a small garden in front of your house."

"I'd rather help you. I'm not really into flowers. I barely mow my lawn. I'm thinking of leaving it another week and just having it baled."

Val laughed. "Oh, I have enough annuals. I put them in a month ago."

Ronnie laughed. "Of course, you did."

"That wasn't a dig."

"No problem. Anyway, I've been wanting to find a place to take Dover. He likes the woods and lakes and another teacher told me of a place close to here. Do you know it? Would you show it to us?"

"I'd love to. It's called Duck Lake. It's a small lake with a park and wooded trail. It's about thirty minutes from town, and a hike would be nice."

"Dover and I'll pick you and Gwen up."

"I can drive," Val said.

Ronnie shook her head. "Dover's going to swim, and I have a system to keep my car cleanish."

"Okay. Oh, my parents have Gwen for the day. They've taken her to Saskatoon to buy her a present. It's sort of an end of school year tradition."

"What's she getting?"

"It's a surprise for her, but she's getting a riding helmet. Her riding instructor says she has to have one."

"Safety first. I'd probably be less mixed up if I'd worn one at her age."

"Are you expecting Gwen to fall off?"

The alarm in Val's voice brought Ronnie the rest of the way awake. "No, no, not at all. The Starview horses are safe. I was working with green horses and they threw me a few times. You know, hit my head, mixed me up?" Ronnie held her breath and waited for Val to pull Gwen out of her riding class.

Val laughed. "Mixed up? You seem normal to me."

"But you don't know me, yet." Ronnie cleared her throat. She'd come very close to flirting. Too close. "Give me forty minutes or so."

"See you."

Ronnie hung up and swung her legs out of bed. She picked up the coffee she'd made when she let Dover out in the morning. The coffee was cold, but she chugged it, needing the caffeine. She glanced in the mirror. It was odd to shower before a hike, but her hair was sticking out in seven directions and there was no way Val could be allowed to see it.

After breakfast and a shower, she dressed in a T-shirt, hiking pants, and boots and drove to Val's house. Val was sitting on her porch step. She leaped up, jogged over to Ronnie's car, and slid in.

"Hi." Val turned and petted Dover. "Hi, Dover. You ready to go for a paddle?" Dover licked her hand and then settled down on the back seat.

"Were you waiting long?" Ronnie asked. "Was I late?"

"You were right on time. I was ready early."

Of course, Val was ready early. "Nice hat," Ronnie said.

Val fiddled with the brim of her ballcap. "You like it? My good friend bought it for me. It fits great and there's room for my hair."

Ronnie laughed, strangely elated that Val was wearing the gift she'd given her. "Which way?"

"East into town and then take the highway north." Val settled back. "Those look like serious hiking pants. Are they the kind where the bottoms of the legs zip off?"

"Yup. I've had them a long time. Dover and I like the trails."

As they drove to Duck Lake they chatted about hiking and Dover when he was young and tearing up the trails. Sharing details of her life was different, and she liked it.

At Duck Lake Ronnie drove in and parked. "A lot of people here today."

"That's the sailing club." Val waved at a tall blond woman. "That's my friend Carrie. She's one of the instructors. The sailors won't be on the trail. If we follow the trail about a quarter way around the lake there's a bench and a nice place for Dover to swim."

"Lead the way." Ronnie snapped on Dover's leash.

"Are you a quiet hiker?"

"Quiet?"

"Some people like to hike quietly so they can see the wildlife."

Ronnie grimaced. "Dover is going to bark at everything. No, we're not quiet."

Dover pushed past Val and sniffed the edges of the trail and everything interesting as they hiked. They chatted as they walked, and thirty minutes later, they arrived at a bench made from roughhewn timbers. "Here we are," Val said.

Ronnie looked around. There were no other people or animals, so she unclipped Dover. He waded in to his belly and lapped at the water. Ronnie dropped on the bench, opened her water bottle, and sipped. Val sat beside her and drank from her bottle.

"Cookie?" Val asked. She opened a plastic container and passed it to Ronnie.

Ronnie peered in. "You made these? How do you get them all the same size?"

Val shrugged. "Practice."

Ronnie munched on a cookie. "These are good. I'm not showing you what I brought."

Val poked her. "You have to share. It's the rule of the trail."

"All right, bossy." Ronnie produced a plastic bag of slightly mangled Double Stuff Oreo cookies.

Val pounced on them. "Oreos. I love Oreos. I can't make these."

"So buy them."

"I try to stick to homemade." She pulled an Oreo apart and proceeded to lick the icing center.

Ronnie watched Val, enchanted by the way her tongue moved, until Dover laid a wet paw on her knee. She shook his paw and pulled out a second bag of dog treats. "No, buddy, I didn't forget your cookies." She set one on his nose. He threw his head back, tossing the treat in the air and then caught the cookie in his mouth.

"Look at you two. Ready for the circus." Val petted Dover when he leaned against her knee.

"That's all we've got." Ronnie finished her oatmeal cookie and reached for a second.

"So, tell me about your family. You know all about mine."

Ronnie winced slightly. Family conversations always made her stomach ache. "We're not very exciting. I'm the youngest of six."

"Six? I would have loved to have brothers and sisters."

"And when I was a kid, I'd have gladly given you a couple of mine. I have two sisters and three brothers. We're scattered around

Canada and the USA at various jobs. One of my sisters still lives in Winnipeg and she has the unfortunate job of watching out for my mother."

"Unfortunate?"

"Mother's a handful. Very demanding and picky. Obsessed with tidiness. Everything in its place. She would hate my house in Thresherton." Ronnie smiled wryly. "Good job she'll never see it."

"What about your dad?"

"My father passed away when I was fifteen."

Val laid a hand on Ronnie's knee. "I'm sorry."

Ronnie watched Dover paddle around and pretend he had a chance of catching the ducks he was chasing. "It was fourteen years ago, but he was too young. One day he's driving home from the shop, next minute he's hit by a drunk driver and killed."

"Did that make you angry?"

"Of course, and it still does. And I won't be in a car unless the driver's sober." Ronnie was frowning and she softened her expression. "Sorry, I'm kind of stuck on that point."

"I agree. Nobody should drive drunk. Lauren's ex-wife was in a car accident last week. The other guy wasn't drunk, but he ran a red light."

"How bad is she?"

"Pretty banged up. Lauren's gone back to Ontario to look after their kids."

"I didn't know Lauren had children."

"Two. Samantha's twelve and William's eighteen. Lauren misses them, but she's settled in Thresherton now and loves Callie and Becky."

"That's nice. I'm taking a third cookie."

"Help yourself." Val pushed the container closer to Ronnie. "Lauren and Callie met at Poplarcreek. Lauren was out there to help with some calving, and bang—true love. I'm oversimplifying, but that's the gist."

"Lucky them. That almost never happens." Ronnie paused with the cookie halfway to her mouth. Val was studying her with her head tilted to the side. In her ballcap, blue T-shirt, and faded jeans, Val couldn't have been more beautiful. Sometimes you could accidentally run into the right woman or her kid could be in your class. Ronnie stuffed the whole cookie in her mouth and almost choked herself. She stood and called for Dover. "Come on, Dover, let's keep walking." Val was a friend, just like Callie and Lauren, and it was best that she remembered that. She was way out of Ronnie's league.

Val followed her and they finished the hike and the drive back to town chatting amicably about families and growing up, but Ronnie couldn't help but wish she could hold Val's hand the way she had the other day.

❖

Ronnie flipped to the next page in her book and smiled. She relished a quiet morning reading in bed. It was her first week off since the end of school and she was going to sleep in every day. So what if her lawn needed cutting? The neighbor had cut his twice since she'd done hers last. She sighed. She was entitled to a break and her mower would disturb the neighbors this early in the morning. Tomorrow, after lunch, she'd cut it, unless she went cycling or spent the day at Poplarcreek. Maybe Val would be around. They'd had such a nice hike on Sunday.

She glanced at the clock. She had to be at Starview Farm at eleven a.m. for the first lesson of the beginners class. She wanted to check on the horses at Poplarcreek, but she'd do that afterward. Ronnie rolled out of bed, dressed, and jogged downstairs. "Dover, come on, buddy. We have time for a short walk." Dover tottered over to her and leaned his old body against her leg. She stroked his head as he peered up at her.

Ronnie hooked the leash on and took Dover outside. It wasn't a walk, but a slow stroll. She sauntered to allow Dover to keep pace with her. She was energetic, and sometimes it strained her patience to wait for Dover, but she loved him. She walked him at least twice a day. Lauren had prescribed stronger arthritis and pain medication for him and told her Dover might live for many more years if he got regular exercise. "Come on, buddy. We need to move to keep your legs going." Dover's ears perked up and he plodded faster.

After the walk they returned home. Ronnie led Dover into the house and he immediately crawled into his bed. She stroked his head. "You have a nice nap, old man."

Ronnie darted upstairs, grabbed her riding boots, ballcap, and jacket and returned. Dover was standing with his nose pressed to the patio doors that opened into her backyard. She filled her water bottle in the kitchen and glanced outside. The neighbor's dog was in her backyard again. "Sorry, buddy. I'll fix that gate this weekend to keep him out of your yard and to keep you from leaving to visit his." She'd been planning to do it for a month now, but she was so busy. Ronnie dropped a kiss on Dover's head and darted out the door into the garage.

At ten thirty, Ronnie pulled into Starview Farm on her bicycle. It took an hour to bike to the stable. The stable owner thought she was crazy to ride her bike from Thresherton, but she'd given up years ago explaining to people how a long cycling trip kept her mind clear.

Ronnie stopped behind Val's car, dismounted, and removed her helmet as she watched Becky and Gwen leap from the car. She switched her cycling shoes for the cowboy boots she stored in the saddle bags of her bicycle. Becky and Gwen were punctual. Their lesson started in thirty minutes, but they had to be early to learn to saddle their horses before the lesson.

"Morning, Ms. Yakimoto," the girls called in unison as they ran to the barn.

"Helmets." Val stepped from the car and held up two riding helmets. The girls circled back, grabbed the helmets, and jogged off. "Morning, Ms. Yakimoto," Val said with a laugh.

"Hey, Val. They're excited."

"First lesson and it's horses and riding."

Ronnie smiled. "I used to feel the same way at their age."

"I bet. No Dover today?" Val pulled on her ballcap as she spoke.

"He can't keep up with the bicycle."

"Oh, of course."

Ronnie smiled at Val and tugged gently on the brim of the ballcap she'd bought her. "Getting a lot of use out of that."

"I am. Still need a bucket of sunscreen, especially for my poor neck."

Ronnie ran a finger along the edge of Val's ear and felt her shiver. "Don't forget your ears."

Val open her mouth and then closed it again.

Ronnie stared into Val's dark blue eyes with their dilated pupils and backed away. "I'd better get in there and help with saddling. Nice to see you." Ronnie turned and strode after the girls. She looked down at her hand. It couldn't belong to her. Some supernatural power must have been operating it because for some reason she'd just caressed Val's ear. She rubbed the tips of her fingers together. They still tingled from the contact and it wasn't a sensation that said friendship. No, the sensation screamed for something more and she wasn't going there. She shoved her traitorous hand in her pocket. "Val is my friend, Val is my friend," she muttered to herself as she almost ran to the barn.

CHAPTER THIRTEEN

"Gwen? Gwen?" Val called. "Gwendolyn Helen Connor, hurry please." Val wished she could take Gwen to riding class like last week, but this Thursday she had to work. She paced and glanced at her watch. "If you want to spend the day at Poplarcreek we have to leave now, or I'll be late for work." Val always aimed to be ten minutes early. She liked to switch into her lab coat and clinic shoes and do a quick tour of the kennels to check on the animals before the veterinarians arrived. Her mother always said if she wasn't ten minutes early then she was late.

"Yes, Mom, I'm coming." Gwen sang her words. "I can't find my riding boots. Lesson two today, yippee."

Val smiled at Gwen's happy sounds as Gwen skipped around the house. Gwen was ecstatic about the riding, which was a far cry from the last time she'd tried it. Becky was a natural and Gwen bounced along doing her best. "They're by the front door, honey."

Gwen hopped along the hall and landed with a wide smile at Val's feet. Val grinned and kissed Gwen on the forehead. Val's parents bet Gwen would be taller than Val's five two by the time Gwen reached twelve years old. It could happen. Today was July eighth, and Gwen's ninth birthday was in two days and she was already taller than Val had been at that age.

"Are you ready, honey?" Val caressed the soft, pale skin of Gwen's cheek. "Do you have your sunscreen?"

"Yes, Mom."

"It has to be reapplied every thirty minutes. Will you do that?" Most people applied sunscreen once and forgot that sweating and time made the product wear off. She had read the labels on the seven different products the local pharmacy stocked and had picked this one as the safest for Gwen, but it needed regular applications to be effective. Their red hair left them prone to sunburn.

"Yes, Mother," Gwen said stringing the word mother to four syllables.

While Val waited for Gwen to collect the tin of cookies they had baked for Callie and Becky, she considered her options. Callie was driving Becky and Gwen to lessons. Maybe Callie would help her move forward with Ronnie? She and Ronnie had chatted a bunch of times over coffee or simple meals, or at the riding lesson, but Val wanted more. Val shook her head. She was supposed to be concentrating on other projects, not thinking about how attractive Ronnie Yakimoto was.

"Let's go. Do you have clothes for later and pajamas?"

"Yes, Mom."

"I'll pick you up after work on Friday."

Thirty minutes later, Val pulled into the driveway at Poplarcreek, Callie's farm. She scanned the farmyard. Callie wouldn't be in the house. Early each morning, she drove her ATV into the fields to check on her cattle.

Val followed Gwen inside to say good morning to Becky. When she exited the house, she saw Callie drive her ATV into the shed and sit on it for a few seconds. Callie crawled off the ATV and trudged toward her house, and Val walked to meet her. "Morning, Callie. Thanks for driving Gwen to lessons today. You know if you want to leave Becky with me some weekend so you can see your friends in Saskatoon, I don't mind."

Callie's shoulders sagged. She jammed her hands in her pockets and kicked at the dirt with the toe of her boot. "Thanks, but I'm not in a visiting mood."

Val slanted her head to catch Callie's eyes. "Have you heard from Lauren this week?"

"I did, and she's not coming home soon." Callie sighed. "The car accident was worse than we thought. T.J. is out of danger and home now, but in rough shape. Lauren hired a home nurse for T.J. but needs to stay and look after Sam and William. They're her children and I get it, but I miss her. We miss her."

"She'll be back soon."

"I hope so. She's been gone two weeks already." Callie shrugged and focused on Val. "Sorry, just a little insecure. I know she loves me. Loves us."

"She does. With all her heart and she's coming back."

"I know it, but I miss her. Okay, pity party over."

Val rubbed Callie's arm and switched to a cheerier conversation. "Are you ready for Gwen's birthday party on Saturday?"

Callie brightened. "We are. Becky and I bought her a present yesterday."

"Thanks." Val sighed and took the plunge. "Do you think you might like to go to the club sometime?"

"When Lauren gets back, sure."

"Not sooner?"

"What's up?" Callie laughed. "Ah, I get it. You want to take Ronnie dancing."

Val blushed. "She's cute. I keep telling myself it's a bad idea, but I can't stop thinking about her."

Callie grinned. "She's perfect for you. Rachel has been trying to coax me to the Rainbow Club. I'll invite Ronnie."

Val frowned. "*You'll* invite her out?"

"She's new to the area, so I'll invite her to the club. She can make new friends if she comes with us. You come too and I'll ask Mitch. We'll just be a group going dancing. All very casual, no awkward setups. What do you think?"

Nothing awkward, but time together. There wouldn't be any pressure. "Awesome idea. My parents will look after the girls. They love Becky too." Val glanced at her phone. She would be late for work as she stole a few minutes to plot with Callie, but she had her priorities.

"Perfect. Let's come home after the dance and not stay in Saskatoon overnight, though. Can I crash at your house and pick Becky up in the morning?"

Val nodded, glancing at her watch again. "Yes, perfect." Callie had perked up and she was smiling. Maybe all she needed was a new project or a night out. "Oh, and Ronnie's dad was killed by a drunk driver when she was fifteen, so we'll need a designated driver."

"How terrible for her. I bet Mitch will do it."

"Good because Ronnie's kind of fierce about not getting into a car if the driver's not sober."

"Message received. So, it's a date. We'll iron out the details later, but I'll ask Ronnie today. When you come back for Gwen tomorrow why don't you two stay over? The four of us can have a girl's night and I have a bottle of wine I need help to drink. And Becky wants to host a birthday breakfast for Gwen on Saturday and make her pancakes."

Val smiled. "She'd like that and so would I. Thanks."

"Good. It's all set."

As Val drove to the clinic, she considered Callie's situation. Callie was sad and missing Lauren, but how typical of her to be thoughtful and devise a way for Val to spend time with Ronnie.

She'd spent an absurd amount of time thinking of Ronnie but hadn't had the courage to get in touch about anything not to do with school or horses. They were too different, but there was something about Ronnie, about her quick, easy smile and confident aura, that Val couldn't stop picturing. Now Callie had orchestrated the perfect situation. She shook her head, suddenly uncertain about the whole plan. No, it was just as Callie said, they were a group going dancing. A little light adult conversation and some laughter, along with a bit of eye candy. Besides, it would do Callie some good to get off the farm and not think every minute about Lauren. It would be good for everyone, and hanging out with friends was better than being alone.

Val slowed at the corner and watched the bicycle speed toward her. It had to be Ronnie. How convenient that Poplarcreek was between town and Starview. Ronnie was pumping fast, as if she was in a hurry, but she slowed beside Val's car and steadied herself with her hand on the roof of the car. "Hello, Val. Thought that was you."

"Morning, Ronnie. I just dropped Gwen at Poplarcreek."

"Lesson number two today."

"You're going to be early at the barn."

Ronnie shook her head. "I'm going to ride a little longer and then stop in to see the horses at Poplarcreek. Adam rubbed off his bandage yesterday. I put it back on, but I'm not sure it stayed."

"Adam?"

"Didn't Gwen tell you? She and Becky named all the horses. The pair of horses in stall *A* are now called Amy and Adam."

Val glanced at her watch. She was really late for work now. There was a little war in her head between being late and spending time with Ronnie. "Would you like some help with Adam?"

"Do you have time?"

"I'll call PVS and let them know. It's been my job to keep an eye on the horses while Lauren's gone."

"And it's been going great. Follow me to the barn if you can. I'll go straight there." Ronnie pushed off and pedaled away.

Val called PVS and spoke to her boss, Fiona. She was supposed to open at PVS, but there were no overnight patients, so Fiona said to help the horses first. She turned around and headed back to Poplarcreek. She waved at Ronnie as she passed her and pulled up at the barn.

Callie jogged over. "Everything okay? Thought you went to work."

"I passed Ronnie on the road and she asked for help with Adam. I said yes."

"Who's Adam?"

"Apparently, the girls have named all the horses. Not sure why they didn't tell us."

Callie nodded. "It's a surprise. There was some major cutting of wood and painting of signs in my backyard the other day."

Val laughed. "And you think they're making name plates?"

Callie shrugged.

"Well, they didn't bring Ronnie in on the secret because she spilled."

"Spilled what?"

Val jumped and turned. Ronnie was beside her, still straddling her bike. "Callie and I aren't sure we're supposed to know the names of the horses, yet."

"And I spoiled the surprise."

Val shook her head. "Not if the three of us keep it quiet and you don't tell us any more names. Can we look at the foal right away? I'm supposed to be at PVS this morning."

"Follow me."

"Need me?" Callie asked.

"I can hold him," Ronnie said.

Val grabbed her kit of supplies and followed Ronnie to the tack room where they pulled on boots and coveralls over their clothes and headed into Amy and Adam's stall.

"It's off again. See what I mean?" Ronnie said.

"Hold the foal, please. Hello, sweetheart." Val took a second to stroke the mare's neck and then she pulled on rubber gloves to check the foal. "It's nearly dry and almost healed. We're okay to leave the bandage off now. There's a little bit of raw skin, but it will heal as long as you keep it clean." She dabbed at the wound with iodine then examined the rest of the burn patches. "Some of these are growing hair back. Adam is such a clever boy, aren't you?" Val petted Adam and then stepped back. "You can let him go."

Ronnie had been cradling Adam against her body with one arm across his chest and the other around his back end. "Clean bill of health for you, buddy." She let him go and he circled over to his mother and hid beside her. After getting her reassurance, he approached Ronnie and nibbled on the sleeve of her coveralls.

"He likes you," Val said.

"He just wants to play, don't you, buddy? Needs somebody his own size." She rubbed his neck. "I've got a few small bruises where his nips went a little far."

Val laughed at Ronnie and Adam as she checked the mare's healing burns, and then she collected her gear and reluctantly left the stall with Ronnie following. "The mare will be fine too. Just keep the open sores clean and all will be good with them. See? I'm trying to forget their names."

"Thanks. I've got your kit." Ronnie hefted the case and carried it to the barn door.

Val ducked into the tack room to remove her boots and coveralls and then joined Ronnie.

"Thanks for your help," Ronnie said. "I hope I didn't make you too late for work."

Val shrugged. "I'm at work. And I like looking after the horses. Everyone else okay?"

Ronnie nodded.

"Then I'll be back on the weekend."

Ronnie followed Val to her car and slid the vet kit in the trunk. Val stood by the driver's door of her car as her mind actively searched for something to say. She wanted to invite Ronnie to the club herself, but the words stuck. What if Ronnie thought it was a date and said no? Then everything would become weird and awkward between them. She couldn't risk it. "Okay, well, have a good day."

"I'm sorry you won't be at the lesson today."

"Me too. I'm hoping for next Thursday off so I can watch."

"Good. I like when you're there." Ronnie stepped away from the car. "Bye."

Val pulled out of the driveway and drove down the road. Ronnie waved and then stood with her hands in the pockets of her coveralls. Val hit the gas and sped back to town. Her mind was full of Ronnie and the possibility of dancing with her. She shivered when she thought of swaying to music and being held tightly. The closest they'd come had been a brief hug after the horse rescue and that was more relief at being alive than anything. Val grinned. She felt alive and excited at the possibilities. As long as she kept things in perspective it would all be fine.

CHAPTER FOURTEEN

Ronnie finished up in the barn and then accepted a lift from Callie for her and her bike to Starview. "Thanks for the lift."

"You're welcome," Callie said and shifted to focus on Gwen and Becky as they jogged to the barn. "Have a good lesson, girls. I'm staying to watch."

Ronnie studied Becky and Gwen as they ran. Becky covered much ground with one stride, but Gwen was fast and kept pace with her.

"Thanks for the help with Adam." Callie slapped her hand over her mouth for a second. "I'm not supposed to know yet, but what are they calling the others?"

Ronnie shook her head. "I gave up two names by accident. I'm keeping quiet about the rest." She removed her bike from the SUV and leaned it against the fence. Cowboy boots with cargo shorts might look a little odd to some people, but Callie worked in shorts and work boots. She wouldn't think it was odd.

"Is Lauren coming back soon?" Ronnie asked.

Callie's face fell and she looked away. "Don't know. She's in Ontario as long as her kids need her."

Ronnie wanted to punch herself as the sparkling, mischievous look fled from Callie's eyes and their blueness dimmed. She searched for something to say, staring at her boots as if the answer were etched there. She barely knew Callie and Lauren and was in no place to offer reassurance.

Callie straightened her shoulders. "So, it's just us at the farm. We've got Val seeing to the horses' injuries and Ian is available if we need him. Anyway, nice day for a lesson." Callie pointed to the bicycle. "And for that."

There was a forced brightness in Callie's voice, and she played along. She glanced at the clear blue of the sky. "Yes, a perfect day for both. I'm looking forward to a long ride home." It was clear Callie was done talking about Lauren, so Ronnie gladly let the topic drop.

"Becky and Gwen are excited about the lessons. How are they doing?" Callie asked.

"Becky is a natural and Gwen is doing well. They'll be fine." Ronnie waved. "Well, I better go help saddle up." She sped off, ashamed of dragging Callie down and then running, but some days she could barely get herself out of bed. She was about as useful to Callie as a grass fire.

Thirty minutes later, her students were mounted and circling her in the outdoor arena. The beginners class was a group of ten eight- to twelve-year-olds. Ronnie gave them time to settle and then began the lesson. "Everyone, think about where your feet are. If you concentrate on proper placement now, it will become a habit. In Western riding, you'll learn to direct your horse with only your feet. Remember people, guiding a horse is not about pulling them with the reins."

Ronnie frowned as she spotted Irene walking toward her. She was busy with a lesson. Couldn't Irene see that? Irene walked toward the line of moving horses as if nothing would dare get in her way. The horse Becky was on was closest to Irene. The horse stopped, laid his ears back, and backed up a few steps. Becky looked perplexed, but after Irene had passed, the horse started walking again.

"Hey, Ronnie."

"Irene." Ronnie nodded and studied her students as they circled.

"What a group of amateurs. I recognize that little redhead. Bounces like a ball."

Gwen's face blanched when she saw Irene, and it made Ronnie mad. Who could be mean to such great kids?

"Good job, Gwen. Squeeze with your knees. Yes, that's it. You're doing really great," Ronnie said. "Irene, I'm kind of busy. Can we talk later?"

"Nope. I just tortured my last student of the day and I'm headed home." She stuffed a small packet in the back pocket of Ronnie's shorts.

Ronnie jumped and spun at the unwelcome contact. "What's that?"

"A present of the smokable kind."

"No, thanks. Take it back."

"Okay, Grandma." Irene yanked the packet out. "When did you get so boring?"

"Bye, Irene." Ronnie moved away to concentrate.

Irene waved as she passed unnecessarily close to the head of Gwen's horse. The horse jerked his head up, snorted, and scrabbled sideways. Gwen grabbed the saddle horn and hung on. She looked terrified as she focused on Ronnie for help.

"It's okay, Gwen. You're okay and Comet's a good horse. You'll be fine. Relax." Part of Ronnie wanted to run to Gwen and comfort her, but if she did that the shying horse would become a bigger deal and eat away at Gwen's confidence. Gwen was stroking Comet's neck as much to calm herself. She would be okay, but would Val when she heard about Irene's prank?

"That was a good lesson, people. Horses are unpredictable and scare easily. Always be prepared for them to freak out and never be afraid to hang on to the horn when you need to. Good recovery, Gwen."

Gwen smiled her thanks.

Forty-five minutes later, the children dismounted and led their horses to the barn. Mandy, the owner's teenage daughter, waited to supervise the grooming of the horses. Assuming an air of nonchalance, Ronnie scanned the arena fence. Callie waved at her and waggled a bottle of water.

"Thanks." Ronnie accepted the cold bottle of water and drank half in one pull.

"Wonderful lesson. I'm impressed. Gwen and Becky are doing so well."

"Horseback riding was primarily about confidence to this point. They're no longer holding the horn and they're smiling as they ride, instead of clenching their teeth. Up to now they've only half listened to my direction. Now they can concentrate on learning."

"You're an excellent teacher."

"Thanks." Ronnie blinked. It wasn't as if she planned the lessons. She just made it up as she went. What she was telling the kids was correct information, but she had no idea what to teach in a beginners class. Fortunately, it was working.

"You're patient and make learning fun. Gwen took lessons last summer with Irene, but Irene yelled at her about bouncing too much and Gwen quit. She tried to squeeze with her legs and hold on, but it was too hard."

"Val told me. I'm sorry she had a bad experience. Most children her age are here for the fun of being with horses and riding with their friends. A teacher ought to keep that in mind."

Callie frowned. "I might not know much about horses, but I saw what Irene just did to Gwen's horse."

"It was an accident."

"You think so? You're very trusting."

Ronnie shrugged. Was she trusting or just inclined to avoid drama? She needed Irene's help with the rescued horses. And to do that, Irene needed to be welcome at Poplarcreek. But it was true that Irene had been out of line.

"Well, anyway, Gwen is happier this year and that means Val is happier. We're going to the Rainbow Club in Saskatoon a week this Saturday. Do you want to come with us? As part of a group?"

"I don't know. I registered for a race that weekend."

"Bicycle race?"

Ronnie nodded. "I train all week and race on the weekends. I decided not to teach summer school this year so I could concentrate on training."

Callie looked suitably impressed. "That's very ambitious, but I wish you'd come. We'll meet with my friend Rachel and Val's friends. It'd be a chance for you to meet new people."

"Is it a gay club?" Ronnie was curious.

"Rainbow is a gay club, but there are gay-friendly people there too. Val is gay, but not all her friends are. My friend Rachel is bi and I never know whether she'll bring a man or a woman."

"I'd enjoy that, thanks. In case you were in any doubt, I'm a lesbian."

Callie shook her head slowly. "I was never in *any* doubt."

Gwen and Becky burst from the barn and sprinted toward them. "Thanks for the lesson, Ms. Yakimoto." Becky and Gwen giggled and bounced into Callie's SUV.

Callie shrugged. "My cue to head home. So, on club night, we'll leave early evening and have dinner in the city. I'll email you the rest of the details. We'll come back to Thresherton after the dance. It'll be two or three a.m. before we're home. Will that still suit you?" Callie asked.

"Yes, thanks." Ronnie grinned. She waved as the SUV drove away. Her summer might be more fun than she had originally thought. She'd made a new friend in Val and now had an invitation for dancing and dinner. A night out with friends, nothing complicated. She switched her boots, then she hopped on her bicycle and shot out of the parking lot. The thought of going dancing with a group of women, especially Val, made her pulse race.

CHAPTER FIFTEEN

Ronnie tried on her fourth jacket and checked it in the mirror. It would do for the Rainbow Club. It wasn't her newest, but at least it had all its buttons, unlike the other three. There was a jar of buttons on her dresser. Sometime when she was watching television, she'd sew the buttons back on. She didn't have many jackets and needed all the ones she owned.

She pulled up her pants leg and experimentally poked the purple bruise on her shin where Adam had kicked her on Tuesday. He'd been playing, but his hooves were sharp. Val had been there treating the horses and switched to fussing over Ronnie. Val had insisted she sit for ten minutes with an ice pack on her shin. She'd been about to refuse until Val presented her with a container of a dozen homemade oatmeal cookies to keep her busy. And if she was honest with herself, she really liked Val fussing over her and giving her cookies. She laughed at the idea.

She jogged downstairs to the front window and watched for Callie, who'd offered to drive. When the SUV rolled into her driveway, Ronnie jogged to the passenger door. She skidded to a halt. Another woman was in the passenger seat.

The window slid down and the woman said, "You're in the back." Then the window went up again.

Ronnie crawled into the back seat. "Hi, Callie."

"Hi, Ronnie." Callie smiled over her shoulder and then backed the vehicle out of the driveway. "This is my friend Mitch."

"Hi, Mitch." Ronnie and Mitch shook hands between the seats. Ronnie had seen Mitch around town but hadn't been introduced to her.

"Mitch is local RCMP. Ronnie is Becky's English teacher."

"English teacher," Mitch said and nodded.

"Ronnie, can you please run in and get Val?" Callie asked when they pulled into Val's driveway.

"Sure." Ronnie had been thinking of Val constantly and couldn't wait to see her in person. Her mental images paled in comparison every time.

The door opened and Val said, "Sorry, I'm not ready. I hate making people wait for me." Val waved Ronnie inside her house.

Val looked worried, like they'd been waiting two days instead of two minutes for her. She needed to relax. "No hurry. We have lots of time."

"The restaurant won't hold our dinner reservations on a Saturday if we're late."

"We have lots of time."

"I need to find Lauren's little cat. While Lauren's in Ontario, I'm taking care of her cats."

"Why aren't they with Callie?"

"They're house cats. Lauren was scared they'd get out and run away at Poplarcreek, and Callie and Becky are too busy to look after them. My old cat passed away this winter and Gwen and I miss the fur people, so here we are."

Val was staring at her and Ronnie had the urge to shoo her away to find the cat.

"Elsa? Where are you?" Val looked around. "I want to shut the bedroom doors, but I have to make sure they're out first."

"Can I help?"

"No, thanks, Elsa's skittish. Best if you wait here." Val walked from room to room. "Elsa, Elsa? Here kitty, kitty, kitty."

Ronnie shrugged and studied a bulletin board by the front door. There was some kind of monthly schedule of chores with boxes neatly ticked off. There was another list of tasks reminding Val to get an oil change on her car and switch batteries in the smoke detectors. Ronnie shrugged. When had she last changed batteries and had she switched oil in her car before Christmas, or before Thanksgiving? There were hair and dental appointments also listed. She brushed her short bangs to the side, happy that the hairdresser had been able to squeeze her in Friday morning.

"You're staring at my schedule. Callie thinks I'm over organized."

"I was thinking I should get one. Can't remember the last time I had my car serviced. It's going to break down and cost me buckets of money if I don't."

Ronnie shifted and focused on Val. Val was elegant in a casual emerald green dress that fell to an inch above her knees. The dress hugged her curves, and she resembled a glamorous 1950s movie star. The slit up the side wasn't matronly at all. When she'd first met her, she hadn't considered how exquisite Val was because she'd assumed Val was straight and married. Now that she knew better, it seemed perfectly acceptable to drool over her like a fool.

"There she goes." Val darted into a room and emerged with a small orange cat she deposited on the floor and then closed the door. "All set. We can go now."

Val slipped into heels that made her almost as tall as Ronnie. She locked her front door and Ronnie followed her to the SUV. She held the door of the SUV open for Val and took her hand while she climbed into the vehicle. The SUV was high, but in heels and a dress Val hopped in with little difficulty. Ronnie jogged to the other side and jumped in. She inhaled and caught the subtle sandalwood-floral scent Val wore.

The drive was comfortable, and they chatted about music interests, laughing at one another's choices. In Saskatoon, the four of them ate dinner at a Greek restaurant Val recommended. They talked about Thresherton and people in the town. They discussed the veterinary clinic and Callie's farm, but nobody mentioned Lauren. "So, Ronnie you're originally from Winnipeg? Has your family always lived there?" Callie asked.

"I'm Canadian of Japanese descent. After World War II, my family settled in Winnipeg."

"How do you like Thresherton?" Callie asked.

"I like it now that people have stopped remarking on how well I speak English, as if it's not my first language." Ronnie forced a laugh.

"English is my only language, and I have a master's degree in English from the University of Manitoba in Winnipeg." She didn't mean to sound bitter, but it came through anyway.

"Ouch," Val said. "Sorry about that. I love my hometown, but we are a little insulated."

"At least when I moved here, I didn't have to explain who the Métis were," Mitch said.

"Where did you train to be a teacher?" Val asked.

"I trained in Winnipeg and afterward moved here to teach. I might do my PhD sometime or move to a large community to teach high school." Ronnie gave a quick smile, hoping she didn't sound flaky. Val's smile slipped and she bent her head to her plate. Ronnie watched Val push food around her plate after eating with gusto at the start of the meal. She shrugged. Maybe Val was just full.

Ronnie laughed, trying to ease the sudden tension. "I don't know what's next for me. Not for sure. I'm not a person with a ten-year plan. More like a ten-minute plan."

Mitch and Callie laughed at her joke, but Val didn't raise her head.

After dinner, Callie drove them to the Rainbow Club. Ronnie glanced around and took in the décor. It was a mixture of western and gay themes. Lots of rainbows and pictures of impossibly muscular cowboys without shirts. A little tacky, but if it was the only gay club in the city, then it was home and nobody would care.

They got drinks and found an empty table. Ronnie picked at the label on her beer bottle and shifted from foot to foot. She only knew the three people she came with and half the club knew them. There were lots of hugs and kisses for Val and Callie. Some days it was harder to be an outsider than others.

Val and Callie introduced Ronnie to many of their friends. She had no hope of remembering all their names, but there were a couple of women she might phone next week. The number of people Callie and Val knew between them overwhelmed her. The group at their table spilled onto the dance floor because so many women gathered around Val and Callie. Ronnie hovered on the periphery of the group and watched, feeling out of place and out of sorts.

When a song started that she liked, Ronnie placed her bottle on the table and approached Val, who had also taken a slight step back from the group. "Val, would you like to dance?"

"Love to." Val took her hand and led her to the dance floor.

Ronnie watched Val's body as Val relaxed and followed the beat with little effort, moving in an organized pattern, but not stiffly. Val put her entire body into the dance. The sway of her hips and the wiggle of her butt when she spun, made Ronnie's throat go dry. The names of the other women in their group drifted from her mind as she leaned closer to Val. "You're an awesome dancer."

Val grinned. "You too."

A burst of heat shot through Ronnie as Val blatantly looked her over.

"Do you like to dance?" Val asked.

"Love it. Though I'm strictly freestyle. No dance lessons."

"Free is good and I like your style."

Ronnie grinned and upped the energy of her moves. Now that was flirting.

When the music turned slow, Ronnie headed toward their table, but Val grabbed her arm. "Dance some more with me?"

"Sure." Ronnie and Val squeezed into the crowd. Val slipped into Ronnie's arms and when their chests connected an electric charge zipped through Ronnie's body. Val peered toward their table and her body stiffened slightly, and Ronnie followed her gaze. It landed on a pretty woman with long brown hair who waved at Val.

"My ex, Christine. I want to stay away from her."

Ronnie frowned. "Was she mean?"

"She was great with me, but we weren't on the same page about other things."

Ronnie refocused on Val's warm blue eyes and full lips. How could somebody not want to be with Val? She was beautiful, sexy, and smart.

Val stopped moving when the song ended. "Like to join me in the lounge for a drink?"

"Sure. What lounge?"

"Follow me." Val took her hand and towed her toward the far end of the club.

Ronnie scanned the room they entered. The Rainbow Lounge was located on one side of the main club. It was much quieter than the club and furnished with chairs, tables, couches, and a big television in the corner.

They picked up drinks at the bar and Val led Ronnie to a table. "What do you think of the club? Is this your first time here?"

"I'm having a great time, and yes, tonight is my first time. I read about it online, but never made it here." Ronnie locked eyes with Val. "Nice of Callie to invite me."

"It was a joint idea, but yes, Callie asked you." Val blushed and studied the liquid in her glass.

Ronnie clasped Val's hand and held it. She couldn't resist. Val's hands were surprisingly soft for a person who worked with them all day. "Thank you for including me. I appreciate it."

"You're welcome. I'm really glad you came." Val bit her lip and looked at Ronnie over the rim of her glass.

"Thanks. So, you were with Christine? The woman at the table?"

"Yes, for almost a year. What about you? You have a girlfriend back in Winnipeg?"

Ronnie shrugged. "Several exes. Fun women, but not serious. Julia was the last one, and I'm not looking for another, not yet." Best to make it clear from the start she wasn't into anything serious. She was too busy and too scared to start another relationship. It was best to keep things light. "Was it hard to break up with Christine?"

"Oh, a little sad. You know the feeling of having failed again. It was less painful than when Margery left me."

"Margery?"

"You don't want to hear all of this."

"I do. Go ahead."

"Margery was my last girlfriend, before Christine. She dumped me after three years together. We met when I was a student at college in Saskatoon and she moved back to Thresherton with me. I thought she liked it here." Val shrugged.

"But she didn't?"

"One day at dinner, she announced that she was moving to Vancouver for a new job. No explanations, no apologies, no remorse, and no invitation to join her. Margery's last words to Gwen were devoid of emotion. She only said, 'See you later, kid.'"

"What a bitch. Sorry."

"No, you're right. She was a bitch. She discarded us, Gwen and me. Gwen loved her. I was hurt, but seeing my child so crushed pissed me off. I wanted to wallow in my pain, but I had to look after Gwen."

"So, Christine?"

"Exact opposite. She refused to even meet Gwen. Pretended Gwen didn't exist, which now appears to have been a blessing."

"Her loss. Gwen's an amazing kid."

"Thanks. What was Julia like?"

Ronnie looked around them. "She'd have hated it here. The last time we were at a club, she accused me of checking out the other women and planning to cheat on her. I tried to calm her, but she started screaming at me. I spent the rest of the evening looking at the floor or into Julia's eyes, as nothing else was acceptable."

"Wow. That must have been rough."

Ronnie shuddered. "She was jealous and controlling. A real headcase and she hated Dover. She wasn't mean to him, but he wasn't allowed to touch her, and she complained about his smell all the time."

"But Dover's a lovely dog. Have you had him long?"

"Change of subject?"

Val blushed.

Fair enough. Talking about exes wasn't exactly flirting material. "My father gave him to me when Dover was a puppy." Ronnie shrugged. "I asked for a horse, but a puppy was all my parents could manage."

"Gwen wants a horse, but it's never going to happen. I don't have that kind of money."

"They're expensive. More so than people realize." Ronnie laughed. "For my next birthday I had planned to ask for a horse. A black one to match Dover."

"You could get a horse now. Board it at Starview."

Ronnie shook her head. "The board is almost as much as my mortgage. I considered robbing a bank to pay for it but thought that'd create new problems."

Val laughed. "Big problems."

"It made more sense to stick with the plan of a second job or a boarder."

"Is that how you ended up teaching riding?"

Ronnie nodded. "I struck a deal with the owners of Starview. If there's enough interest I'll carry on and teach riding in the fall too. I love working with horses."

"Gwen and Becky would sign up again."

"They'll have to toughen up because I might be teaching the intermediate class," Irene said as she dropped uninvited into a seat at their table.

Ronnie liked Irene, but she always appeared when not wanted. "It's an ongoing discussion. The Trevors like the job I'm doing." Ronnie smiled at Val, but Val was watching Irene with a nearly murderous expression on her face. The story of Irene spooking Gwen's horse had clearly reached home.

Irene punched Ronnie in the shoulder. "You're too soft. The kids need a tougher teacher. Speaking of tough, I've got time after lessons on Thursday to look at the SPCA horses you have. They looked rough, but it's been a month. Let's see what we can do."

"They're beautiful and sweet. Every one of them, and they don't need tough," Val said.

Val's eyes were flashing now and had turned a dark blue. In ten seconds, she would be coming across the table at Irene. "Okay, thanks, Irene," Ronnie said.

Irene jumped up. "There's somebody I need to talk to. See ya."

Ronnie glanced at Val and back at Irene. Irene hadn't acknowledged Val's comments or even her existence. It didn't surprise her that Irene had left when there was somebody more important to talk to.

Val leaned toward Ronnie when Irene had left. "We don't need her help. Tell her to fuck off."

Unsurprised by Val's vehemence, Ronnie picked at the label on her beer bottle. "I need her help. Everyone is expecting me to work miracles with these horses. Irene knows horses and she's not going to be mean to them. She just likes to joke and sound tough."

Val snorted. "And FYI, Gwen is never taking a class with that bitch. Tell Starview if you're not teaching, we won't be there and I bet most of the other parents will think the same."

"There you are," a woman said, darting into the room. "I found her. Come on, Val." Three women grabbed Val and tugged her, laughing, from her seat. "We haven't seen you in months. You're not allowed to hide in here."

"You come too, Ronnie," one of the women said.

Fierce Val was gone. Ronnie grinned with relief and followed them back to the dance floor. Val was stunning and vibrated with energy, but getting involved with someone who had a kid was risky. A little kid could get hurt by partners who left. She sipped her beer and studied Val. Kids didn't scare her, but was she ready to be an adult? Like, that kind of adult? And what if she hurt Gwen? She'd never want to hurt either of them.

She watched Val dance two fast songs with her friends, then she took Val in her arms for another slow dance. She pushed serious thoughts aside to enjoy being with Val. When Val relaxed into her and rested her cheek against her shoulder, Ronnie's senses shot into overdrive. How could she yearn to explore possibilities with Val while having the urge to run far and run fast?

Tomorrow, after sleeping in and having a light breakfast, Ronnie planned to dig out her racing bike. A long ride would help her clear her mind and organize her thoughts and desires. Val was cute, but she played for the long haul, and serious drama wasn't in the cards. After Julia, it was all about fun and freedom.

She pushed the thoughts from her head and pulled Val closer. Tomorrow, on her bicycle, she would figure it out. Tonight, she would enjoy Val's company.

CHAPTER SIXTEEN

Callie was falling-down drunk by the time they dragged her from the club. Ronnie and Val drank in moderation, but weren't safe to drive. Mitch had volunteered to be designated driver, so was still stone sober. Val tucked Callie into the front passenger seat and wrapped a blanket around her. Callie was asleep before they left the city.

In the back seat, Val and Ronnie huddled together and whispered to keep from disturbing Callie although it would take an explosion to wake her.

"She's wasted," Ronnie said.

"I should've kept a better eye on her," Val said.

"She's not your responsibility."

Val leaned away and frowned at Ronnie. "She's my friend and she's missing Lauren. She doesn't normally drink like that."

Ronnie shrugged. "She's a grown woman."

"Wow." Val shook her head. "You really don't care."

Ronnie studied Val. "Wait. That's not it. I just think people should be left to make their own choices."

"That's the point. She was too lonely to make sensible choices. She needed a friend and I was…"

"With me?"

"Maybe, for some of the time. It's not your fault or mine." Val sighed. "I just wish I'd stopped her sooner."

Ronnie scrutinized Val. "You really do care about her. Sorry for the distraction."

Val slid close and leaned against Ronnie. "From the time I was old enough to go places with my friends, my mom drilled into me the importance of looking out for each other and never leaving a girl alone or in a vulnerable situation. I failed tonight and she'd be disappointed."

Ronnie tentatively slid her arm around Val's shoulders. Val smiled at Ronnie's hesitation and settled in. Curled against Ronnie, she was able to let the guilt go. They lapsed into silence, but Val didn't mind. Her brain was full of how close Ronnie was and all her senses were alert.

An hour later, Mitch pulled into Val's driveway. "You're home, Val."

"Callie? Callie?" Val shook Callie's shoulder, but she barely stirred. "Mitch, I need help to get her inside."

Mitch stepped out of the SUV and moved to Callie's door. "Come on, Callie." Mitch scooped her from the SUV and carried her inside, and Ronnie got the doors.

Val grabbed Callie's overnight bag and purse. "Put her in my bedroom. First door on the right." Mitch carried her in, Val pulled back her duvet, and Mitch plopped her onto the bed. "I'll take it from here. Thanks."

"Night, Val." Mitch waved and exited the room.

Ronnie shuffled from foot to foot and scanned the room. She jumped when Mitch disappeared, and Ronnie headed for the door too. "Night, Val," she called over her shoulder.

Val smiled at Ronnie's departing back. It had been a fun night and she wished she could have invited Ronnie to stay for a sandwich and maybe something else, but she had Callie to look after. She wouldn't let her down again.

Callie lay back in her dress and began to lift her feet onto the bed.

"Hold it." Val wrestled with Callie and removed her shoes. She tugged Callie's arm until Callie sat up again. "Want to sleep in your dress?"

"No, thank you." Callie pawed at the straps of her dress.

"Wait." Val opened Callie's overnight bag and fished out a long T-shirt. She slipped it over Callie's head and helped her slide the dress straps off her shoulders. Val averted her eyes to avoid seeing Callie half naked.

When the shirt was on, Callie reached to the middle of her back. "Help me unhook my bra?"

Val cupped Callie's cheek. "Honey, you weren't wearing one."

"Forgot. Don't need one." Callie laughed and clasped her own breasts. "I have the same tiny breasts I had at puberty. They're almost not here, but you have nice breasts. Nice big breasts." Alcohol had washed away Callie's inhibitions and she tried to cup Val's breasts.

Val nudged Callie's hands away from her chest. "Stand up so we can remove your dress."

Callie staggered to her feet and leaned on Val. "You have nice big breasts. Did they get big when you were pregnant with Gwen?"

Val ignored the drunken ramblings. "Callie, please. Can you help *a little*?"

"Lauren has nice breasts. Nice big breasts." Callie held her hands six inches from her chest, to show the size of Lauren's breasts, but she overbalanced and stumbled against the dresser. "Don't you think Lauren has nice breasts?"

When Callie's dress fell to the floor, Val sat her on the bed, then she left and returned with a damp cloth she handed to Callie. "Wipe your face."

"Val?" Callie wiped her face.

"I will not discuss Lauren's breasts, or mine or yours or Ronnie's or anybody's."

"Oh, you noticed Ronnie's." Callie smirked. "Hers are small like mine. She's little, like you, but small-breasted." Callie laughed.

"Go to sleep, Callie."

Callie lay down and an instant later, bolted upright. Her skin blanched, and she looked panicked as she put her hand over her mouth.

"Oh no, you don't!" Val hauled Callie to her feet, not troubling to be gentle.

Val dragged Callie to the bathroom where Callie was sick. Callie's hair was still up, so it wasn't a complete disaster. She fetched a toothbrush and Callie stabbed at her teeth until satisfied, then she stumbled into the bedroom and collapsed on the bed. Val tucked the comforter around Callie and dropped a tender kiss on her forehead.

Val sighed with relief at getting Callie to bed. She collected a clean nightdress from her closet and changed in Gwen's room. She removed her makeup and used the bathroom, then she checked on Callie and discovered her crying.

Val perched on the edge of the bed and placed her hand on the Callie's shoulder. "Hey, what's wrong?"

"Sorry to be so much trouble. I'm gross and a pain." Callie gasped the words between sobs.

"You're unhappy and drunk." Val rubbed her shoulder. "Everybody's been there. I don't mind taking care of you."

"I miss Lauren. I wanted to dance with Lauren the way you were with Ronnie. You two were so close together. Looked so beautiful. I wanted Lauren to hold me like that again. Why isn't she here? Why isn't she holding me now?" Callie's sobs filled the bedroom.

Val rubbed Callie's back. "Callie, Callie, hey, my friend."

"I've loved two women in my life. One died and one abandoned me." Callie rolled over and peered at Val with red puffy eyes. "What's wrong with me?"

"Nothing. You're an awesome woman and Lauren did not abandon you. She went ho—to Ontario for a bit. That's all," Val said firmly. She meant it. There was nothing wrong with Callie Anderson. Callie was sweet, smart, hard-working, and a great mom.

"I'm stupid. I'm a stupid woman. She has ties to Ontario. What if she doesn't come back to me? What if she realizes I'm not enough and she doesn't want to live on a farm?"

"You're not stupid and Lauren's coming back. I'm sure."

"Is she? We had four months together. Four amazing months, but how can Becky and I compete with Dr. T.J. the wonderful, their two kids, and ten years together? What if…what if she doesn't love me anymore?"

Callie wrapped her arms around Val's waist and buried her face against Val's stomach. "It's just the alcohol making you think this. It'll all be okay in morning. You're just missing her and she's missing you." Alcohol always brought fear barreling to the surface, but daylight could chase away those shadows.

Val slid into the bed and gathered Callie in her arms. Callie curled into a ball and nestled her head against Val's chest. She rocked

Callie until she cried herself to sleep, then she slipped from bed and headed to Gwen's room. Callie would be all right in the morning.

Val crawled into Gwen's bed and hugged a pillow to her chest. She shivered at the memories of being held tight against Ronnie, but Ronnie wasn't girlfriend material even if she was beyond cute. She sighed. Ronnie had looked stunning in dark blue jeans and a tight, V-necked T-shirt, with her black jacket.

Val longed to let her attraction loose, but what if Ronnie left Thresherton? She'd never mentioned the possibility before, but what if she and Gwen got attached to Ronnie and she left? Callie had told her to go for it anyway. But what if she did and it all fell apart again? She was exhausted and needed to sleep yet her brain was spinning out of control, not to mention her body was on fire from all the close slow dancing. She took a deep breath. It had been a nice, low-key evening. She should keep things between them casual and friendly. Keep things safe.

Val woke to sunlight streaming through the window. She got ready and woke Callie. "Sorry, honey, but it's time to get up. We have to be at my parents' by ten. We have church this morning."

Digit lay stretched along Callie's legs and Elsa was curled on the end of the bed. It was unusual behavior for Elsa, as Lauren's small cat never slept on beds and she kept her distance from people, other than Lauren.

Callie shoved up to a seated position, hunched over, and cradled her head, then she lay down again. "Am I dead?"

Val laughed. "No, honey. If you were dead it wouldn't hurt so much."

"Are you sure?" Callie's voice was faint and rough from the crying and sobbing. Digit crawled into Callie's arms. She kissed him on the head and cuddled the big orange cat. "Are you missing your mom? She's coming back."

"Time to get up and put the questions away for a while. We have to fetch your SUV from Mitch. Do you want a shower or breakfast?"

Callie sat up and grimaced. "I'll shower at home and no breakfast, please. No food ever again."

Val handed Callie the jeans from her bag. Callie rose to her feet and leaned against the dresser as she tugged her jeans on and tucked her long T-shirt in.

Callie petted Elsa. "I remember some of what I said last night. Sorry for all the drama and grabbing at you."

"It's okay."

"I intended to quit drinking sooner, but too many people asked me about Lauren. Smiling and saying, 'My girlfriend is in Ontario, but coming home, soon,' was exhausting. So, I just drank."

Val rubbed Callie's upper arm. "You miss Lauren. It's okay."

Callie nudged Val. "Successful night for you, though. You and Ronnie looked gorgeous dancing together *and* you snuck away for half an hour."

"We were in the lounge, talking."

Callie smirked. "Perhaps that's the truth."

"It is." Val shoved her gently when Callie grinned. "Stop it, you. Get dressed."

Callie zipped up her jeans. "I can't wait for Lauren to come home and take me dancing. I danced some fast dances last night. But no slow ones, because I'll only do that with Lauren. I love resting my head on her shoulder."

Val tried not to look at her watch impatiently. "That's very sweet, but please hurry. I hate being late for church. Everyone stares at you when you're the last in."

"Sorry." Callie darted into the bathroom.

Val packed Callie's bag while Callie brushed her teeth. Her body craved sleep, but she still looked better than Callie. She'd showered and put on fresh makeup and a nice sundress. She had even managed coffee and a slice of toast, and she wasn't any worse for wear from their night out.

They drove to Mitch's house and Val ran to the door and returned with Callie's keys. Callie climbed into her SUV and followed Val to her parents' house.

"Mommy!" Becky and Gwen yelled in unison and then took turns hugging Val and Callie

"Mommy, are you, all right?" Becky peered up at Callie.

"We'll talk later, honey. But I'm fine, promise," Callie whispered.

Her mom hugged Callie. "How are you, dear?"

"Tired, Helen. How are you and Andrew?"

Her mom held Callie at arm's length and scanned her face. "Oh, we're as good as ever. Dear, you are a little pale. Are you sure you're not ill?"

Val slipped between them and gave her mom a hug. "We had a big night at the club and arrived home late."

"Good for you. You girls work hard and deserve a night of fun." She kissed Val, but her expression shifted to worried as she focused on Callie again. "You might have a cold. You sound a little scratchy."

Callie's face turned pink. "Hmm, maybe. Thanks for taking care of Becky."

"See you." Becky hugged Gwen, grabbed her knapsack, and bounced out the front door after hugging the rest of the Connors. "Thank you, Mr. and Mrs. Connor."

Val hugged Callie and kissed her on the cheek. "We'll talk next week."

Callie nodded and left with Becky.

Val studied Callie as she shuffled to her truck. Callie was hurting and a reminder that getting involved with a woman from another province was risky. Val nodded to herself and absorbed the inadvertent warning from Callie. Lucky for her she wasn't planning to get involved with Ronnie, even if she was desperately cute.

CHAPTER SEVENTEEN

A slender figure on a bicycle passed Val as she drove to Poplarcreek to pick up Gwen after her riding lesson. The cyclist flew by fast, but it looked like Ronnie. Who else wore a professional cycling outfit in Thresherton? And Val recognized the red and black helmet.

It had a been five days since their night at the club. She'd thought Ronnie would call, but maybe it was better that she didn't. She and Ronnie had seen a lot of each other over the last two months, but they hadn't been on a real date. Maybe she was imagining a connection where there wasn't one. Maybe they were just friends? Val sighed. This felt more complicated than a regular friendship should.

A few minutes later, an ATV traveling in the same direction as the bicycle roared toward her. The ATV was in the middle of the road and Val swerved until she was half driving on the shoulder to let it past. The driver raced along the road at a reckless speed and tossed her a jaunty wave. "Stupid kid!" Val yelled.

When Val arrived at Poplarcreek, she parked and entered Callie's house.

"Hello, you. Just in time for lunch." Callie grinned.

"I just about ran some kid over on an ATV. Who would that be?"

"Don't know." Callie shrugged. "Every farm has one or two ATVs."

Val shook off her irritation. "You look happy. Nice having Lauren home?"

"I picked her up at the airport last night and we made out in the car. Kissed for like twenty minutes before we left the airport parking." Callie hugged Val. "It was the best. I can't believe I was worried. What a drama queen."

"You're allowed to be insecure. Everyone is sometimes, even you. Is Lauren home now?"

"No, she had a meeting with Ian and Fiona this morning to talk about scheduling and catch up. She'll be back after lunch."

Val returned the hug and the kiss on the cheek from Callie. Callie was so happy to have Lauren home, Val thought she might break into a dance. "I wish we could stay, but I have a mountain of laundry and housework. Thanks for the lunch invite." It was Thursday and she had the day off, which meant she had time to do a thorough clean and reorganize of the kitchen cupboards. It also meant she could've watched the riding lesson, but she'd chosen to hide at home.

"Maybe next time." Callie turned and called upstairs. "Gwen, your mom's here. Time to go, honey."

Gwen jogged down the stairs followed by Becky. "Aren't we staying, Mom?"

"Not today." Val interrupted when Gwen opened her mouth to protest. "Please, get your bag."

Gwen shot a forlorn look at Becky and snatched her knapsack off a kitchen chair. "Bye, Callie. Thanks for taking me to the riding lesson today." She scowled at Val and stomped outside.

"Bye, Callie." Val headed outside and propelled her pouting daughter into the car. Gwen preferred to be with Becky, but today Val didn't feel social. She wanted space and lacked the will to interact with people, even Callie. Hiding from the world and burying herself in chores was the plan. If she and Ronnie were just going to be friends, then she needed time to regroup and learn to be content with her own company.

On her way to Thresherton, Val spotted a bicycle lying at the side of the road and Ronnie sitting hunched on the edge of the ditch. She slowed the car and opened her window. "Hello? Ronnie? Everything okay?"

Ronnie glanced over her shoulder. "Hey, Val, hey, Gwen."

"Are you injured?" Val asked, hoping Ronnie was okay so she could drive away, while simultaneously hoping she needed someone to tend to her.

"I fell and skinned my elbow. I've had worse." Ronnie held up her arm and studied the scrape.

"Ouch. Do you want a lift?" Val prayed Ronnie would say no. She hated being even a little attracted to a woman who was surrounded by question marks, but she had to keep their interactions mature. They lived in a small town and in an even smaller lesbian community. She'd seen the tension between Mitch and Lauren because they barely tolerated each other. She refused to develop such a dynamic between herself and Ronnie. Polite friendliness was the best option. It would have to be when that's all there was.

"Thanks. I was just about to try hitchhiking. Somebody always stops."

"You've done this before?"

"Oh, yeah."

Val parked and climbed from her car. They lifted the bike and set it on its wheels. "Looks okay."

Ronnie spun the front wheel. "The front wheel's bent. That'll be expensive to fix. I wish I knew who that kid was."

"Kid?"

Ronnie frowned and stared down the road. "A kid passed too close on an ATV and sent me into the ditch. We had the whole road to share. I'm not sure why he drove so close."

"I passed him after I saw you."

"Did you recognize him?"

"No, sorry, but he was driving like an idiot." Val helped load Ronnie's bicycle into her trunk. She smirked to herself as she recalled the story about Lauren meeting Ronnie on the road. This time Ronnie accepted the offer of help to lift her bike. She wasn't trying to impress her, and on some level, Val was disappointed.

Ronnie rinsed her scraped elbow with bottled water and blotted it dry with a scrap of cloth she yanked from her pocket. "Ouch, ouch. Dang kid."

"I have a first aid kit. Do you want help?"

"No, thanks. I'll clean it again at home."

"What about your other elbow? Your shirt is torn there too."

Ronnie laughed. "That's from last summer."

"You mean last year?" Val cringed at how judgmental her comment sounded, but she couldn't picture leaving a shirt for a year without mending it and *still* wearing it.

Ronnie shrugged. "Yeah. I always meant to patch it, but maybe now there are two torn elbows it might be time to give up. I'll get some new cycling shirts at the back-to-school sales."

"Back-to-school?"

Ronnie winked. "I buy my tops in the boys' department. Hadn't you noticed?"

"No." Val climbed into her car, Ronnie following, and they continued the drive to town. Ronnie's clothes fit perfectly and showed off her slender figure, but Val wasn't about to admit it.

Ronnie chatted with Gwen about riding lessons and they discussed how Gwen was enjoying her summer. Val remained silent and concentrated on her driving. She struggled to ignore the subtle scent of fresh air and healthy living that wafted off Ronnie. It made her long for Ronnie the way the smell of fresh baking made her hungry.

Val grinned at Ronnie's infectious laughter and looked her over. Big mistake. Ronnie sat turned in her seat so she could look over at Gwen while they talked. Val had a quick flash of tight shorts and strong thighs. There wasn't enough housework in the world to dispel the picture of her head nestled at the junction of those thighs. Val's head snapped forward, and she groaned inwardly, forcing herself to focus on the conversation.

"I didn't love school and I skipped off a lot. High school was worse," Ronnie said.

"Mom never skipped," Gwen said.

"Never?"

Val shrugged. "I didn't see the point. I wanted my grades to get into—grades to move on."

"To where? University?"

"Maybe." Val caved and peeked at Ronnie. She registered a dazzling smile of perfect straight teeth and cheeks rosy from exercise. She had the urge to run her fingers through the hair plastered to Ronnie's forehead with sweat.

Val focused on the road as they passed the ATV from earlier. "There's the idiot."

Ronnie looked through the side window and then straightened in her seat. *"Wait! Stop!"*

Val slammed her brake pedal to the floor and her car skipped to stop at the side of the road. For a second, she thought Ronnie had read her mind and wanted out and away from the objectification of her body.

"What is it?" Val scanned the area but saw nothing. She turned to Ronnie, but Ronnie had already leaped from the car and was sprinting back up the road.

As Val watched in the rearview mirror, Ronnie dropped from sight into the ditch. Val turned and drove back. As she neared the spot where Ronnie had disappeared, Ronnie popped up from the ditch waving her arms.

Val parked and jumped out to investigate. The ATV had overturned in the ditch and the boy was underneath it. The boy was still, and Ronnie stood beside him holding him by his shirt to keep his head out of the small creek. The water reached the middle of Ronnie's calves.

Ronnie said, "I saw him go off the road. A second ago, he was holding his head up and trying to hang on to the ATV, but he's not talking now. We have to get him out of here."

Val tried her phone. "No cell signal. I'd prefer not to move him, but can we move the ATV?"

"You hold his head and let me try."

Val slid into position and winced as she kneeled in the cold water. She placed her arms on either side of his head and held the top of his shoulders to stabilize his neck. His eyes were closed, his skin pale. He was a skinny teenager, a few years older than Gwen. He looked a little familiar, but she couldn't place him.

"Mommy, what's wrong?"

Val glimpsed Gwen at the edge of the road staring down at her. "This boy hurt himself. Stay in the car please, so I don't have to worry about you."

Ronnie heaved on the ATV. "Too heavy for me, but we might do it together."

"It's more important for me to keep his head above the water and stabilize his neck and spine. Take my car and go back to Poplarcreek. Tell Callie to bring a tractor and tow ropes or something."

"Why don't I stay?"

"I have him now and we shouldn't move him more than we have to. You go. Please, make sure Gwen wears her seat belt."

"Back soon."

Ronnie scrambled up the ditch and sped away in Val's car. At least the water level wasn't rising, but Val was cold and the boy would be hypothermic soon. She talked to him and told him what she was doing, and although she wasn't sure how much he heard, it calmed her.

Val prayed while she waited for Ronnie, hoping someone would hear her silent call for help. She couldn't, wouldn't, let this boy die.

Chapter Eighteen

Val looked up as a car stopped. It felt as if Ronnie was gone for an hour, but she'd returned quickly.

Ronnie hopped from the car and descended to Val. "Gwen's at Poplarcreek and Becky's calling an ambulance. Callie's right behind me."

Callie appeared on her small tractor within minutes. It had big wheels and was fast on the road. She parked and slid down the slope of the ditch to land beside Val. "Are you all right, Val?"

Val's teeth chattered. "Yup, just freezing."

"We'll get you out of there, soon," Callie said.

Callie and Ronnie inspected the ATV. They attempted to lift the machine and roll it off the boy in an effort to do it more quickly, but they weren't strong enough. Instead, Callie attached her tow rope to the ATV and climbed the ditch to attach it to her tractor. Ronnie followed and removed her bike from Val's trunk. She lifted the spare tire out of the trunk and rolled it into the ditch, then she rolled over a large rock.

"What are you doing?" Val asked, trying to keep her hands from shaking.

"We'll raise the ATV and I'll shove the rock and tire underneath, on either side of the boy, so the ATV won't trap him if it falls."

"Is that safe?" Val asked.

Ronnie stuck out her hands, palms up, and grimaced. "That's all we've got. Do you think we should wait for professional rescue?"

"No. He can't wait." Val gestured with her chin toward the water surrounding the boy. "The water's turning pink. He's bleeding from somewhere. We need to get him out of this."

Callie slowly started to drive. The four-wheeler rose slightly and then the rope slipped to the side and the machine came down on the boy. "Shit," Ronnie said. "Did we get you, Val?"

"I'm okay. Try again. Hurry, I see more blood."

"Callie, back up a bit and I'll put the rope on again." They tried again.

When the ATV was high enough, Ronnie pushed the tire and rock underneath. As the ATV rose higher, she shoved them farther. When they had it two feet above the boy, Ronnie signaled to Callie to stop.

Ronnie crouched beside Val. "We can't pull the ATV all the way because it could tip and scoop you and the boy up as it flips."

Callie parked and ran to Val and Ronnie.

Ronnie regarded Val. "Val, what do we do now?"

Val glanced from Callie to Ronnie. "Why ask me?"

Ronnie shrugged. "You have the most medical training."

"On dogs and cats." Val's answer ended on an astonished squeak.

"What would you do if he were a dog?" Ronnie asked.

"You can do it, Val," Callie said. "We can't let him die."

Val shook her head and concentrated. "We have to pull him out of the water, but we need to keep his spine straight. The best choice we have is to drag him straight up the ditch."

Ronnie nodded and she and Callie cleared away debris between Val's back and the road, then Callie pried Val's frozen hands open until she could let go of the boy. Ronnie scooted in and held the boy the way Val showed her. "Don't let go, Ronnie. If we didn't have to move him I wouldn't. There is a big risk of spinal injury, but we have to stop the bleeding."

Val was too stiff to move. "Pull me up the hill, Callie." She put her arm around Callie's shoulder and half-walked, half-dragged her way up the hill as gravel and twigs scratched at her bare legs.

When they reached the road, Callie hauled Val to her feet, and set her on the bumper of her car. Val flexed her legs and ankles. Callie slid back down the ditch and she and Ronnie got a hold of the boy's clothing. They dragged him slowly and carefully from the ditch to the road with Ronnie walking backward and stabilizing his neck the entire time.

When they had the boy on the road Val draped a blanket over him and grabbed her emergency medical kit. She kneeled and checked his pulse and breathing. Blood pooled beside his leg and she looked more closely. "He has a gash near his femoral artery. If it extends into the artery, he'll bleed to death."

Val pulled on sterile gloves and wiggled her fingers into the hole in his leg and applied more pressure. The bleeding slowed to a trickle.

"Want some help with the blood?" Callie asked.

"No, you hold his head. Keep his neck nice and straight. I'm worried about paralysis."

He stirred and moaned and looked up at Callie. "Mom?" he said before his eyes closed again.

"What now?" Ronnie asked. "What about a tourniquet?"

"Like in the movies?" Val shook her head. "No, much too dangerous. A tourniquet is a last resort. If done improperly you can cut the skin or damage nerves and blood vessels. The bleeding's under control with just the pressure of my fingers. That's the best way to go."

"What should I do?" Ronnie asked.

"Watch for the ambulance and make sure nobody runs us over. People drive too fast when the roads are straight and flat."

Ronnie leaped to her feet and scanned the road in each direction. Five minutes later, an ambulance appeared with lights and sirens on. Two paramedics jogged over and focused on Val.

"We found him pinned underneath his ATV in the ditch. He was unconscious. We stabilized his neck and dragged him out of the ditch. He's bleeding near his right femoral artery. I put pressure on his wound, but it's still bleeding a little."

"He been unconscious the whole time?"

Val shook her head. "He woke for a second, asked for his mother, and fell unconscious again. Do you think he has a brain injury?"

"That's up to the doctors, but it's good that he was conscious."

"I did everything I could. I'm only a vet tech," Val said.

"And a good one. You saved my dog," the paramedic said. "We can take it from here, Val."

Val struggled to move out of their way, and she stumbled as she tried to rise, too stiff to stand. Ronnie's arm slipped around her waist and lifted her to her feet. The sensation of the slender, powerful arm around her body was jarring in the best way. Val gasped, unprepared for the immediate surge of electricity and warmth. For a second, she forgot she was cold and sore from kneeling in the water and on the gravel road. She allowed herself to relax into Ronnie's warm embrace as they watched the medics do their job.

The paramedics put a pressure bandage over the bleeding, but it had mostly stopped. Next, they strapped on a neck collar. "Let's get him inside for the IV," the paramedic said.

When they were ready, the paramedics strapped the boy on a board and lifted him onto the stretcher and then into the ambulance.

Val, Ronnie, and Callie watched as the paramedics hooked up an IV and oxygen.

"Will he be okay?" Val asked.

Ronnie gently propelled Val toward her car. "You did your best. I think he'll be fine."

Val stopped and brushed tears from her cheeks. She was shaking as the adrenaline wore off. "How do *you* know? You don't get it. If I screwed up, then he dies or is paralyzed or loses a leg." Val shook her head. "I'd never forgive herself. This is why I picked being a vet tech over human nursing. It's sad when a pet dies, but this is somebody's *child.*"

"You did your best." Callie squeezed her shoulder.

"Do you recognize him?" Val asked. "He looks familiar and it's bugging me."

Callie shook her head. "Don't know him."

Ronnie shrugged. "He was in my English class, but his name escapes me."

Mitch appeared as the paramedics drove off. She had questions and agreed to follow them back to Poplarcreek. Val tried to ignore the disappointment that ran through her when Ronnie let her go and took the wheel, since Val was still stiff and shivering. She wanted to be held and just allowed to cry. How did nurses do this? She'd be a basket case every night. She shifted close to Ronnie until their shoulders touched.

Ronnie took her hand and smiled. Val bit her lip to keep from weeping like a fool. Ronnie understood Val's need to connect with her.

"You were amazing," Ronnie said.

Val shook her head.

"You were, and stop arguing, woman. Nothing's going to change my mind."

Val laughed quietly and took a deep breath. She had done her best and time would tell if it had been enough. Ronnie had been calm and present the whole time. They made a good team.

When they arrived at Poplarcreek, Val pointed toward the horse barn. "Is that Irene's truck?"

Ronnie parked and glanced over. "It is. That's odd. I wasn't expecting her today."

"She showed up after Val left. She said she'd talked to you. I don't like this," Callie said. "I'll go run her off."

"We need her help with the training," Ronnie said.

Callie scowled. "She lied to me."

"Maybe I got it wrong." Ronnie sighed. "Can we leave it for now? Val's freezing."

"I'm okay. Get rid of Irene."

Ronnie pulled on her hair. "Okay, okay. I'll go over there right now and tell her to go home. To just fuck off and then I'll do all the work. I'll groom and exercise seven horses twice a week. I'll give up everything else and Dover and I'll move into Callie's spare room. That suit you two?"

Val bit her lip. She wanted to laugh, but Ronnie wasn't ranting to be funny. "Sorry, Ronnie."

"I'm sorry Irene's a pain and sorry to be petulant, but I'm freezing too," Ronnie said.

Callie frowned in Irene's direction. "Okay we need her help, but I'm talking to her later. I don't like to be lied to and there are other horse trainers in the world." Callie exited the car. "Come on, let's get you two inside."

After hot showers and donning dry clothes at Callie's place, they met in the kitchen where Becky had hot coffee ready for them.

Mitch joined them at the table. "I called the hospital. The boy's awake and crying. They're still testing his spine, and he has a broken ankle and the severe cut to his leg. The soil in the creek must have been soft enough that the ATV pushed him into the mud, instead of crushing him. Congratulations on saving his life. Val, you were correct. The boy nicked his femoral artery. They think he landed on a sharp tree branch. If you hadn't put your finger in there, this would be a different meeting."

"He could have bled to death." Val swallowed. "He could have died." She smiled weakly at Ronnie. "Ronnie saved him from drowning."

Ronnie shook her head. "You stopped the bleeding."

"Who is he?" Callie asked.

"Kenny Williams," Gwen said. The adults focused on her. "I saw his face. He's in the class ahead of Becky. He's not a nice boy. Kenny is always shoving and pushing the little kids."

"Kenny Williams. You're right. I recognize him now. He squeaked through my English class by doing an extra credit project." Ronnie shrugged. "His father threatened to keep him out of hockey this fall if he didn't pass."

Mitch talked as she wrote her notes. "Missing hockey is a serious punishment. Most of the boys and many of the girls play."

Val opened her mouth to tell Mitch that Kenny had forced Ronnie off the road, but Ronnie gave a subtle shake of her head. Val frowned but stayed quiet.

When Mitch left, Becky and Gwen sprinted upstairs to Becky's room. Callie said, "What was the look that passed between you two?"

"Kenny drove too close to me and there was no reason to be that close. He may have forced me off the road," Ronnie said.

Callie frowned and tapped the tip of her finger on the table. "Tell Mitch."

"I agree with Callie. What if he tries something else?" Val asked.

"I'll speak with his parents first. Getting a young boy in trouble with the police leads to more trouble. He's out of hockey with a broken ankle and I don't believe he meant to harm me."

Callie leaned back and crossed her arms. "If Kenny is a bully now, how much of a jerk will he be in five or ten years? Will he become another Kyle Kruger?"

"We have to give him a second chance. Bullies are often angry, and getting him in trouble with the police isn't going to make him less angry. Just give me time to talk to him and his parents. If I have to, I'll talk to Mitch." Ronnie gave her usual mischievous grin. "And I'm not in any worse shape than all the other times I've fallen off my bike. Competitive cycling is dangerous business. I'm tough."

Shocked as she imagined Ronnie lying wounded at the side of the road, Val scooped Ronnie's hand off the table. She longed to hold her hand against her cheek. Val absorbed the strength and comfort in Ronnie's grip, and was glad she just smiled instead of pulling her hand away. Ever since the club she'd been trying to keep away from Ronnie, but now all she wanted was to curl up in her arms. So much for independence and waiting for the right woman.

CHAPTER NINETEEN

A fter Mitch left, Val and Ronnie declined an invitation to stay at Poplarcreek and rose from Callie's table. Gwen joined them and they headed to Val's car.

Ronnie glanced toward the horse barn relieved to see Irene's truck was gone. Confrontation avoided.

Val held out her hand. "Do you still have my car keys, Ronnie?"

"You kneeled in the water the longest and had the hardest job. You deserve a rest. How about I drive?"

"Thanks. I *am* tired." Val climbed into the car. Gwen jumped into the back and Ronnie settled behind the wheel. Val sat hunched in her seat with her arms wrapped around her and shivered. Gwen passed Ronnie a blanket, and she tucked it around Val.

Ronnie stole glances at Val and shook her head in wonder as they drove home. Coping with the emergency and issuing orders came naturally to Val, and she had been right about the femoral artery. Kenny could have bled to death, but Val had been calm and had known exactly what to do. It was beyond impressive.

When they arrived at her house, Ronnie leaped out and dashed around to Val's side of the car. She opened Val's door and helped her out. Val shuffled around her car and dropped behind the steering wheel. "Thanks. I'm stiff like an old woman."

"We worked hard," Ronnie said. She removed her bike from the trunk, but something in her rebelled against parting from Val, though she had avoided her since the night at the Rainbow Club. She wanted to say or do something important. Should she invite Val for coffee? At the very least she could do that.

Ronnie leaned against Val's window. "Thanks for the lift."

"I thawed spaghetti sauce and left it simmering," Gwen said. "Do you want to have dinner with us, Ms. Yakimoto? Mommy, is it okay if Ms. Yakimoto comes for dinner?"

Val raised an eyebrow at Ronnie. "I like the idea."

"Thank you, Gwen. What time is best?" She was tired of her own cooking, and a meal with friends sounded nice.

Val smiled. "We eat at five but come sooner and visit first."

"Thanks."

After Val drove away, Ronnie tried to wheel her bike but then lifted it and frowned at the damaged front wheel. "Stupid kid." She carried her bike into the garage and leaned it against the wall, then she entered the house and met Dover on his way to the sliding patio door.

After letting him outside, Ronnie dropped into a chair at her kitchen table. She was still navigating her way through the events of the night at the club. She had enjoyed her quick visit to Val's bedroom when she and Mitch had carried Callie in. The walls were light green with matching curtains and bedspread. No clothes littered the floor or hung over the chair. Val had even made the bed. Why make a bed when you'd be back in it in another sixteen hours?

Ronnie shivered, not sure if she was cold or coming down off the adrenaline high. Competitive cycling was tense, but this was different. They had saved a child. Mostly Val, but together they'd done it. It had been hard to drive off and leave her in the cold water, but Val had been right. Without Callie they'd never have gotten Kenny out.

Ronnie stood and shook her arms out. They were a little numb and her hands shook slightly. She let Dover in and stumbled upstairs to shower again and change. After a nap, she dressed and headed to her front door. Someone had pushed a paper bag through the mail slot. She opened it, and as the odor hit her nose, Ronnie ricocheted backward into the wall. It was a bag of pot. Dover could have eaten it. She stomped into the bathroom and flushed the bag and then texted Irene.

You leave me a bag?

Surprise. Enjoy.

Flushed.

That was expensive!

Listen—told you I don't smoke. Don't do it again.

Whatever, Grandma.

Obviously, Irene hadn't grown up. She was a good trainer, but she didn't listen, and clearly, she wanted her old pot buddy back. Ronnie jammed her phone into her pocket. She was having dinner with Val and Gwen and looking forward to it, and that was all she needed to think about right now. On the way to Val's, she stopped at the bakery for fresh garlic bread and purchased a small cake.

Gwen opened the door. "Hi, Ms. Yakimoto."

Ronnie followed Gwen into the kitchen and exchanged greetings with Val. She accepted a soda and leaned against a cupboard as mother and daughter prepared the meal. "Something smells good."

"That's the spaghetti sauce we made on the weekend."

"Weekend?"

"On Saturdays, Mom and I make all the meals for the next week and freeze them." Gwen opened the freezer and pointed. "See?"

Ronnie scanned the neat stacks of containers. Each was labeled with the contents, date, and cooking directions. She couldn't imagine being that prepared. Where was the spontaneity? She forced excitement into her voice. "Very cool."

Gwen hugged Val. "It takes lots of time, but it's fun."

"It is, and you're doing more and more of the work."

"I even got some new recipes to try," Gwen said as she set the table.

"You two are very organized." Ronnie pictured her own refrigerator and freezer. Both were nearly empty.

"I didn't want us to eat fast food." Val smiled warmly at Gwen. "And I love the time we spend together. We talk about everything as we cook. My mom and I cooked a healthy dinner every night, and I want to raise Gwen that way."

What would that be like, to chat to someone while cooking a meal? Ronnie couldn't fathom, and the thought brought on an unfamiliar melancholy. She shook it off, and Val returned to preparing a salad while Gwen finished setting the table.

"How do you survive without pizza?"

"That's only for special times, like after basketball," Gwen said.

"I brought a cake and garlic bread from the bakery." Ronnie shrugged. "You probably have your own."

Val pounced on the bag. "The bakery's garlic bread is better than mine. I'll freeze mine to have with the leftovers."

"But if the bakery's is better why make your own?"

Val shrugged. "I always have. You think I'm weird, don't you?"

Ronnie held up her hands. "Not at all. I'm simply curious."

Val sighed. "I'm a little sensitive. It's been a long day. The cake is wonderful too. I didn't bake today. Now let's eat before I fall over."

Ronnie wisely decided not to ask Val why she didn't occasionally buy her cakes from the bakery. She just quietly helped carry the food to the table, and then slid into her chair.

"Do you cook too, Ms. Yakimoto?"

"Not as often as you two. My mom cooked dinner for us after spending a long day working in our shop. She'd bang pots around and grumble and she preferred to do it by herself. I like to cook and it's usually edible, but I have to be motivated and I don't force myself. I confess I eat too many frozen dinners and pizza." Ronnie took in Val's expression. "Sorry. Was that too much information?"

"No. But I can see why you don't cook much. It must seem like a chore when it can actually be fun."

"Maybe I'll cook for you sometime."

Val blushed. "I'd like that."

It wasn't a peaceful dinner. Ronnie spent most of the rest of the meal answering Gwen's questions about Kenny's rescue and taking quick mouthfuls of the excellent food. They recounted the details of the rescue, but omitted the part where Ronnie suspected Kenny drove her off the road on purpose. Kids shared information, and she didn't need that going around the town.

After dinner, Val put the leftovers away and Ronnie helped stack the dishes.

Val pointed to the dishes. "I'll do those later."

"Tomorrow?"

"No, tonight before bed. I never let dishes sit overnight. They're too hard to clean the next day."

"Good point." Ronnie pictured the three days of dirty dishes at her house and was glad Val couldn't see them.

Gwen hooked her knapsack off the couch. "Time to go, Mom."

Val slipped on her shoes. "Gwen's visiting a friend this evening, and I promised to walk her there."

Ronnie scratched the back of her neck. "I should go home then." Being alone with Val felt more charged than when Gwen was present and she wasn't sure it was a good idea. Gwen was a great buffer and her constant chatter and questions prevented awkward silences.

Val squeezed Ronnie's forearm. "Do you want to walk with us?" Ronnie jumped. Did Val realize she'd made contact? For some women, it was a habit to touch people when they spoke. Ronnie felt her hand and the warmth it left behind on her skin. Her gut told her to run away, but the rest of her was in no hurry for the night to end. "Sure." She walked with them to Gwen's friend's house, enjoying the chatter and warm evening air. After dropping Gwen off, they strolled back toward Val's house.

"Should I go home and let you sleep? How tired are you?" Ronnie asked.

"When we got home from Poplarcreek, I showered again and crawled into bed for an hour. I'm tired, but please, don't go."

When they arrived at Val's house, Val dropped onto her couch. "I deal with animals more wounded than Kenny every day, but this was many times more stressful. I don't understand why."

Ronnie sat beside Val and held her hand. "You saved a *child*. He could have died."

Val flicked tears off her cheek. "Why aren't you unsettled? Why so calm?"

"Like Callie said, you had the harder job. The more important one." Ronnie slipped her arm around Val's shoulders. "You saved his life. You're amazing."

Val wrapped her arms around Ronnie's neck. Ronnie stopped breathing as Val slid in tight against her. "Hmm," Val murmured as she laid her cheek against Ronnie's shoulder. After a minute, Val leaned back. "How about I take off my pants?"

Ronnie's eyes widened and her jaw dropped. Val wore blue cotton capri pants and a frilly white sleeveless blouse.

Val focused on Ronnie's face and then laughed. "Not that. Twigs and slivers stuck into my legs when Callie pulled me from the ditch. I can't reach them. While we were walking, something kept catching on the fabric of my pants. Can you please help me?"

"Okay," Ronnie croaked.

"Thanks. Wait here." Val disappeared upstairs.

A minute later, Val reappeared with a bath towel draped over her arm and a first aid kit in her hand. Val's legs were elegant and shapely, and she wore the shortest pair of shorts Ronnie had ever seen. Val placed the first aid kit on the table and located the tweezers. Ronnie helped position a lamp until one end of the couch was well lit, then Val spread the towel over the couch and lay on her stomach with her legs on the towel.

Ronnie gasped. "Oh, Val, oh no."

"What?"

Ronnie dropped to her knees beside the couch. "Your legs are more scraped than my elbow." She scowled at the red marks and scratches. "I didn't realize you were getting so scratched up."

"I'm fine, really. My right leg below the edge of my shorts is the most irritated."

Ronnie extracted four slivers and thorns and one small piece of glass. She smoothed her hands along Val's legs to search for more prickles and located two more. She found it hard to breathe. Val's legs were full and soft.

It was a cool evening but sweat beaded on Ronnie's forehead, and she stopped several times to wipe her damp palms on her jeans. She was in so much trouble and just barely suppressed the urge to slide her fingers underneath the edge of the shorts. When the slivers were out, Ronnie dabbed each scrape with iodine. "I'm finished."

Val rested her cheek against a pillow and sighed. "Much better. Thanks."

Ronnie groaned inwardly. It had taken sixty kilometers of hard cycling to burn off the sensation of Val's body pressed against hers at the dance. Now she'd touched Val's smooth skin, taken care of her, and soothed her. How many kilometers would it take this time?

Ronnie dragged herself off the floor and stumbled into the bathroom. She washed her hands and splashed cold water on her face, then she leaned against the wall until her breathing slowed. She returned to the living room and plopped into the chair across from Val. "How are your legs?"

"Perfect." Val smiled at Ronnie. "You've got gentle hands. They aren't soft, but still delicate."

Ronnie swallowed. Her job was to comment on how soft Val's skin was, then Val would comment on Ronnie touching her, escalating the exchange. The sexual energy in the room was already scary. If they continued flirting, Ronnie didn't trust herself to stay sensible.

"Ronnie?" Val's forehead creased in confusion.

Ronnie rose to her feet. "I guess I should go."

"I'm having a beer. Want one?"

Say no. She needed to leave. "Sure, thanks."

"Shall we sit outside? Want a jacket?"

Ronnie nodded. When had she lost the power to speak coherent sentences? It had happened ten seconds after she'd touched Val's bare legs.

Val tilted her head and grinned as though she knew what Ronnie was thinking. Val darted from the living room and returned in jeans and holding two jackets. They slipped them on and snagged two beers before strolling into Val's backyard.

Ronnie scanned the neat yard and registered a colorful garden with a collection of plants arranged in a wagon-wheel pattern of color. Had Val laid out her garden with a ruler?

She scanned the yard as they walked. She'd find no weeds lurking along the edges of this lawn or in the gardens. Trimmed, edged, and weed-free, Val's lawn was golf-course perfect. Ronnie's lawn needed mowing, and she'd be lucky to get to it this week. Her grass was so long it was a scavenger hunt to locate Dover's poop to scoop it up.

Val settled on the bench to watch the sunset and Ronnie sat beside her.

Val searched Ronnie's face. "Beautiful."

The sunset was beautiful, but still unable to arrange words in a sentence, Ronnie only nodded.

"Do you read poetry? I wish I did." Val looked at the sky. "A night like this in a quiet garden deserves poetry."

"I read poetry at university."

"Will you go back there to do your PhD?"

Ronnie shrugged. "I doubt I'd be welcomed. I actually started my PhD. Did two semesters, but I didn't work very hard and flunked out. Teaching children was my second choice of career."

"And how do you like it?"

"I love it. Never thought I would, but I really do."

"Gwen says you're awesome. Plan to be principal some day?"

"Don't know about that. Might not be here that long. My friend Theresa told me there's a spot teaching at a high school in Winnipeg in another year. But there's a lot to consider."

"Such as?"

"I like Thresherton. I'm content right here right now." Content with Val in her backyard, and whatever it was slowly developing between them. "There are straight, flat roads for cycling close by. Thresherton has the stores I need, and houses are affordable. The school has a relaxed atmosphere and the teachers are friendly. And now I have horses to play with. I'll stick around for a while." The distance between Thresherton and her painful memories of Winnipeg was a bonus. "And besides, the four-bedroom house I own here would be too expensive for me in Winnipeg."

"You could've rented a house."

"Maybe I should've, but I got excited when I saw it. I looked at places to rent but they were either apartments or had postage-stamp backyards, and those aren't good enough for a dog."

"You bought a house so Dover could have a large yard?"

"Crazy, eh?"

Val tilted her head to the side. "It's sweet."

"But it wasn't financially sensible. I had to get a second job to pay for it. You'd never make such a rash decision."

"I didn't have to. I had time to look around for the right place and my parents helped me with the down payment."

"Have the Connors lived in Thresherton long? Where did you come from?"

"The Connors are Canadian mutt. A mixture of English, Welsh, Scottish, French, and Irish. One branch of my family was United Empire Loyalists who settled in Ontario after the American Revolution. My father's family homesteaded in Thresherton over a hundred years ago." Val sipped her beer. "My maternal grandmother was a war bride. She met my grandfather during World War II and after the war she moved from Scotland to Canada to marry him. Later they moved to Saskatchewan." A yawn interrupted Val's story. "Sorry. Still tired. That was a long answer."

"It was interesting. I like hearing about your life." Ronnie picked at the label on her beer bottle. "You've got deep roots in Thresherton."

"I can't imagine living anywhere else. I'm happy to be right where I am."

Ronnie leaned toward Val "What's that feel like?"

"Like this." Val took Ronnie's hand and squeezed it. "It's sitting quietly outside on a warm night and feeling content."

Ronnie read compassion in Val's eyes and smiled back. "Sign me up."

They sipped their beers in companionable silence for a few minutes. Ronnie enjoyed the clear night and sitting with Val and holding her hand. This was the first time they'd been really alone and it occurred to Ronnie how peaceful she felt with Val. Was peaceful the correct word? She wasn't calm. Every nerve in her body fired and her mind spun with possibilities. Did Val want a kiss? Did she expect a kiss? The idea scared her and she leaped to her feet. "I should go."

They slipped inside and put the bottles in the kitchen. After shedding jackets, they headed to Val's front door and paused at the threshold.

Val leaned toward Ronnie like she was going to kiss her. A wave of panic surged through her. She stepped back and almost fell backward out the door. She clutched the doorjamb and wondered if she left impressions of her fingertips in the wood. "Thanks for dinner and the beer. I enjoyed myself."

Ronnie charged down the front steps. Something dangerous happened to her nervous system when she was near Valerie Connor. She jumped in her car and headed home. Dinner had been a mistake, or at least staying afterward had been. Val had wanted a kiss and although Ronnie was interested, she didn't see Val as the casual lover type. Val was a nester and she wasn't. Just because she owned a house didn't mean she was going to stay. No, as attracted as Ronnie was, she would never mess with Val's feelings. That meant casual fun was out and that left just being good friends.

CHAPTER TWENTY

Val organized the instruments on the five squares of blue autoclave towel. All the instruments from the previous day's surgeries were washed, waiting to be sorted, packaged, and put through the autoclave.

Val smiled as she packaged the instruments. She'd last seen Ronnie four days ago and they'd had a lovely evening together, even if it had happened on the heels of their rescue of Kenny.

"Hello, Val?"

"Yes?" She turned and contemplated Minnie.

Minnie squinted at her. "You didn't hear what I said, did you? I asked if you needed help with the surgery packs. You're usually done by now."

Val doled out the last of the instruments and quickly folded and taped up the packages. "I'm good. We had five spays yesterday and Lauren used extra instruments to—"

"Help me, please! My dog is dying." A woman's panicked shout burst from the waiting room into the treatment room.

Val dropped the instruments on the counter and charged into the waiting room with Minnie on her heels. "What happened? Ronnie?"

Ronnie was practically vibrating as she ran her hands through her hair. "Dover's sick. I can't carry him on my own. He walked to the car, well staggered. But now he can't get up."

The terror in Ronnie's voice tore through Val. "Minnie, bring the stretcher." She and Minnie grabbed the stretcher and wheeled it to the front door of the clinic. Val followed Ronnie to the back seat of the car. They each lifted one end of Dover and carried him to the stretcher. Dover gasped for air and his chest heaved. Minnie and Val rolled him into the treatment room and Ronnie followed.

Val petted Dover. "Good boy. Poor old man." She examined Dover and noted his symptoms. She was in charge when there were no veterinarians in the clinic. Besides his increased respiratory rate and heart rate, Dover's gums appeared as white as a piece of paper. "What happened to him?"

"I'm not sure. I came home after cycling and found him lying on the kitchen floor. He could barely move, and he was panting as if he'd run around the block. Dover doesn't run anymore. He barely walks."

Ronnie shot Val a pleading look, and she registered brown eyes full of naked vulnerability.

"Did anything happen to Dover yesterday or today or earlier?" Val studied Ronnie. She wore tight cycling shorts that emphasized her muscular thighs. Her legs were bare and her calf muscles pronounced. The skintight top showed off her flat stomach and small breasts. She was an alluring blend of fitness and femininity. *Eyes on the dog, Connor.*

Ronnie's voice trembled. "Dover escaped from my backyard yesterday. I'm so stupid. I've been meaning to fix the latch on my gate all summer. I'm supposed to look after him."

The pain in Ronnie's eyes told Val she needed comforting, but Val needed to keep Ronnie on track so they could help Dover. "Could he have been hit by a car?"

"No. I'm sure. When I got home last night, he was lying on the front porch acting normal."

"Did he eat anything he shouldn't have?"

"Dover broke into my neighbor's garden shed. He knows how to push doors open with his nose and paws."

Val gritted her teeth and asked again, "Did Dover eat anything he shouldn't have?"

"My neighbor doesn't keep food in his shed, but he could have gotten into something else, I guess."

Garden sheds were notorious for being full of poisons, chemicals, and pesticides. They were as dangerous as drug cabinets in the home. People never disposed of expired products. Val pictured several poisons capable of causing Dover's symptoms. "Ask your neighbor what Dover ate and, if possible, to bring the package to PVS."

Ronnie stepped away to use her phone. She returned a minute later and stood beside Val. "My neighbor told me Dover probably ate rat poison. The sack has teeth marks in it. Will he die? You have to save him, please."

"What poison? You must tell us what poison so we can tailor our treatment to fit the poison." Val's words were harsher than she intended, but she needed details. "Tell your neighbor to bring the package to the clinic." The poison would be warfarin or a similar compound, but it was important to know exactly what kind of poison.

Val phoned Ian. "A dog just came in. He's in respiratory distress and I suspect he's consumed a large amount of rodenticide."

"I'll be at PVS in fifteen minutes," Ian said.

Val hung up and asked Janice, PVS's full-time receptionist, to move Ian's next scheduled appointment to another day. She needed his help.

Dover lay still and puffed. The speed of his breathing was rapid, as if he'd run across the park. Val put her stethoscope on and listed to several areas on his chest. She heard a crackling as if his lungs were filled with blood. She collected a blood sample and did tests to determine if his blood clotted normally. It didn't. More proof of poisoning.

When her phone rang, Ronnie darted from the room, the cleats of her cycling shoes clicking as she ran. A moment later, she jogged back into the treatment room. "I have it." Ronnie waved a package with the picture of a rat on it.

Val snatched the package and read the active ingredient. "It's bromadiolone. The poison works against an enzyme that keeps vitamin K in the body. Mammals require vitamin K for proper blood clotting and without it they bleed. In Dover's case, he's bleeding into his chest. The blood is taking up space in his chest and making it difficult for him to breathe. Also, with less blood he's not moving enough oxygen around."

"Can you save him?" Ronnie's eyes dilated with worry and she stared at Dover.

Val longed to hug Ronnie and tell her everything would be all right, but it was premature. "We need to replace the vitamin K until the poison breaks down and disappears. But we have one problem."

Ronnie's pleading expression focused on Val. "What?"

"I'm not a veterinarian and the rules say Dr. Ian must examine Dover before we treat him. He'll be here soon. He's the only veterinarian working today. Your options are to take Dover to another clinic or wait. I don't blame you if you want to go and I'll call the other clinic and tell them what we've discovered."

"I trust you. You know what you're doing and you spoke with Dr. Ian. If I leave, it'll just take longer to get Dover treated. I'll wait."

Ronnie took Dover in her arms and rocked him. Val watched Dover's breaths coming in more strained gasps. They needed Ian to return soon. Val watched Dover slowly dying and considered treating him without Ian's input. She could lose her veterinary technician license, but Dover couldn't be allowed to die.

An agonizing ten minutes later, Ian burst through the back door of PVS. "I'm here. What's the plan, Val?" He pulled out his stethoscope and examined Dover and, then he reviewed the treatment program Val designed. He checked her math on the dose of drug to administer. "I agree one hundred percent with Val's diagnosis. We'll treat him now. Do you have questions?" Ian asked.

Ronnie shook her head. "No."

Val and Minnie lifted Dover off the stretcher and placed him in a large kennel on the bottom of a stack of kennels. Val crouched beside Dover. "The vitamin K injections have to go in multiple places under his skin. I'm sure he's a good boy, but Minnie has to hold his head while I do this."

Ronnie reached for Dover. "I'll hold him. He won't bite."

Val squeezed Ronnie's forearm. "At PVS we restrain dogs for injections. If we do it each time, a scared dog will never bite us." It wasn't entirely true, and Val bore the scars on her right wrist to prove it.

Ronnie nodded and stepped back. Minnie squatted and held Dover's head. He was a well-behaved dog and too weak to struggle, but animals in pain were unpredictable.

As Ronnie predicted, Dover didn't even blink when injected. Val lifted his skin to create a pocket, slid the needle into the pocket, and injected vitamin K. She injected in several locations along his back to disperse the vitamin K and speed the rate of absorption. When they had finished, Val and Minnie stood, and Ronnie scooted back to Dover. She sat on the floor and laid his head in her lap.

"Okay, good," Ian said. "Call me if you need me." Ian picked up his bag and left to go to his next appointment.

"He's a good boy. Aren't you, Dover?" Val squatted and stroked Dover's soft fur and locked eyes with Ronnie. Ronnie's long black eyelashes mesmerized her. She had the urge to stroke her face and run her fingers through the sweat-dampened hair on Ronnie's forehead. Instead, she shook her head and chided herself for mooning over a client.

"It'll take a while for him to clear the poison out of his body," Val said. "Because the effect lasts a long time, we'll send him home with an oral vitamin K product. Squirt it onto canned food twice a day and let him eat it. Dr. Ian wrote you a prescription for vitamin K which you need to take to the pharmacy in town."

"Thanks." Misery filled Ronnie's eyes as tears slid down her cheeks.

Val carefully brushed the tears off Ronnie's cheeks. "If you want to leave, Minnie and I'll watch him."

"May I stay?" Ronnie asked. "Am I in the way?"

Val stared at Ronnie who was crouched over Dover as if protecting him from injury. Ronnie loved Dover and Val admired that. She loathed people who didn't care for their animals. "You can stay, and you're not in the way. We'll tell you if that changes. Okay?"

Ronnie nodded. "Thanks."

Val left Ronnie with Dover and continued her other tasks. An hour later, she crouched beside Ronnie and rested her hand on Ronnie's knee. Val told herself she held Ronnie's knee to help her balance, but she wanted to touch her. To comfort her. "The clinic isn't staffed through the night. It's better if you take Dover home with you later, then you can call Dr. Ian if there are problems through the night. I'm here until we close at seven p.m. Will you leave Dover with me for a few hours?"

Ronnie squinted at her as if she would protest.

Val was prepared for the argument. "Go home and get his bed ready. Keep him on the main level of your house. He's too weak to use the stairs. The pharmacy closes at five p.m. and you need to fill his prescription. Why don't you take care of all of that and then come back? That way you'll be ready when it's time to take him home."

Ronnie nodded. "Okay."

"Would you like help to take him home or do you have other help?" Val blushed. She cursed her red hair and the blushing that went with it. Her offer was legitimate. She often helped clients, but because it was Ronnie, the offer felt somehow laden with meaning.

"Thanks. That would be awesome." From her spot on the floor Ronnie stared up at Val. "Dover's a big boy. I'm strong enough to carry him, maybe."

"Please, don't try." Val shook her head. "You don't have to do it by yourself and you don't want to risk dropping him. I'll come back with you and help you get him settled."

The rest of the afternoon was uneventful. Val checked on Dover and Ronnie often. At four thirty p.m., Ronnie left PVS and returned at six. Appointments were over for the evening and Dr. Ian, Minnie, and Janice had gone home. Val would stay until seven and lock the clinic. If needed, she could call Ian and he would be back in ten minutes.

In the busy clinic during the day with other people around, Val didn't feel nervous around Ronnie. But alone with her in the quiet, shyness overcame her.

"Val, are you still available to help me? I know you have Gwen and other responsibilities."

"Gwen's staying at Poplarcreek. I'll help you get Dover home."

Ronnie shuffled her feet and looked at the floor. "Thanks. I know I'm asking a lot."

"I want to help." Val meant it. She felt an extra level of excitement at being alone with Ronnie, but she offered to help because she helped everybody. More than once she'd helped take a pet home and get them settled after a rough treatment or surgery. Thresherton was Val's hometown, and everyone knew her in the small community. People even called her when they couldn't get a pet to swallow a pill. Sometimes people phoned to tell her about their pet and ask if she thought it was sick enough to take to PVS. She never minded.

Val sighed. She could justify the offer to assist with Dover, but helping Ronnie was special. She liked being near Ronnie and talking to her, and it had been oddly comforting to have her in the clinic for so much of the day, but she was just a friend who needed help. She would never be girlfriend material.

When the clinic closed, Val helped Ronnie carry Dover to her car.

Ronnie kissed Dover on the head. "Be home soon, buddy." She turned to Val. "Thanks for your help."

"Give me a second to lock up." Val jogged inside and emerged a minute later with her coat and purse. She locked the clinic and waved at Ronnie as she jumped into her car.

At home, Ronnie backed up her driveway and then pulled her car in. She bounded up the steps of her house, opened her front door, and ran back to the car. She and Val carried Dover into the living room and lowered him into the bed Ronnie had ready for him. He curled into a ball on the soft fleece blanket and slept.

"His respiratory rate is slower than when you brought him into PVS. He's improving," Val said.

"Can I feed him?" Ronnie asked.

"Sure."

Ronnie entered her kitchen and opened a can of dog food. With Val's help Ronnie shifted Dover into a seated position to eat. After he ate and drank, he struggled to stand.

"He has to go outside," Val said.

"Hey, Dover, try to get up old man." He struggled halfway to his feet before he collapsed. "He fell. What do I do?" Ronnie crouched over Dover and petted him. "Should we take him back to the clinic?"

"Between the weakness from the bleeding and his arthritis Dover can't stand. Let me show you a trick. Do you have an old bath towel?"

"A towel? Okay." Ronnie darted upstairs and returned with a threadbare bath towel she handed to Val.

Val folded the towel lengthwise into a wide strap and slipped it under Dover's abdomen. "Try to get him up."

Ronnie coaxed Dover to stand and Val held either end of the towel strap and lifted until he was on his feet. Val gave him enough support to stand up and from her position she controlled most of his erratic movements.

Ronnie grinned. "Good trick."

"Watch what I do so you can do it yourself."

They led Dover outside through the sliding door. They lifted him and carried him down the two steps into his yard. Val held the towel, and Dover stumbled a few more feet. When he stopped, Val removed the towel, and he squatted to pee.

"Is that blood?" Ronnie asked.

"The blood in his urine will clear up when his blood is clotting normally."

When Dover finished, Val replaced the towel, and they reversed the process until Dover arrived back in his bed. His chest heaved as if he'd run a marathon.

Ronnie hovered over Dover and with great effort held back her tears. He looked like he might die, and her heart felt like it might tear in half. "He can't breathe."

"It was the exertion. He'll tire easily for a while and needs lots of sleep for the next few days."

Ronnie studied him. "It's like he's taking his last breaths. He's my best friend. I'll have nobody if I lose him."

"Hey, Ronnie." Val slid her arm around Ronnie's waist. "He's going to be okay. Look at his breathing now. It's calmer."

Ronnie took a deep, shuddering breath. "I need to calm down too. Thanks for helping me bring him home. Am I keeping you from something?" Ronnie dropped to the floor beside Dover and petted him. "I feel like—like Dover's safer if you stay and I like having you here."

Val didn't want to go home. She wanted to be there for Ronnie. "I can stay for as long as you need me." She sat beside Ronnie and held her hand while they watched Dover snuggle into his blankets.

After Dover fell asleep, Ronnie stood and edged away from him. She looked at Val with her eyes brimming with tears and then whirled and ran into her garage. Val followed and found Ronnie rummaging through a box of tools. "What're you doing? Can I help?"

"I'm fixing my gate. Dover got out because I procrastinated about fixing the latch on my gate. It's been coming open for months. I should have taken better care of him. He almost died because of me. I almost killed my best friend in this whole stupid world."

"But he'll be okay."

"I'm not fit to have him. I don't deserve him. He almost died because I'm a lazy shit." Ronnie's chest heaved and she struggled to speak.

Val had seen meltdowns over pets before and Ronnie was in a bad way. Ronnie and Dover needed help and support and Val was happy to be there for them. "You're not lazy. You do a lot. And yes, the gate got missed and that's unfortunate, but anyone can see that you love Dover." She smiled encouragingly as she ran her hand up and down Ronnie's arm. "You're his great friend. He's happy, healthy, and well looked after. You take great care of him."

Ronnie shook her head and charged out of the garage into the backyard.

"Ronnie, wait!" Val snagged a flashlight off a shelf and followed. When she caught up to Ronnie, she was viciously prying the old latch off her gate with a hammer. Val shone the light on the work, but it wasn't bright enough. "It's too late at night for this. You're going to hurt yourself with that hammer and then I'll have two patients."

Ronnie dropped the tools at her feet. "Couldn't fix it anyway. I never got around to buying a new latch."

"Do you have some rope to tie it shut?"

"I have about a dozen bike locks." Ronnie ran back to the garage and returned. She gave Val a half grin then wrapped the chain around both sides of the gate and locked it. "That'll work."

Val took Ronnie's hand. "He won't get through that unless he can hold the key between his teeth."

Ronnie lifted Val's hand and held it against her wet cheek. "Thanks, for everything."

"I'm here to help. I—I care about Dover and—well, a lot. Now come inside. Dover might worry if he can't find you." She took Ronnie's hand and led her inside.

CHAPTER TWENTY-ONE

After they entered through the patio door, Ronnie checked to make sure Dover was still sleeping. "I need a minute," she said and ran upstairs into the bathroom and closed the door. She leaned on the sink and stared at her face. She looked like a wild animal with tears, and dirt and rust from the old gate on her cheek.

Ronnie yanked off her stained T-shirt and washed her face. She brushed her hair and snagged a fresh T-shirt before heading downstairs. She found Val siting on the couch watching Dover sleep. "Freak-out over, sorry about that."

"He's sleeping really peacefully," Val said. "And you're okay. I get it. You love him."

Ronnie hovered in the doorway. What should she do next? She'd trapped Val in her house and then fallen to pieces. "What should I do?"

"Let him sleep." Val smiled. "But I wouldn't say no to dinner."

Ronnie charged into her kitchen happy to have a productive chore. "I can make a stir-fry. How does that sound?"

"Perfect and I can help."

Ronnie pulled her frying pan out of the cupboard. Luckily, she'd shopped the day before and there was actually fresh food in her refrigerator. Before going back for Dover, she'd washed a week's worth of dirty dishes but couldn't help the overflowing draining rack where she'd left them to dry. The house wasn't too messy, though it wasn't anywhere near as neat as Val's.

Ronnie sliced the vegetables while Val cubed three chicken breasts. Ronnie turned the heat on under her pan and dropped the chicken into the hot oil. "I've never seen chicken so evenly and squarely cubed. It could have been done with a ruler."

"They brown more evenly if they're the same size."

"Good point." Once Ronnie had browned the chicken, she dropped the vegetables in. She added soy sauce and seasoning to the mix, hoping Val would like one of the only dishes she really made well.

While their food sizzled away Ronnie pulled a bottle of wine and a beer from the refrigerator. She held up both for Val to see. "Drink?

"Beer, please."

Ronnie popped the tops on two beers. She poured Val's into a chilled glass and handed it to her. She took a deep pull of hers from the bottle. When dinner was ready, she plated the food. They carried their drinks and plates to her kitchen table.

"This is delicious," Val said. "I'm impressed."

"You and Gwen sort of inspired me. I've been cooking more and remembering how much I like it." Ronnie shrugged. "Haven't had pizza in a week."

Val laughed. "And I have. I forgot to defrost something for Monday's dinner, so I ordered a pizza and had it delivered. And you know what else?"

Ronnie smiled and shook her head. Val was trying to be funny to cheer her up, and it was working. "What?"

Val leaned toward Ronnie. "Gwen and I ate it directly from the box sitting in front of the television while we watched cartoons," she whispered.

Ronnie gasped comically. "No, you didn't? Somebody call child services."

"And we didn't make a salad. We were positively savage. Don't tell my mom."

Ronnie laughed and focused on the flecks of yellow that danced through Val's eyes as she laughed. She could get used to having her around. Val filled her house with light and warmth even on a day where she'd almost lost Dover. Ronnie stood and cleared their plates. "Like another beer?"

"Water, please."

Ronnie returned with two waters and sat across from Val. She was pleased she'd taken an extra fifteen minutes to clean her house when she'd come to get Dover's space ready. She didn't know why, but in her house, items accumulated on surfaces. There were two boxes in her front closet full of newspapers, clothing, and other items she'd scooped off the furniture and hidden away.

Val looked around the living room. "You all set for the night?"

Ronnie nodded. "I'm going to sleep down here so I can watch him."

"That's good planning."

Ronnie looked up and paused with her glass halfway to her mouth. Val studied her as if solving a riddle. Suddenly uncomfortable, she spoke to fill the silence. "Gwen's an awesome kid. I enjoy teaching her."

"She adores the riding lessons."

Ronnie laughed. "I mean in school."

"Oh, thanks." Val grimaced. "Her teachers say she talks too much."

"She has a lot to say but talks more when she has nothing to do. Gwen's quick with her work and sometimes I give her extra. You saw the day you visited that she doesn't mind helping the others." Ronnie grinned. "She's a great kid. I'd be happy with a whole class of Gwens."

"It would be a noisy class."

"But a fun one." Ronnie paused for a beat. "Gwen's proud of you. She tells the class about you and the animals at PVS, but she never mentions her father."

Val grimaced. "Gwen sees him once or twice a year and told me it's like she's visiting with an uncle she doesn't know. Don works in Fort McMurray in one of the oil plants. He has a girlfriend and they're getting married next year."

"Was he around when she was little?"

"Don and his parents had already moved to Edmonton when I discovered I was pregnant. I raised Gwen alone, with help from my parents. He wasn't around much."

"You must have been a kid when Gwen was born." Ronnie raised a hand in front of her face, mortified at the personal line of questions. "Sorry, wait. Don't answer that. Cancel the interrogation."

Val laughed. "I don't mind. It's impossible to have secrets in this town. Don and I were seniors in high school. We only had sex once and I got pregnant. I was two months shy of seventeen when I had Gwen. It was ridiculous, my being with Don. I had a crush on a girl the whole time Don and I dated."

"You liked girls and had a boyfriend?"

"My relationship with Don was a teenage mistake. I was always a lesbian, but just didn't see it." Val raised an eyebrow and grinned crookedly.

"Well, Gwen's a wonderful kid."

"My parents helped me so much. Not just with money, but they looked after her so I could finish school. They were mortified to tell their friends I was pregnant at sixteen. I never want to disappoint them like that again."

"Look at all you've done. How on earth could they be disappointed? You're an accomplished vet tech with your own home, and you're an awesome mother. They've got to be proud of you."

"I try to be a good mom. Do everything the way my mom did, but sometimes it's hard. She was home all day. I can't be."

"Well, my mother would trade you for me any day. What a pain I was as a teenager. Messy, sloppy, thoroughly wedded to a grunge phase and the colors I put in my hair…It was my revenge for her inflexible strictness."

"Revenge? You were just being you." Val rested her chin in her palm. "What colors?"

"Purple mostly, sometimes rainbow. I told you I skipped class a lot. You wouldn't have liked me when we were kids."

"I don't know about that." Val leaned back and tilted her head to the side to study Ronnie. "I might have been afraid of you. Afraid that your wildness would rub off on me. I was a bit judgmental when I was younger."

"It's okay. We wouldn't have crossed paths in high school. I didn't do any sports then and I bet you did."

Val blushed. "Not sports exactly…"

Ronnie pointed at Val. "Oh my God, were you a cheerleader? You were, weren't you?"

Val covered her face with her hands. "I was for two years. And Don played football. We were a teenage cliché."

Ronnie opened her mouth, but just then Dover struggled to a sitting position and vomited. Ronnie flew over and hunched over him. "Is he dying? Dover, buddy, please, get better. Can you do something, Val? Should we call Dr. Ian?"

Val squatted beside Ronnie and petted Dover. "He's all right. Just an upset stomach. He's had a rough day."

Ronnie fetched paper towels from the kitchen. When she returned, she found Val cuddling Dover half in her lap. Val held out her hand for towels and wiped the vomit off his snout and front legs. Ronnie cleaned the floor and replaced the bedding in Dover's bed with a fresh fleece and fresh blankets, then they lifted Dover into his bed.

Ronnie collected the dirty bedding and ran it to the basement. When she returned, she washed her hands and dropped to the floor beside Dover. She tucked Dover underneath a fleece blanket and stroked his head until he relaxed. "You rest now, buddy. You're all right, old man."

Val emerged from the bathroom. "How's he doing?"

Ronnie stared at Val for two seconds and then looked away. Ronnie shrugged. Her voice was tight with unshed tears and her lower lip trembled. If she opened her mouth, she would cry, and she refused to cry in front of Val again.

"Cry if you want. You love Dover and he almost died." Val sat cross-legged beside Ronnie and held out her hand. Ronnie accepted it and they rested beside Dover. They held hands and their other hands caressed Dover. When Ronnie lifted her arm to swipe it across her eyes, she didn't let go of Val's hand.

"Just a second." Val jumped to her feet. She fetched a box of tissue and returned to her seat beside Ronnie.

Ronnie wiped her eyes and blew her nose. She grimaced at Val as she did.

Val rubbed Ronnie's back. "Dover will be fine now. He's responded to the vitamin K. Look how easily he's breathing now compared to earlier."

Ronnie stared at Dover. "I can't lose him. He's my pal and I love him."

"Everybody needs a pal."

"He's always been there for me." Ronnie blew her nose. "I cried many nights into his fur after my father died."

"Dover's sleeping and should be fine tonight."

"I've no right to keep you. You've done so much for Dover and me already." Ronnie hardly ever had an issue with being alone, but tonight of all nights, she really hated the thought of it.

"It's no problem, but can I stretch out on your couch? I give you fair warning, I'm beat and if I fall asleep, you'll be stuck with me for the night." Val blushed.

Val was cute, especially when she blushed, and that was often. Her question was innocent, but Val's face betrayed her. Ronnie shook her head to clear unsafe thoughts. Val was being a helpful friend. Nothing more. "Thanks, and please, sleep if you want to."

Ronnie jumped to her feet and raced upstairs. When she returned, she handed Val a long T-shirt, a towel, and a new toothbrush she'd picked up but never bothered to unwrap. "There's a bathroom with a shower in the bedroom by the kitchen if you can find your way through the moving boxes I've got stashed in there.

While Val used the bathroom, Ronnie made up a bed for her on the couch, then she bounded upstairs. Twenty minutes later, she returned to the living room, dressed for bed. She ogled Val who was stretched out sound asleep on her couch. She'd only ever seen Val's hair up, but now it flowed down her back in one long fiery waterfall. Hell, but Val was breathtaking.

Shocked by the sudden urge to curl on the couch with Val, Ronnie moved away. She put her sleeping bag beside Dover and crawled inside. This wasn't how she'd imagined sleeping in the same house as Val, but it was something.

The next morning, Ronnie woke to a wet, sloppy tongue on her face. Dover danced beside her and with a cheer, she threw her arms around him and gave him a kiss. Dover stood by himself and his breathing was almost normal. "You all right, buddy? Thank you, thank you, thank you."

Ronnie spied Val's bedding folded in a neat pile on the couch. She discovered a note on top of the pile: *I examined Dover this morning. He looks better. His breathing is more relaxed and his gums are pink. He needs his first dose of vitamin K at breakfast. Thanks for dinner. Call me anytime if you have questions about Dover, or just call anytime. You've got my number. Val.*

Ronnie walked Dover outside. When he came back in, he followed her into the kitchen. She put a small amount of canned food in his bowl and dribbled the vitamin K on it. Dover ate the food in one bite and licked his bowl, then she gave him a proper breakfast. After breakfast, he snuggled into his bed and slept.

Ronnie made coffee and settled to read and watch Dover. At ten, somebody knocked on her front door. She opened the door and smiled widely. "Hi, Val, I'm glad you're here." She nearly hugged her.

"I dropped by to check on our patient."

Ronnie stepped aside and Val entered the living room. Val wore a pale blue sundress with strappy white sandals. "You look nice." The words emerged without permission and were way too bland for how pretty she looked.

"Thanks. I'm on my way to Poplarcreek to help Callie weed her garden and pick berries. She planted some Saskatoon berry bushes and they're doing well." Val ran her hands over the dress. "I'll help you with your gardens if you want. Flowers or something else."

"Maybe, but I'm into low maintenance and not the kind of structured flower gardens you have."

"Mine might be *too* structured. Callie has a garden of mixed perennials and wildflowers. They come up every year. She has to weed, but that's all. It looks natural and a little wild. I think it would suit you."

"I'd like that." Ronnie smiled. Val was starting to equate her with wildness. She wasn't sure if that was good or bad.

Val squatted beside Dover. She shifted a T-shirt and shorts from her bag and removed her stethoscope. She put it on and listened to his chest, then she lifted Dover's lip and pushed on his gums with the end of her index finger. "His color is better."

Ronnie longed to hug Val again. She'd adored holding Val while they danced, but that was nothing compared to the feelings she had for her now. Val was her hero. "You saved Dover's life, and I can't thank you enough."

"I had help. Now have a look at his gums."

Ronnie kneeled beside Val and squinted at Dover.

"When I push on his gums, the area under my finger goes white. See? When I lift my finger, the blood rushes into the spot. The pink is a sign he's replacing the blood he lost." Val squeezed Ronnie's forearm. "It's a good sign. His lungs sound much clearer, too. Did he get the vitamin K this morning?"

Ronnie grinned. "Yes, and he also walked outside, without help, and I only saw a little red in his pee." *Oh, very sexy. Well done, Yakimoto. Babbling about dog pee is the way to impress the ladies.*

"That's good news." Val placed her stethoscope, shorts, and T-shirt back in her bag. "Well, I should go. Thanks again for dinner last night."

Ronnie followed Val to her car, watching the sway of the dress over her quite perfect butt. The dress wasn't gardening attire, but she'd spotted that she had a shirt and shorts in her bag. "Thanks for your help."

Val smiled for a few seconds and stood with her hand on the door handle. "You're welcome. Have a good day." Val gave Ronnie a quick half-hug, then climbed into her car and drove away.

Ronnie groaned as she watched Val's car roll down the street and out of sight. She'd had the most incredible woman in her house and the chance to say something important. Too bad all she managed to say was, "Thanks for your help." She was pathetic and terrified. There was nothing scary about Val, so why was she terrified? Deep down, she knew. Val was special, and beautiful, and smart. And so many other things that made her someone Ronnie wanted to be around all the time.

Ronnie turned and trudged back into her house. Val had been wonderful and saved Dover, but it was no reason to get all sappy about her. She glanced at Dover and wished she could leave him for a short ride, but it wasn't safe. She rolled her shoulders and headed upstairs. A couple of hours on her stationary bike would push romantic thoughts of Valerie Connor right out of her brain.

CHAPTER TWENTY-TWO

After Val left, Ronnie called her friend Theresa in Winnipeg and told her all about Dover's episode of poisoning.

"I'm glad Dover's okay. I know how much he means to you," Theresa said.

"I don't know what I'd have done if something had happened to him. I thought I'd lost him, but Val saved him."

"Val sounds special."

"She's smart and caring and beautiful." She could go on and on about Val, but she stopped herself.

"Is that how you met Val? Through the vet clinic?"

"No, her daughter is a student of mine."

"So, she's older. How much? You like the older ones."

"Actually, Val's only twenty-five."

"What? Younger than you?" Theresa chuckled. "You always dated older women."

"Age doesn't matter. You should meet her. Val's so beautiful."

Theresa laughed "You said that."

"She has vibrant red hair and the bluest eyes, and when she dances, wow, can she move. So sexy."

"She sounds amazing. Did you ask her out?" Theresa asked.

Ronnie groaned. "No, I didn't."

"Dude, why not? Is it the kid?"

"Gwen's awesome and doesn't worry me. I mean, I don't know that I'm parent material, but she's not the issue."

"What'll you do?" Theresa paused. "Are you scared?"

"Terrified." Ronnie's next words burst out in an exasperated rush. "I'm not sure I can do it again. I'm not sure I'm wired properly to have a relationship. I loved Julia and it never worked with her."

"Julia? I was there, remember? You couldn't trust her. She was cruel and shitty to you. You had no chance to be happy. You sure you were in love with her?"

"Yes. Wasn't I?"

"Ron, if you don't know…"

"I'm such an emotional cripple. I'm relationship poison, thanks to my mom and to the other women I've been with. I should stay away from every woman on the planet. I should stay away from Val." Ronnie rested her forehead on the table for a beat and then sat up. "But what if I can make it just for fun and there's no romance getting in the way? Then I could see Val."

"Dude," Theresa said, drawing the word out to three syllables. "Now's your chance to be happy with an honest woman who treats you well. And even if it's not Val, you can't stay single because of one bad relationship and your cranky old mother."

That might be true, but she had her doubts. She'd never been in a good relationship. But maybe that needed to change. Ronnie squared her shoulders. "I'll invite Val out to dinner. Somewhere nice to thank her for saving Dover." She slapped her forehead. "Now I need to find my suit and get it cleaned. I wish I'd labeled my boxes when I moved."

"Stay with me, Ron. So, Val's interested in you. Why not ask her out because you enjoy being with her and not just because she saved Dover?"

"I should." Ronnie took a deep breath. "I will, but this is so stressful I'm getting a migraine."

"That's what your mother says all the time. You don't get migraines and neither does she. Just relax. Talk to me some more. So, how's the training going? You must have lots of spare time this summer to race."

"I am racing, but it's been a while since we talked. And before you ask, I'm not writing. No time."

"Too bad."

"I'm riding again and teaching beginners western riding. It's a lot of fun and I know most of the kids from school. Val's daughter is in my class."

"Hey, I bet you're good at it. You could've taught back in the day."

"When we were in high school?"

"Yes, but Irene Schmidt pushed her way in and got the job instead. I don't think she even liked the kids, but she couldn't lose at anything."

"You didn't like her, did you?"

"Sorry, I know you were crushing on her, but she led you around by the nose and I think…"

"What?"

"Well, she's the one who got you started on pot."

"Maybe, but it's my responsibility now and I don't smoke anymore. And she understands that." As least she hoped so.

"You're still in touch with her?"

"She happens to work at the stable I teach at. Irene's a horse trainer. She gets results, but she's not very popular." Ronnie told Theresa about the riding lessons and the horses at Poplarcreek.

"I don't trust her. You be careful."

"You too? Doesn't anybody like her?" In truth, Ronnie wasn't totally sure she liked her either. So why was she okay with keeping the old relationship intact?

"You trust Val and Callie and they don't like Irene. I'm just saying keep that in mind."

"Val *loathes* Irene. She never curses when she talks about anyone else."

"Val sounds cool and like a good judge of character."

"I'm going to ask her out as soon as I can find the nerve." They chatted a while longer before ending the call.

When Ronnie hung up the phone, she changed and spent two hours on her stationary bike until she felt calm enough to phone Val. "Hi, Val, I was wondering if maybe…" She cleared her throat and tried again. "Will you have dinner with me on Friday?"

"Thanks for the invitation, but I'm busy Friday night."

"Okay, maybe another time." Her enthusiasm fled. She looked at her toes expecting to see her confidence oozing out.

"How about Saturday night? Friday night's a baby shower for my cousin."

Ronnie brightened. "Should we drive into Saskatoon? We have the Thresherton Diner, but you deserve somewhere nicer."

"I like the diner, but there's a great restaurant not too far from Thresherton. Do you trust me?"

"Yes." Ronnie realized with a jolt it was true.

"I'll make the reservations. The place is dressy. Pick me up at six thirty, please."

Ronnie couldn't disguise the glee in her voice. "Saturday at six thirty, then. Thanks." She hung up and her stomach tightened. She launched into panic mode and contemplated another hour on the stationary bike. What was she thinking? She'd gone over the reasons she couldn't date Val and now she was throwing them to the wind.

At six twenty-five on Saturday night, Ronnie stopped in front of Val's house. She blinked in astonishment to see Val outside, in a knee length cobalt-blue dress, barefoot, parting the bushes in her front garden as if searching for something.

Ronnie walked up to Val. "Hi."

Val whirled and stammered. "Digit. He's gone. Digit escaped."

Ronnie's breath caught in her chest and warmth poured into her body. Val was pretty every day, but with her face flushed from exertion and hair mussed, she was beyond sexy.

Ronnie smirked. "You have a mountain gorilla?"

"What?"

"Digit the gorilla." Ronnie cringed. Starting the date with a lame joke was nerves.

Val's expression was puzzled. "Digit's the name of Lauren's big orange cat. She asked me to hang on to her cats for a while longer." Val continued to check in her front garden as she spoke. "Digit, Digit," she called. "He's taken it into his head to go exploring, and if I leave him outside, I'm afraid he'll run away or get hit by a car. Digit, Digit. Here, kitty. I opened the front door, and he bolted. He's an indoor cat and has zero street smarts."

Ronnie helped search for Digit and finally cornered him between Val's house and the neighbors' fence. He crouched on his belly, his pupils dilated with fright as he stared at her. "Val? Is this him? Big orange cat?"

Val sprinted to the side garden. "Hey there, Digit. Hey, big guy. Don't you want to go inside? It'll be dark and scary soon." Val whispered in soothing tones and edged closer until he rose and padded toward her. Val scooped him up and held him against her stomach with his feet pointed away from her dress. "Got you, Mr. Digit. Now keep your dirty paws off my dress."

Ronnie opened the front door, and they slipped inside Val's house. Val set Digit on the floor and pointed to Ronnie's shirt. "We match. Okay with you?"

"Pardon?" Ronnie glanced at her light blue shirt, and then Val's dress and grinned. Val looked young and alluring.

"I'm okay, are you?" Ronnie asked.

"Sure. We look cute. I just need a minute to finish getting ready." Val smiled and focused on Ronnie but didn't move.

A trickle of sweat slid down the middle of Ronnie's back. She wore a light cotton shirt, but she craved air. Was she supposed to kiss Val? Did Val expect a kiss? Val was delectable, and she imagined kissing her, but her shoes had fused to the floor. Now Val just stared at her, but her gaze dropped briefly to Ronnie's hand. "Oh, for you." Ronnie shoved the bouquet she'd brought for Val into her hands.

Val smiled. "Thanks for the flowers. I'll put them in water, then I ought to clean the cat hair off my dress…and my feet are dirty." Val disappeared with the flowers. Ten minutes later, Val returned looking less flushed and with her hair tidy. She looked as put together as she usually did, but Ronnie couldn't help but miss the tousled look. What did Val look like after sex?

Val directed Ronnie to drive east out of Thresherton. "The restaurant's in the next town. It serves lunch and dinner four days a week. The owners are two chefs who moved from Vancouver. They were tired of the noise and traffic and moved to Saskatchewan where the air smelled fresher. I suspect sometimes the prairie is too quiet for them, but they have a peaceful life and have Welsh terriers they treat like their children."

Ronnie squinted at Val.

Val smiled. "Yes, they're a gay couple."

When they arrived at the restaurant Ronnie parked and jogged to the passenger's side of the car. Val already had her door open, but Ronnie held out her hand and Val clasped it. She felt the instant intense heat their joining made. Ronnie pictured her hand with a scorch mark the shape of Val's fingers. She didn't let go of Val's hand as they walked into the restaurant.

"Valerie," a booming voice announced as Val entered ahead of Ronnie. "How's my favorite veterinary technician? It's been much too long since you've allowed us to feed you. Now we get to spoil you. But I see you have company." The man winked and he and Val kissed each other on the cheek. "My name is Thomas. Marcus lives in the kitchen, but he promised to appear later to say hello."

Ronnie shook Thomas's hand, once again slightly bemused at the fact that Val seemed to know just about everyone.

Thomas showed them to their table in a dim, romantic corner of the restaurant. He gave them menus and recorded their drink orders. He returned five minutes later with their drinks. "Valerie, I see you've not opened your menu."

"You pick for me, please, Thomas. Whatever you think is the best tonight." Val grinned at Ronnie.

"Me too, please." Ronnie closed her menu. "And will you please select the wine that best complements our meal? Okay with you, Val?"

Val nodded.

Thomas smiled at them. "Oh, you two are fun. You're going to have a fabulous dinner. Anything for Valerie. She saved our boy Maurice. He ate a whole chocolate cake and Valerie saved him."

Val raised her hands. "I didn't do it alone."

"We know you did all the work. Howard and Forster would've been miserable without Maurice."

Ronnie chuckled.

Thomas regarded her with an eyebrow raised.

"I like the names. I have a master's degree in English from the University of Manitoba."

Thomas smiled and nodded.

"For the record, Val saved my dog too. Dover ate rat poison on Tuesday, and she saved him." Ronnie looked at Val. "I love him and it would've crushed me to lose him."

Val blushed a deeper shade of red.

"Valerie, I approve of your Ronnie. Ronnie, you have my consent to date our wonderful girl." On that note, Thomas disappeared.

Ronnie's stomach flipped. Were they dating now? Was this a one-time thing?

Thomas returned with six small serving dishes of different foods. He arranged them on their table and let them serve themselves. The meal fell into a category beyond delicious, but Ronnie knew she wouldn't remember a day later what she ate. Val captivated her and held her full attention.

"How's Dover doing?"

"Much better, but still tired. My neighbor's staying with him this evening. Sorry I got so crazy when he was sick."

"It's okay. He was in danger." Val shook her head. "It's been a dangerous summer hasn't it? First, we saved the horses, then Kenny—"

"And now you saved Dover."

"I hope that's it. I'm ready for a couple of ordinary months."

"This doesn't feel ordinary."

Val blushed. "Well, I—not ordinary, just not dangerous."

Ronnie opened her mouth, but her words got stuck. This evening was dangerous for her. The fear she'd had under control blossomed in her chest. She drained her wine glass, but the fear lay there, growling and waiting for a chance to pounce.

Val started talking again, and her voice soothed Ronnie until she found herself relaxed. They discussed many surface topics, but when the conversation flagged, they ate in companionable silence for a few minutes.

"Dreams?" Ronnie asked and wondered why she did.

"Pardon?" Val blinked at Ronnie.

"Dreams. What are your dreams? What do you want to be when you grow up?"

Val tilted her head, looking thoughtful. "You first."

"I've wanted to write professionally since I was a kid. I just need to find a topic. My current dream has to do with placing well in the cycling circuit. I also want to travel. Maybe travel and write. I've had a job, at least part-time, since I turned thirteen and I plan to take a break at some point. You?"

"A vacation sounds nice, but I would always return to Thresherton." Val rolled the stem of her wineglass between her fingers and stared at the red liquid. "My dream is to go to veterinary school. Is that too crazy?"

Ronnie shook her head. "You'll be an awesome veterinarian."

"Thanks. Lauren says I'm a great veterinary technician and would be an amazing veterinarian. She's sure I can do it." Val shrugged. "I'm worried it would be too much work, but they have a veterinary school in Saskatoon so at least there wouldn't be too much travel."

"Outstanding. When will you do it?"

"It depends on many factors. I'll wait until Gwen's older, but not much older because I'd prefer to graduate in the next ten years. Also, Gwen's going to vet school, so if I don't hurry, I'll still be there when she starts." Val laughed. "Six years ago, Don visited Thresherton to see us and ever since has been paying me child support, although I never asked for it. I'm saving it for Gwen's university education. I've done the math and been through my budget. I'll have to sell my house if I go back to school and I'm not sure how I feel about that. What about you?"

"I'll finish my PhD if I return to school, but going back to school full-time is a hard decision. I like living here and I enjoy my sport and the time teaching gives me to train. And yes, I'd have to choose between my house and another three years in university." She hadn't done the math like Val, but she could barely afford her house now.

Dinner ended with coffee, and Val and Ronnie shared a slice of thick, rich chocolate cake. Ronnie paid the bill and Thomas winked at her. Marcus appeared for a quick visit to kiss Val and fuss over her.

Ronnie smiled. The evening with Val had been perfect. Their conversation had been genuine and real. When Val looked at her, she really looked. She made Ronnie feel special, which was dangerous. It was a feeling she could get used to.

CHAPTER TWENTY-THREE

There's nowhere to sit, but we can stroll along the edge and look at the view." Val refused to let the evening end. She suggested a place to stop and watch the sunset on the way home from the restaurant.

"The Thresherton area of Saskatchewan is a flat prairie, but deep river valleys, carved by the glaciers, wend their way through the wheat fields and grasslands." She flushed as she realized how much like a travel documentary she sounded. "Here we are. Park where we can watch the sunset."

Ronnie pulled in and parked on the edge of one of the valleys as the sun set. "This is beautiful."

Val was happy to see they were the only vehicle present. When she was in high school, they called this place the Hang. It was the favorite make out spot for students. The Hang sat between the road and the edge of the valley and there was enough room for fifteen cars.

"Nice stop," Ronnie said and reached to start the car again.

Val laid a restraining hand on Ronnie's. She didn't want to go, and her brain scrambled to find a topic of conversation. "How are the horses doing?"

"Good. Coming along and gaining weight. We're riding three of them, and Irene said two more'll be ready soon."

"Why'd you pick teaching English and not horses?" Val needed desperately to steer the conversation away from Irene. Ronnie's obvious admiration for Irene was like a knife in her belly. But Val had no claim on Ronnie. They were just friends, and other than a nice date, there had been no suggestion of anything more, yet.

Ronnie leaned back. "I suck at math and science and I like reading." She laughed. "That's a lame answer. I usually come up with a more scholarly reason."

"It's an honest answer. So, no career in horses?"

Ronnie shook her head. "I didn't want to train them and couldn't afford to buy and sell them. I just liked looking after them." She grinned. "I loved the foals."

Val grinned back. "Babies. Who doesn't like babies?"

"Would you like more children?"

"At this point no, but I might change my mind. I love Gwen and she's all I need. Gwen won't miss out on siblings because Don will have more children. What about you?"

"I've never given it much thought." Ronnie held her hands up to ward off the concept of being pregnant. "I could see myself with kids, but not pregnant."

"Bet you'd be a great parent."

Ronnie shrugged. "Don't know about that. My mother told me never to have children."

"What? Why?"

"She didn't get along with her mother. Called her the Dragon Lady. And my mother didn't get along with me. She thought it would just carry on to the next generation. She said it was a waste of time and resources."

Val was fuming and struggled to control her ire. She had no right to trash Ronnie's mom, but she couldn't let that go. It was too evil. "Who would say that to their child? I'm sorry, but that's just cruel. Maybe it was all her. She was the common denominator between you and your gran."

"Grandmother, yes."

"I notice you always call her Mother, not Mom or Mommy."

Ronnie shook her head. "Her rule. It was Father, Mother, Grandfather and Grandmother, always."

Val shook her head and slowly released her clasped hands. Her rings had left red marks on her palms.

"My mother wasn't all bad. She was honest and hard working. People respected her."

Val wanted to scream. First, they'd talked about Irene now about Ronnie's mean mother. They should move on to the devastation caused by global warming and make the evening truly romantic. "Well, she's wrong. You should have kids." Val forced a laugh. "You'd look cute pregnant, but it'd be hard to race your bicycle."

"Probably." Ronnie scanned the horizon and brought Val's hand to her lips. "I'm enjoying this."

"Me too." Val studied their joined hands and relaxed. She was content holding Ronnie's hand and Ronnie held it so naturally. She enjoyed the heat and roughness of Ronnie's hand as it surrounded hers.

Val observed Ronnie in profile with her chin up to face the sunset. She yearned to prolong the night and searched for a topic of conversation. She considered discussing books because Ronnie was a reader. Val's eyes dropped to her lap. The joke at dinner about the dogs' names was the second comment Ronnie had made Val didn't understand. In her bathroom at home Val had googled Digit and mountain gorilla on her phone. What did Maurice, Howard, and Forster have to do with English? She wasn't stupid, but her education had been specific. The world was full of books she'd never heard about, much less read.

Ronnie squeezed Val's hand, and Val shifted to gaze at her. She scooted closer and Ronnie slipped her arm around her. Val nestled into the crook of Ronnie's arm. She didn't want to discuss books and Ronnie's expression told her she wasn't thinking about books either. Desire mixed with fear filled Ronnie's eyes. Val craved a kiss, but sensing Ronnie's skittishness, she waited. Ronnie searched her face until Val fidgeted, then she leaned in for a kiss meeting Val's lips halfway.

An electric current flowed between them. Val felt a buzz and a little light-headed. Ronnie's soft lips contrasted with her hard, athletic body. She wrapped her arms around Ronnie's neck. She had the urge to lie down and drag Ronnie on top of her.

Ronnie pulled her closer and deepened the kiss. When they parted Ronnie looked a little stunned.

"Are you all right?"

"Yes. Fantastic." Another car pulled in ten feet from them. Ronnie glanced over. "I better not get caught making out in public. It might not impress the school board." She grinned and shifted to start the car.

Val bit her lip to keep from screaming that it was the summer and Ronnie should do what she liked. She'd tasted Ronnie and longed for more. She didn't care if people saw them. The other couple would be busy and not paying attention to them. "It's too dark for them to see us clearly."

"Still, better if we go."

When they arrived at her house, Val rested her hand on Ronnie's thigh. "Do you want to come in for a drink? Gwen's not here." Five minutes after Ronnie had asked her out, Val had called Callie and asked her to take Gwen. Just in case the night took a pleasant turn.

Ronnie studied her lap and slid her hands up and down the steering wheel. "Thank you for the invitation. I want to visit with you more, but then I need to go home. I'm not up for anything else tonight."

Message received. Shit. Slow was good. Val was capable of going slowly. She wasn't a hundred percent sure what they were doing anyway. She'd sworn off women to concentrate on her plan for veterinary school and a stable life, and somehow forgotten about that when Ronnie asked her out. "I want to visit with you more too."

Ronnie climbed out and jogged around the car. She opened the door and Val gave Ronnie her hand. She could get accustomed to this. She led the way into her house. "What would you like to drink?"

"I'll stick with plain lemonade, please. The wine at dinner was enough for me and I have a long bike ride tomorrow."

"Go into the living room and I'll bring the drinks." Val poured two ounces of gin in her lemonade. She needed something to dull her senses.

Val arrived with the drinks and smiled at Ronnie. Digit lay stretched across Ronnie's lap.

"Digit insists on constant attention. If he's not sleeping in the sun, he's cuddling with people. His orange fur is making a mess of your suit." Val handed Ronnie her drink. Ronnie wore a black suit with low-slung slacks and a jacket that appeared tailored for her body. Val settled beside Ronnie on the couch and curled her legs under her.

"Kenny will be all right. I spoke with his parents and he's doing well."

Startled by the sudden topic change, Val frowned as she gathered her thoughts. "Did you tell them what happened to you?"

"I did, but I don't know if he meant to run me off the road. He landed in the ditch, so clearly he's a crap driver."

"Will they pay for your wheel?"

"The wheel was old, so we split the cost. Kenny will earn the money to pay them back." Ronnie shook her head. "I hope it's a good lesson for him and not something he'll resent. He's not all bad. Few people truly are. Everyone deserves a second chance."

"Everyone?"

"Yes, even Irene. She had a rough childhood and it made her the way she is."

Val took several deep swallows. Back to Irene again. She sighed and studied Ronnie. "You're a very forgiving person."

"I am?" Ronnie stared for a second and then shrugged. "Thanks for coming with me tonight. I had a great time."

"Me too. Thanks." Val focused on Ronnie and licked lemonade off her lips. Ronnie's eyes followed the path of her tongue. Val set her glass on the coffee table and leaned in for a kiss. Ronnie enfolded her and tugged her closer.

Val's heart pounded, and she throbbed between her legs. She caved in and did what she had longed to do. She hiked up her dress and shifted to straddle Ronnie's lap. The amazing kisses grew more demanding. On her knees, Val was higher, and she dipped her head to capture Ronnie's mouth.

After she had waited forever, Val sighed when Ronnie caressed her hips, ass, and legs. When her hand stole under her dress, she moaned and grew wetter. She longed for this more than anything. It was crazy and way too soon, but she hungered to have Ronnie on top of her and inside her. As if reading her mind, Ronnie repositioned them with Val on the bottom. Breathing raggedly and eyes dilated, Ronnie looked at her.

Val arched against Ronnie and slipped her hand under the waistband of Ronnie's pants. Ronnie stiffened, then jumped off Val like she'd been burned. Shocked, Val remained frozen on her back with her legs spread wide, her dress rucked up to the top of her thighs.

Ronnie stood beside the couch staring down at her. Her body trembled and she shook her head hard. "I can't. Not now. I'm sorry."

Val rose to her feet and swayed for a second with desire. She smoothed her dress over her hips. "Sorry, I pushed you. I broke our deal." The words went unheard, though as Ronnie turned and fled from the house.

In all her life, nobody had ever run off on Val during foreplay. She glanced down the street, not sure what she expected to see. Ronnie's face had been filled with confusion and fear. What was Ronnie so afraid of?

Val closed her door and headed upstairs to change. It was probably for the best. Hadn't she just been thinking about concentrating on veterinary school? Val dropped onto the end of her bed and laced her fingers over her stomach. The fluttering in her belly told her it was Ronnie's slender athletic body, her warm brown eyes, and shiny black hair that filled her thoughts. Not her future and not veterinary school. Just another woman she couldn't have.

CHAPTER TWENTY-FOUR

"Good job everyone. You've improved a great deal." Ronnie congratulated her riding class, proud of their accomplishments. "You've improved a hundred percent, Gwen. Well done."

"Thank you, Ms. Yakimoto."

Ronnie grinned. The confident way Gwen spoke and made eye contact reminded Ronnie of Val. It had been five days since she'd taken Val to dinner, since she'd run off with no explanation. She'd wanted to call Val but was still embarrassed at the way she'd behaved.

Ronnie watched the children lead their horses to the barn. They unsaddled and groomed the horses at the end of each lesson. Val had asked for some Thursdays off, which meant she sometimes brought Becky and Gwen. She held her breath, searching for Val, and expelled it noisily when she spotted her waiting by the fence.

"Fabulous lesson, Ms. Yakimoto."

Ronnie tried casual. "I saw you watching. What do you think of Gwen?"

"She's awesome. She's wanted to learn to ride since she was four years old. You're a good teacher," Val said and sipped from her bottle of water.

Ronnie fixated on Val's tongue as it traced the edge of her upper lip to catch a stray droplet of water. The energy flowing between them was off the scale and Ronnie had no earthly idea what to do about it.

Gwen and Becky ran over and thanked Ronnie in unison before racing each other to Val's car. They switched their boots for running shoes and jumped in.

"Will you come?" Val said.

Ronnie raised an eyebrow, unable to resist.

Val blushed. "Come and have lunch with us at Poplarcreek."

"Really? I thought maybe after last weekend..." Ronnie whispered.

"I'm sorry for my behavior."

"*Your* behavior?"

"Yes, now please forgive me and come to lunch."

Ronnie shook her head in confusion. "Thanks. I'd like that." She lifted her bike into the trunk of Val's car, and they drove to Callie's farm.

"Callie and Lauren are away for a few days. I have Friday off and I'm staying at the farm with Gwen and Becky so the animals aren't left alone."

Ronnie's stomach clenched. She'd assumed Callie would be at Poplarcreek for lunch. She wasn't sure she was ready to be alone with Val. Their one date had been a lovely evening until she'd run off like a scared little rabbit. They hadn't talked properly since. This lunch was probably Val's plan to get her alone for a conversation she wasn't ready for.

"Ronnie, are you there?"

"Pardon?"

"I said your name three times. Where were you?" The glint in her eye suggested she knew the answer.

Ronnie exited the car without answering.

"Mom, play soccer with us, please," Gwen said.

"You too, please, Ms. Yakimoto," Becky said.

Ronnie scanned Val from her pretty dress to her open-toed sandals and laughed. "*Do* you play? Or do you cheer?"

Val rested her hands on her hips and frowned. "Why're you laughing, Yakimoto? I'm not completely devoid of athletic ability."

Ronnie did a goofy dance. "Show me your moves, Connor." Two children made excellent chaperones. She wouldn't be alone with Val and didn't have to worry about how to respond if Val kissed her.

"We've played before with Callie, but soccer's not her sport," Val said. "She prefers volleyball and basketball."

"Mark, Mom, and I poured a concrete pad and hung a basketball hoop," Becky said. "Mom's drilling Gwen and me this summer so we make the school basketball team again." Becky fetched her soccer ball from the patio. "Gwen's even scoring some baskets."

"Shut up." Gwen playfully punched Becky in the stomach and raced away with the ball to Callie's grassy backyard.

Val went inside to change and came out wearing a T-shirt and shorts that made Ronnie salivate.

Gwen pointed to Becky. "Me and Mom against you and Ms. Yakimoto."

"Girls, how about we drop the Ms. Yakimoto bit outside of school? Call me Ronnie, please?"

Gwen blushed and Becky shrugged, then Gwen knocked the ball out of Becky's hands and dribbled away with Becky chasing her. As the game progressed, Becky and Gwen impressed Ronnie, but Val astonished her. Val was nimble and dodged Becky with ease. Ronnie hooked the ball from Val a few times, but it was difficult. They agreed on a tied game. Nobody kept score, but she suspected team Gwen won.

Ronnie contemplated Becky and Gwen as they continued to chase each other after the game. "Gwen's an outstanding player. Fast and agile. She playing soccer anywhere?"

"No, the school doesn't have a girls' soccer team. There's no coach. But as you know she's a sub on the basketball team."

Ronnie peered down and brushed a piece of grass off her shirt. "Oh, right. I remember."

"What're you thinking?"

"Why does Gwen play basketball? She'll never be tall. Sure, she plays now, but in high school she'll be too short."

"I suggested as much to her, but she prefers to be with Becky and there's no soccer team. At least she's playing sports and participating which, at her age, is the most important thing."

"You're right." Ronnie scuffed at the dirt, her mind racing.

"What're you thinking, now?"

"What if I coached a girls' soccer team? Most of the teachers do one extracurricular activity."

Val looked surprised. "Awesome idea. The girls ought to have another team sport that involves running. They have basketball and volleyball, but a lot of girls don't play." Val grimaced. "Becky plays both. Soccer is a better fit for Gwen, and it would help with her self-confidence."

"I'll talk to the school. The indoor soccer club in the winter is popular, so there must be interest already among the students."

"It's very generous of you, but won't you be busy with cycling, riding lessons, and teaching English?"

"Maybe, but I'd like to do this. I wouldn't have played any sports at their age without soccer. I mean I had riding, but I worked at the barn to pay for that."

"So why soccer?"

"Cheapest. Only needed cleats and I saved for those."

"Were you very poor?"

"Not at all. We had everything we needed, just not everything we wanted. My parents only had a small shop. We all took turns helping in the store, but we never got paid for it." Ronnie brushed grass off her shorts. "Enough about me. How about we work with the horses now."

"A little lunch first?"

Ronnie nodded and followed Val inside. Soccer and lunch led to spending the afternoon at Poplarcreek, and Ronnie reveled in feeling so relaxed and part of something.

The four of them spent time together working with the horses, and each horse got a good grooming. Ronnie had booked Irene to help, but she didn't show up. It was just as well. She wouldn't have found Val or the girls welcoming.

Ronnie approached Becky and Gwen when Val went in the house. "You two almost finished the name plates for the horses?"

"We were done ages ago, but Becky wanted to repaint them. She's an artist. They look beautiful now," Gwen said.

"We're going to put them up so they're a surprise when Mom and Lauren come home."

"Val's busy in the house. Want some help now?" Ronnie asked.

Gwen and Becky raced off to get the signs and Ronnie helped them nail them up.

When Val had Gwen and Becky organized to make dinner, Ronnie prepared to leave. "I'm heading home now."

"Please, stay for dinner, Ms. Yakimoto. I mean, Ronnie." Gwen nudged Becky with her elbow.

Ronnie glanced at her phone. "It's five o'clock and I've been here all day. I should go."

"Why?" Val shrugged. "We'd like you to stay."

Ronnie wavered. "I'm intruding."

"No, you're not. Stay." Val glanced up at her from where she was cutting a carrot, then looked down again.

Torn between going and staying, Ronnie caved. It had been a wonderful afternoon, and with Val smiling at her, how could she leave? "Okay, thanks."

Becky and Gwen giggled and leaned until their shoulders touched.

Ronnie registered the laughter and looked at Val.

"We're not a secret, Ronnie. Gwen knows we were on a date." Val sighed and focused on Gwen and Becky, her expression warm and full of love. She held Ronnie's upper arm as she whispered in her ear. "People have seen my car parked at your house, overnight."

"But that was for Dover!"

Val shrugged. "Small town, and I don't hide anything from Gwen. Hey, I forgot. Will Dover be all right? Should you go get him?"

"I'll call my neighbor. He'll let Dover out, and he sleeps most of the time anyway. Not like Max." The border collie hovered near Becky and Gwen in the kitchen and had chased them up and down the soccer field.

After dinner, Gwen and Becky disappeared to play in Becky's room. They'd cooked dinner, so Val and Ronnie cleaned the kitchen. When the dishes were done, they carried their coffee into Callie's living room and settled on the couch.

"So, are we going to talk about what happened after our date?"

"Happened?" Ronnie squirmed. Would it be too obvious is she bolted from the house? She was backed into a corner.

"I invited you into my house. And then we—well, I—I'm sorry. What I did was wrong. I shouldn't have kissed you when you'd already made it clear you weren't interested." Val covered her face with her hands. "And I sure shouldn't have climbed into your lap."

"I was participating."

"You were…and wow, were you. As I recall, I ended up on the bottom."

Ronnie hung her head. "Then I ran away."

Val rubbed Ronnie's upper arm. "You did. You looked terrified and I feel terrible. Can you tell me what happened?"

"It's ancient history."

Val shook her head. "It's still important if it makes you react like that."

"It's hard."

"I know. We all have our triggers. Mine is infidelity. My ex, before Christine, cheated on me. I told you Margery lived in Thresherton and then moved to Vancouver without us. Afterward, I ran into a woman at the club who'd also been seeing Margery."

"You must have been furious."

"Oh, I was pissed all right even though we had already broken up. Instead of being left by a girlfriend who moved for a better job, I had an ex who moved for a better job *and* because she was tired of me. Bored with me."

"You're not boring."

"Okay, not boring, but all I do is work, raise my kid, and once a month I make it to a party."

"You're a busy single mom—"

"I have that on a T-shirt."

"Well, I like talking to you and you're interesting." Ronnie pointed to herself. "Look at me, I teach and I ride my bike. End of story. No dating. It was hell last time."

"I get it. I won't push you anymore." Val laughed, though her eyes looked sad. "Or jump you. I didn't realize you were fresh off a bad breakup."

"After Julia and I broke up I went to teachers' college and then moved here. It's been three years."

"Three years?" But you can't *stop* living because of one bad relationship. Look at me, I had Don, Margery, and Christine, and clearly I haven't given up." Val tilted her head slightly. "I'm more careful now. Less likely to jump in, although after our date you might not believe that."

"I'm sure you're right." Being more careful was good advice. Val was wonderful, but could Ronnie live with a neat freak, someone who liked ultimate organization and control? Her mother had been obsessed with tidiness and Ronnie refused to live that way. She grimaced. "Lame, I know. But I'm starting my third semester in Thresherton and just starting to feel centered."

"It's not lame, and you must take whatever time you need to feel safe." She gave Ronnie's hand a gentle squeeze. "No pressure. We can do what we want when we're ready. And if it doesn't happen, we stay good friends."

Ronnie leaned toward Val intending to give her a friendly kiss, but their mouths met in a soft kiss that sent bolts of lightning shooting through her. She recoiled in reaction to the intensity and read desire in Val's eyes. The connection was scary, but she adored Val. Around Val she felt alive for the first time in years. She slipped in for a deeper kiss, even though her brain was flashing warning signs.

Val slid her arms around Ronnie's neck and angled her shoulders to press her chest against Ronnie's. Ronnie shifted her weight and lowered her body on top of Val. An instant later, she leaped off the couch. "Not here. Not now. I can't."

"Can't what? Can't kiss me?" Val's tone was casual. "All we're doing is kissing."

"This feels more important, or at least it could be." Ronnie paced in Callie's living room. "I don't know what I'm saying. Ignore me." She snatched her jacket off the chair and shoved her arms into it. Anger surged through her veins, but she didn't know why.

Val remained seated with her hands folded in her lap.

Ronnie stuck her hands out, palms up. "Why're you so calm and serene?"

"Because there's nothing to freak out about. One kiss and we're done. You don't have to go."

"I don't want to go." Ronnie's body exploded inside with desire. She craved Val, but terror crushed her confidence. Could she trust Val? Trust herself? What if they got together and Val dumped her or she ran away? What if she couldn't get it right? What if she ended up being the one to hurt Val?

"Then don't go."

"I won't have sex on Callie's couch."

"Hold on there." Val raised her hands. "We weren't talking about sex. But what do you want? Right now?"

Ronnie hung her head. What did she want? Val was wonderful. Emotions warred inside her. How could she be both aroused and terrified at the same time?

"Stay and visit." Val winked. "I promise not to jump you again. Let me find more wine and you pick a movie."

"No, thanks."

Val shrugged and turned toward the kitchen. "Go or stay, whatever you need to do. If you stay, I'll keep my distance. And I wish you'd stay," Val said over her shoulder as she left the room.

Ronnie followed Val and crept past her to the mudroom.

"You're still going?" Val carefully placed the dishes on the counter. She whirled to face Ronnie and rested her hands on her hips. "You're right. You better run. Your innocence and honor are in danger. I won't promise not to jump you and tear off your clothes."

Ronnie smiled, not put off by the flare in Val's temper. "Thanks, Val, but I won't promise the same for you." She winked and left. She heard Val sputtering as she hopped down the stairs. The flippant remark had been funny, but it wasn't the truth. Or was it?

Ronnie leaped onto her bike and switched on the lights. She peddled off the Poplarcreek property and flew down the road toward town. She had to concentrate to stay out of the ditch and avoid the potholes in the dark, which was a perfect way to clear her head and stop thinking about Val. She peddled faster as sweat poured down her back. If she pushed hard, maybe she could wash the desire away.

Later, her heart pounding with exertion, Ronnie collapsed on her front lawn. She'd cut ten minutes off her time. Her thighs screamed and her chest heaved as she struggled for air. She would pay for this ride in the morning when sore muscles refused to cooperate.

She stood and hobbled into her house. She stowed her bike and fed Dover, then she showered and fell into bed. Ronnie yanked the covers over her head as sleep eluded her. She wanted to scream. She had run off again. After a kiss she'd instigated, she'd run away and left Val. She was a mess and Val was better off without her. If she couldn't manage to stay in the same room as Val, what use was she? She'd kissed Val twice and run off twice. But she simply couldn't risk her heart, not when she had no idea where she'd be emotionally next week, next month, next year. And she wouldn't risk Val's heart, not ever.

CHAPTER TWENTY-FIVE

When Ronnie arrived at Poplarcreek the next morning, she waffled about sending Val a text. Maybe she should just go straight to the horses and not bother her. Was Val annoyed at how the evening ended? Annoyed that Ronnie had run off? She took a deep breath and sent Val a text. She didn't want to knock and wake anybody.

Are you awake?

Yes, making breakfast.

I'm outside. Just going to check on the horses.

Come in first.

Thanks. I have Dover.

He's welcome too.

Ronnie slid her phone into the pocket of her shorts and headed up to the house. She entered the mudroom, kicked off her shoes, and stepped into the kitchen. "Early morning here."

"We're making breakfast," Gwen said. "Pancakes."

"Are you here to see the horses?" Becky asked.

"I am."

"Becky and I are going to take them trail riding next summer," Gwen said as she petted Dover.

Becky nodded. "Down to the creek and along it. I'm going to cut a trail first."

"And now that we can ride, everything's perfect," Gwen said.

Ronnie smiled at their ambition and certainty. At least someone in the house knew what they were doing.

Val approached with a carafe of coffee and motioned Ronnie to sit. "I'll get cream and sugar."

Ronnie perched on the edge of her chair and watched Val. She tried to catch her eyes to see what mood she was in.

Val leaned down. "Stop looking so hunted. You and I are fine. No drama," she whispered in Ronnie's ear.

When breakfast was done, they all trooped to the barn to feed the horses, then Becky and Gwen ran off to feed the cattle. Ronnie and Val walked back through the horse barn and watched the animals eat.

"We're getting lots of donations for the horses," Val said. "The Thresherton Farm Store donated thick horse blankets. Keeping the horses warm this winter would be a challenge without blankets, and good ones are expensive."

Ronnie nodded, unsure what else to say. Things unsaid still hung between them.

Val filled in the silence. "I'm worried about Becky and Gwen's plan to go trail riding next summer. I don't know if all the horses will still be here. They're expensive to feed even with donations. Callie and Lauren might have to give some away."

"Sorry, but girls her age dream about horses, especially when they have a barn full of them. Would you like to learn to ride?"

Val tilted her head and stared at Amy and Adam for a minute. "Never thought about it, but yes. I bet Callie and Lauren would too."

Ronnie smiled. "I think that could be arranged."

"Thanks."

"I'm hoping Irene can come around this afternoon to help with the horses."

"Awesome."

Ronnie squinted at Val. The tone of Val's voice didn't sound like she thought it was awesome. Ronnie pointed to the young filly. "Frieda looks so much better than when she arrived."

"Frieda? Oh, my goodness, they all have name plates."

"We put them up yesterday after you went in the house. Horse *F* is now Frieda."

Val leaned against the stall door. "Frieda's a sweetheart, aren't you, honey? You've had a bad time, but you're safe now."

Ronnie scanned the young horse. Frieda, the chestnut filly was white to both hocks and both knees and had a white blaze. She stretched her neck and pressed her muzzle to the bars of the stall door. Ronnie slowly raised her hand and caressed the muzzle. The filly froze for two seconds, then snorted, and scurried to the back of her stall.

"She's still afraid of us, but that will pass. She'll let Becky pet her muzzle for longer. Becky's in love with the little filly."

Val frowned. "As long as the kids are safe with her."

"They are."

Val slipped her hand through the crook of Ronnie's arm and they continued their stroll.

"The boys are Ernie and Dave. Ernie is black with the star and Dave is the bay," Ronnie said. "Amy and Adam are the mare and foal. They've both healed now. You and Lauren did wonders."

"They'll be beautiful when their hair grows back."

"This is Courtney, and oh yeah, Becky and Gwen named the pregnant mare Bella."

"Good names. I'm glad they kept all the letters associated with the medical records."

"The boys are gentle, and the other horses are well-behaved. Frieda is untrained, but not mean. Becky's keeping her own records of Frieda's recovery. She's disappointed we can't continue to weigh Frieda. I do my best to guess Frieda's weight every time Becky and Gwen ask."

"Is that daily?"

"Oh, if only they asked that infrequently." Ronnie smiled.

"I love their enthusiasm. Gwen is here all the time and she and Becky are watching no television, which makes me happy. So, what's the plan for today?"

"Dave and Ernie are ready to ride. Irene and I've had them out a few times. The girls would be fine."

"I trust you, and Callie does, too." Val stopped and rubbed her thighs. "I'm glad you thought of riding. We were about to be challenged to another soccer game, kids versus adults."

When Gwen and Becky returned, Val got them suited up and they mounted Ernie and Dave. Ronnie kept them to a walk as they circled the paddock. It was helpful watching how the geldings interacted with the children. They were perfectly calm. Even Max's sudden appearance at their feet only startled them a little.

After a good grooming, Dave and Ernie were left to munch their oats. Val threw together a quick lunch and then Gwen and Becky took the dogs outside to play.

"Will you have dinner? With me, I mean?" Ronnie asked. "I'll cook."

Val stood and busied herself clearing the lunch dishes off the table. "I don't know. Didn't we try this twice?"

Ronnie hung her head. "I'd like to make it up to you, but maybe it's a bad idea."

"I don't want to rush you. What if we just stuck to being friends?"

Ronnie approached Val and stooped to look in Val's eyes. "Is that what you want?"

"I don't want you to run off again."

"Can't. It'll be my house."

Val shrugged and managed a half smile. "Would this be a date?"

"Yes, I think—of course—if you…"

Val took Ronnie's hands. "You're running again. I can hear it in your words."

"A date. A date then. Please." Ronnie locked eyes with Val and gave her warmest, most confident smile. Her stomach was tying in knots, but she wanted this. Or did she? She told her chicken side to shut up and quit spoiling things.

Val studied her. "You still seem a little uncertain. Nervous? Scared?"

Ronnie dropped Val's hands and stepped back. "I'm no good at this."

"Shit," Val said as she grabbed the front of Ronnie's shirt and pulled her close. "Don't make me regret this."

Ronnie's knees wobbled as Val kissed her. She slowly slid her arms around Val and then pulled her close and deepened the kiss.

Val backed up, panting. "Okay, when?"

A blast of terror welled up in Ronnie, but she tamped it down. She was ready for this date. Forget all the crap in her life. She could do this. She could have a satisfying adult relationship, especially with Val. There was nothing to be afraid of. "How about Wednesday night?"

"Perfect."

"Thanks." Ronnie searched for a distraction and pointed to the counter. "Can I help with the dishes? I'm washing my dishes more often. It's nice not wading through stacks of dirty dishes every time I want something." She'd washed dishes last night and liked the flash of accomplishment so much she went around and tidied the clothes strewn here and there too.

Val waved her hand at the counter. "These can wait. Come outside."

Hand in hand, they strolled around Callie's backyard and looked at her gardens.

Val pointed. "Here's Callie's wildflower garden. What do you think?"

"I'd like that at my house. Don't suppose we can dig it up and transplant it?"

Val laughed. "No, but I'd be happy to help you design your own."

"Thanks." Ronnie smiled and fished out her phone when it buzzed. "It's Irene."

Val dropped her hand and moved away.

Ronnie read Irene's text.

Want some help today?

Please. What time?

Two thirty and you can buy me dinner.

Meet me at Poplarcreek.

Ronnie scowled as she stuffed the phone in her pocket. She needed Irene's help, but she didn't want her around. Complicated stuff was irritating.

"Everything all set?" Val asked.

"She'll be here about two thirty or so."

"I'm going to take the girls and head into town for a bit. Water my gardens, pick up some groceries and clean clothes…" Val shrugged.

Ronnie wasn't fooled. Val was avoiding Irene and who could blame her? "Would you like a text when Irene leaves?"

"Yes, please."

"If I could do it without her help I would, but Frieda—"

"Is a little green and there's nobody else. I get it. And I don't want you to get hurt trying to do it all." Val kissed Ronnie on the cheek then turned and called for the girls who were playing fetch with Max. Dover was standing in the shade barking in encouragement.

When Val left Ronnie headed into the horse barn to clean stalls. Just after three p.m. Irene strode into the barn. "Hey, Ronnie."

"Hey, Irene."

"Come here Dover, you remember me," Irene said. Dover backed away and glanced at Ronnie.

"Go play," Ronnie said, and Dover hurried out of the barn.

"What's his problem? Bad memory? He getting senile?"

Ronnie swallowed her retort with difficulty and felt disloyal to Dover for not telling Irene where to go. Dover had an excellent memory. What had happened to make him dislike Irene?

Max hopped over and looked up at Irene. "You go too," she said and waved her arms in a shooing motion. "Go, dog. You scare the horses."

"That's Max. This is his home and he's good with the horses."

Max cringed when Irene shooed him again and then he took the hint and followed Dover.

"Why would Callie keep a dog with only three legs? What a waste of space."

"They love Max."

"Love him?" Irene looked perplexed by the comment and then shrugged. "Whatever."

Ronnie looked out the window and watched the dogs. Dover was plodding toward the shade of Callie's backyard and Max was running loops around him. What was it about Irene that made her capable of offending everyone? She should try harder to find somebody else with experience to help her. Maybe Claire or Mandy Trevor from Starview? Somebody who wouldn't send the whole farm into hiding just by showing up.

CHAPTER TWENTY-SIX

After work on Wednesday, Val had rushed home and jumped in the shower. That had been an hour ago, and now her bedroom and bathroom were a mess, but she was ready. She slipped on her shoes, then collected her purse and the food basket. She was nervous, and that surprised her. She was never nervous around women, but perhaps that had been the problem. Nervousness signaled strong feelings, and she'd never had feelings this powerful for another woman.

Val paused with her hand on the front doorknob. She put down her purse and basket and sat on the couch. She clutched a throw cushion against her chest and rocked. What was she doing? Was she really going to try to date Ronnie? It was tiring being pushed away. What if Ronnie were fine for a month and then ran off? Gwen was already more attached to her than just as a schoolteacher. Could she risk letting Ronnie into her family?

Val stood and paced. Ronnie didn't think ahead. Didn't plan sensibly. Took on too much and wasn't great about follow through. But maybe it was because Ronnie was always trying to help people and animals?

Val shook her head. She liked her organized life. It was set out in small, manageable chunks that fit together. She bought something when she could afford it. When there was a mess, she cleaned it up. Ronnie was clearly struggling with some emotional issues, and did she really want to become entangled with a grown woman who still couldn't manage her finances? A woman whose approach to housework was to take off on her bicycle? Val took a deep breath. She was being judgy and overthinking, and that was unfair.

Val squared her shoulders. She'd accepted the offer of dinner and would go. Maybe they could have a nice evening, a nice meal, and a nice conversation. A shiver of pleasure shot up her spine as she pictured kissing Ronnie and maybe more. "No, Valerie, don't go there." She would just see how it went. If she could manage to keep from jumping on Ronnie, maybe she wouldn't be so frightened. Damn but Ronnie was cute, and fun, and sweet. Was she worth the risk? Maybe yes, maybe no, but she was committed to this evening now. Val loaded everything in her car and drove to Ronnie's house.

Val knocked and Ronnie opened the door. "Hello, Val."

Val stepped inside. "Thanks for the invitation to dinner, but it should be my turn to cook. You're spoiling me. You made me stir-fry the other day."

"It was only right to feed you when I trapped you here to look after Dover."

"I wasn't trapped. I volunteered."

"Well, anyway, I like cooking for you."

"Well, that's something we share. We both like cooking."

"Okay." Ronnie looked puzzled.

Val bent her head and pretended to look for something in her purse, unable to stop overthinking their situation. They had very little in common. Ronnie talked a lot about the horses and Val couldn't keep up. Even the children could contribute to those conversations. Val didn't even know how to ride. Horses weren't something she could share with Ronnie. Nor was cycling or old university days, or even books.

"And we both like hiking, and animals, and I'm going to teach you to ride and you're going to teach me to garden," Ronnie said. "What's up, Val?"

Val smiled, determined to banish second thoughts from their evening. She handed her basket to Ronnie who set it on the couch and turned back to face her. There was an awkward pause until she kissed Ronnie on the cheek. Ronnie's fear was back and as clear in her eyes as a cloud in a blue sky. Val sighed. Maybe she'd provoked it, but she was hoping they'd passed this hurdle.

Val followed Ronnie into the kitchen. She took in the tidy kitchen and empty dish drainer. "Did you get out cycling today?"

"I don't do the long distances every time. Today I did a short trip and increased my speed. I switch it up sometimes. I wish there were a few hills for me to practice on."

"You need to go north for hills." Val inhaled. "Wow, something smells wonderful."

"Thanks. It has another thirty minutes. Drink?"

"Please, whatever you're having."

Ronnie poured wine into a glass and pointed to the basket. "What's in your basket, Red?"

"Red?" Val accepted the wineglass from Ronnie's trembling hand with thanks and forced a smile. "Nobody has called me Red since grade seven."

Ronnie laughed. "Sorry. Lame Little Red Riding Hood joke. You have red hair and a basket…" She tugged at the collar of her shirt. "Warning. Lame jokes mean I'm nervous."

"No need to be. And the basket is full of cookies. I know you like the oatmeal ones I make, but there are a few others in there. I didn't know your cookie preference, so I brought a basket with a variety of types." Val blushed and sipped her wine. "Gwen and I needed cookies for a bake sale at church, so we baked cookies for hours on Monday night."

"Sounds as if you prepared a ton."

"We did, and it was for a special event which makes sense, but I'm starting to wonder if it's worth the time. Maybe Gwen and I should find activities to share outside of the kitchen."

"Like ironing?"

"Funny woman. I was thinking more of furniture polishing."

Ronnie laughed. "You wouldn't?"

Val shook her head. She could still be a good mom even if she didn't bake as often. It was about sharing activities with Gwen and staying connected as her daughter sprinted toward her teenage years. "The SPCA in the city is always looking for people to foster litters of orphaned kittens or puppies who need to be bottle fed."

"You two would be so good at that. And the babies would have neatly ironed bedding."

How nervous was Ronnie? It was like they were a stand-up comedy duo about to be booed off the stage. "I bet you don't even own an iron."

"Nope. I don't like golf."

"Stop it." Val playfully punched Ronnie. "So, what *is* your cookie preference?"

Val had the urge to crawl under the table and disappear. She'd asked about a cookie preference? What she was burning to learn about Ronnie wasn't her favorite flavor of cookie. She wanted to know how Ronnie liked her nipples pleasured. Val's mind ran amuck, and she gulped her wine, which led to a fit of coughing. *Cool, Connor. Well done.* She wanted to scream. Now she was nervous and aroused. Neither emotion was permitted tonight.

Val excused herself and went upstairs to use the washroom and dab cool water on the back of her neck to cool down. After the washroom, she peeked into Ronnie's room through the door she'd left open. One wall was lined with boxes, the hamper was overflowing with clothes, and a pair of gym shorts were draped over a stationary bike. It was not the bedroom of a woman expecting company for the night. Too bad.

She returned to the kitchen and almost chugged the next glass of wine Ronnie handed her. Val grimaced. When her glass was low, Ronnie had refilled it as if watching a woman throw an entire glass of wine down her throat was normal. "Okay if I grab a glass of water?" She needed to stay sober and save a glass of wine to have with dinner.

Ronnie checked on the contents of the oven. "Needs more time. Let's go outside for a bit." Val picked up her water and followed Ronnie into her backyard. When Dover saw Val, he hobbled over to greet her.

"Dover's idea of a greeting is standing beside a person and letting them fawn over him," Ronnie said. "When he was a puppy, I had a tough time teaching him not to jump up on people."

Val petted Dover. "He's a good boy. Aren't you, Dover?" Val looked around. "Your yard looks very tidy."

"I spent hours cutting it yesterday. You know if you leave it to get too long it takes twice as much time to cut? I also bought a weed-wacker and trimmed the edges. And look at this?" Ronnie pointed down. "Is that basil?"

"And oregano and parsley."

"I found a secret herb garden. I'm going to tidy it up and see what else I have. I decided I want the wildflower and perennial garden in the backyard where I can see it. Maybe over there in the corner."

Val glanced at the garden gate, noted the bike lock and quickly looked away, but not fast enough.

"Busted."

"I'm not judging you for not fixing your latch."

"No, it's busted. Come see." Ronnie pointed to the hinges. "They're pure rust. And that night I attacked the latch I must have broken a hinge. It's a two-person job now, so I'm going to ask the shop teacher at the school to help me. His son's in my riding class with Gwen."

"Brad's a good guy. He'll help."

"Do you know everyone in Thresherton?"

Val shrugged. "I didn't know Kenny."

"One out of six thousand." Ronnie laughed.

After their short stroll, they returned inside for dinner. Famished, Val filled her plate. When her plate was clean, she sat back and held her full stomach and discovered Ronnie staring at her.

"That was delicious. Sorry, busy day at PVS. I didn't have time for lunch. I should have warned you I planned to stuff myself." When she was hungry, she ate, and she didn't apologize.

Ronnie grinned, looking unusually shy. "Glad you enjoyed it."

After dinner Val helped clear the table. She offered to wash dishes, but Ronnie just stacked them, saying she'd do them later. Ronnie shoved the half-full serving dishes of food into her refrigerator. Val was about to say the food would keep better in sealed containers and take up less space, but she saw the vast space in Ronnie's refrigerator. There was room for six dishes in the empty appliance. Did she only shop when she was having people over?

"Let's take our drinks to the living room. Or are you ready for dessert?" Ronnie asked.

Val headed into the living room. "Let's wait on dessert." She scanned the bookshelves waiting for Ronnie to sit first so she could sit near her.

Temped to crawl into Ronnie's lap, Val stuck to her end of the couch. If she hung on to the arm of the couch, it would be better. Too bad couches didn't have seat belts. She'd been the aggressive one so far and needed to keep her distance or she'd risk spoiling the evening and sending Ronnie running. This would be a friendly hands-off dinner. Val took a deep gulp of the excellent coffee and burned her tongue.

After ten minutes of nonsensical chatting, Ronnie slid close and touched one of the curls Val had artfully left loose from her updo. "This is cute."

Val cracked. All the thoughts about keeping her distance disappeared as she lifted Ronnie's hand, and held it to her lips. Her hand trembled. "Are you okay?" Ronnie nodded but didn't say anything. Val held their joined hands in her lap and leaned in for a kiss.

Ronnie jumped to her feet and practically threw herself across the living room. "I don't know. I don't know. Shit, shit, shit."

"You don't know what?" Val stood. When she got close, Ronnie stepped back. "You don't want to do this, do you?"

"I'm struggling."

"And I'm sorry. I thought you wanted to kiss me." Val gave an embarrassed little chuckle. "Do you want me to leave?"

"Please, don't go."

"Do you want to talk about why you're struggling?"

"I suck at relationships."

Val smiled encouragingly. Hadn't she heard this before and convinced Ronnie that she should try again after Julia? "Tell me more."

Ronnie gave no answer, just bit her lip and looked at Val with wild eyes.

"Sit down, Ronnie." Val waited for Ronnie to sit and then she took the armchair. "We all struggle."

"It's about pot." Ronnie studied her feet. "Marijuana."

"Do you want pot?"

"No!" Ronnie held her hands up for protection as if Val were stabbing at her with a hot poker.

"A little isn't a big deal at a party, but I don't have any. I don't keep any anywhere near Gwen. It doesn't do much for me. I can take it or leave it."

"I'm glad you can, but any amount, party or otherwise, is a big deal to me. I smoked a mountain of pot in Winnipeg when I lived with Julia. It was how I coped with her craziness, and pretty much any emotion I had to deal with. I'd smoked pot since high school, but with her it was every day. When I became a teacher, I quit. But it was hard."

Val clasped her hands, her heart pounding a little at the admission. "Did you do anything else? I'm not into drugs."

"Just pot. Nothing else."

Val perched on the edge of the chair and leaned toward Ronnie. "What does that have to do with why you're struggling? Is it that you're struggling with an…"

"Addiction. It's okay to say it." Ronnie grinned crookedly. "Bet *you're* scared now. You should leave if you want to."

"Only if you want me to go. You're my friend and I don't want to leave you like this. If you don't want to talk anymore, we'll just eat cookies."

Ronnie kneeled at Val's feet, clasped her hands, and kissed them. "I've never been with a woman when I wasn't high. It's scary, or maybe it's always been scary and pot just dulled the fear for me. As you've seen, without it I freak out."

Val extracted her hand and caressed Ronnie's head. She sifted soft black hair though her fingers and sighed. "So, take the fear away."

"How?"

"What would you do if Frieda was scared of Max and was rearing up and kicking out every time she saw him? Would you drag her closer to Max? Would you let him bark at her and chase her?"

"Not at all. I'd take her away and when she was calm, I'd slowly expose her to Max. A little bit at a time until she wasn't scared anymore. In fact, that's what I did."

"I know it. So, we go slow or we stay friends. Having you terrified accomplishes nothing." Val caressed Ronnie's cheek and brushed tears from her eyes. "I need to be honest though. I'm attracted to you and I can keep it together, but not if you kiss me or caress my ear again."

Ronnie sat back on her heels. "Don't know what came over me except that you have beautiful ears."

"Stand down, Yakimoto. I'm a woman on the edge." Val was laughing but every nerve was begging for attention.

Ronnie returned to the couch and watched Val.

"What would you like to do right now?" Val asked.

"Is rewind the clock about twenty minutes an option?"

Val shook her head.

"How about twenty years?"

"Is this you being nervous again? The lame jokes?"

"Were they lame?"

Val stood up. "Stay there for a minute." She went to the patio door and called Dover in. He headed over to Ronnie and laid his head on her knee.

Ronnie petted him and kissed him on the nose. "You having a nice time in your yard? Now that you can move around? I swear the long grass was tripping him up."

Val smiled at Ronnie as she did everything but pull Dover into her lap. "Thought so."

"Thought so what?" Ronnie asked.

"Dover calms you down. Pets have that effect on people." Val shrugged. "I forget why."

"I appreciate your patience while I work out my crap. I didn't even realize I had so much baggage. Sorry." Ronnie stood and reached for Val's hand. "Let's eat some cookies." Dover gave a woof. "You too, buddy, but the ones Val brought are for me."

Val followed Ronnie to the kitchen. They got out plates and soft vanilla ice cream that they squished between cookies. Val ate so many cookies she thought she was going to be sick. But Ronnie was having fun. Val nibbled as she listened to Ronnie's stories. The serious part of the evening was over, and it was clear Ronnie was done talking about her struggles with relationships. But Ronnie now felt free to tell stories about her teenage years. Too many of them started with "We were so wasted that," but Val refused to let that worry her. She was just glad that Ronnie had survived and was clearly in a different place now.

"I love your stories, but I have work tomorrow." Val stood. "I'm going to head out now." Ronnie walked her to the front door. "Will you be okay?" Val asked. "You can call me if you want to talk. That's what friends are for."

"Are you my friend?"

"Since that time you called begging for help with sports day. No, before that. When you took the time to pick some books out that are now Gwen's favorites."

Ronnie kissed Val on the cheek. "Thanks for coming."

"Thank you for dinner. Talk soon." Val didn't remember the drive home, but suddenly she was on her couch, rocking with a throw pillow in a crushing embrace. In the beginning, she'd thought their problems were that Ronnie might move away or that Ronnie was immature and lived like a frat boy. But Ronnie was cleaning up her house and yard. She was showing no signs of moving and was crawling into the adult world.

Having a child when she was a teenager had forced Val to grow up quickly. Ronnie had stayed a kid longer. Val kept up with her chores to set an example for Gwen and because she was responsible for her daughter, someone she wanted to grow up to be just as responsible and aware as Val was.

An addiction to marijuana had run Ronnie's life, but she was in charge now. Clean and finding a new way to live. Sure, she was in over her head, but Ronnie was reaching out with both hands for life and laughing as she did it.

Did she dare become involved with a person who admitted to a drug dependency? Even if it was in the past? Didn't those people relapse and go back to drugs? Her aunt had coped with her uncle's alcoholism and too-frequent relapses. That wouldn't happen to Ronnie. She was too strong to fail.

Val tossed the pillow away and jumped to her feet. She shook her head as she paced. Could she trust Ronnie around Gwen and Becky? "Absolutely."

Ronnie said she didn't use it anymore, and she'd looked so beautiful and vulnerable as she'd asked for patience. But this was about more than attraction now. She needed to get her feet back on the ground and her head out of the lust-clouds. She would be hands-off with Ronnie for now. And Ronnie would have her support for whatever she needed, because that's what friends did.

Chapter Twenty-seven

Val stopped to investigate the crowd gathered beside a truck parked and spilling into the road in a residential section of Thresherton.

Gwen's riding lesson was yesterday, and as usual, she was spending Friday at Poplarcreek with Becky. She really needed to get Gwen out with her parents for the day, before they started to feel neglected.

As she walked toward the truck, she heard Ronnie's voice. It had been two days since their last attempt at a date and Ronnie's reveal about her previous pot use. Since then, they'd only shared a few friendly texts and it had been Callie's turn to take the girls to their riding lesson yesterday.

Val rolled her shoulders. Life was complicated. Part of her was still worried about Ronnie's past and how that might interfere with her life. If Ronnie slipped back to pot would it hurt her and Gwen, or just cause huge embarrassment? An embarrassment that Ronnie could run away from, but which Gwen, Val, and her parents would have to weather. She was full of compassion for Ronnie and ready to be her friend if that was all they could have. But really, she wanted more.

Val listened to the voices raised in argument and couldn't help smiling at the prospect of seeing Ronnie even if she appeared to be involved in a fight.

"*Stop it!* Don't do that again," Ronnie shouted. "You have no right to kick that dog. If you hate it so much, find it a new home."

Val recognized her dentist's teenage son Dillon standing beside his pickup truck holding the end of a dog's leash, and towering over the crowd.

"Screw off, bitch." Dillon directed his comment at Ronnie and shoved her. Ronnie stumbled but didn't fall.

Val gasped and pushed through the crowd. She could see Ronnie clearly and grinned at the familiar cycling shirt but with two elbow patches instead of holes. The patches didn't match the shirt, but they matched each other. That was something.

Dillon opened the door of the truck, but the dog didn't move. "Get in the truck, stupid dog." He screamed at the animal and yanked on its leash. The terrified dog emitted a strangled whining cry.

"You're hurting him. *Stop!*" Ronnie gripped Dillon's arm and tugged, but she couldn't budge it. He was far larger than she was. All she did was piss him off and he took another swipe at her. This time he connected with her cheek and she staggered backward and fell on the road.

The crowd, as useful as a flock of birds in a carwash, parted for Val as she strode up to Dillon. "Hi, Dillon." Val struggled to appear casual, but he was abusing a dog *and* he'd struck Ronnie. She itched to punch him in the stomach, or lower. But the situation called for calm.

Dillon turned. "Hi, Ms. Connor." He sounded as exasperated as only a teenager could.

"How's Barney doing?"

"He's being a pain as always. He won't get in the truck." Dillon sighed as though it was the most difficult thing in the world. "And that lady is sticking her nose in."

With Herculean effort, she kept her voice calm and reasonable. Words she didn't want to say in front of children were her words of choice, but she restrained herself. "Barney's old. I don't think he can jump that high anymore."

"Well, he has to. I'm not picking him up. He stinks."

"Sorry about your grandmother. She was a kind woman."

Ronnie stood and edged closer, her expression furious and her hands balled into fists.

Val subtly signaled Ronnie to stay back. "Barney was your grandmother's, wasn't he?"

"Yes, and Mom told me we have to look after him now. He's old and not cool to walk. He walks stupid slow and I have to drag him."

Ronnie sucked in her breath, prepared to attack at any minute.

"Do you mind if I take Barney for the day? He needs a bath, and I'd like to do it in memory of your grandmother." Val contemplated the old dog at their feet. Dillon's abuse had terrified Barney into peeing where he stood, and now he lay in a puddle of urine, looking desperately miserable.

Dillon looked surprised, and then relieved. "That would be real nice. Thanks, Ms. Connor." Val accepted the leash and Dillon leaped into his truck. He drove slowly past the crowd of people and gave Ronnie the finger as she glowered at him.

Ronnie squatted in front of Barney. "Hey, Barney. Hey, buddy. It's okay. You're safe now. Val will protect you," she said gently, then popped to her feet. "Hello, Valerie," she said perkily.

With one eyebrow raised, Val rested her hand on her hip. "Have you taken up public brawling?"

"I rode by on my bike and that thug wannabe was beating Barney. I tried to get him to stop."

Val took a deep breath and spoke with a calm she didn't feel. "Looked as if he beat you too."

Ronnie examined her elbow. "He knocked me down and I tore off my new elbow patch. It was kind of fun having them and not looking so much like a hobo." Ronnie shrugged. "Maybe it's time to give up on this shirt."

"How's your face?" Seeing Ronnie take a hit like that had made her stomach lurch, and looking at the red mark made her queasy.

Ronnie gingerly touched her cheek. "I'm fine. I egged him into hitting me to distract him from hitting Barney." She laughed. "I'm kidding. You did a good job of getting Barney away from him. Thanks." She shook her head, her eyes hard. "The bastard was practically choking him with that leash."

Val's hand dropped from her hip as she regarded Ronnie with interest. "Do you want Barney?"

Ronnie peered down at him. "I never considered it, but yes, I'll take him. Dover might enjoy the company. Dover gets along with everybody."

"We're two blocks from your house. Put your bike in my car and drive it to your house. I'll walk Barney, and I'll call the family to let them know we'll take him. They won't put up a fight, I'm sure."

Ronnie reached for Barney's leash. "I can walk him home."

"No, thanks. While we walk, I'll examine him and ensure Dillon didn't do any damage."

It took a long time to get to Ronnie's house. As an old dog, Barney's fastest speed was amble. But the walk also gave her time to steady her nerves as she prepared to be back in Ronnie's orbit again. As expected, Barney's family was happy to give him up to a better home. "He's sore, but otherwise healthy, except for being wet with urine and needing a good clean," Val said when she arrived in Ronnie's backyard.

"I have everything ready." Ronnie had a dog bath set up in her backyard. "I designed it for Dover so he could walk up two stairs and then down two stairs into the tub. I've even got hot water out here."

"What about your cheek? It needs ice." Val reached out to touch Ronnie's face but let her hand drop. "Wait. Don't tell me. You've done worse falling off your bicycle."

Ronnie grinned. "Yup."

Val shook her head. "Let me help you with Barney."

Ronnie scanned Val up and down. "Beautiful." Ronnie cleared her throat. "You're wearing a nice dress. Too nice for dog bathing."

Val shivered as Ronnie's eyes caressed her body. She liked the way Ronnie looked at her and regretted that the desire she'd seen would go no further.

"Want to borrow a tracksuit?"

"I grabbed my gym bag from my car." Val started toward the house and stopped with her back to Ronnie. "Is it okay if I change my clothes?" Val froze at the steps, uncertain if she was welcome in Ronnie's house.

"Yes, and help yourself to whatever you need. Please, leave Dover in the house though. I want to wash Barney before they meet."

Five minutes later, Val returned, and they bathed Barney together, each rubbing soap into their side of him. "Your cheek needs ice. Do it now. The sooner the better." Val kept talking to take her mind off how close she was to Ronnie. If she leaned forward, she could touch her, and she ached to touch her. Val's body sizzled with electricity whenever she was within two feet of her. She took a deep breath. Acting on her attraction wasn't possible. Ronnie needed time, not her lust.

"Are you going to report Dillon to the police? He assaulted you." Ronnie shrugged. "Perhaps."

Val nodded. "You don't want to get Dillon in trouble with the police in case it makes him angry and he becomes a bigger criminal?"

"I'll talk to his parents first."

They rinsed Barney and Ronnie helped him out of the tub, then they kneeled across from each other drying Barney with old towels. "That's what you did with Kenny."

"Everyone deserves a second chance, don't they?"

"How do you know Kenny and Dillon haven't attacked people before?" Val asked. "How do you know they won't do it again if there aren't any consequences?"

"I'll get their parents to tell me, then decide what to do. And if they do it again, then there can be consequences."

"What if you'd been caught with marijuana when you were a kid?"

"I probably wouldn't be allowed to teach school. But that's all behind me, I promise."

They finished in silence, and Val couldn't think of a thing to say that wouldn't sound forced. Relationships whether between friends or lovers were always so complicated.

When Barney was dry, they let Dover into the backyard. Dover and Barney sniffed each other until Dover wandered off to roam his backyard with Barney plodding after him. "Old Barney is getting the tour." Ronnie focused on Val.

They sat on the steps of Ronnie's patio. "Giving Barney a home is generous of you." She'd thought that Ronnie was generous so many times since meeting her, and it kept proving true.

"Thanks for your help today."

"Sure. No problem." Val picked at the seam on the leg of her yoga pants as the silence of unsaid words swirled between them.

"Val, I—"

"Ronnie, I—"

They both spoke at once, interrupting each other. At Ronnie's nod, Val continued. "I'm sorry about the other night. I should've been more understanding."

Ronnie rocked with her arms wrapped around her knees. "But you were great. I'm a pothead and you needed to know."

"Are you smoking again?"

"I had the urge after you left, but I have no plans to go there again. I went for a long ride and painted half my house instead." Ronnie shook her head. "Pot has smoothed my way through life and relationships since high school. I won't let it anymore, but I have to learn how to do things without it, too."

"Thank you for telling me. It helps me understand. And for the record I trust you."

"You trust me?"

Val smiled. "Yes."

"Thanks, Val. Hello, boys." Ronnie spoke to the two Labradors now sitting at her feet. She petted them and smiled over her shoulder at Val. "Look, bookends."

Val scrutinized Ronnie's face and registered the lame joke.

"Is everything okay?" Ronnie asked.

Val shook her head.

"Say whatever you want."

Val raised her eyebrow.

"Do it." Ronnie clasped Val's right hand in both of hers.

"I'm a bit conflicted. But I can't seem to focus on anything but you." Val glanced at her watch. "Sorry, but I need to get going. I'm not running away."

"I understand."

Val rose and entered the house to change into her dress. When she returned to the living room, Ronnie waited for her. She looked at Ronnie with longing.

"Would you like to have dinner with Gwen and me tonight?" Val asked. Gwen was the most important person in her life, and she loved how well Ronnie and Gwen got along.

"I would. Thanks. I like being with you and want to be friends."

Friends. At least she knew where they stood now. "I'd like that."

Ronnie stepped toward Val and embraced her. "Thanks for the help with Barney."

After a minute Val spoke into Ronnie's shoulder, not wanting to move away. "Don't thank me yet. I helped you get an old incontinent dog with permanent diarrhea."

Ronnie leaped away from Val and stared outside at Barney in horror.

"You're so easy, Yakimoto."

"Does that fiendish cackle mean you're joking?" Ronnie called after her.

Val laughed as she slid into her car, then she sent Ronnie a text. "Just kidding about Barney. See you for dinner."

She drove home excited at the prospect of hanging on to her friendship with Ronnie. She wanted more, of that she was sure. Even though Ronnie had plenty of things to work through, she didn't want just friendship. But if that was all that was on the table, she'd accept it. Anything to have her close.

CHAPTER TWENTY-EIGHT

On Saturday, Irene showed up at Ronnie's house. "You ready to work with the horses again?"

"Sure, but I didn't know you were coming." She'd planned to take Barney and Dover for a walk. She'd only had Barney a day and she wanted to make sure he settled in.

She also planned to unpack the last of her boxes. There were only ten left and she'd made two trips to the thrift store with donations, and one very satisfying trip to the dump. She'd be moved in before Val visited again. No more piles of boxes like she was a nomad ready to run.

But the boxes would have to wait. When she had Irene available, she'd go for it. There'd been some good training sessions, but far more cancelations or instances of Irene just not showing up. Ronnie was getting Irene's help for free so she could hardly complain, but it was still annoying. "Thanks. I could use some help."

"Surprise. And I come bearing gifts." Irene pulled a small paper bag from her pocket and swung it in front of Ronnie's nose.

Ronnie had the urge to bat it down and stomp it into the ground. She settled for scowling at Irene. "I told you not to bring any here. I don't use any more. I told you before and I texted you after I found that last bag. What aren't you getting?"

"Come on. We've been smoking since we were kids. It's only pot. Harmless."

"Not harmless. Not for me. I'd like you to leave and take it with you. I can't be around you if you're going to keep hassling me like this." She'd find a way to manage the horses without Irene's help.

"Come on, really?" Irene squinted at Ronnie for a second and then shrugged. "What if I leave it in my truck and take it home?"

Ronnie gritted her teeth. "Fine. Park on the street. We'll take my car to Poplarcreek."

"You won't be in my truck with it? You're serious?"

Ronnie leaned closer. "Deadly. And I need you to *hear* me this time. Really *hear* me. *Never* offer me any again."

Irene held her hands up. "Sorry, message received. Didn't realize you'd turned into a stodgy old woman. I guess it comes with the territory."

"Territory?"

"Being a teacher in this little backwater town. We always hated our teachers in school."

"Not all of them, and that's in the past. Maybe I'm finally growing up. It's about time."

"Okay, okay. Be right back." Irene ran to her truck, jumped in, and moved it to park on the street.

Ronnie grabbed her gear and headed to her car. She tried to relax and forced herself to smile. Irene was doing her a favor helping with the horses, and now that they had the issue with the pot sorted out, they could concentrate on the horses.

They arrived at the barn and changed in the tack room.

"How about a ride this morning?" Irene said. "The geldings?"

"Sure."

They saddled Ernie and Dave and took them outside. Irene chose to ride Ernie. That didn't surprise Ronnie. Irene always chose the taller horse. Was it because she wanted to be taller or because she liked to dominate the biggest animal? Ronnie shrugged and watched Irene work.

"I could never get Dave to do that," Ronnie said and watched in awe as Ernie galloped, did rollbacks, changed gaits, and walked backward. She had pretty good luck with Dave, but his movements weren't as crisp.

"That's because you're too soft. Work him harder. Dave can do it, but he's not going to if you don't make him."

"Maybe." Ronnie stroked Dave's neck. He was more relaxed than Ernie today. She liked the idea that the ride should be fun for the horses too.

When they were done, they returned to the stable to groom the geldings.

Ernie shied away when Irene reached to remove his bridle. "I'll get it." Ronnie slid the bridle off and studied the gelding. She hadn't seen Irene hit Ernie, not once, but he was still jumpy. Or maybe there was a dark energy around Irene that made animals not like her? Ronnie shook her head. Maybe Ernie was just tired?

"Well, I'll leave you to groom them. I've got to get going. Got a lesson at Starview." Irene slapped Ronnie on the back and left. The sound made both horses jump. Ronnie stretched her back to dispel the sting from Irene's hard slap.

Ronnie removed Dave's tack and hung it up. Dave was barely wet from his ride, but Ernie was the opposite. His chest was wet and he was soaking under his saddle. Maybe she was too slack with Dave? Irene had certainly put Ernie to work.

Two minutes after Irene left, Becky skipped into the barn with Max on her heels. "Need some help, Ronnie?"

Clearly, Becky, or maybe Callie, had been waiting for Irene to leave. It was just as well. More peaceful for everyone. "Thanks. Can you get their legs and bellies? Then they need to be walked for a bit to cool down."

"One day I'll be taller than you and you'll have to get the low parts." Becky laughed good-naturedly and set to work.

"Of that I have no doubt." Ronnie enjoyed the company. She and Becky made quick work of the grooming, and after a walk, the boys were returned to their pen with an extra helping of grain. Ronnie felt guilty for some reason she couldn't put her finger on, but she was pretty sure it had to do with Irene.

❖

"Well done everyone." Ronnie handed out the red ribbons she and the owners of Starview had collaborated on. They said *Starview Beginners Class* and she gave one to each of her students.

"Look, Mommy. Look at my ribbon." Gwen practically bounced up and down with excitement. "I'm going to put it up on the wall in my bedroom."

Val kissed her cheek. "Good for you."

"Thanks, Ronnie." Gwen bounced away to mingle with the other kids.

"That was nice of you."

Ronnie shrugged. "Starview bought them."

"But it was your idea. I get it. You're always so thoughtful." Val blushed and turned to watch the children admire their ribbons.

"They earned it. They're good kids. And they're all coming back in September for intermediates with me and I have another full beginners class. I didn't even advertise."

Val squeezed Ronnie's forearm. "You still don't understand small towns and word of mouth. The kids have been telling their friends and their parents about the lessons. People have heard how great you are. I'm not surprised there's so much interest. If Starview had an indoor arena you could teach all winter too."

"For now, I'll just hope it's not too cold in October to be outside. The last lesson is right before Halloween."

"Gwen and Becky will be there." Val straightened her ballcap. "We'll just hang out until you're ready to go."

"I'm ready now." She'd left her car and dogs at Poplarcreek and hitched a ride to the lesson with Val. Callie had invited the whole class for a barbecue to celebrate the end of riding lessons. Any time she could spend with Val was special, and she looked so beautiful with her hair loose. She wanted to run her fingers through it and see Val's eyes close in pleasure. She cleared her throat and focused on the party ahead. She could return to that image tonight, alone in her bed.

Ronnie smiled at her garden gate. She opened and closed it and opened and closed it. It was a good job and she'd done most of it.

Even used the drill. Brad, the shop teacher at the school, had helped her. They'd fixed her gate and enjoyed a beer in the shade before he left.

"Look, boys, your gate is fixed. Two new hinges and a new latch." She'd been looking at that bike lock on the gate for a month. It was satisfying to have it fixed and she was even going to buy her own rechargeable drill now that she could work one. There were other jobs around the house she was itching to tackle. She'd already nailed the baseboards back on in her living room and organized her computer games on shelves. She was feeling pumped.

Ronnie reached for her phone as it rang. "Hello?"

"Hi, Ronnie, it's Val."

"Hey, you're back. How was the camping trip?" She'd missed Val and almost told her so.

After the last riding lesson of the summer, the Connors had left town, planning to squeeze in a week of vacation before school started.

"So much fun. My Dad and Gwen and I went trail riding one day. One of those places where you rent a horse for an hour. I had fun, but I need lessons. Gwen was showing me how to steer the horse."

"It's more of a guiding thing. I'm still willing to teach you to ride."

"It wouldn't be an imposition?"

"Not at all. We'll take Ernie and Dave out and ride around at Poplarcreek."

"Thanks. So, I was wondering if you'd like to have coffee with me and maybe talk? Sorry, that sounded more serious than I meant it to. I just need your help with something I'm working on, please."

"Coffee? Okay. And I'm happy to help."

"Thanks. This town is full of people with big ears, so how about my house? It's short notice, but my parents have claimed Gwen for tomorrow afternoon and I'm free."

"Sounds mysterious. What time?"

"Two work?"

"Perfect, see you then." They hung up and Ronnie sat smiling at her phone as she swigged absently from her warm beer. Val was special, but was she special to her? Ronnie grinned and put her hand on her chest. Was it excitement or panic that made her heart want to beat out of her chest? She needed to find out and soon. Excitement she could handle, but panic made her crave a joint.

Ronnie poured the rest of her beer down the sink, grabbed another box, and headed upstairs to her new home office. She'd have it all organized before school started again in eleven days. No more piles of assignments all over her kitchen table. She set the box down and moved her desk to take advantage of the afternoon sun and the view of her backyard. Maybe she'd even get assignments marked early this year. Life was different, in a good way. She was different, and she was liking the person she saw in the mirror. Being around Val had made her think, and being without Val had made her lonely. It was all about Val, and she liked it. A lot.

CHAPTER TWENTY-NINE

After Gwen left with her parents, Val headed into her laundry room and pulled the bedding out of the dryer. It was slightly damp, perfect for ironing. She clutched the bedding to her chest and rolled her eyes. It would take hours to iron it all and it'd be wrinkled again soon.

It seemed like a Ronnie kind of thing to think, and it made her laugh. Val shrugged. She sorted the bedding and removed the pillow slips, then she stuffed the sheets back in to finish drying.

She had fifteen minutes. She snagged the pillow slips, tossed them into the dryer with the sheets and headed to her bedroom to change her clothes. She ironed too much and today she wouldn't waste her time.

She splayed her fingers over her belly in an attempt to stop the flutters. She'd barely seen Ronnie since they rescued Barney from Dillon two weeks ago. She was going slow and trying to give Ronnie some space, but it was hard. Being gone for the last week had helped, but she'd thought a lot about Ronnie during her vacation.

At exactly two p.m., Val opened her front door to a smiling Ronnie. "Hey, you."

Ronnie hugged her warmly. "I missed you."

Val looked at Ronnie for a few seconds, taking her in. "Sorry, come in. Let me take your coat."

"Here." Ronnie handed her a white cardboard box and removed her jacket.

Val pointed to a coat hook as she experimentally hefted the box. "You stopped at the bakery."

"I did." Ronnie's smile slipped. "Is that okay? I didn't think. You probably have home baking to go with the coffee."

Val sighed. "Not today. I like baking, but it should be for fun and I was making it another chore, and there are already too many mandatory chores in my life." She shrugged. "Gwen and I do more store-bought desserts or none at all these days. A bowl of popcorn in front of the television after dinner suits us fine." Val ushered Ronnie into the kitchen. "Coffee?"

"Or tea, whatever you're having."

"Coffee." Val switched on the coffee maker. She placed mugs and sugar on the table, then she pulled a milk carton from the refrigerator. "I hope milk's okay. I shopped when we got back, and I forgot cream." One day back home and her refrigerator was full. She would work through some of the food she already had before shopping again. She was hoarding food like a squirrel before winter and it was a pain fitting everything in her refrigerator.

"You okay, Val?"

Val looked at Ronnie in confusion. "Yes, why?"

"I don't know. You're usually very organized, but today there's no baking and no cream—" Ronnie gasped. "I just heard how that sounded. Please let me retract that ridiculous statement."

Val laughed at Ronnie's shocked expression. "I'm fine. Maybe I'm rethinking some things." She put the pastries Ronnie had purchased on a plate and set them on the table, then she fetched plates and forks.

"Things?"

Val blushed and pulled a file folder from under a stack of books on the table. "I'm looking at courses to prepare for veterinary school. I probably have to do four or five university-level science courses. I've been kind of caught up in the planning lately."

"Cool."

"Would you have a look? Maybe you have some suggestions about university?"

"I'm happy to. I didn't do science, but I can look at what you've got."

Val rose to fetch the coffee and returned.

"Ah, here we go." Ronnie showed Val a list. "Here are the courses you need. You've got that, but to take this one you need the prerequisite course."

Val poured the coffee and shifted her chair closer to Ronnie. "Prerequisite?"

Val took notes and listened while she and Ronnie pored over the requirements for veterinary school. She leaned back after forty minutes and sighed. "Wow, thanks for your help. I have a plan now. I'll need two semesters of basic classes before I can apply. I guess that's okay. It'll give me a chance to see if I'm ready to be a student again. Would you like more coffee?"

"I'd prefer a glass of water, please."

Val cleared the table, tucked away her schoolwork, and set two glasses of water on the table. She casually shifted her chair away from Ronnie's now that the school preparations were done.

"What did you want to talk about?" Ronnie asked.

Val took a deep breath. "I appreciate the school advice, but I wanted to talk about us." She bit her lip. "It's hard to start. How're you doing these days?"

Ronnie sat forward in her seat and leaned her elbows on the table. "I've done a lot of thinking and you've given me the space to do that. Perhaps too much."

"Have I been ignoring you?"

"No, the phone calls and the texts are fun, but I miss seeing you in person. Sitting across from you like this."

Val nodded. By talk Ronnie meant they hadn't discussed the elephant in the room. Were they friends forever or could there be more between them.? "And what did you figure out?"

"That I like kissing you, holding your hand, holding you in general…and that I want to be more than friends. Or at least try to, if you're ready."

Val had the urge to crawl across the table into Ronnie's lap. She was ready. She took a deep breath to slow her racing heart and head. "I'd like that. What's the next step?"

"A redo. You come to dinner at my house and I don't freak out this time."

She was proud of Ronnie, impressed that she been through some tough times with drugs and her crazy past, but had survived with her health and sense of humor. She was a great teacher, a good friend, and brave. And she was awesome with Gwen. There wasn't a woman she wanted to date more in the world. Ronnie was still struggling with intimacy, but Val could be patient. Ronnie was worth it. "I'd like that if you're ready."

"Thanks. I'm on track for about the first time in five years." Ronnie clasped Val's hand.

"So, what's next for us?"

Ronnie scooted her chair close to Val and Val met her halfway for a kiss that sent electricity skittering through her body.

Val left Gwen and Becky at Callie's house and headed toward the horse barn. She squared her shoulders. Now was her chance to catch Ronnie alone. Since the meeting for coffee in her kitchen, they'd been on three nice dates and had some more casual visits. Sometimes Ronnie cooked and sometimes Val and Gwen cooked. Most of the visits ended with some excellent make out sessions that left them both panting like teenagers. The last time Ronnie had pulled her into her lap and hinted at more to come.

"Hello, Ms. Yakimoto."

Ronnie glanced over her shoulder. "Even Gwen and Becky don't call me that when we're at Poplarcreek. I thought you were working tonight."

Val kissed her on the cheek. "Only every second Thursday night now that I have to work some Saturdays." She patted the horse Ronnie was grooming. "Hi, Ernie. You're looking sharp."

Ronnie smiled with pride. "He is, isn't he? Look how glossy his coat is. Will you be bringing the girls to their lesson this Saturday?" It was the first week of school and Ronnie had moved riding classes to Saturday mornings.

Val couldn't be bothered with small talk. "Do you know we kissed for the first time over a month ago?" It had really been almost six weeks, but she'd sound too desperate if Ronnie knew she was counting.

"Six weeks this Saturday, actually." Ronnie continued to groom Ernie. "That was when we stopped to watch the sunset."

Val moved behind her and splayed her fingers on Ronnie's back. She trembled as she smoothed her hands over the hard muscles. It had been ages since that first perfect kiss at the Hang. "You ever consider doing anything more?"

"All the time." Ronnie turned and pulled Val close. "I can't stop thinking about you. Imagining you naked. But I want to be certain."

"Certain?" Val wrapped her arms around Ronnie's waist and rested her chin on her shoulder.

"I don't know. That I won't hurt you, I guess."

Val placed a line of kisses on top of the tight thermal shirt over Ronnie's collarbone. "I have to plan ahead." It was impossible to be spontaneous with a nine-year-old bouncing through the house.

Ronnie rested her hands on Val's hips. "If we have sex too soon, our relationship will become all about when we can have sex again. Life will revolve around stolen moments and quick fucks. And I want more than that."

Val's lips parted and her breath hitched. Oh, how she would adore a quick fuck right now. Her judgment blurred as she imagined Ronnie crushing her against the wall and sliding her hand down the front of her jeans. She moaned and grew wet as her breasts pressed against Ronnie's. There wasn't an ounce of fat on Ronnie, and her lips were impossibly soft. It was a heady combination. Val shuffled backward and dragged Ronnie with her. She yearned for Ronnie to take her.

Ernie shifted in the crossties. He snorted and stamped one foot with impatience. Ronnie broke contact and spun to face the gelding so he didn't hurt himself. "There, there, Ernie. Almost done, big guy."

Val darted from the barn while Ronnie was busy. She was desperate for cool air. Her cheeks burned, and she groaned in frustration. She covered her face with her hands and leaned against the outside wall of the barn. She'd promised herself to be patient and not push, but her body wasn't in tune with her mind.

Val pressed her forehead against the cool glass of the barn window and groaned. She jumped as hands landed against the wall of the barn on either side of her as she waited. Her breath caught in her chest. Ronnie pressed Val against the barn, her body strong and hard against her. Val trembled and spread her legs in invitation, but

Ronnie's hands remained planted against the wood. Val moaned as hot breath caressed her ear.

"I'm certain now. Can you get away tomorrow night?" Ronnie asked.

Val attempted to speak but failed. She tried again as her body quaked under the pressure from Ronnie's body. She longed to be pinned under her, crying out her name. Her answer emerged as part of a strangled breath. She repeated it louder and firmer. "Yes."

"Then I'll see you tomorrow," she whispered, and nipped at her earlobe.

An instant later, Val's body chilled. Ronnie had vanished and taken her warmth with her. Val dug her fingernails into the soft wood of the barn to stay upright. She yearned to sink to the ground and pull Ronnie down on top of her. Her legs shook with the effort of remaining standing. When her legs could once again support her weight, she let go of the barn. She swayed for a second before stumbling toward Callie's house. She had arrangements to make.

Val entered the mudroom of Callie's house and hung up her coat. She kicked off her boots and stepped into the kitchen. Callie glanced at her and returned to the meal preparations.

"Dinner's almost ready. The soup just needs another ten minutes." Callie peered over her shoulder. "Val?" Callie smirked and a broad smile lit up her face. "Oh, Valerie," she said, stretching Val's name to a full three syllables. "Come here." Callie clasped Val's hand and tugged her toward the kitchen table. They dropped into chairs with their knees touching. "You're red as a beet. What happened?"

Val blushed harder and opened her mouth, but nothing emerged until she tried again. "Tomorrow night."

"Tomorrow night?"

"Ronnie and I have another date, and I think I'm staying over."

Callie crossed her arms over her chest, leaned back, and grinned. "Good for you."

Val playfully slapped Callie's knee. "Stop looking so smug." Callie deserved to act smug. She had more dating experience with women than Lauren, Ronnie, and Val put together.

Callie raised her hands in surrender. "So, it's all set."

"Mostly."

"Mostly?"

"Am I safe to be in a relationship with her? What if she picks up again? Should she be around children? Our children?"

"You know the answer to that."

Val cradled her face in her hands. "You're right. Ronnie's put all that stuff behind her. Besides, pot is no big deal. You smoke it in moderation."

"So, let her move on and be happy."

"That's the same conclusion I came to, but I wanted to check with you." Val squeezed Callie's hand. "Can I bring Gwen to you tomorrow evening, please?" Val blushed. "I'm hoping she can stay here overnight, and I'll pick her up on Saturday after riding lessons."

"We love having Gwen here, but let her come home on the bus with Becky. You'll need time to prepare."

"Yes, a long bath and serious work with the razor." Her emotional balance restored, Val looked around. "Where are Becky and Gwen?"

"They're with Lauren in the cattle barn. There's a litter of kittens that need socializing." Callie put air quotes around the word socializing.

Val scoffed. "Socializing is Lauren's code word when there are kittens she wants to cuddle."

"I know it." Callie's grin exuded love.

"Lauren's a marshmallow inside that not-so-tough exterior."

Val laughed with Callie, but not unkindly.

"Gwen and I'll head home after lunch today. We're having dinner with my parents and my cousins tonight. But it'll be a struggle to keep my mind in the conversation, and Gwen prefers to be at Poplarcreek with you guys and the animals."

"Gwen likes a crowd of people to talk to. She's tired of the three of us. We're a quiet crew at Poplarcreek."

"We like your quiet crew. You're a good friend. Thanks." Callie stooped, and they gave each other a quick peck on the cheek. Val slipped her boots and coat on and skipped off in search of Lauren and the girls. *It's tomorrow night, tomorrow night.*

On the way to the barn, she mulled over the significance of this next date. Ronnie said she was ready so Val would trust her. She would enjoy their date and only move as fast as Ronnie wanted, even if Val was ready for a night of all out, sweaty fun.

❖

Val pirouetted in front of the mirror and tugged her clothes into place. The dress looked amazing. It wasn't new, but it was a nice mixture of modesty and sexy. It showed cleavage but covered enough to be a mystery. And the elegant blue made her eyes pop.

She spent no time picking the right purse. Ten seconds after she entered Ronnie's house, she would discard it in a corner of the room. In the past that wouldn't have stopped her. She'd have insisted on making the best impression and picked a fussy little purse that held nothing. With Ronnie it didn't matter, and there was something wonderfully freeing in that. She selected her biggest black shoulder bag and popped her items into it.

Tonight was the night Ronnie would take her to bed, she hoped. To Val, making love meant staying until morning, so she'd be ready. She focused on her preparations, determined not to overthink the evening.

Val slipped her sexiest nightdress into her bag. It showed a generous amount of cleavage and left nothing to the imagination. She dropped in her small travel toiletries bag and fresh panties, then she scampered downstairs and pulled on her boots. She collected the items she had purchased and stuffed her shoes in her bag.

Her knee bounced as she drove to Ronnie's house. She moved her hand from the steering wheel and struggled to hold her knee steady, but her hand trembled. Her nervous system was on overdrive and she took deep breaths to calm herself. As much as Val longed to make love, she now believed Ronnie had been right to make them wait. But she was definitely done waiting.

Chapter Thirty

R onnie opened her front door and waved Val into the house. "Val's here and I'm cooking. I need to hang up. No, that's private. I've got to go. Yes, I've got it. More work for Frieda and the boys and rest Abby and Bella. Got it."

"Hi." Val stepped inside and handed Ronnie the flowers and the bottle of wine.

"Thanks." Ronnie smiled and tucked the phone under her chin while she took the gifts. "Sure. See you next weekend. Yup…Yup… Yup."

Val took her coat off and hung it up. She glanced at her watch to see if she was early. She didn't want to interrupt, and Ronnie was trying to end the call.

"Got to go. Yup. Val's here, I have to go. Right, talk next week, right, tomorrow." Ronnie laughed. "I promise. Bye, Irene. Yup… Yup… Hanging up."

Val kicked off her boots and slipped on her black pumps. The shoes had a low heel, but they showed off her legs to their best advantage. She also felt sexy as her heels clicked on the tile of Ronnie's hall. She didn't feel very sexy with Ronnie on the phone with Irene, though.

Ronnie walked toward the living room and Val followed her. The euphoric high she'd been on was crashing.

"Bye, Irene. Yup. Val's here. None of your business. Going now. Bye." Ronnie slid her phone into her pocket and sighed dramatically before smiling widely. "You look fantastic. I'm glad you're here."

Ronnie's eyes traveled over her body. Val's stomach flipped and tensed with nerves. She leaned in for a light kiss, but Ronnie deepened it. After a minute, she summoned enough control to step back.

"You look awesome yourself." Val's words sounded breathless to her own ears and for good reason. Ronnie wore simple black jeans and a red shirt that outlined her lean figure. She was wearing a little mascara that emphasized her dark brown eyes while her straight black hair shimmered and caught the light.

"Thanks for the wine and flowers. I'm always the flower giver."

"That's not fair. You deserve flowers." Val followed Ronnie into the kitchen. "You said to bring white wine, but I'm no expert. I like that one and I chilled it at home." She scanned the room. "Did you paint?"

"I've been planning to since I moved in and I just did it. I liked having it done in the living room and decided to jump to the kitchen too. You like it?"

"I do. What's that shade?"

Ronnie shrugged. "Some kind of light yellow. I never remember all the goofy names of the shades."

Val laughed. "Well, I like the way it brightens up the room. I was thinking of painting my kitchen. Something bright and cheery."

"Your kitchen's nice."

Val wrinkled her nose. "A nice tidy, boring, neutral beige. You've inspired me. I'm tired of neutral. I want color and pictures of Gwen on the wall." Colorful, vibrant Ronnie was making Val want more color in her own life, too.

"I'll help you if you like. And how about a picture of Gwen on horseback? You could take some at the next lesson. Or Becky could. She's into photography. Or what about Gwen and Becky on Ernie and Dave?" Ronnie grinned. "Imagine, Gwen could see them every day in her own kitchen."

"It's very thoughtful of you to think of Gwen."

Ronnie shrugged. "She's a great kid and deserves to feel special."

Val sensed the sadness in that statement and pursued it. "Do you have pictures of you on horseback at Gwen's age?"

"I had some in my mother's house, but she did a big clean out a few years ago and I lost them. She told me to pick up my stuff and I didn't get around to it." Ronnie shrugged. "Other than that, I've got a couple somewhere that my boss took for some advertisement. They're okay, but we could do better for Gwen. I mean you could. She loves Comet. He's a big bay. Very solid and build like a brick house."

Val wanted to cry for Ronnie. What mother would toss out pictures of her children? She'd have Gwen's forever. "Comet sounds safe."

"The safest."

Val focused on Ronnie for a beat, touched again at how much she cared about Gwen and looked out for her. More than anyone had looked out for Ronnie at that age. "Thanks. I may take you up on that." Val grinned, already plotting to get pictures of Ronnie on horseback. "Something smells good."

"Since I was feeding the two of us, I decided a small chicken might be nice. And there'll be enough for my lunch for a few days." Ronnie uncorked the wine and poured them each a glass. "The chicken has another twenty minutes to go. I'm roasting small potatoes with it and only just stuck them in a little while ago. I figured there wasn't any hurry." Ronnie clasped Val's hand and led her into the living room.

Dover and Barney rose from their beds and tottered to Val for petting. She put her wineglass on the table and cupped Dover's face to study him. "Dover is looking good."

"He is." He pressed against Ronnie's leg and she played with his ears. She looked at Val and her eyes flashed with vulnerability. "Thanks again for everything you did for him. I don't know if I'd have survived if I'd lost him this summer."

"Hey." Val rubbed her hand up and down Ronnie's arm. "You take excellent care of him." She liked Dover and hated to see the sadness in Ronnie's eyes.

After his visit, Dover tottered back to his bed. He collapsed with a grunt and rested his head on his paws. He appeared content to watch them and not be in the thick of the action. After Val petted him, Barney followed, lying beside Dover, resting his head on Dover's shoulder.

Ronnie sank into the couch and motioned for Val to join her. She longed to slide her dress up and straddle Ronnie's lap, but she settled for sitting with their thighs touching.

Ronnie put her wineglass on the coffee table, took Val's from her, and set it on the table.

Val ran her tongue over her lips, ready for anything.

Ronnie studied their joined hands and caressed the back of Val's hand with her thumb. "About tonight…"

A wave of anxiety swept through Val's body. Another excuse was on the way. There'd been too many over the last few weeks. Her brain screamed as she turned her face away from Ronnie. *Be patient.*

"Don't worry," Ronnie said.

Val slowly brought her eyes back to Ronnie's. In Ronnie's eyes, she saw affection and desire.

"I want to have a nice dinner and take you to bed. You're welcome to stay and have breakfast with me. I'm usually stupidly spontaneous, but I have a plan tonight, if that's okay."

Val tried not to show how relieved she was. No need to appear desperate. "I love your plan, and now you'd better kiss me again or I'll do something foolish."

Ronnie smiled and leaned in to capture Val's lips. The kiss started softly and then deepened. Oh, but Ronnie was such an amazing kisser. Val was crazy aroused and tried to hold back, but the kiss overwhelmed her and she angled to press her chest against Ronnie's.

Val craved more, yearned for more, insisted on more. She adored Ronnie's slight weight on top of her and wanted to lean back farther. *Not yet, not yet. Don't ruin the moment.* Val broke the kiss, her breathing ragged, and her heart rate through the roof.

Conversation, interspersed with kissing, filled their time while dinner cooked. For the most part, though, Val couldn't concentrate on Ronnie's words. As their kisses grew more ardent, she gave herself points for not crawling into Ronnie's lap.

When the oven timer rang, Ronnie kissed Val once more and rose. "I'll check on dinner."

Val followed on rubbery legs, reluctant to let Ronnie out of her sight. She sat at the table as Ronnie finished preparing dinner. Ronnie arranged the serving dishes in front of her and then dropped into a chair. Val spooned food onto her plate and ate enough to comment on how delicious it tasted, but her nerves had tied her stomach into knots, destroying her appetite.

Ronnie cleared the table of their half-eaten food. Val rose with surprise. It felt as if they had sat down ten seconds ago, and clearly, Ronnie's appetite was for something else too.

Val helped carry the leftovers and dishes to the kitchen, then she opened the patio door and let Dover and Barney amble into the backyard. She watched them for a few moments before turning to focus on Ronnie. They held each other's eyes and grinned. Val grabbed the door handle as an anchor. She refused to fling herself at Ronnie, but her desire was at war with her good sense.

Val yanked the patio door open. "Hey, Dover, hey, Barney. Hurry please, boys." When the longest five minutes of her life was over, they tottered in. She closed the door and turned to Ronnie, catching the grin that Ronnie couldn't hide.

Ronnie tipped her head toward the refrigerator. "I have dessert."

Val nodded, but her brain and her voice declined to cooperate to form even incoherent sentences.

"It'll keep," Ronnie said.

Val nodded faster. She linked her arms around Ronnie's neck as desire trumped control. Now was the time to lose control, and she aimed to in a big way. Ronnie kissed her and slipped from her embrace, then took Val's hand and led to her bedroom.

"I finally finished this room too."

Val gasped at the tidy bedroom. The room was clean and there were no boxes lining the freshly-painted walls. There was no stationary bike, and Ronnie had hung small white lights above the bed that looked like twinkling stars.

Val pulled Ronnie close, impatient for the next phase of their evening. She craved Ronnie on top of her and inside her in the worst way.

Ronnie caressed Val's shoulders and back. "You're so elegant. It's a shame to undress you."

"I'll do it."

Ronnie shook her head and with trembling hands, unzipped Val's dress and slid it off her shoulders, leaving goose bumps in the wake of her trailing fingertips. Ronnie scooped the dress off the floor and laid it on a chair, then tore off her pants and yanked her shirt over her head.

Val caught the briefest glimpse of Ronnie in a gray sports bra and boxers before their bodies crashed together again and Ronnie guided her down onto the bed.

Val trembled under Ronnie's hands and lips. She could come without being touched, she was so worked up. The build up to tonight was maddening, but she concentrated on relaxing. Ronnie needed to go slowly after confessing she'd never made love without being high.

"Val? What would you like?"

"Forget slowly. You, inside me, now." Val sounded desperate, and she didn't care. "Next time, we'll go slow, but I need your hands on me."

Ronnie slid Val's panties off and slipped two fingers inside causing Val to moan and arch her back. It was amazing to have Ronnie's fingers inside her after staring at them for weeks and imagining.

Ronnie thrust faster while Val's passion built. It didn't take long. She teetered on the edge and crashed without Ronnie even touching her clit. She came with a small cry and clutched Ronnie to her. "On top. I want your weight on me." Ronnie shifted. "All your weight."

"You have all my weight."

Val shuddered a few more times as Ronnie slowly stroked her inside. Ronnie slid off her and kissed her face.

Val whispered, "Now you."

"I'm not done with you. I'll take my time with the next one." Ronnie removed Val's bra and the rest of her own clothes.

Val grinned. "I can make the next last longer. A little longer." Her second orgasm only took a little more time than the first. It might even have been part of the first. At least Ronnie got to touch her clit before she came. How long had she needed this?

Ronnie held Val while she trembled with aftershocks. "Should I stop?" Ronnie asked.

Val shook her head. "You now." She pushed weakly at Ronnie trying to propel Ronnie onto her back.

Ronnie showered Val's face and neck with kisses. "I'm not done. Please, may I explore?" Ronnie nipped at the skin of Val's shoulders. "You have so many interesting curves and dimples to visit."

Val blinked and smiled. She dropped her arms and relaxed into the soft bed. Ronnie caressed her breasts, sucked her nipples, and caressed each curve and dimple. She ran her finger along the pale line low on Val's abdomen.

"Gwen was a C-section," Val said, strangely not self-conscious under Ronnie's adoring scrutiny.

Ronnie nodded and kissed the scar, stringing a line of kisses from one end to the other.

Val's third orgasm took a long time to build, but when she crashed, she fell deeper than the first two.

She woke feeling luscious, used, and more than a little pleasantly sore. Ronnie slept on her stomach, her face turned toward Val. She had the longest black eyelashes. Val's lips curved into a wicked grin as she moved onto her back. She counted three orgasms after dinner. There might have been more, but her head had exploded after number three. When she shifted to focus on Ronnie's face, she discovered soft brown eyes gazing at her.

"Hey," Ronnie said.

"Hey back."

After their witty exchange, Val fell silent and continued to gaze at Ronnie. They were both grinning like fools. Val broke the mood with a wink. Ronnie laughed and slipped from the bed.

Val grasped Ronnie's forearm. "Why're you leaving?"

"To make you a snack."

Val tipped her head toward the clock glowing beside the bed. "At two thirty?"

"I saw how little dinner you ate."

Val's face flushed. "Sorry. It was delicious, but you distracted me. You're so gorgeous and all I could think about was being here with you."

"Wait here." Ronnie edged out of Val's grasp, slipped into a simple black robe, and headed downstairs.

Val hugged Ronnie's pillow and listened to Ronnie doing something with dishes in the kitchen, then the patio door opened. The boys were awake too. A pot scraped on the stove and the lid clanged. Val snuggled into the covers. They smelled wonderfully of Ronnie's floral soap and sex.

Fifteen minutes later, the patio door closed, followed by more muffled conversation. Ronnie entered the bedroom with a small tray and set it on the end of the dresser. Val sat up and tucked the sheets over her breasts.

"Milk or water?" Ronnie asked. "I didn't make coffee."

"Milk please."

Ronnie set a glass of milk on the table at her side of the bed and a matching drink beside Val. Ronnie bent and kissed her on the forehead. "Now for dessert."

Ronnie sashayed to the dresser and scooped up a dessert bowl. She tilted it so Val could see the contents, a thick chocolate brownie with a large scoop of French vanilla ice cream on it. Val licked her lips and reached for the bowl.

"Not yet, you." Ronnie raised the pot. "Some sauce?"

Val nodded.

"Peanuts, almonds, both, or neither?"

Val pointed to the clear jar of peanuts and a generous amount landed in each bowl.

"Whipped cream? I only have the kind in the can, sorry."

Val shook her head. She accepted the bowl and spoon and cradled the warm bowl between her palms. Ronnie sat cross-legged on the end of the bed with a second dessert bowl.

Val dipped her spoon in and scooped up a piece of brownie, ice cream, sauce, and a peanut. She put the spoon in her mouth, cleaned it, and moaned in appreciation. "This is delicious. I'm going to have a chocolate-induced orgasm."

Ronnie took a spoonful herself and chuckled. "Sometimes simple is best. Hard to beat good chocolate. I'm glad you passed on the canned topping. I planned to prepare the real kind, but I couldn't wait to get back to you."

"The dessert is perfect just like this. I'm full of sugar and bursting with energy."

Ronnie winked. "I'm happy to hear you say that."

They ate in silence, staring at eat other with happiness and enjoying the sundae. When Val scraped the bottom of her bowl, Ronnie offered her more. Val declined. Her current sugar high satisfied her, and if she ate more, she'd suffer a sugar crash. She didn't want to crash and refused to fall asleep. Her ideas for the rest of the night involved her tongue on and in Ronnie.

Ronnie stacked the dishes on the dresser, shed her robe, and crawled into bed.

Val rolled on top of Ronnie and placed her elbows above Ronnie's shoulders. "I fell asleep on you. Did I leave you hanging?"

"I was all right, then."

"And now?"

Ronnie nudged Val's head until Val's lips hovered above Ronnie's nipple.

"Awesome." Val brushed the sensitive tip with her tongue. She wanted to please Ronnie, make her squirm and cry out like she had. After everything Ronnie had been through, she deserved the best. She deserved the world.

Chapter Thirty-one

Ronnie stirred and woke to the buzz of her phone as it vibrated across her bedside table. She looked at Val, naked and curled in her arms. It had been a wonderful evening and Val had surprised her with an adventurous side. How could she have ever thought Val was matronly and boring? She wanted to spend a few more hours in bed and then have a leisurely breakfast before riding class. She sighed and reached for the annoying phone.

"Ignore it," Val whispered groggily. "Sleep. Nobody should call this early on a Saturday."

After the fifth buzz, the phone quit and went to voice mail. Ronnie sighed with happiness and started to drift off again, only to wake when it started again. "It might be important. I should answer it." She looked into Val's warm eyes, and thoughts of anything except Val, disappeared. She leaned in to kiss her and shifted on top of her. The phone ceased buzzing. She kissed Val's forehead and face, then nestled between Val's spread legs.

A minute later, Val's phone buzzed. "Shit," Val said.

"Ignore it."

"When you have a child, you can't ignore the phone. Clearly, someone's trying to get hold of us."

Ronnie slipped off Val with a snort.

Val rolled to grab her phone. "Hello? Callie?"

Ronnie was close enough to hear both sides of the phone conversation.

"Oh, my God, Val!" Callie said.

Val sat up in bed. "What, Callie? What's, oh my God? Is Gwen all right?"

Ronnie sat up and tucked the blanket around Val's shoulders.

"Sorry, sorry. I'm calling about the horses and Ronnie's not answering her phone."

"Callie, slow down."

"Lauren said to call Ronnie. Is she there? Can I talk to her?"

Val blushed and passed the phone to Ronnie. "It's Callie, for you."

Ronnie accepted the phone and pushed the speaker button so Val could hear more easily. "Hey, Callie."

"Ronnie, thank God. Something's wrong with Bella. She's sweating, agitated, and pacing her stall. There's a white sack, like a balloon, under her tail. I called Lauren and she's sure Bella's foaling. I know nothing about foaling. I only learned about calving this winter. Lauren is busy on an emergency call and can't get away."

Was Callie excited or terrified? Either way, she needed to calm down. "Bella will be all right. We'll be there soon." Ronnie leaped to her feet and started pulling on clothes. "Keep talking, Callie."

"Lauren told me most foalings are quick and you never see them, but to call you anyway. Lauren is busy dealing with two colics at Starview. Some horses broke out and gorged on grain last night."

"We're on our way."

"What do I do?" Callie's voice was high and panicked.

"Stay quiet and stay out of her stall. She's a calm mare, but she'll be uncomfortable right now. And grab a couple of old towels so I can dry the foal off."

Ronnie and Val ran downstairs and yanked on boots over bare feet. They pulled on coats and dashed outside. Val had parked behind Ronnie so Val took the wheel and Ronnie settled beside her. She crossed her fingers and hoped they wouldn't pass any RCMP as they sped to Poplarcreek.

Twenty minutes later, they arrived at Poplarcreek after a tense drive. Ronnie had stayed quiet, thinking of all the things she needed to consider and what she'd do if something went wrong, and Val remained quiet to let her think. They parked and jogged into the barn. Gwen and Becky, wearing coats, boots, and pajamas, stood on upside down feed pails and were peeking over the solid side of Bella's stall. Callie stood behind Gwen and Becky with her arms around them. Callie turned and smiled at them when they entered the barn.

Ronnie's anxiety level dropped three notches. Callie was smiling. She and Val sidled up beside the trio. Gwen saw Val and opened her mouth to speak, but Val motioned for her to be quiet. Ronnie and the rest peered into the stall. Bella stood at the back of the stall nuzzling her black foal who raised its head to touch noses with its mother.

Ronnie watched, enchanted as Bella nudged her foal to encourage it to stand. The foal tried to stand, but it was awkward and nosedived into the thick layer of straw covering the floor. The others uttered shocked noises and focused on Ronnie, wanting her to do something. She gave the group two thumbs-up and continued watching.

After the third attempt, the foal rose to its feet, and on wobbly legs stumbled to the mare's udder. The group watched enchanted as the black foal took its first drink. "Can we pet the baby?" Gwen whispered.

"It's too soon. We don't want to upset Bella." They watched Bella and her foal for another ten minutes. When Gwen and Becky grew restless, Callie and Val took them to the house.

Ronnie waited until the barn had quieted and then stepped into Bella's stall. Bella was a gentle horse with beautiful sad eyes. Ronnie couldn't wait to see how gorgeous the mare became when she had gained back all her weight and reached normal body condition. She quickly and gently toweled off the foal. It was beautiful, but this wasn't how she'd wanted to spend her morning.

Ronnie could see that Callie had already done the morning feedings, so she exited the barn and jogged to the house. She left her coat and boots in the mudroom and washed her hands in the bathroom. Four pairs of eyes were locked on Ronnie when she emerged from the bathroom. "They're both fine."

"Okay if we stay for breakfast?" Val asked. "Gwen and Becky are preparing their famous berry pancakes."

Ronnie nodded. It would have disappointed Gwen and Becky if they'd left, even if she really would have liked more time in bed with Val.

After Callie had Gwen and Becky organized in the kitchen and working away on breakfast, she sauntered up to Val. She did an exaggerated examination of Val and winked at Ronnie. "Sorry for dragging you out of bed," Callie whispered.

Val blushed and pushed at Callie's arm. "Stop it."

Callie grinned. "Did you have a nice evening?"

Val blushed more deeply.

"Sorry for the panicked phone calls."

"I'm just glad Bella's okay and has a healthy foal," Ronnie said.

"Me too." Callie walked to the window. "Lauren's home."

Ronnie jumped to her feet. "I'll go."

"Tell her we're making pancakes," Gwen said.

Ronnie jogged across the yard and met Lauren on her way into the horse barn. "Morning, Lauren."

"Hey, Ronnie. How's Bella?" Lauren asked.

"A proud mama of a beautiful foal." They tiptoed up to the edge of the stall and peered in.

"Everything go okay?"

Ronnie shrugged. "Perfect as far as I can see. I ran my hands over the foal."

"Good. She trusts you. Let's let her rest." Lauren led the way to the house and Ronnie followed.

"Hello, everyone," Lauren said. They all greeted her with warmth and then sat to eat the breakfast Callie and the girls had prepared. The primary topic of conversation was the new foal. Gwen and Becky hammered Lauren and Ronnie with questions.

"Buddy's the baby's name," Gwen announced with finality.

Val gave Gwen a one-armed hug. "That's an interesting name. Does it matter if the foal is a girl or a boy?"

"Buddy is for both," Gwen said with assurance. "And it's a cool name. Ronnie calls Dover Buddy all the time."

Val looked into Ronnie's eyes. "Well, I guess Buddy it is. It's a great name."

Callie nudged Ronnie with a shoulder. "You haven't told us the sex of the foal."

"Oh sorry. We have another little filly," Ronnie said. She couldn't get the image of Val in the throes of an orgasm out of her head and was utterly unfocused on the conversation.

"Another girl. Yahoo. Bella and her baby, Buddy," Gwen shouted as she and Becky danced in their chairs.

"The baby is all black," Callie said.

"Bella is a gray and their babies are often black at birth. Buddy is also a gray and will lighten each year as she ages," Ronnie said. Lauren smiled and nodded her agreement.

When the meal was done, Ronnie and Val cleared the plates away. Gwen and Becky headed upstairs.

"Try to sleep some more, girls. It's going to be a long day," Callie called after them.

"Not much chance of that," Val said. "Did you see how excited they were?"

"Sorry to run off, but I need to head back to Starview," Lauren said. "The horses there are still sick, and I want to look them over. I'll be back as soon as I can."

"Bye, you. See you soon," Callie said softly, giving Lauren a long hug. She turned to Val and Ronnie. "It's only eight and class is at eleven. What's your plan?"

Val blushed and looked at Ronnie.

Ronnie grinned. She had some ideas. "I left my gear at home and I need it for the lesson. We'll head back to town and see you later. Okay with you, Val?"

Callie laughed. "Have fun."

Val and Ronnie headed back to Ronnie's place, and Val slipped her hand into Ronnie's as they drove.

"So, Ronnie. Here's the thing. Tomorrow is my parents' anniversary. It's a little short notice, but would you like to come to dinner with Gwen and me?"

"And meet your parents?"

"Yes, but no pressure. All casual, not a big meet the parents thing."

"I'm trying to be more organized this semester and return assignments within a week."

"Good for you."

"I scheduled three hours for marking on Sunday night." She'd thought it would be stressful organizing her time more, but it turned out to be less stressful because she somehow had time for all her tasks.

"That's okay, sure. Another time."

There was no mistaking the disappointment in Val's voice. "I could do the marking tonight, but that only leaves me a couple of hours at Poplarcreek after today's lesson."

"You know Callie's going to invite you to stay for a barbecue."

Ronnie grimaced. "Help me work out the timing." Being organized was great, but it was still unfamiliar territory.

Val's smile lit up her face. "We'll go to the barn after the lesson and two hours later, you go home. I'll keep Dover and Barney so they can play with Max. Later, I'll bring you the dogs and dinner from the barbecue and then Gwen and I'll go home and prepare our meals for the week."

"So, Gwen won't be staying at Poplarcreek?"

Val grinned. "She could. She loves it there. Could you pencil me for some time this evening?"

"How about at seven ten for forty minutes?"

Val slapped Ronnie's knee. "Do better."

"Bring dinner at eight and don't go home."

Val smiled. "I like that."

Ronnie started to cough.

"You okay?"

"Just a little dry." Ronnie focused out the window of the moving car and watched the landscape fly by. It had just sunk in that she was having dinner with Val's parents. She was meeting Val's parents. Val's perfect mom. What would she think of her? How much had Val told her? She concentrated on her breathing. Maybe she should take up meditation and calm down? Val said it was no pressure. No pressure for Val, but she was the perfect daughter of the perfect mother. Ronnie hadn't been taken home to meet anyone's parents since her undergrad years. Suddenly, she felt like the hinges she'd removed from her gate. Old, tired, rusty, and a little cracked.

CHAPTER THIRTY-TWO

Ronnie rolled over and snagged the book off the table beside her bed. She read a page three times and then gave up. She'd been trying to read since Val left twenty minutes ago.

It was meet the parents day, and for a second, she considered running. She needed an activity or a project to get her mind off it. Not to mention she couldn't stop thinking about how good Val had felt against her when she'd woken up with her in her arms again. She could always review her English lessons for tomorrow, but the idea fell flat.

She leaped out of bed and pulled on her cycling clothes. She'd scheduled cycling for the morning, and a good bike ride hadn't failed her yet. She headed downstairs and let Barney and Dover out while she ate breakfast.

When her phone buzzed, she glanced at the texts, hoping for one from Val. It was Irene suggesting they work with the horses today. Ronnie arranged to meet her at the barn and hopped on her bicycle for a short ride that would bring her to Poplarcreek.

Ronnie headed into the barn and switched into boots and coveralls. She slowly approached Bella's stall. There was a new name plate sitting by the entrance. It said *Bella and Buddy*. The girls had been busy. She was glad they'd left it for her to put up. She didn't want Bella disturbed. "Hello, Bella. How's Buddy today?" Buddy moved awkwardly on her spindly legs.

Bella walked over and Ronnie patted her. She got a quick peek at the foal, but Buddy was shy and hiding behind her mother. She talked softly until the foal stretched out her neck to tentatively touch Ronnie's hand with her nose.

"How're they doing?"

Ronnie jumped at the unnecessarily loud volume of the question. Buddy scurried behind Bella and Bella backed up. "You could have seen her if you'd been quiet. Now Buddy's hiding." Irene was a loud talker, probably because she thought what she had to say was so important that everyone should hear her.

Irene stepped into the opening of Bella's stall. Bella focused on Irene and pawed the ground with her front foot. "I can see her back there. Nice foal. Squirrelly mare." Irene backed out and closed the stall door. "Let's get to work."

They worked with Frieda. She was still young, but not as nervous as when she'd first come to Poplarcreek. She did have her favorites though. Ronnie could walk right up to her, but she shied away from Irene. It didn't matter because for the most part Irene was directing Ronnie. She was being trained as well as Frieda, which meant one day she might be able to do what Irene did, so they wouldn't need her.

After Irene left, Ronnie groomed Frieda, put up the new name plate, and then cycled home. She was a little tired from the day, but her stress level was lower. It was only dinner with Val's parents. It wasn't like she was meeting the Queen.

At home, Ronnie showered and changed. She picked her good black jeans, a button-down shirt, and a charcoal gray jacket. She experimentally buttoned the jacket. She wouldn't wear it buttoned, but she liked the idea that she could. It had been a project and a half, but she'd replaced all the missing buttons on her dress jackets. It was nice to have choices.

Shortly after five, she knocked on Val's front door.

Gwen opened the door. "Hi, Ronnie, Mom's almost ready."

"Hey, Gwen, you look pretty."

Gwen blushed. "It's my new dress for summer. Mom said I could wear it tonight."

Val walked into her front hall. "Hi there. Zip me up?" She turned her back, and Ronnie grazed her fingertips down the length of Val's spine as she zipped it up. "Go get your shoes, honey," Val said to Gwen.

After Gwen left Val leaned in and kissed Ronnie soundly. She brushed her hands down the front of the jacket, making sure she grazed Ronnie's nipples on the way. "I like this jacket."

"Stop that, you. There are children present." Ronnie stepped out of reach of Val. "I don't have anything to give your parents."

"Gwen and I got them a present and I picked up a bottle of wine they like. You can give the wine to them."

Ronnie was going to suggest that next time Val just tell her the brand to buy, but she let it drop. She was nervous enough and one less thing to do was probably better. This was Val being kind.

Val tilted her head to the side. "I like that shirt."

"But?"

"It has a few wrinkles. You break your iron?"

Ronnie laughed. "I don't have an iron. I had one in Winnipeg, but I kept packing it and moving it without ever using it. I finally gave it away."

"Okay, give me your shirt." Val held out her hand.

"No, it's fine." Ronnie tried to laugh it off.

"You're meeting my parents for the first time. You'll want a pressed shirt. My dad's will be." Val bit her lip. "Please."

Ronnie looked into Val's eyes. She was nervous too. Apparently, it was a big thing to meet her parents after all. Probably would have been easier to meet the Queen. "Okay." Ronnie headed into the bathroom. She removed her shirt and pulled her jacket back on, buttoned it, and then she exited and handed Val her shirt.

She followed Val into her bedroom where the ironing board was set up. Val ironed the shirt, moving it quickly and expertly until the only creases were the ones she meant to be there. "That's better." She handed it back to Ronnie.

Ronnie returned to the bathroom and winced as she pulled the hot shirt on. She turned to admire herself in the mirror. She looked sharp in a pressed shirt.

"Hurry please, Ron."

Ronnie slung on her jacket and darted out of the bathroom. She stood patiently while Val used a sticky roller to remove the dog hair from her jacket and pants. Ronnie was relieved that she'd polished her shoes or Val would have taken those too. When Val was satisfied with everyone's appearance, they headed outside, jumped in Val's car, and drove to her parents' house. Ronnie was certain there'd be sweat marks on the back of her shirt, given how nervous she was. No one spoke, and the tension was killing her.

Gwen leaped out when they arrived and ran inside.

Ronnie rubbed her sweating palms on the legs of her jeans. The front of the house was immaculate, like something from a rural living catalogue. There were decorative chairs on the front porch and the lawn was mowed and edged. "Did your dad use a ruler to edge the lawn? It's so straight." She'd had a postage stamp lawn as a kid, and they'd trampled it so much it never needed mowing. What planet was this?

Val shrugged. "I never noticed. Let's go."

Ronnie shook her head, panic welling in her chest. She didn't belong in this world.

"It's okay, Ronnie. They're nice people." Val kissed her cheek. "I would never do anything to embarrass you."

"This is a bad idea." Ronnie felt her pulse in her wrist. It was racing. Was she about to have a heart attack? If only she had a joint, just a small one or a couple of puffs to calm her. Maybe a drink? A couple of shots?

"It's not a bad idea. It'll be fine. I won't embarrass you, but I make no such promises for Gwen. You're her schoolteacher and her riding instructor."

"And soccer coach."

"And soccer coach." Val kissed her softly. "Come on, honey. I'll take the wine. Can you bring the gift, please? It's nonbreakable."

"Oh, you're funny. A scream a minute." Ronnie grabbed the wrapped gift and followed Val to the front door.

They entered the house and Ronnie was introduced to Helen and Andrew Connor. She opted to let Andrew hang her jacket up. Her shirt was too nicely pressed not to show off. Besides, Andrew wasn't wearing a jacket and his shirt was also ironed.

She handed the bottle of wine to Andrew as Val gave the present to her mother. "Happy anniversary," Ronnie said.

She took the beer Andrew offered and then perched on the edge of the armchair. She picked at the label and looked toward the kitchen for Val, willing her to come back, but she'd disappeared with Gwen and her mother. For a second, Ronnie thought she was in a 1950s movie, sitting with her girlfriend's father and expecting him at any moment to ask her what her intentions were.

Ronnie focused on Andrew. He was smiling. Somewhere in the dictionary beside the word average was a picture of Andrew Connor. Brown graying hair. Not fat, but not skinny. Tall, but not overly so.

"What's your plan?" Andrew asked.

Ronnie sipped her beer to stall and then coughed when it went down the wrong way. It was happening. He wanted to know what a pothead was doing with his perfect daughter. She floundered for an answer. "Date some more. Get to know each other."

"Date?" Andrew smiled. "I was asking about the horses."

Ronnie didn't blush, but she went cold. She'd missed something. "The horses?"

"Val and Gwen praise your abilities with horses. I used to ride a lot when I was younger, so I was curious."

"You're welcome to come and watch Gwen at her lesson some time." Ronnie told Andrew about each of the rescue horses. He asked intelligent questions, and twenty minutes later, she found herself relaxed, leaning back in her chair and laughing about some misadventure he'd had on horseback in his twenties. It shouldn't have surprised her that he'd set out to put her at ease. It was exactly what Val had done.

When dinner was ready, they sat to eat. Helen Connor was as sweet as Val. A little taller and with brown hair, but they had the same laugh. Val had probably grown up listening to her mom laugh. What must that have been like?

Andrew smiled fondly at Val and Helen and Gwen and called them his best girls. Ronnie warmed to the family scene, but it was like being abducted by aliens. It was like nothing she'd experienced before. Could families really be this happy? Could Val's parents really be as pleased with her as they were? Her father and mother said several times how proud they were of Val and Gwen.

Ronnie's father had been proud of her riding abilities, but her mother had never commented except to tell Ronnie she smelled of manure. She was a little envious, but happy for Val and pleased to be included in the happy scene. Would her father still be proud of her if he were here? She pushed the melancholic thoughts away. This wasn't the time for that.

Ronnie dug into her dinner. The potatoes were served chunked with butter and herbs. She grinned and bet herself that each piece was the same size. "This is delicious, Mrs. Connor."

"Call me Helen, please. The potatoes are Valerie's recipe. She experimented with the seasoning and it's perfect."

"Just trying to follow your example," Val said.

Ronnie paused with her fork halfway to her mouth. She glanced at Val's parents but everyone was peacefully eating. It wasn't a dig, just a comment.

Helen laughed. "Valerie, you're better than me. At your age I was still smoking. Only two or three a day. But I was still hooked on nicotine."

Gwen stared at her grandmother. "Do you still smoke, Grandma? Mommy says it's bad."

"Your mom's right, and no, I don't. Gave it up years ago, before your mom was born."

"And she never smoked the bad stuff," Andrew said to Gwen.

Ronnie lowered her fork and caught Val's eye. Val was blushing and subtly shook her head.

"I never would," Gwen said.

Ronnie shifted, uncomfortable with the new topic.

"So, Dad, Mom tells me you're fishing next weekend," Val said quickly changing the subject.

"Me and a couple of the guys from work. Do you fish, Ronnie?"

Ronnie took a large sip of water to loosen her tongue. "Not in years. I used to fish with my dad."

"Val told us he's gone. I'm so sorry," said Helen.

"Thanks." Ronnie continued to eat and participate in the conversation about the best places to fish in Saskatchewan and Manitoba. Val's parents didn't interrogate her about her background, which was what she'd expected. Instead they talked about horses, pets, dogs, soccer, and school.

Helen was particularity impressed that Ronnie had rescued Barney. "Dillon's not a bad boy, but he's not patient with animals."

Ronnie smiled. Dillon had smacked her in the face, but she let it go. If Val hadn't told them, then she wouldn't. "Barney's great and he's settled in really well with Dover. I like that Dover has company because I have to leave him alone so much."

The rest of the evening passed uneventfully, and after dinner they headed back to Val's house. Gwen was sent in to get ready for bed since there was school the next day.

Ronnie kissed Val. "Thanks, I had fun. I like your parents."

"I'm glad and I can tell they liked you."

"I'm relieved." She kissed Val again. "Good night."

"Don't go. Can you stay and talk for a bit? I'd like to make sure you're okay."

"I'm fine." It wasn't true. She was out of sorts and feeling less-than, but Val didn't need to know that.

Val took her hand and led her around the back to the garden bench. "I could see you were uncomfortable, and I'm really sorry."

"Bottom line is to stay away from pot, then there can never be a problem." Ronnie kissed Val again. "I have school tomorrow as well." She didn't mention that she had an hour of work to do before bed. She'd planned to prepare for her lessons, but she'd spent too much time with Irene at the barn. She didn't need to give Val another reason to think she wasn't good enough.

"Are you sure, you're okay?"

"I'm positive. Thanks again. I'll call you tomorrow." She kissed Val and strode away. The garden bench in the dark with Val was tempting, but not if Val just wanted to pick the evening apart. It had been okay. She'd had fun and Andrew and Helen liked her. She shook her head. She'd spent an evening with the perfect family that made hers look even more dysfunctional.

How were they ever going to tell the Connors that Ronnie had been a drug addict? Never, was the answer. They couldn't. It would cause a rift, and she wasn't willing to be the cause of it.

But it was part of who she was, of the person she'd been. She didn't want to be ashamed of her past and have to hide it, even if she wasn't necessarily proud of it. So where did that leave them?

Chapter Thirty-three

Val closed the curtains in Ronnie's living room. They had the evening to themselves. Gwen was at a birthday party and sleepover.

After finishing the delicious dinner Ronnie cooked, they'd cleaned up the kitchen and moved to the living room. Ronnie was perusing her collection of movies. "What do you feel like?"

"Not a movie." Val had other ideas and kissed her with all the pent-up passion building inside her. She planted a series of kisses along Ronnie's chin. A movie dropped from Ronnie's limp hand to the floor.

Val's lips glided over her neck as Ronnie caressed her shoulders. She slid her hands over Ronnie's skin under the collar of her shirt and pushed the edges apart to expose her throat. She kissed her way down Ronnie's chest, popping one button at a time. Ronnie's hands combed Val's body from her back to the curve of her waist and down to her ass.

Val moaned with pleasure when she discovered Ronnie wore a simple black silk bra, a delicious change from the utilitarian sports bra. She lifted Ronnie's shirt off her shoulders and dropped it on a chair, then slid her hands over Ronnie's stomach and sides. Never had she made love to a woman who displayed such perfect muscle definition. She had made love to thin women, but never one as fit. She found it exciting and shivered as she unhooked Ronnie's bra and it dropped to the floor. Val grinned as she kneeled and popped the button of Ronnie's jeans as she rubbed her cheek against the smooth skin of

Ronnie's torso and looked up into dark, luminous eyes dilated with desire. "Should I stop?"

In answer, Ronnie rested her hands on Val's head and closed her eyes.

Val smiled and moaned in appreciation as she slid her fingers under the waistband of Ronnie's jeans and stroked her perfect ass. She smoothed the jeans down Ronnie's legs and admired the well-defined muscles of strong thighs and calves. Ronnie stepped from her jeans and Val tossed them on a chair to discover skimpy black panties to match the bra. She leaned back to admire the view.

Ronnie squirmed under the scrutiny and reached for her. Val raised her arms to allow Ronnie to remove her top. She craved Ronnie's skin against hers. When Ronnie tried to unclasp Val's bra, she pressed Ronnie against the closed door to the spare bedroom.

Ronnie's breath caught. "Should we go to bed?"

Val shook her head. "Now. Here." She grinned as Ronnie stepped from her panties.

Ronnie caressed Val's shoulders and sifted her hair between her fingers.

Val kissed and caressed Ronnie's stomach and the inside of her thighs. Ronnie groaned and rested her back against the door. Val dragged a low stool close and lifted Ronnie's leg, directing her left foot to the top of the stool. She longed to spread Ronnie open to her eyes, to her tongue, and to her roving fingers.

"Oh, Val, oh, honey."

Honey was right. Val drank in Ronnie's sweet scent and scanned the wonders uncovered. She was perfect.

"Val…" Ronnie grasped Val's head and brought her in close.

Val circled her slit with the tip of her tongue and then abandoned it to lavish attention on her lips.

Ronnie's hands closed in Val's hair. She removed Ronnie's hands and placed them on the doorjamb. Some women needed to grasp something as their orgasm built, but now she demanded control and refused to have her head held. She wanted to do this her way.

Ronnie cooperated and sucked in her breath as Val's tongue glided inside her. She drank in the wetness and swirled her tongue into Ronnie's hot softness.

Ronnie moaned and her knees buckled. "Need down."

Val smiled as the English teacher's grammar departed.

Ronnie gasped. "I no up, no longer."

"But you must."

Ronnie chuckled and gripped the doorjamb harder.

Val continued her probing. She pressed her lips against Ronnie's clit and reveled in her sexual pulse. She explored Ronnie with her tongue, taking her time.

Ronnie's knee trembled with the effort it took to stand with all her weight on one leg. "I can't."

Recognizing Ronnie had reached her limit, Val rose to her feet. She stretched Ronnie, stomach down, over the back of the couch, then she glided in behind and thrust gently into her. One-handed, she unhooked her own bra and lowered her chest until her breasts skimmed the perfect body beneath her. She kissed Ronnie's back and nibbled her hard flesh. She pushed two fingers inside Ronnie's wetness as she spread her legs wider in invitation.

Ronnie collapsed over the back of the couch and rocked back against her fingers. Val adjusted her thrusts to match Ronnie's movements. As she thrust, her breasts glided over Ronnie's back now slick with sweat. Painfully aroused, Val thought she might orgasm just from enjoying Ronnie. That was all right as long as Ronnie crashed first.

"Now, please," Ronnie said.

Val ignored the request and kept thrusting. "Are you enjoying this?"

"Don't stop. Please."

Ronnie's breath shot out in loud gasps when Val moved her fingers to thrust at a different angle. She could tell by the moisture dripping off her hand that Ronnie was close. She adjusted her thumb to rub against Ronnie's clit with each thrust.

Val nipped Ronnie on the shoulder as Ronnie was about to come. The bite was painful enough to distract her so that Val got to thrust into her and rub while Ronnie's orgasm built again. A minute later, Ronnie let go with a cry, arching and calling out Val's name. She slipped her fingers out and lay bent over her, their slick skin pressed together as they both began to breathe regularly again.

After a few minutes, Ronnie straightened and turned. She cupped Val's face and kissed her. "Wow. That was unexpected and very sexy."

Val pressed her body against Ronnie's. "Glad you enjoyed it."

"I have one question." Ronnie scanned Val from top to bottom. "Why're you still wearing clothes?"

"I'll take care of that." Val dragged off her skirt and panties and stood naked in front of Ronnie. "I'm on the edge. I need you to finish me."

"Meet me in the bedroom in three minutes."

"What?"

Ronnie smiled and dashed upstairs as Val stood with her mouth open. She waited two minutes and rushed after her.

Val opened the door to a dark room except for a light in the corner set low. The base of sexy music pulsed against the soles of her feet. She discerned the shapes of furniture in the room but not Ronnie. A second later, hands caressed her shoulders.

"Nothing has to happen you don't want to happen." Ronnie pressed against Val's back.

Val's breath caught, and she whispered, "How do you want me?"

"Wouldn't you like to decide that?"

"No."

Ronnie walked forward and propelled Val to the end of the bed. Ronnie slid her arm around Val's waist, and with the other hand in the middle of her back, nudged Val's face toward the mattress. Val was bent with her head down and ass in the air. She spread her legs in expectation and trembled when Ronnie parted her. "You're dripping wet."

"Ronnie, please. Don't make me wait." Ronnie slowly filled Val with a dildo. Sliding in an inch, pulling out, and then sliding in farther. Val longed for this. She was desperate for Ronnie to take her fully, to make her cry out. Her hips bucked to meet Ronnie as she plunged into her. Their speed increased until Ronnie met each backward motion with a thrust. "Oh, Ronnie, you feel so good inside me." She moaned. "Yes, yes," Val called as her orgasm built.

Ronnie withdrew. "I need to see your face. To be closer."

Val crawled onto the bed and lay on her back. She smiled as Ronnie slipped between her legs. Ronnie kissed her lips and eyes.

Val spread her legs, not as an invitation but as a demand. She raised her knees as Ronnie slid the dildo into her again. Ronnie was right. This was better. She could now reach Ronnie to caress her face and back. Ronnie had drawn her close to an orgasm, then dropped her, and now brought her back to the edge. Val bit her lip.

"I want to hear you."

Val moaned as she pitched over the edge, letting her passion explode in the cries she couldn't have held in if she tried. She pulled Ronnie on top of her and wrapped trembling legs around her. She relished the pressure on her abdomen and Ronnie still inside her.

Ronnie slipped her hand between them to circle Val's clit. It didn't take long and Val crashed again.

"You're breathtaking. How many orgasms can you have?"

Val squeezed her legs around Ronnie's waist. "I want..."

"What do you want? I'll do anything."

Val pushed Ronnie onto her back and straddled her. She rose high on her knees and lowered herself onto the dildo. Val's eyelids slammed shut in ecstasy as she took all of Ronnie in again and rode her. "Thrust into me." Ronnie drove into her and Val moaned in approval.

She circled her own clit with two fingers, but Ronnie pushed Val's fingers away.

"More," Val demanded. She groaned and cursed as she rode Ronnie hard. She'd not felt this wonderful in years, if ever. When Val's fingers splayed over her clit, again, Ronnie's fingers pushed in to take their place. Ronnie circled and tugged. Val rode Ronnie until she came with a scream of deep, gratifying ecstasy.

Spent, Val rested her hands on either side of Ronnie. She panted and slumped, exhausted, onto her side of the bed. Ronnie undid the harness and dropped it beside the bed before taking Val in her arms.

"Wow. That was amazing."

"You're amazing."

Val kissed her. "Thanks."

"You're so exciting. You're so beautiful. You're so...everything."

Val blushed as she curled against Ronnie. She dropped light, lazy kisses on Ronnie's chest as her heart surged with satisfaction and contentment. In Ronnie's arms, she had come home. She had found peace and caring. She didn't know what next month or next year would bring, but for the moment, she didn't care. That could wait. For now, she wanted to sink into the feeling of this being exactly what she wanted.

CHAPTER THIRTY-FOUR

Ronnie jogged downstairs when someone rapped on her front door. Maybe Val had come back. She'd said this was her Thursday night to work, but plans changed.

Ronnie pulled open the door with a flourish. "I'm glad you're back."

Irene pushed past Ronnie into her house. "You're crazy." Irene laughed. "Thought you were going to kiss me, and I don't play for your team." Irene dropped onto the couch. "I'd never play on the losing team."

Ronnie summoned every ounce of nonchalance her body possessed. She dropped into her armchair and slung a leg over the arm. "Why losing?"

"Cause your lot is outnumbered."

"Whatever."

Irene laughed. "You know, cause you're ten percent. Get it?"

Ronnie ignored the ridiculous conversation and moved on. "So, what's up? Didn't expect to see you tonight."

"Passing through on my way home from Winnipeg."

"You go to see your parents?"

Irene cackled. "Only if I had a shovel. They're dead. Nah, dropped in on my little sister to see the new baby. She's really happy. Her husband's a good guy and they have three kids now." Irene shrugged. "I don't get why she wants a house full of brats, but that's her call."

"I like children."

"Let's go to the barn and check on the horses. I want to see how much the foal's grown."

"You saw her four days ago." Ronnie smiled at the eagerness in Irene's voice. Human babies and children didn't interest her, but a foal and she was all over it. "Okay. The foal's called Buddy and I could use a break."

"From what?"

"I was grading papers."

Irene leaned back and laughed so hard she started to cough. "You hated school. Never did your homework. Now all you have is homework."

Ronnie closed her eyes and counted to five. Irene was being an extra pain tonight. She wished she'd never answered the door. "I'll just go up and change."

"Okay if I grab a soda?"

"The fridge is yours. Anything you want."

Ronnie jogged up the stairs, not surprised Irene hadn't thanked her. She summoned another nonchalant shrug and changed into a T-shirt and jeans.

When she returned, Irene was standing in her living room eating a sandwich and dropping crumbs everywhere. The dogs would clean it up.

"Where's Dover?"

"Upstairs," Ronnie said.

"Thought I saw him under the table, but it's a yellow dog. You get another old mutt?"

"That's Barney." Ronnie walked over to the table. Barney was curled under the table with his head under a chair. He was scared, probably of Irene's loud voice. She opened the patio door and he trotted outside. She listened for Dover, but he didn't come. He probably didn't want to walk past Irene. When Barney was done, he came back in and settled under the table. It bothered her that her dogs were unhappy. She needed to tell Irene to meet her somewhere else from now on.

"Let's go." Ronnie followed Irene to her truck, and they headed to Poplarcreek. Ronnie texted Callie and her reply was brusque. There'd be no welcome this afternoon.

"Hey, Callie. Here we are again." Ronnie entered the horse barn with Irene following.

"Hey, Ronnie. Irene," Callie said.

"I'm staying with Ronnie tonight. Nothing like great cooking and good company."

"Oh?" Callie focused on Ronnie as she spoke. "A good cook, eh?"

"What?" Ronnie stared at Irene. There'd been no invitation and she'd never cooked for Irene, nor did she want to.

"She's a great cook." Irene grabbed Ronnie's hand and pulled her toward the end of the barn. "Time to get to work. Let's have a look at Bella and Buddy first. We'll get Buddy's halter on her," Irene said.

Ronnie frowned. She'd said she wanted to see the foal, nothing more. Still, they were already there so they might as well do something.

Ronnie hooked a lead on Bella and led her into the walkway. Buddy pranced after her.

"You hold Bella, Callie. Ron, you help me."

Ronnie cradled Buddy against her body and Irene approached with the halter. An instant later, Bella pushed between Irene and Buddy.

"Stop, Bella, honey," Callie said. "Sorry, I thought I had her."

"Let's try again." Irene moved to the other side of Ronnie and reached toward Buddy with the halter. Bella pushed in again, this time knocking Irene back a step.

Callie stroked Bella's neck. "She mustn't want the halter on Buddy."

"It's not her choice," Irene said.

"But Buddy's only five days old," Callie said. "Is this necessary?"

Bella pushed between Irene and Buddy again and Irene raised her hand to slap Bella, but Ronnie jumped in the way and the slap meant for Bella landed on Ronnie's shoulder.

"Callie, put Bella in her stall if you can't control her," Irene said.

Ronnie glanced at Callie and caught the look of annoyance in her eyes, but she followed directions. "Okay, okay. And there's no need to slap Bella," Callie said. "She's just a scared mom."

"Irene, we don't hit the horses at Poplarcreek," Ronnie said quietly as she rubbed her stinging shoulder.

"Whatever."

When Irene approached Buddy again, the kicking and angry whinnying started. Bella thumped repeatedly against her stall and tossed her head in agitation.

Callie put her hands over her ears. "Bella's too upset. We can't do this."

"Some mares are just fussy about their foals," Irene said as she snugged the halter on Buddy.

Bella pounded against the wall of her stall so hard that Ronnie felt the vibrations. "This is no good. She'll hurt herself."

"She has to learn."

Ronnie shook her head. "Stop. Now!" She slipped the halter off and walked Buddy to Bella's stall. Callie was ready and opened the door for Buddy to run in. The mare immediately calmed down as she ran her nose over Buddy, checking for injuries.

"Why'd you do that?" Irene asked. "Buddy needs to get used to a halter."

"Do you need my help anymore?" Callie asked.

"Nope, we're okay." Irene shrugged, looking irritated.

Callie studied Ronnie with one eyebrow raised. "Ronnie? Do *you* need my help?"

"I've got this."

"Okay, I'm with the cattle if you need anything." She strode away.

Ronnie studied Bella, pleased to see that the mare had calmed down and Buddy was happily nursing. "That was bad."

Irene laughed. "You're out of practice. You've gone soft. Remember mares are odd about their foals. Bella's just being protective. She'll calm down when Buddy's older."

"But it's extreme behavior. She hasn't behaved like that before."

"Never mind. Let's get Frieda out."

Ronnie glanced once more at Bella, then shook her head and followed Irene. Irene was standing at Frieda's stall and the filly was circling in agitation. Ronnie sighed. Another female who didn't like Irene. It was time to put an end to this. "Irene, wait. That's enough for tonight."

"But we've been here like ten minutes. Come on." Irene started to open Frieda's stall, but Ronnie blocked her.

"We're done. You're done. I'd like you to leave. I appreciate your help, but this isn't working anymore."

Irene's eyes narrowed and she crossed her arms. "You can't do it on your own. You're nothing without my help. You've been following me around since we were kids, leeching off me."

"I haven't even seen you in the last decade. Please go."

"You don't know shit about horses. You need me." She moved closer, invading Ronnie's space.

"Stop yelling and leave, now. Everyone's upset. The horses are upset."

"Upset? Who? Your dyke girlfriend? Miss Perfect?"

"Shut up and get out." Val's voice came from behind them and her tone brooked no argument.

Ronnie jumped and turned toward her.

"I'm here with Ron," Irene said.

Ronnie shook her head. "Go, please. And don't come back."

Irene threw her hands in the air. "All right, all right. You do it all and try not to get killed." Irene's scorn was obvious.

Ronnie stood between Val and Irene, figuring she was saving Irene's life. "Bye, Irene."

"I don't need friends like you. Don't need some dyke for a friend." Irene stomped out, slamming her hand against the door, and setting the horses off. Before the barn door closed behind her, she turned. "Oh, and, Val, don't let her near your daughter. She almost killed her sister's kids."

"Liar," Val yelled.

"Ask her." Irene sneered at Ronnie and left.

"She's such a bitch. I just saw Callie and she told me what Irene did to Buddy and Bella. Are they okay?" Val peered into the mare's stall. "Mama and baby look fine. Hi, Bella, sweetie." The mare snorted softly in greeting.

Ronnie stood still. She couldn't move. It was as if monsters had reached up from hell and were holding her feet in place. Irene's accusation was a punch to the gut.

"Ronnie? Baby?" Val kissed her and caressed her face. "You okay? Did Irene hurt you? Callie said she hit you." Val scanned her face. "Ronnie?"

"It was an accident. I'm not hurt." Ronnie stumbled to the end of the alley and collapsed on a bale of straw. She lowered her head, hid her face in her hands, and waited for her world to implode. Waited for Val to look at her with the loathing she'd only seen directed at Irene.

Val sat beside her and handed her a cold soda from the refrigerator in the tack room. "You're as white as a sheet." Val cupped Ronnie's face and looked into her eyes. "Baby? I'm sorry you lost a friend, but she's a jerk."

Ronnie turned away. She couldn't make eye contact. "I know." She gulped down the soda.

"And she's a shit and a liar. My gran would say, 'good riddance to bad rubbish.'"

Ronnie shook her head. "Not lying, or not completely."

"The comment about almost killing your sister's kids?"

Ronnie nodded and looked at Val. Val wasn't pulling away. She was holding Ronnie's hand. Her expression was deadly serious, but she wasn't running. Ronnie wanted to. She glanced at her feet. The earth hadn't opened, but she almost wished it would.

"Tell me," Val whispered.

Ronnie sipped the soda and began. "I was nineteen and high as a kite. I had my nieces in the car. They were six and seven. I ran a red light. I don't remember doing it, but the girls told their mom, and she told me to go home. I wasn't allowed to see them for a month." She'd yelled at her sister, not out of anger, but from fear because she'd come so close to killing her nieces.

"But you were only nineteen."

"A kid, but old enough. You're too kind. You don't have to cut me any slack on this one. I've been preachy about drunk drivers and then you find out I was driving high. It's just as bad. Could have killed the kids, or someone else."

"Was anybody hurt?"

"No."

"Did you do it again?"

Ronnie leaped to her feet. "No never. Not even close. I've never driven high since."

"Then it's in the past. We all make mistakes—"

"Not you. Not like this."

"No, I've never driven drunk or high, but I'm not perfect. I've let people down. I got pregnant when I was sixteen, remember."

"That's not a crime."

"My parents sure thought it was. Thought I'd bring the wrath of God down on them. They didn't go to church for a month after I told them."

Ronnie sat down and took Val's hand. "You never told me. They seemed so wonderful on Sunday. Supportive, proud, and caring."

"Oh, they are, but for that first month, whew. I thought they hated me and that would have been better."

"Better than what?"

"The disappointment. I'm their only child." Val smiled wryly. "Their perfect child. An A student and a cheerleader. I was going to be a doctor. The first one in our family, and then I let them down."

"I'm sorry."

"Me too. It's in the past now and they love Gwen. Everyone makes mistakes."

"You can still be a doctor. A veterinarian."

"Maybe." Val stood. "Are you done here tonight?"

Ronnie nodded.

"I'll get Gwen and we'll take you home. Do you have Dover and Barney with you?"

Ronnie shook her head. "I didn't think we'd be here long."

Val kissed her. "Back soon as I find Gwen."

Ronnie stared at her feet. Hell hadn't come up to claim her. Val had let her off, again. She glanced at the door Val had gone through. Hell hadn't found her, but an angel had. And she'd do everything in her power to be worthy.

CHAPTER THIRTY-FIVE

The next day, Val pulled into Ronnie's driveway to see Ronnie and Gwen getting out of the car in front of her. Val stepped from her car and got an immediate hug from Gwen.

"Hi, Mommy. Guess where we were?"

"Judging by the white box in Ronnie's hand I'd say you were at the bakery."

Ronnie stepped close and kissed Val on the lips. "You look stunning and you smell wonderful."

Val ran a finger down Ronnie's cheek to her chin. "You too. Thanks for bringing Gwen home from school."

"I'm going inside if you two are going to do that," Gwen announced.

Val laughed and backed away. "What did you buy?"

"We got a cake. It looks nice, but it won't be as good as yours," Gwen said.

"That's my girl." Val kissed Gwen on the forehead. "Thanks, honey, that's a sweet thing to say."

"You're welcome. Ronnie, can I let Barney and Dover out, please?" Gwen asked.

"Please do." Ronnie and Val laughed as Gwen darted through the front door calling for the dogs.

Val kissed Ronnie again and didn't care if the neighbors saw them. Didn't care if the whole world saw them. She followed Ronnie into the kitchen.

"How's your shoulder?"

"Shoulder?"

"Where Irene hit you yesterday." She wanted to stay the night with Ronnie but hadn't made arrangements for Gwen. She'd thought about her all night, though.

"I've had worse—"

"Falling off your bike. I get it. I can't believe you're cooking for us. We're so spoiled."

"You deserve to be spoiled. Besides, I like cooking and you've inspired me to do more of it. Look." Ronnie opened her freezer and proudly pointed to six plastic containers. "Leftovers. All ready for my next meal." She shrugged. "I kind of like having ready meals. If I remember to defrost them, they're as fast as pizza."

"And better for you."

Val moved in close against Ronnie and wrapped her arms around Ronnie's' neck. Ronnie slipped her hands under Val's ass and lifted her onto the counter.

Val broke the kiss and pushed Ronnie back a step. "Steady on. There are children present." She hopped down and straightened her shirt with shaking fingers. She did up two buttons and stared at Ronnie. "How'd you do that so fast?"

Ronnie shrugged. "Sorry, I got carried away."

"You're all right. Now, what're you feeding me?" Val opened the refrigerator and discovered four salmon steaks marinating in a glass tray. "Those look good."

"I got a new barbecue to complement my new tidier backyard. Callie said if I keep an eye on them, they won't get overcooked. I'll put the veg on first."

Gwen came in with Dover and Barney. "That was fun, but they want to rest. The new garden you and Mom planted looks great."

"Thanks. We had fun doing it," Ronnie said.

Val blushed. It had been a start and stop job as there'd been some rolling around in Ronnie's backyard that ended up with her on the bottom.

"Ronnie, do you have something I can read, please?" Gwen asked.

"Living room. Third shelf from the top. Help yourself."

"What've you got?" Val asked after Gwen left.

"Some of the classics, geared to kids mostly. I found them in the last box I unpacked."

"You're unpacked?"

"Yes, finally. I finished a week ago. Unpacked and here to stay."

Val smiled. It had been ages since she'd worried about Ronnie moving away, but it was nice all the same to hear she was settled in. "I'll go see what Gwen picked." She headed into the living room and stopped to pet Dover and Barney.

She spotted Gwen kneeling in front of the bookshelf. "What're you doing, honey?"

"I spilled Ronnie's little bag. It was sitting in front of the books and I knocked it off. It's really hard to pick up. Come here, Dover. Lick this up for me."

Val squinted at the substance on the floor. She moved in front of Dover. "Dover, go lie down."

Dover blinked at her, clearly startled by the sharp tone of her voice, but he crawled into his bed.

Val took a big book off the shelf and lay it over the spill. "Come with me." She took Gwen's hand and led her upstairs

"What's wrong, Mommy?"

"I just want you to wash your hands." She turned the water on and held Gwen's hands under as if she were three years old instead of nine. "Did you get any in your mouth? Touch that stuff and then touch your mouth?"

"No, Mommy. You came in just as I was starting to clean it up."

"Did the dogs get any?" She couldn't breathe past her anger.

Gwen's' eyes filled with tears. "Why're you so mad, Mommy? Barney and Dover didn't get any. I'm sorry I spilled Ronnie's little bag."

"Oh, honey." Val kneeled and pulled Gwen into her arms. "I'm not upset that you spilled it. It's just that I don't want you or the dogs to eat any."

"Is it poison?"

"You remember that movie we watched where those kids were smoking and sharing?"

"You said it was a joint."

"And joints are full of marijuana. I think that's a bag of marijuana you spilled. I didn't want any inside you."

"We should tell Grampa. He says it's bad stuff."

"I don't totally agree with Grampa on that, but I do want to talk to Ronnie about it. Can you take Dover and Barney outside again, please?"

"Okay, but we just came in and they're tired."

"Let's try." They headed downstairs and Val herded Gwen and the dogs outside.

"Hey, didn't they just come in?" Ronnie asked.

"Follow me, please," Val said and marched into the living room.

Ronnie stood beside Val at the bookshelf. "Is there something you disapprove of? I told Gwen to pick from the third shelf. The erotica is too high for her to see—"

"There certainly is something I disapprove of." Val tapped the book on the floor with the toe of her shoe. "Look under that."

Ronnie lifted the book, then dropped it, and backed away as if the book were on fire. "Why'd you bring pot into *my* house? I don't touch it anymore. I told you that."

"*I* didn't bring it. Gwen *found* it here." Val pointed to the bookshelf. "She said she knocked it on the floor by accident. I just came in and found my daughter picking up your poison with her fingers and just about to let Dover lick it up."

"It's not good for dogs."

"I know that and the dogs didn't get any. Why's it here? You told me you quit. Were you lying? Did you relapse?"

"It's not mine."

Val scowled at Ronnie. "Did Santa Claus bring it? The tooth fairy? It was on *your* bookshelf. I won't have that stuff around Gwen. And I won't be with an addict. A little is okay for most people, but you can't handle it. You said so yourself." She held her hand up. "I was okay when you were off it, but back on is a deal breaker. You know Gwen's going to tell my parents? I wouldn't disappoint them again, and you heard their thoughts on pot."

"Your parents don't know me. Stop trying to be like them. Be your own woman for once. Make up your own mind."

They turned as the patio door opened and Gwen entered with the dogs. "What's wrong, Mommy? You and Ronnie look upset."

Val struggled to soften her features but only managed a grimace. "Ronnie just remembered she has some work to do, so we're going home for dinner." Val wanted to scream. Now she was lying to Gwen. Her parents hadn't lied to her and she never lied to Gwen. Screw Ronnie and her stupid addiction and all her lies.

"No, Mommy, I want to stay."

"Let's go, Gwen." Val grabbed her purse and Gwen's hand and headed for the door.

"Take the cake," Ronnie said.

"You keep it. I don't want it." Val shot over her shoulder.

"Because it's not homemade? That's obsessive even for you, Miss Perfect. I don't need your organized nonsense in my life," Ronnie shot back.

Gwen tugged on Val's hand. "Ronnie had it made specially."

"Come on, Gwen." Val fumed, still stinging from Ronnie's criticism.

Gwen dug her heels in. "But I helped pick it out. It's a birthday cake for you."

Val rolled her eyes. She'd turned twenty-six on Wednesday and hadn't put two and two together when she and Gwen were invited to Ronnie's. She hadn't told Ronnie about her birthday, but Gwen must have.

She glanced at the book on the floor covering the marijuana and squared her shoulders. "Come now." Val frowned. "Gwendolyn Helen Connor, move it." She loaded a weeping Gwen into the back of her car. She hadn't wanted to upset Gwen, she just needed to get away from Ronnie and the disappointment sweeping through her. It had felt so real, so…right. Now she needed to get home and hide in her bed.

Ronnie approached her with the cake box. "Can I please give Gwen the cake?"

Val opened the back door of the car and Ronnie handed the box to Gwen. "Sorry, Gwen. I forgot about this work I'm supposed to do, and I'll be in trouble with the principal if I don't get it done."

"Got to do your homework. Mommy says."

"Your mom is right."

Gwen swiped at her nose. "I'm sorry I spilled your marijuana. That's why Mommy's mad at me."

Ronnie shook her head. "Your mom loves you more than anything in the world. She's not mad at you. She's disappointed in me for having that bad stuff in my house. She loves you."

Val listened to Ronnie console Gwen and felt the tears welling in her eyes. She needed out of there now. She liked Ronnie so much, but she had drugs around Gwen. Would she bring them into Val's house next? Had she already? Gwen must be protected. Val had reached the end of her patience and understanding. "Close the door please."

Ronnie backed up. "Sorry, Val, sorry, Gwen."

Gwen sniffled but held the box carefully. "Bye."

Val closed the door and turned just as Ronnie reached her front door. She'd never seen a more dejected sight. Maybe she should help Ronnie clean up? No, it was Ronnie's mess and her job to clean up.

Val climbed into her car and turned to focus on Gwen. "I'm sorry I upset you. I'm not mad at you."

"Ronnie explained."

"I love you, honey, and I'm sorry we don't get dinner with Ronnie." Val turned and gripped the wheel, trying to crush it. "We'll come back another time." She started the car and backed down the driveway. She doubted very much if she would be back. Dear God, she'd been driving Gwen around town. What if Ronnie were high now? Val shook her head. She certainly didn't seem high. She seemed…despondent.

When they got home, she went through the motions of making them some scrambled eggs and toast. She tried to eat, but the food caught in her throat.

"Should we do the cake now?" Val asked.

Gwen shook her head. "Can we wait for Ronnie please?"

Val nodded. She didn't feel like celebrating and couldn't have eaten a bite anyway. She tossed the leftovers in the trash and the dishes in the sink. She left Gwen watching television and headed into her room. She slipped off her clothes and crawled into her bed. Life sucked. She and Ronnie were getting along so well and finally building something and then wham, Ronnie trashed it all. She buried her face in her pillow and wept for what might have been.

Chapter Thirty-six

Ronnie sank to her couch and groaned. Immediately, Dover and Barney put their heads on her knees. She petted them both. "What just happened?"

Dover gave a quiet woof.

"You don't know either do you?" Ronnie glanced at the book lying on the floor. It was a coffee table book about veterinarians in practice around the world. She'd bought it for Val's birthday, but Val wasn't going to want it now. Val wasn't ever going to want anything from her again.

But where did the pot come from? She hadn't purchased it. Had she? Was she sleep-walking and buying drugs?

Dover sniffed around the book. "Stay away from that. Come here, boy."

He returned with a small paper bag in his mouth. Ronnie snatched it from him and peered inside. It was half full. She jammed the bag under her thigh and cupped Dover's face. She peeled back his lips and looked in his mouth for any sign of pot. Thankfully, there was none. "Good boy."

She extracted the bag and opened it again. It was hard looking at the stuff and the small whiff she caught made her head pound. She scrunched up the bag, wanting to throw it across the room. Her saner side told her that would make a bigger mess. She needed to get rid of it, now.

Ronnie stood and then sat again. "What was that?" She opened the bag and removed the scrap of paper, careful to shake the pot off into the bag. She jammed the bag back under her thigh and read the note.

Surprise. Have fun. I.

Irene fucking Schmidt. The bitch had brought pot *again*, and she'd probably left it there when Ronnie had gone upstairs to change. "But how come I didn't see it? Did you guys see it?"

Why had Irene done it? She'd told her half a dozen times she didn't smoke anymore. That she'd had a problem with it. Still, Irene had brought some and left it in her house. Did Irene want her to smoke again? Become an addict again? Live her life in a fog where finding money to buy more pot was all that mattered? A life where her education didn't matter, her health didn't matter, her girlfriend didn't matter, her family didn't matter and even where Dover barely mattered? No, it likely wasn't even that deep. She just didn't want to feel like Ronnie had left her behind. Irene couldn't stand the thought that someone might be better than her.

Dover sensed her pain and laid his head on her knee. She sank to the floor and pressed her forehead against his. She let the tears go. She didn't try to hold them back. Not anymore. Maybe if she let the pain go through tears she wouldn't want to smoke anymore?

Ronnie turned around and stared at the small bag. She wanted a joint so much. Just a small one, even just one puff and she'd be done. Surely after all this time she could handle it. And after Val's tirade she deserved it. She just wanted to numb the emotions she'd thought she could deal with, but evidently couldn't.

She tipped some out onto the scrap of paper with Irene's note and proceeded to roll it. It was a crappy joint, but she didn't care. Now all she needed was a lighter. Matches. She had matches. Ronnie sprinted into the kitchen. She'd been going to light candles at dinner, but she had another use for the matches now. She stuffed the joint between her lips and pulled out a match.

The joint dropped from her lips when she cried out. "Dover, what the hell? Did you just *bite* me?" She looked down at Dover. He was still holding her pants leg between his teeth. He'd never bitten anyone in his life. He hadn't bitten her hard, but it still hurt. She backed away from him and then caught her reflection in the window. It was a familiar sight from her past. She looked dead in the eyes and desperately unhappy. Tears ran down her face. She didn't look like a successful teacher. She looked like a scared teenager.

She stuffed the joint into the bag with the rest of the pot and then she dropped onto a kitchen chair. The pot would blot the pain out. Had wiped it from her mind and body for years. But at what cost? This time it had cost her Val. She shook her head to try to dispel unwanted memories, but they punched their way in anyway.

Before she'd given up pot, she'd only reacted one way to hurt and fear especially after her father died. Whenever she thought about her mother's rejection, she'd smoked. Whenever she pictured her father taking her fishing, she'd smoked. PhD down the toilet, she smoked. Relationship with a lover imploding, she smoked. Fear, fear, and more fear, she'd smoked.

But she'd been dealing with her fear, until tonight. She wasn't afraid with Val. But there was that moment when Val had called Gwen by all three of her names and Ronnie had flashed back to her mother, but didn't all parents do that occasionally?

With a deep sigh, Ronnie carried the bag to the toilet and flushed it. Joint, note, and all. Gone. She hurt. Hurt so badly it felt as if her heart were trying to dig its way out of her chest, but she wouldn't hide in marijuana. Not anymore. She headed into her bedroom and grabbed her cycling gear. A second later, she stopped and glared at the garments in her hands. Not anymore. She'd face the fear this time. She'd feel it. She wouldn't take her pain to the road and exercise it away. That was healthier than pot but not a solution for life. She needed to work this out, mentally and emotionally.

She dropped the clothes on the floor and sat on her bed. "Hi, buddy." Dover had followed her upstairs. She petted his head, then lay down and scooted to the side. "Come on. Up." She grabbed Dover around the shoulders and helped him crawl in. He settled, lying in front of her and she pulled him into a hug. She cried into his fur and cursed her bad luck with life, her bad luck with friends, and her bad luck with women.

After a while, she sat up, rubbing her head and blinking against the soreness of her eyes. The only proof she had that it was Irene's was in the note she'd flushed. Val wasn't going to believe the "it's not mine" story, clearly.

She scrambled to retrieve her phone from her pocket when it rang. "Hello? Val? Val? I'm so sorry. I—"

"Ron, dude, time out."

She lay down and curled around Dover. "Hey, T."

"You expecting Val to call? I can call another time."

"No, T, I'm not expecting Val to call ever again."

"Ron, what did you do? You sound like your world just came to an end."

Ronnie moaned. "It just did, or I'm hoping it's going to. T, will you look after Dover and Barney?"

"Fuck no! What the hell are you saying?"

"Sorry, sorry, not that. Life's never gotten that bad." She gave a half chuckle. "I was thinking of cycling to Vancouver. The boys might need a home for a while."

"It's thousands of kilometers, but you could do it. In stages. So, once again. Where's Val and what did you do?"

"Val found a bag of marijuana at my house. Correction, *Gwen* found it."

"Oh shit," Theresa said, stretching the word out to three syllables.

"Yeah, right? And Val was pissed."

"What're you doing with pot? Thought you gave it up? You know if you slip it doesn't have to be the end of the world. Just kick it again. You're strong. You can do it. I believe in you."

The tears started again. Ronnie swallowed several times until she could speak. "Thanks T, you're the best."

"No, you are."

"I haven't slipped, though. Irene left it in my house. She was over last night. I left her alone for like five minutes while I changed. She left this little bag of pot on my bookshelf, where Gwen found it tonight."

"Damn Irene. When're you going to dump her? She's bad news."

"The dumping is done. I sent her away from the horses last night. I can safely promise you never to speak with Irene again. We're done. What did Val say? 'Good riddance to bad rubbish.'"

"Glad to hear it. Now go tell Val."

"Can't. No proof."

"Proof?"

"Irene left a note, but I flushed it."

"Val will believe you."

Ronnie shook her head. "Don't know why she should." She kissed the tip of Dover's nose. "Dover saw the note. She'd believe him, but he can't communicate."

"He communicates just fine. It's English he struggles with."

Ronnie laughed sadly and then snuggled in with Dover. She and T made plans to talk again the following week, and she felt a little better. At least she had one friend left in the world.

She woke when Dover shifted. Her bedroom was dark, and Dover was trying to get off the bed. She helped him down and he plodded downstairs. She searched the bedding for her phone, grabbed it, and jogged after Dover. She found him and Barney at the patio door and let them out.

Ronnie sat at the kitchen table and rubbed her eyes, then wet some paper towels under the tap and headed into her living room. She picked up Val's book, carefully brushed it off, and returned it to the shelf. She used the damp towels to clean up the last of the pot.

She washed her hands, digging under her fingernails and scrubbing until her hands were red. She wanted every last bit of pot gone. Every hint of the scent of it gone. She did a final wash with Val's shower soap and held her hands to her nose. That was all she wanted to smell.

Ronnie returned to the kitchen. When the dogs came in, she fed them and then headed upstairs. She thought about getting on her exercise bike but felt too weighed down. She stripped off her jeans and slid into bed. When Dover returned, she helped him up and wrapped her arms around him. Barney lay on the floor by the bed and she petted his head. "You're a good boy too, but there's not enough room for three of us up here."

She lowered her head to the pillow and prayed for sleep to take her. She wasn't completely cured from her desire to run and hide. But tonight, she'd faced her emotions and let them run through her. She won against her addiction and become, at least a little, the person she wanted to be. Ronnie brushed fresh tears from her eyes. If only there was a way back to Val, life would be perfect.

CHAPTER THIRTY-SEVEN

Val spilled her purse as she tried to stuff it into her work locker. "Shit, shit, shit." She blinked to clear away the threatening tears. She'd woken up thinking about Ronnie on pot again and felt like she'd been crying ever since. Now she was forty minutes late for work and even her locker was being a pain in the ass. At least it was Saturday and they closed at two.

She jammed her purse in the locker and slammed the door. It was Margery and Christine all over again. How was she here again? Involved with the wrong woman. This time, though, it hurt deeper.

Val shuffled through the clinic and did her job on autopilot. She was thankful when the morning flew by in a blur of appointments and sick animals. Val concentrated on her job and only spoke when asked a question. She forced herself to be polite to everyone but spent no more time interacting with her colleagues than necessary. She had no energy.

Lauren motioned for Val to follow her into the room with all the cat kennels. "Are you okay? What's going on? Can I help?"

Val opened a kennel and petted a stray cat. "I'm fine."

"No, you're not. I'd like to help."

"I can't talk now. Later? Okay?" Tears filled her eyes and she blinked them away.

"Whatever you need." Lauren hugged her and left.

At lunchtime, instead of eating the yogurt and fruit she'd brought from home, Val cleaned the treatment room. One shelf at a time, she removed the equipment and drug bottles, then she washed the shelf and wall behind it and returned the items. When the pill bottles stood in tidy rows in alphabetical order, she turned them until the English side faced out. She stepped back to admire her work and wanted to laugh or cry, she wasn't sure. What a waste of time. The shelves had been cleaned two weeks ago and who needed the labels all straightened? She just managed to stop herself from flinging all the bottles onto the floor.

Forget Ronnie. She had good friends, great parents, a home to look after, and a wonderful child. Her life was full, just as it was. Ronnie Yakimoto was a complication she didn't need. Val's eyes stung with the many tears she'd yet to shed.

But it was torture being away from Ronnie. She loved her, and the thought surprised and depressed her. How had Ronnie let this happen? Why had Ronnie stomped on something so special?

Why wasn't she in bed with Ronnie now? She loved it when Ronnie scooted in behind her and snugged an arm around her waist. It was heaven to be in Ronnie's arms and there was nothing better on the planet than being held by the woman you loved.

After work, she avoided Lauren's questioning eyes and headed over to her parents' house.

"Hello, Valerie. What a nice surprise." Her mother kissed Val on the cheek and gave her a warm hug. Val sunk into the hug. Twenty-six or not, sometimes a girl just needed her mom.

"Hi, Mom. Dad here?"

Her mother shook her head. "He's fishing up north today. Remember? Is Gwendolyn with you?"

"I dropped her off at Poplarcreek. She has riding."

"Oh yes, she loves the horses and Ronnie seems like she'd be a wonderful teacher."

"Ronnie's awesome. Come and watch next weekend." Val sighed. "I'm rethinking my work schedule. I feel like I never see Gwen." A wave of guilt washed through her. Between work and spending as much time as possible with Ronnie, Callie and Lauren had practically been raising Gwen.

Her mother kissed her cheek. "You do look tired. You need to work less."

Val nodded. She didn't need to work less, she needed to sleep more. Last night it had been impossible to keep thoughts of Ronnie from her head. When she was lying in the dark, willing sleep to take her, she was at her most vulnerable and the tears came so hard she thought they'd never stop.

"Your father and I enjoyed meeting Ronnie last weekend. We'd like you to come again. Tomorrow maybe?"

Val shook her head.

"Well, you let us know when you're free."

Val collapsed into a chair and dropped her head in hands.

"Your eyes are red. Have you been crying? Can I help?"

Val didn't want to talk about Ronnie. Didn't want to see the pity in her parents' eyes. "We're over, Mom. We broke up." Val's voice cracked on the last word and she struggled to keep from crying. The only upside to having Ronnie gone from her life was the extra time she could spend with Gwen. Val rolled her shoulders and tried to get control of herself. Gwen needed a happy mother, not a sad and miserable one.

"Oh, honey, I'm so sorry." Her mother slid her chair closer and laid an arm across Val's shoulders. "We thought she was perfect for you."

"Perfect? Why perfect?" Val's eyes widened, and she stared at her mother, incredulous. How could her mother be positive when she was uncertain?

"She respects and admires you. Her eyes light up when she talks about anything you do. You're her hero. Did any of your other girlfriends look up to you? Respect you?"

Val shook her head. "I thought Ronnie was different from the rest. She seemed happy here, with me, but it doesn't matter now. She'll leave to finish her PhD or to teach school in Winnipeg."

"You told us she might leave, but that was when you first met. Ronnie never mentioned leaving to your father and me. She chatted about how great Thresherton was. It was her way of telling me she liked you but was too shy to say so. Look at her now. She owns a house and teaches school and riding. She's made new friends and now she's coaching soccer. She sounds like a woman who has a home." Her mom lifted Val's chin with two fingers and looked into her eyes. "Or wants one."

"Mom, am I a fool?"

"Valerie, dear, I don't approve of you putting yourself down and I would never use that word to describe you."

Val studied her mother and waited.

"I don't know what happened, but is it possible you misread signs and jumped to conclusions?"

Val cringed. She'd let her mom think she was worried about Ronnie moving. She'd never have the guts to tell her about the pot use or driving high with children in the car. "I'm not sure we suit each other. We're too different. She's messy."

"There're more to life than a tidy kitchen."

"You don't think that."

"I do, and people can change their habits."

Even if their habit was drugs? Val glanced at her phone. "Thanks, Mom. I should get going. I need to pick up Gwen." She hugged her mother and left.

Val dodged the invitation to dinner at Poplarcreek by saying she was ill. Gwen's shoulders drooped in disappointment. Gwen wanted to be with Becky every second.

"Can I visit Buddy before we go?" Gwen asked. "She belongs to me too."

Val winced. "Horses are expensive."

"Not here." Callie winked. "I have a horse barn with lots of feed and my own personal vet."

"You can visit Buddy, but then we need to go," Val said.

Gwen bolted out the door before Val could change her mind, quickly followed by Becky.

Callie squeezed Val's upper arm. "I'm sorry you're leaving. Do you have a headache? Would it help to rest in my spare room for an hour? I'll bring you soup or herbal tea." Callie leaned close to Val. "Or painkillers and a hot water bottle if that's what you need."

"No, thanks." Val was in pain, but it was nothing drugs would solve.

Callie studied her. "You've been crying. What's going on?"

Val sat at the table. "She's smoking pot again. Gwen found a baggie at her house last night."

"But a little pot—"

"But it wasn't a little when she lived in Winnipeg. It was all the time. It ran her life. What if it goes that direction again?" Val squeezed Callie's hand. "Sorry, Callie, it's just a big thing."

"What does your mom think?"

"They don't know. I don't want them to think poorly of Ronnie or be disappointed in me for exposing Gwen to her. It's a shame. They liked Ronnie a lot."

"And she's awesome, except for the pot."

Val nodded. "Except for the fucking pot."

Callie hugged her. "Then you have to let her go, if that's what you need to do. Look after yourself and Gwen first."

Val brushed at her eyes. "Thank God you get it. Gwen comes first. Before romance with Ronnie. I'd walk through a fire to save Gwen." It was true, but deep down she simply couldn't believe that anyone needed to be saved from Ronnie. Sweet, gentle, mischievous Ronnie, who flipped her world upside down and made her happy beyond reason.

Chapter Thirty-eight

"As I recall, you hate being offered a ride, but when I drove by twenty minutes ago, you were sitting here."

Ronnie squinted toward the voice and stared into beautiful blue eyes. Too bad they were the wrong blue eyes. "Hi, Callie. I fell."

Ronnie had fallen off her bike when she hit a pothole and now she sat at the side of the road nursing a scraped knee. She didn't know where she was. She'd been cycling for hours trying to run away from herself. It never worked for long. Sure, she could ride the fear away, but it always came back. Her mind had been spinning since Val left. How had something so wonderful crashed and burned?

Callie parked, exited her truck, and squatted by Ronnie. "Are you hurt? Did you break or twist something?

"Only scrapes, but I can't stand up." Ronnie grimaced as she rubbed her knees. Her leg muscles were seizing up. She needed to drink some water and move. "I rode too far today, and I'm wiped. Don't even know where here is." *Don't care where here is.*

Callie straightened, crossed her arms over her chest, and shifted her weight to one hip. Her scowl made Ronnie quake. She was a dead woman. The RCMP would discover her body in this ditch a week from now and she deserved it.

"Hmm, I see. Running away, were you?" Callie's arms dropped to her sides. "Val told me what happened, and I feel sorry for you. Addiction must be hard, but if you lose Val because of it, then you're a fool. Run toward Val, not away."

Ronnie stared at Callie. Callie really had no clue. It wasn't about the addiction. It was about not being good enough for Val, not fitting into her neat little world.

Callie contemplated Ronnie for a few seconds. "You're my friend, but right now I'm not sure if you need a hug or a hard shake."

"Probably both," Ronnie muttered.

"Come on then. Stand up." Callie dragged Ronnie to her feet. She gave her a hug and then with little care, shoved her into the cab of the truck. Ronnie winced when a loud clang announced that her racing bicycle had landed in the bed of Callie's rusty, dirt-encrusted farm truck. At least she hoped it was dirt.

Callie climbed in. "Wow. Your bike's light. Did you see me toss it into the truck?"

Ronnie grimaced and Callie chuckled.

"Need a lift home?"

Ronnie mumbled, "Thank you, as long as—"

"I wouldn't have offered if it was a problem."

Callie's voice held no softness the way it usually did. She was pissed.

"Well?"

Ronnie kept her helmet on to protect her head. Callie wasn't a violent woman, but just at this moment she didn't want to test her.

"You've been messing with one of the people I care about most in this world. Callie frowned. "I really thought you two were perfect together, but you blew it. Why are you smoking pot again? And why would you store it where Gwen might find it?"

Ronnie shook her head. "No...yes."

"Oh, that's a good answer. Well thought out and very articulate," Callie said sarcastically. They drove in silence for several minutes. "You don't have much to say do you?"

Ronnie hung her head. She had nothing to say. There was nothing to say that didn't sound like a teenager's excuse. "You wouldn't believe me anyway. Val doesn't. Why try?"

"There's no reason to lose Val. She and Gwen are an amazing pair, and you're lucky to have them. You must admit that your judgment is questionable. You were friends with Irene. It's clear now she can't be trusted."

How did Callie know about the pot Irene had left? "What do you mean?"

"It's obvious Irene can't be trusted to be nice to children or animals."

"I don't trust Irene. It was hers."

"What was?"

"The pot. She left it at my house right before that last visit when she was mean to Bella. She left a stupid note with it. I didn't know it was there." Ronnie groaned. "And then Gwen found it."

"Irene?" Callie almost spat the name. "So, you're not smoking?"

Ronnie shook her head with enough force to rattle her brains. "No, never again."

"Then tell Val."

"I did, and I flushed Irene's note with the pot."

"Val's unhappy too." Callie shook her head. "You two are so frustrating. I'm going to lock you and Val in my garden shed until you have an adult conversation and make up."

"There's no point. Val and Gwen are better off without me." Ronnie wanted to shrink into the seat. She fingered the door handle and contemplated leaping out when Callie stopped at the next corner.

"Do you love Val?"

Ronnie nodded. "More than I want to breathe."

"That shows some good judgment, at least. But I'm not going to tell her for you. And if you want her to know it was Irene's pot, you'll have to tell her."

They drove in silence until Callie delivered Ronnie home. Callie's parting words were good advice on any day of the week. "Don't be a fool, Ronnie."

Ronnie carried her bike inside and propped it against the wall, then she limped to her bedroom with Dover following. She stripped off her clothes and stood in a hot shower before pulling on a T-shirt and shorts and crawling into bed.

She pulled Dover into bed. It wasn't just about the pot. It was more than that. How could she be good enough for a woman like Val? Good enough for Gwen? She came from a different world than theirs, no matter what Callie thought. Ronnie groaned, picturing the scowl on Callie's face. There was no help there, but was locking them in the garden shed an empty threat? You could never tell with Callie.

She pulled Dover close and wrapped her arms around him. It was comforting. His soft fur and soothing heartbeats were calming. What would she have ever done without him? What would she do without Val?

Ronnie sighed as the tears came. "Sorry, buddy. Here we go again." She didn't want to be without Val. She loved her. Loved her so much she almost leaped out of bed and ran to Val's house. Her muscles tightened as if to eject her from bed, but her head won again. The fear came and drowned out her best intentions. Drowned out her future with Val.

Chapter Thirty-nine

Val kneeled in the garden and viciously attacked the weeds. There was no place for weeds in her yard. Her garden needed to be perfect. She would get the order back in her life if it killed her.

"Mom, those aren't weeds," Gwen said.

Val sat back on her heels and studied the green plants in her hand. They were wildflowers. She'd gotten some when they went looking for wildflowers for Ronnie's garden. Tears glided down her cheeks, and she impatiently brushed them away.

"You need some water," her mom said.

"I'm fine."

"I can see that." She squeezed Val's shoulders. "Let me fix that."

"I can do it."

"I know you can, my girl. You can do anything you want."

Val glanced at her mother and read only love and honesty in her eyes.

"I mean it. Now you need water and a rest. And where's your hat? Gwen's wearing one."

Val smiled at the gentle admonishment and looked at Gwen. She was wearing a white ballcap with *WCVM* on the front in green lettering. It was for the *Western College of Veterinary Medicine* where Gwen, and maybe Val, would go to school one day. Thoughtful as always, Ronnie had purchased it for Gwen and now she rarely took it off.

Ronnie was kind and generous. Looked out for everyone but herself and was now smoking pot and setting out to ruin her life again. Very soon she'd stop showing up for class and the principal would fire her. Starview would give up on her. She'd be arrested for possession and that would be it. If only she could help her. Save her.

Val shoved up from the ground and stood in defeat. Defeated by her garden and defeated by her traitorous heart. She couldn't fix this. Couldn't tidy Ronnie's problems away. No matter how much she cared about Ronnie, she couldn't save her from addiction or the consequences of addiction. It was up to Ronnie.

"Thanks, Mom." She grabbed a cold glass of iced tea from the house and dropped into a patio chair in the shade. Gwen and her mom were carefully repairing the carnage, digging holes, and rescuing the little wildflowers.

Val sighed. Her head wasn't into gardening today. She tucked an errant strand of hair behind her ear. The green hat Ronnie had bought her was in the bottom of her dresser. As if by burying the hat she could forget how much she hurt. "Stupid."

Her mom walked over and sat beside Val.

"Do you want a water, Mom?"

"No, thanks." She patted Val's hand. "I like your new flowers. They're very you."

"Wildflowers are me?"

"Yes, of course. You like nature and they're going to be even more beautiful next year when they're all flowering."

Val pointed to her side garden. "You don't like the annuals I planted?"

"Yes, I do. It's all lovely and it's all you. You're not one thing, honey. And you're allowed to change. Maybe next year you'll want more wildflowers and fewer annuals. You'll decide. Just give it a chance."

"Mom, do you still iron your sheets?"

Her mom laughed. "No, honey. I stopped that years ago. They just get wrinkled again. I iron pillow slips sometimes, but that's all."

"Ronnie doesn't own an iron."

"Fabrics are wonderful these days. All kinds of drip-dry. I don't iron most of your father's shirts anymore. Just for church or special occasions."

Val gaped at her mother. "You don't iron his shirts? What would your mom think? What would his mother think?"

"Don't know. Don't care. There's a point in life where you adjust your priorities and change things to live the way you want to, not the way your parents did. It's called growing up. Don't do anything just because I did or do. Do what you want."

Val contemplated that. She *would* do what she wanted. She'd been learning to since shortly after meeting Ronnie. Ronnie had helped her take a more relaxed and easy approach toward life. Val rolled her shoulders. She'd loosened up some of her standards and found she was happier. Sure, there were things in life where there was no compromise, like anything that protected Gwen and made her happy. But some things she could let go. No more ironing for one. She'd bake less, paint more of her house bright colors, and sometimes leave her dirty dishes sitting for a couple of days. And next year she would plant more wildflowers. She'd survive and so would Gwen. Nobody would say she was a bad mother because Gwen didn't have fresh baking and pressed sheets. She'd been so worried about what her parents might think that she'd failed to ask what they actually *did* think. Ronnie had been right; it was time to live life the way she wanted to and put all the what-ifs aside.

"Mom, could you stay with Gwen for a little while, please? I have an errand." She'd wouldn't give up on herself or Ronnie. There had to be a way forward.

"Happy to. We're going to garden a little longer and then head over to my house."

"Thanks."

"Anything I can do?"

Val shook her head. "I'm going to go see Ronnie."

She patted Val's knee. "That's wonderful. Good luck, honey." She stood and walked over to where Gwen was planting seeds.

Val followed and told Gwen the plan and then headed inside. After washing her face and changing her clothes, she jumped in her car and drove to Ronnie's house, practicing the things she wanted to say. She sat in the car for a few minutes and then knocked on Ronnie's door. She waited, but there was no answer. Maybe Ronnie was cycling? She knocked again and was about to turn away when the door opened.

"Hi, Val," Ronnie said.

Val forced a smile to her lips. Ronnie looked pale and disheveled and she stood leaning against the door as if she couldn't stand up on her own. "Hi, Ronnie. Can we talk?"

Ronnie pulled the door open and walked slowly away with one hand on the wall as if she couldn't keep her balance. Barney greeted Val for a petting and then sat at Ronnie's feet.

Val entered the living room and surreptitiously sniffed the air. It smelled a bit of dog, but nothing else. She perched on the edge of the couch and studied Ronnie, who was sitting in the armchair petting Barney who was resting his head on her knee.

"Where's Dover?" Val asked.

Ronnie shrugged. "Sleeping, I guess."

"How're you doing?"

Ronnie shrugged.

Val took a deep breath and launched in. "I want to help you, if you're ready. You're such a wonderful woman. So much more than your addiction."

"More?"

"You're warm and funny and smart and thoughtful. You really care about people and animals. You saved Barney and the horses. You're amazing with kids. You're sexy and kind and generous...." Val wanted to cry when tears slid down Ronnie's cheeks.

"Thanks."

"I'd like it if you took care of yourself too. Tell me what I can do to help you kick this once and for all."

"Do you think I'm a good person?" Ronnie looked at her, her head tilted.

"The very best. You just have one wrinkle in your sheets. Most of us do."

Ronnie smiled. "Not you. You iron them."

Val shook her head. "Not anymore. I haven't for two weeks and I'm not going to again." She raised her hand. "And I'm stopping because I want to, not because my mom stopped years ago."

Ronnie laughed. "Years ago? You thought she still was ironing sheets."

"Very true. But I don't have to be my mother or live up to my parents' standards. I'm my own woman and will be with who I want. And that's you."

"Me?" Ronnie barely whispered it.

"Yes, now tell me how to help you because I want you to put this behind you and be my Ronnie again. The fun, generous, happy Ronnie is the real you. Not this one." Val waved a hand around and took in Ronnie's appearance.

"You think I'm high?" Ronnie laughed. "I was asleep. I've seen you in the morning and you're not all pressed and perfect, either. I was out at five a.m. cycling and I went too far. Callie had to bring my carcass home." She rubbed her thighs. "I'm so sore I can barely walk. I'll be paying for this for a few days."

"Oh, I see." Val bit her lip, ashamed at her assumption.

"No, you don't. Val, I'm not smoking again. Irene left the pot here. Whether you believe me—"

"Of course, she did. That night you chased her out of the horse barn." Val leaped to her feet and paced. "She was here first. You drove to Poplarcreek together. She's been pushing pot on you all summer. What a bitch." Val dropped into the couch. "Why didn't you tell me?"

"I—"

"You tried that night and I wouldn't listen. Is that it?"

"I—"

"I'll kill her. Next time Irene comes to Thresherton I'll kill her. Did you want to say something?"

Ronnie held up her hands. "Irene's not coming back to Thresherton."

"I hope she figures things out in her life, but I don't want to see her again."

Ronnie nodded. "Me either. She had a rough childhood and never grew up. Emotionally, she's still a child."

"You're not."

"Perhaps in some ways. But, well, I've outgrown Irene, anyway. I'm done with her craziness."

"I'm so happy for you. Wait, so you're still you? Why did you say perhaps you're not emotionally still a child?" Val couldn't stop the stream of questions long enough to let Ronnie answer.

"I saw a therapist for a few years in university. Saw her professionally, I mean. She told me stuff I didn't want to hear so I quit and spent her fee on pot. Now that I look back, I can see the sense in what she said. I've had some time to do some thinking."

Val forced herself to be patient and quiet. She wanted to dance around the room because Ronnie wasn't smoking pot, but she pinned her hands under her thighs and leaned back into the couch. Ronnie wanted to talk, needed to talk, and appeared to be ready to.

"I'm not sure I understand it all, but it's about not learning to form close attachments when I was young. I won't lay this all at my mother's feet because I'm a grown woman, but it started there. I was really close to my dad. When I lost him, I went into a tailspin. Thing is, he and my mother were in love, deeply. They always said they were best friends and spouses. Imagine her struggles? Six kids, a business, and dealing with the loss of the man she loved."

Ronnie dug a tissue from her pocket and blew her nose. "Maybe if I'd been more understanding or she had been, we could've helped each other. She's closer to my older sister, which is good, but that whole experience made me feel like I wasn't good enough, and that I never would be. I became a cliché of self-fulling prophecy. I often still don't feel good enough, and deep emotions scare me."

Val ached for her. And to think she'd made her feel that way yet again. "How do you feel now?"

"Still a little scared, but I'm doing better. I want to be with you. Some days I feel like I can do this. Like I can get it right this time, as long as I keep the fear at bay."

"We can be happy together." Val put her hand over her heart. "I know it right here. And I'm so sorry I didn't let you speak, and that I didn't believe you. It was incredibly unfair."

Ronnie took a deep, shuddering breath. "I love you, Val. Love your warmth, and strength, and big heart. I love your ambition and I'd like to help you become a veterinarian. I love the way you care about Gwen. I love the way you never forget to greet everyone, including the animals when you enter a room. You see people. You see me, or the me I can be. And you make me want to be that person."

Val grabbed a tissue and blew her nose. "I love you, too. Your generous heart, caring nature, and your tight ass."

Ronnie laughed. "Did you say you loved my ass?"

Val winked. "And your legs. Best legs in town. Best in the province."

Ronnie laughed.

"And I love your laughter. Seriously though, I'll take you the way you are now and I'll take the woman you become. I love you."

Ronnie struggled to stand, and Val pulled her up.

"Still stiff," Ronnie said.

"Too bad, because according to the romance novels, now is when you carry me to bed and we make crazy love."

Ronnie grinned. "What if I just led you quickly to bed and made crazy love to you?"

Val poked Ronnie in the stomach. "Close enough. Lead the way."

Upstairs, Ronnie froze outside her bedroom door and whirled to face Val, making her laugh. "I don't care how messy your bedroom is, as long as I'm the only one in there with you."

Ronnie blanched and focused on the floor. "Maybe we shouldn't—"

"Ronnie? What the hell, Ronnie!"

"Give me thirty seconds."

Ronnie hobbled into her bedroom and Val followed. "Down please, Dover. Come on, old man."

Val laughed until tears came. Curled into the comforter with his head resting on Ronnie's pillow was Dover. He was snoring loudly, oblivious to the urgency of the situation.

"He almost never sleeps with me. We were sad about losing you." She grinned at Val. "Don't laugh at me, help me." They lifted Dover off the bed and Ronnie walked him downstairs.

Val had been gardening and wanted to clean up. After a quick shower, she stepped into the bedroom. Ronnie had stripped the bed and was remaking it.

"I lust after women who can make hospital corners," Val said. She posed seductively against the doorjamb and winked. She was only wrapped in fluffy blue towel.

Ronnie glanced up, stumbled, and rammed her toe into a leg of the bed. "Shit." She dropped onto the end of the bed and grabbed her foot. "These are my best sheets. The ones I bought for us, for the first time." She hung her head in frustration.

"Scoot over."

Ronnie perched on a table beside the bed, and Val felt her eyes follow her as she finished making the bed.

"All done." Val peered at her. "Ronnie?"

"I bought those towels because they match your eyes. You're exquisite. I love you in my towel."

Val wiggled her hips. "How much would you love me out of your towel?"

Ronnie stood and crossed the room in two steps. She put her arms around Val. "I love you so much."

"And I love you."

Ronnie kissed her forehead and then her lips. She kissed Val's bare shoulders and licked droplets of water off Val's skin. "Have I mentioned that I also love all your freckles?"

Val tossed the wet towel on the floor, lay down on the bed, and opened her arms in invitation. "Come here and prove it."

About the Author

Nancy Wheelton graduated over twenty years ago from the Ontario Veterinary College in Guelph, Ontario. She spent the first few years after graduation working in a mixed animal practice in a small town in the province of Saskatchewan. Then she settled in the Great Lakes region of Ontario, where she is a practicing veterinarian.

When Nancy's not kayaking, photographing wildlife, or working on her beach house, she enjoys the crashing waves and sunsets while writing.

Website: http://Nancywheelton.com

Books Available from Bold Strokes Books

His Brother's Viscount by Stephanie Lake. Hector Somerville wants to rekindle his illicit love affair with Viscount Wentworth, but he must overcome one problem: Wentworth still loves Hector's brother. (978-1-63555-805-0)

Journey to Cash by Ashley Bartlett. Cash Braddock thought everything was great, but it looks like her history is about to become her right now. Which is a real bummer. (978-1-63555-464-9)

Liberty Bay by Karis Walsh. Wren Lindley's life is mired in tradition and untouched by trends until social media star Gina Strickland introduces an irresistible electricity into her off-the-grid world. (978-1-63555-816-6)

Scent by Kris Bryant. Nico Marshall has been burned by women in the past wanting her for her money. This time, she's determined to win Sophia Sweet over with her charm. (978-1-63555-780-0)

Shadows of Steel by Suzie Clarke. As their worlds collide and their choices come back to haunt them, Rachel and Claire must figure out how to stay together and most of all, stay alive. (978-1-63555-810-4)

The Clinch by Nicole Disney. Eden Bauer overcame a difficult past to become a world champion mixed martial artist, but now rising star and dreamy bad girl Brooklyn Shaw is a threat both to Eden's title and her heart. (978-1-63555-820-3)

The Last First Kiss by Julie Cannon. Kelly Newsome is so ready for a tropical island vacation, but she never expects to meet the woman who could give her her last first kiss. (978-1-63555-768-8)

The Mandolin Lunch by Missouri Vaun. Despite their immediate attraction, everything about Garet Allen says short-term, and Tess Hill refuses to consider anything less than forever. (978-1-63555-566-0)

Thor: Daughter of Asgard by Genevieve McCluer. When Hannah Olsen finds out she's the reincarnation of Thor, she's thrown into a world of magic and intrigue, unexpected attraction, and a mystery she's got to unravel. (978-1-63555-814-2)

Veterinary Technician by Nancy Wheelton. When a stable of horses is threatened Val and Ronnie must work together against the odds to save them, and maybe even themselves along the way. (978-1-63555-839-5)

16 Steps to Forever by Georgia Beers. Can Brooke Sullivan and Macy Carr find themselves by finding each other? (978-1-63555-762-6)

All I Want for Christmas by Georgia Beers, Maggie Cummings, Fiona Riley. The Christmas season sparks passion and love in these stories by award winning authors Georgia Beers, Maggie Cummings, and Fiona Riley. (978-1-63555-764-0)

From the Woods by Charlotte Greene. When Fiona goes backpacking in a protected wilderness, the last thing she expects is to be fighting for her life. (978-1-63555-793-0)

Heart of the Storm by Nicole Stiling. For Juliet Mitchell and Sienna Bennett a forbidden attraction definitely isn't worth upending the life they've worked so hard for. Is it? (978-1-63555-789-3)

If You Dare by Sandy Lowe. For Lauren West and Emma Prescott, following their passions is easy. Following their hearts, though? That's almost impossible. (978-1-63555-654-4)

Love Changes Everything by Jaime Maddox. For Samantha Brooks and Kirby Fielding, no matter how careful their plans, love will change everything. (978-1-63555-835-7)

Not This Time by MA Binfield. Flung back into each other's lives, can former bandmates Sophia and Madison have a second chance at romance? (978-1-63555-798-5)

The Dubious Gift of Dragon Blood by J. Marshall Freeman. One day Crispin is a lonely high school student—the next he is fighting a war in a land ruled by dragons, his otherworldly boyfriend at his side. (978-1-63555-725-1)

The Found Jar by Jaycie Morrison. Fear keeps Emily Harris trapped in her emotionally vacant life; can she find the courage to let Beck Reynolds guide her toward love? (978-1-63555-825-8)

Aurora by Emma L McGeown. After a traumatic accident, Elena Ricci is stricken with amnesia leaving her with no recollection of the last eight years, including her wife and son. (978-1-63555-824-1)

Avenging Avery by Sheri Lewis Wohl. Revenge against a vengeful vampire unites Isa Meyer and Jeni Denton, but it's love that heals them. (978-1-63555-622-3)

Bulletproof by Maggie Cummings. For Dylan Prescott and Briana Logan, the complicated NYC criminal justice system doesn't leave room for love, but where the heart is concerned, no one is bulletproof. (978-1-63555-771-8)

Her Lady to Love by Jane Walsh. A shy wallflower joins forces with the most popular woman in Regency London on a quest to catch a husband, only to discover a wild passion for each other that far eclipses their interest for the Marriage Mart. (978-1-63555-809-8)

No Regrets by Joy Argento. For Jodi and Beth, the possibility of losing their future will force them to decide what is really important. (978-1-63555-751-0)

The Holiday Treatment by Elle Spencer. Who doesn't want a gay Christmas movie? Holly Hudson asks herself that question and discovers that happy endings aren't only for the movies. (978-1-63555-660-5)

Too Good to be True by Leigh Hays. Can the promise of love survive the realities of life for Madison and Jen, or is it too good to be true? (978-1-63555-715-2)

Treacherous Seas by Radclyffe. When the choice comes down to the lives of her officers against the promise she made to her wife, Reese Conlon puts everything she cares about on the line. (978-1-63555-778-7)

Two to Tangle by Melissa Brayden. Ryan Jacks has been a player all her life, but the new chef at Tangle Valley Vineyard changes everything. If only she wasn't off the menu. (978-1-63555-747-3)

When Sparks Fly by Annie McDonald. Will the devastating incident that first brought Dr. Daniella Waveny and hockey coach Luca McCaffrey together on frozen ice now force them apart, or will their secrets and fears thaw enough for them to create sparks? (978-1-63555-782-4)

Best Practice by Carsen Taite. When attorney Grace Maldonado agrees to mentor her best friend's little sister, she's prepared to confront Perry's rebellious nature, but she isn't prepared to fall in love. Legal Affairs: one law firm, three best friends, three chances to fall in love. (978-1-63555-361-1)

Home by Kris Bryant. Natalie and Sarah discover that anything is possible when love takes the long way home. (978-1-63555-853-1)

Keeper by Sydney Quinne. With a new charge under her reluctant wing—feisty, highly intelligent math wizard Isabelle Templeton—Keeper Andy Bouchard has to prevent a murder or die trying. (978-1-63555-852-4)

One More Chance by Ali Vali. Harry Basantes planned a future with Desi Thompson until the day Desi disappeared without a word, only to walk back into her life sixteen years later. (978-1-63555-536-3)

Renegade's War by Gun Brooke. Freedom fighter Aurelia DeCallum regrets saving the woman called Blue. She fears it will jeopardize her mission, and secretly, Blue might end up breaking Aurelia's heart. (978-1-63555-484-7)

The Other Women by Erin Zak. What happens in Vegas should stay in Vegas, but what do you do when the love you find in Vegas changes your life forever? (978-1-63555-741-1)

The Sea Within by Missouri Vaun. Time is running out for Dr. Elle Graham to convince Captain Jackson Drake that the only thing that can save future Earth resides in the past, and rescue her broken heart in the process. (978-1-63555-568-4)

To Sleep With Reindeer by Justine Saracen. In Norway under Nazi occupation, Maarit, an Indigenous woman; and Kirsten, a Norwegian resister, join forces to stop the development of an atomic weapon. (978-1-63555-735-0)

Twice Shy by Aurora Rey. Having an ex with benefits isn't all it's cracked up to be. Will Amanda Russo learn that lesson in time to take a chance on love with Quinn Sullivan? (978-1-63555-737-4)

Z-Town by Eden Darry. Forced to work together to stay alive, Meg and Lane must find the centuries-old treasure before the zombies find them first. (978-1-63555-743-5)

Bet Against Me by Fiona Riley. In the high stakes luxury real estate market, everything has a price, and as rival Realtors Trina Lee and Kendall Yates find out, that means their hearts and souls, too. (978-1-63555-729-9)

Broken Reign by Sam Ledel. Together on an epic journey in search of a mysterious cure, a princess and a village outcast must overcome life-threatening challenges and their own prejudice if they want to survive. (978-1-63555-739-8)

Just One Taste by CJ Birch. For Lauren, it only took one taste to start trusting in love again. (978-1-63555-772-5)

Lady of Stone by Barbara Ann Wright. Sparks fly as a magical emergency forces a noble embarrassed by her ability to submit to a low-born teacher who resents everything about her. (978-1-63555-607-0)

Last Resort by Angie Williams. Katie and Rhys are about to find out what happens when you meet the girl of your dreams but you aren't looking for a happily ever after. (978-1-63555-774-9)

Longing for You by Jenny Frame. When Debrek housekeeper Katie Brekman is attacked amid a burgeoning vampire-witch war, Alexis Villiers must go against everything her clan believes in to save her. (978-1-63555-658-2)

Money Creek by Anne Laughlin. Clare Lehane is a troubled lawyer from Chicago who tries to make her way in a rural town full of secrets and deceptions. (978-1-63555-795-4)

Passion's Sweet Surrender by Ronica Black. Cam and Blake are unable to deny their passion for each other, but surrendering to love is a whole different matter. (978-1-63555-703-9)

The Holiday Detour by Jane Kolven. It will take everything going wrong to make Dana and Charlie see how right they are for each other. (978-1-63555-720-6)

Too Hot to Ride by Andrews & Austin. World famous cutting horse champion and industry legend Jane Barrow is knockdown sexy in the way she moves, talks, and rides, and Rae Starr is determined not to get involved with this womanizing gambler. (978-1-63555-776-3)

BOLDSTROKESBOOKS.COM

Looking for your next great read?

Visit BOLDSTROKESBOOKS.COM
to browse our entire catalog of paperbacks, ebooks,
and audiobooks.

Want the first word on what's new?
Visit our website for event info,
author interviews, and blogs.

Subscribe to our free newsletter for sneak peeks,
new releases, plus first notice of promos
and daily bargains.

SIGN UP AT
BOLDSTROKESBOOKS.COM/signup

Bold Strokes Books
Quality and Diversity in LGBTQ Literature

*Bold Strokes Books is an award-winning publisher
committed to quality and diversity in LGBTQ fiction.*

www.ingramcontent.com/pod-product-compliance
Lightning Source LLC
Chambersburg PA
CBHW021951010726
47494CB00003B/682